WENDY CORSI STAUB

SCARED TO DEATH

AVON

An Imprint of HarperCollinsPublishers

By Wendy Corsi Staub

SCARED TO DEATH
LIVE TO TELL

AVON BOOKS
An Imprint of HarperCollins*Publishers*
10 East 53rd Street
New York, New York 10022–5299

Copyright © 2011 by Wendy Corsi Staub
Excerpt from *Hell to Pay* copyright © 2012 by Wendy Corsi Staub
ISBN 978-1-61129-242-8

First Avon Books paperback printing: January 2011

For Morgan and Brody,
who enabled me to write the theme of this book—
maternal love—straight from the heart.

And for Mark,
father of said children and keeper of said heart.

Acknowledgments

With gratitude to John Gullo, Gregg and Kristin Casalino, Wendy Zemanski, and Michael Dwyer, all of whom patiently answered my research questions; to my editor, Lucia Macro, and the many talented folks at Avon Books who had a hand in this endeavor; to my agents, Laura Blake Peterson and Holly Frederick, Tracy Marchini and the rest of the gang at Curtis Brown, Ltd.; to Carol Fitzgerald and staff at the Book Report network; to Peter Meluso, who keeps www.wendycorsistaubcommunity.com up and running . . . and, most of all, to my loyal readers, who make it so worthwhile.

It is a fearful thing to love what death can touch.

—Anonymous

Prologue

Dallas, Texas
September

"Mind if I turn on the TV?"

Hell, yes, Jeremy minds.

Minds the disruption of television, and suddenly having a roommate.

Until an hour ago, when an orderly pushed a wheelchair through the doorway, Jeremy had the double hospital room all to himself. He should have known it was too good to be true.

Most good things are.

An image flashes into his head, and he winces.

Funny how even after all these years, that same face—a beautiful female face—pops in and out of his consciousness. He doesn't know whose face it is, or whether she even exists.

"Hey, are you in pain?" the stranger in the next bed asks, interrupting Jeremy's speculation about the face: *Is she a figment of my imagination—or an actual memory?*

He almost welcomes the question whose answer is readily at hand.

Am I in pain?

He feels as though every bone in his face has been broken. That's pretty damned near the truth—and not for the first time.

"I can ring the nurse for you," the man offers, waving his good hand. The other hand—like Jeremy's face—is swathed in gauze. Some kind of finger surgery, he mentioned when he first rolled into the room, as if Jeremy might care.

Reaching for the bed rail buzzer, he adds, in his lazy twang, "That Demerol's good stuff, ain't it?"

"No, thanks." Jeremy starts to shake his head.

Bad idea. The slightest movement above the neck rockets pain through his skull. He fights the instinct to scream; that would be even more torturous.

"You sure you're okay, pal? You look like you're hurting."

His jaw tightens—more agony. Dammit. Why won't this guy leave him alone?

Jeremy closes his eyes.

He's in another hospital, long ago and far away. In pain, terrified, surrounded by strangers . . .

"You don't have to be a hero, you know," his roommate rambles on.

But there's another voice, in his head, the one that belongs to a face he still sees in nightmares even after all these years: "All you have to do is triple up on his pain meds tonight. Maybe quadruple, just to be sure. Then tuck him into bed . . ."

"If you're in pain, pal, all you need to do is call a nurse and she'll give you something for it."

Jeremy's eyes snap open.

"I'm fine. Really. Just—go ahead, turn on the TV."

"You sure? Because if it'll bother you I don't want to—"

"I'm positive. Watch TV."

"Yeah? Thanks." Working the remote with the healthy hand, his roommate begins to channel surf.

Face throbbing, Jeremy gazes absently at the barrage of images on the changing screen, half hearing the snippets of sound from the speaker. Audience applause, country music, stock reports, a sitcom laugh track, meaningless words.

" . . . *ladies and gentlemen, please welcome . . .*"

" . . . *be mostly sunny with a high of . . .*"

" . . . *and the Emmy-nominated drama will return on . . .*"

His roommate pauses to ask, "Anything in particular you feel like watching?"

"Nope."

"You a sports fan?"

"Sometimes."

"Rangers?"

"Sure," Jeremy lies.

"News should be on. Let's see if we can get us some scores."

More channel surfing.

More fleeting images.

More meaningless sound, and then . . .

" *. . . in Manhattan today indicted the congressman for . . .*"

"Here's the news." The clicking stops. "I'll leave it. Sports should be coming up soon."

"Great." As if Jeremy gives a damn about sports, or the news, or—unlike the rest of the world, it seems—television in general.

"You don't know what you're missing," someone said to him in a bar not long ago, when he professed ignorance about the reality show finale playing on the television overhead.

True. And when you grow up deprived of something, you can't miss it.

Or can you?

"*. . . kidnapping the seven-year-old son of Elsa and Brett Cavalon. In an incredible twist, the child . . .*"

A close-up flashes on the screen: a photograph of a striking couple. The woman . . .

Jeremy gasps, his body involuntarily jerking to sit up.

"What?" Glancing over, his roommate immediately mutes the volume. "What's wrong? Pain, right? I knew it!"

Jeremy can't speak, can't move, can only stare at the face on TV. It's as if the pain exploding inside Jeremy's head has catapulted a piece of his imagination onto the screen. Of course, that's impossible.

But so is this, unless . . .

As suddenly as she appeared on the screen, she's gone, and the camera shifts back to the anchorman.

Unless . . .

Unless she's real.

She was there. On TV.

She does exist. She has a name—one he's heard before, in another place, another time . . .

Now, the name—*her* name—echoes back at him from the cobweb corners of his mind.

Elsa.

CHAPTER
ONE

Norwich, Connecticut
June

Another day, another dollar . . .
Which about sums up my salary, Roxanne Shields thinks as she cuts the incredibly loud engine of her aging car, desperately in need of a new muffler—or something.

"You need to get that fixed," her boss at the agency told her just yesterday. "It's just not appropriate to visit clients in a muscle car."

"*Muscle* car?" She snorted. "It's a seven-year-old Hyundai."

"Well, it sounds like a muscle car. Fix it."

Yeah. Sure. She'll get right on it—as soon as she's taken care of two months' back rent on this dumpy apartment, her overdue utility bills, and the student loan that's about to default.

How ironic that she was the first in her family to go to college, yet she can't even afford a nice wooden frame to display her bachelor's degree in social work from Southern Connecticut State. The BSW is still in its cardboard folder, tucked away in the back of her underwear drawer since graduation last May—over a year ago already.

"When I grow up, I just want to help people. I don't care about money," she always liked to say, mostly because it made her mother beam with pride as Roxanne's less-noble siblings rolled their eyes.

These days, her brother—a welder in Waterbury—is driving a BMW and her sister—a cocktail waitress at some fancy Newport restaurant—just bought a waterfront condo.

Meanwhile, how is Roxanne supposed to help people—namely, kids—when the agency is so underfunded and understaffed that she can't possibly keep up with a caseload that grows larger by the day?

She gets out of the car, opens the trunk, and picks up a box filled with client files.

"Looks like somebody's got a pile of homework to do tonight," a voice calls, and she looks up to see old Mr. LoTempio waving from his aluminum lawn chair under a tree across the street.

"Not really," she calls back. "I just don't want to leave anything in the car overnight. It's been broken into a few times lately."

"Who'd want to steal a big box of papers?"

"You never know—next time, they might want to steal the car itself."

"That bomb? Anyway, the whole neighborhood would hear it driving off down the street."

She can't help but grin at that. Mr. LoTempio isn't one to mince words.

"You know," he continues, "this isn't the kind of weather for you to be wearing all that black."

Here we go again.

"Would it kill you to try on a little color sometime?"

"It might," she replies tartly.

"You must have been sweating all day in that."

She was, but she'll never admit it.

After a cool spring, summer weather literally arrived overnight. Today has been freakishly hot—particularly when one is wearing leather boots. But her style isn't about fashion or comfort—it's a way of life. She doesn't expect an eighty-year-old man to understand that, though. So few people do.

"Have a good night, Mr. LoTempio."

"You too, Morticia."

Morticia. He's been calling her that since the day they met last fall, not long after she moved in. She doesn't mind, considering she never much cared for her real name, inspired by the old Sting ballad. "I just liked the song. Who knew it was about a hooker?" Ma would say with a helpless shrug.

Roxanne lugs her box of files across the patch of dandelion-sprinkled grass to the two-family house sorely in need of a paint job—as well as a handyman to fix the wobbly wrought-iron rail and the broken lock on her bedroom window.

If she ever manages to catch up on her rent, maybe she'll dare to mention it to the landlord. For now, she'll deal with what she's got.

The stairwell smells of Pine-Sol and roast pork, courtesy of the downstairs tenants, who cook three hot meals on even the most sweltering day of the year.

In her apartment, Roxanne plunks the file box on the floor just inside the door and bolts it behind her. As she starts for the kitchen, trying to recall whether there's anything edible in the fridge, a floorboard creaks behind her.

Seized by a paralytic rush of fear, she realizes she's not alone.

Then the knife slashes deeply beneath her right jaw, and her left, and it's over.

* * *

Groton, Connecticut

"Mommy . . ."
Elsa Cavalon stirs in her sleep.
Jeremy.
Jeremy is calling me.
"Mommy!"
No. Jeremy is gone, remember?
There was a time when that realization would have jarred her fully awake. But it's been fifteen years now since her son disappeared, and almost a year since Elsa learned that he'd been taken overseas and murdered shortly afterward.

The terrible truth came as no surprise. Throughout the dark era of worrying and wondering, she'd struggled to keep hope alive while harboring the secret belief that Jeremy was never coming home again.

All those years, she'd longed for closure. When it came last August, she braced herself, expecting her already fragile emotions to hit bottom.

Instead, somehow, she found peace.

"It's because you've already done your grieving," her therapist, Joan, told her. "You're in the final stage now. Acceptance."

Yes. She accepts that Jeremy is no longer alive, accepts that she is, and—

"Mommy!"
Jeremy isn't calling you. It's just a dream. Go back to sleep . . .

"What's wrong?" Brett's voice, not imagined, plucks Elsa from the drowsy descent toward slumber. Her eyelids pop open.

The light is dim; her husband is stirring beside her in bed, calling out to a child who isn't Jeremy, "What is it? Are you okay?"

"I need Mommy."

"She's sleeping. What's wrong?"

"No, Brett, I'm awake," she murmurs, sitting up, and calls, "Renny, I'm awake."

"Mommy, I need you!"

Elsa gets up and feels her way across the room as Brett mumbles something and settles back into the pillows. With a prickle of envy-tinged resentment, she hears him snoring again by the time she reaches the hallway.

It was always this way, back when Jeremy was here to disrupt their wee-hour rest—and when his palpable, tragic absence disrupted it even more. All those sleepless nights . . .

Brett would make some halfhearted attempt to respond to whatever was going on, then fall immediately back to sleep, leaving Elsa wide awake to cope alone with the matter at hand: a needy child, parental doubt, haunting memories, her own demons.

"Mommy!"

"I'm coming, I'm coming." Shivering, she makes her way down the hall toward Renny's bedroom.

The house is chilly. Before bed, Elsa had gone from room to room closing windows that had been open all day, with ninety-degree sunshine falling through the screens. The weather was so glorious that she and Renny had spent the whole day outside, even eating their lunch on a blanket beneath a tree.

Now, however, it feels more like March. Late spring in coastal New England can be so unpredictable.

And yet, Elsa wouldn't trade it for the more temperate climates where Brett's work as a nautical engineer transported them in recent years: Virginia Beach, San Diego, Tampa. It's good to be settled back in the Northeast. This is home.

Especially now that we have Renny.

Technically, she isn't their daughter yet, but optimistically thinking, it's only a matter of time and paperwork. As far as Elsa and Brett are concerned, Renata Almeida became Renata Cavalon on the October day she came to live with them.

Or perhaps just Renny Cavalon. Elsa isn't crazy about the given name bestowed by the abusive birth mother who has since, thank God, signed away her rights.

Renata—it's so lofty, pretentious, even—better suited to a European princess, or a supermodel, than a cute little girl who looks far younger than her seven years. Elsa and Brett shortened it immediately, with Renny's blessing. Maybe they'll make it official on the adoption papers.

Any day now . . .

Elsa will feel a lot better when the adoption process is behind them and they're on their way to Disney World for a long-planned celebratory trip with Renny. Until then, with all of them under the close scrutiny of yet another new caseworker—the overburdened, underpaid agency staff seems to turn over constantly—there's always the nagging concern that something will go wrong.

No. Nothing can go wrong. I can't bear to lose another child. I just can't.

Renny's bedroom door is ajar, as always. Plagued by claustrophobia, she's unable to sleep unless it's open. That's understandable, considering what she's been through.

Whenever Elsa allows herself to think of Renny's past, she feels as though a tremendous fist has clenched her gut. It's the same sickening dread that used to seize her whenever she imagined the abuse Jeremy had endured—both before he came into their lives, and after he was kidnapped.

But Renny isn't Jeremy. Everything about her, other

than the route she traveled through the foster system and into Elsa's life, is different.

Well—almost everything. She's a docile child with a sunny personality, unlike Jeremy—but with her black hair and eyes, Renny resembles Elsa as much as he did. No one would ever doubt a biological connection between mother and child based on looks alone.

Their bond goes much deeper than that, though. From the moment she saw the photo on the agency Web site, Elsa felt a connection to the little girl whose haunted eyes stared out from beneath crooked bangs.

And yet . . . had she felt the same thing when she first saw Jeremy?

I just don't know. I can't remember.

There was a time, not so long ago, when her memory of her son was more vivid than the landscape beyond the window. Now, it's as if the glass has warped, distorting the view.

Now.

Now . . . what?

Now that I know Jeremy is dead?

Now that there's Renny?

Elsa pushes aside a twinge of guilt.

Her daughter's arrival didn't erase the memories of her son. Of course not. She'll never forget Jeremy. But it's time to move on. Everyone says so: her husband, her therapist, even Mike Fantoni, the private eye who had finally brought the truth to light by identifying Jeremy's birth mother.

"Why would you want to meet her now?" he'd asked Elsa the last time they'd seen each other, over the winter.

"I didn't say I want to . . . I said I feel like I should know more about her. About *him*."

"Has she been in touch with you?"

"No."

"Then let it go," Mike advised, and for the most part, Elsa has. Just once in a while . . . she wonders. That's all. Wonders how the other woman is feeling, and coping. Wonders whether she has questions about Jeremy; wonders whether she can answer some of Elsa's.

She finds Renny sitting up in bed, knees to chest. Her worried face is illuminated by the Tinker Bell nightlight plugged into the baseboard outlet and the canopy of phosphorescent plastic stars Brett glued to the ceiling.

"What's wrong, honey? Are you feeling sick?" Elsa is well aware that her daughter had eaten an entire box of Sno-Caps at the new Disney princess movie Brett had taken her to see after dinner.

"Why would you let her have all that candy?" Elsa asked in dismay when he recapped the father-daughter evening.

"Because we wanted to celebrate the end of the school year, and it's fun to spoil her."

"I know, Brett . . . but don't do it with sugar. She's going to have an awful stomachache. She'll never get to sleep now."

Renny proved her wrong, drifting off within five minutes of hitting the pillow. And right now, she doesn't look sick at all . . .

She looks terrified. Her black eyes are enormous and her wiry little body quivers beneath the pink quilt clutched to her chin.

"I'm not sick, Mommy."

"Did you have a nightmare?" It wouldn't be the first time.

"No, it was *real*."

"Well, sometimes nightmares *feel* real."

And sometimes they *are* real. Renny knows that as well as she does. But things are different now. She's safe here with Elsa and Brett, and nothing will ever hurt her again.

Elsa sits beside her daughter and folds her into an embrace. "Do you want to tell me about it?"

"It wasn't a nightmare," Renny insists, trembling. "A monster was here, in my room . . . I woke up and I saw him standing over my bed."

"It was just a bad dream, honey. There's no monster."

"Yes, there is. And when I saw him, he went out the window."

Elsa turns to follow her daughter's gaze, saying, "No, Renny, see? The window isn't even—"

Open.

But Elsa's throat constricts around the word as she stares in numb horror.

The window she'd closed and locked earlier is now, indeed, wide open—and so is the screen, creating a gaping portal to the inky night beyond.

Not a creature was stirring, not even a mouse . . .

Which nursery rhyme was that?

Does it matter?

Really, right now, the only thing that matters is getting away from the house without being spotted.

Yet this is far less challenging than escaping Norwich earlier in broad daylight. That went smoothly; no reason why this shouldn't as well. At this hour, the streets are deserted; there's no one around to glimpse the dark figure stealing through the shadows.

Not a creature was stirring . . .

Damn, it's frustrating when you can't remember a detail that seems to be right there, teasing your brain . . .

Sort of the way Jeremy had forgotten Elsa Cavalon

until, by chance, he caught a glimpse of her on television back in September.

Anyone who doesn't understand what Jeremy's been through might wonder how a person can forget his own mother.

How, indeed.

The human mind doesn't just lose track of something like that, like the name of a nursery rhyme. More likely, out of self-preservation, the brain attempts to erase what's too painful to remember.

What's too painful to remember . . .

Hmm . . . Wasn't that a long-ago lyric?

Maybe. But the song title, too, is elusive—and unimportant.

One thing at a time.

Not a creature was stirring . . .

Leaning on the terrace railing, gazing at the smattering of lighted windows on the Queens skyline across the East River, Marin Hartwell Quinn finds herself wishing the sun would never come up.

When it does, she'll be launched headlong into another exhausting, lonely day of single motherhood, a role she never imagined for herself.

At this time last year, the storybook Quinn family was all over the press: Marin, Garvey, and their two beautiful daughters—Caroline, a striking brunette with her father's coloring, and Annie, a blue-eyed blonde like her mom. They were destined to live happily ever after on the Upper East Side, and—if the expected nomination came through and the election turned out predictably—in the governor's mansion . . . and someday, perhaps, the White House.

But in a flash—a flash, yes, like those from the ever-present paparazzi cameras—Garvey was transported from Park Avenue to Park Row, the lower Manhattan street that houses the notorious Metropolitan Correctional Center.

Naturally, the photographers who had dogged Congressman Quinn along the campaign trail were there to capture the moment he was hauled away in handcuffs on a public street. And when the detectives had driven off with their prisoner, sirens wailing, the press turned their cameras on Marin, still sitting, stunned, in the backseat of the limousine.

Later, she forced herself to look at the photos, to read the captions. One referred to her as *the humiliated would-be first lady*, another as *a blond, blue-eyed Jackie Kennedy, shell-shocked at witnessing her husband's sudden downfall on a city street.*

That wasn't the first time the press had drawn a Kennedy-Quinn comparison. But while the slain JFK had remained a hero and his wife was lauded as a heartbroken, dignified widow, the fallen Garvey Quinn was exposed as a coldhearted villain—and his wife drew nothing but scorn from his disillusioned constituents.

No one seemed to grasp—or care—that Marin herself had been blindsided; that the man she loved had betrayed her—and their children—with his unspeakable crime. That Elsa Cavalon wasn't the only mother bereaved by Jeremy Cavalon's kidnapping and murder. Marin, his birth mother, grieved as well. And, unbearably, her own husband—Jeremy's own father—was responsible for his death.

What the hell is she supposed to do with that knowledge, and the accompanying guilt? How the hell is she supposed to move past it?

So far, she's come up with only this: Force herself to get up every morning—if she manages to stay in bed that long—and face the wreckage of her life.

One foot in front of the other, one day after another. Just move on, blindly, preferably not looking back, not looking ahead.

With a sigh, Marin turns away from the railing. Still no hint of sunrise on the eastern horizon, but it will appear any moment now, and the day will be under way.

Time to get moving: Shower and dress, make some coffee, check her e-mail . . . Oh, and the cleaning service comes today.

Marin had felt only mild disappointment when Shirley, their longtime housekeeper, gave notice two months ago. She wasn't one of those warm and fuzzy domestic employees who become part of the family. No, she kept her distance, even amid all the upheaval—not as much out of professional discretion, Marin suspects, as because she just didn't give a damn.

It's just as well. The last thing her daughters needed was another shakeup on the home front, however small. Marin was pretty sure no one was going to miss Shirley, and she was right. It took a few days for the girls to even realize she was gone—and even then, it was only the growing pile of laundry that tipped them off.

"Aren't we going to hire a new maid?" Caroline had asked, dismayed.

"Nope," Marin heard herself say, shocking Caroline—not to mention herself.

Until that moment, she'd been meaning to get around to calling the domestic agency her friend Heather Cottington recommended. But suddenly she couldn't bear the thought of bringing a new person into the household—someone who'd undoubtedly be well aware that this is Garvey Quinn's family. Someone who'd wonder—and maybe talk—about the "episodes" Marin suffers with more and more frequency.

She figured she was perfectly capable of running the house herself, at least until this fall, after the move. What else did she have to do?

On good days, she's done a fairly decent job on the basics—laundry, emptying the dishwasher, running the vacuum. On bad days, the girls came home from school to drawn shades and toast crumbs still on the countertops, and their mother in bed.

On occasion, Marin even made her daughters help around the house, something they'd never had to do and weren't particularly happy about—particularly Caroline, who tends to make a scene over the smallest imagined slight.

"Don't you think you're being too hard on them?" Heather asked when she heard. "They've lost their father. They've been through hell. You're planning to move them out of the only home they've ever known. And now you have them cleaning toilets?"

Maybe she was right.

Maybe not.

All Marin can do is feel her way through one day at a time. And now, with Realtors about to descend, every room has to be scrubbed from floor to ceiling.

Marin just doesn't have it in her. She spent all day yesterday boxing up every framed family photograph and most of the contents of Garvey's home office—anything that might negate the seller anonymity clause in the real estate contract and thus betray their identity to prospective buyers.

In the master bedroom, she smooths the lavender coverlet on her side and arranges the floral print European throw pillows. She bought new bedding after Garvey left; would have bought a whole new bed if she could have disposed of the old one privately. But she could just imagine photographers snapping photos of the California king–sized mattress being moved out, and printing them above a caption like: *The wishful widow Quinn purges her upscale digs of everything jailbird hubby touched.*

Wishful widow . . . one of the tabloids gave her that nickname, assuming she thinks she'd be better off if Garvey were dead.

They're right. Bastards.

Anyway, public contempt is nothing compared to the rest of it: mourning her firstborn; helping her surviving children cope with the realization that their father is a criminal; preparing to sell an apartment that's too big, too expensive, and holds too many memories; looking Garvey in the eye through protective visitors' room glass and telling him she'll never forgive him, and that even if he manages to be found innocent when the case goes to trial, he won't be coming home to her.

She strips out of her nightgown and hangs it on a hook in her walk-in closet.

Beside it, Garvey's closet door remains closed, as it has been for months now. His expensive suits and shirts, shrouded in dry cleaner's plastic, are presumably still inside, along with dozens of pairs of Italian leather shoes and French silk ties.

What is she supposed to do with any of it? Burn it? Give it away? Save it? For what? For whom?

She has no idea, and doesn't have to make any decisions until the move, and so his clothes hang on in a dark limbo, like Marin herself.

In the large marble bathroom—her dream bathroom, she once told Garvey, when they were walking through as prospective buyers, a lifetime ago—she showers, brushes her teeth, blows her hair dry.

Same routine every morning, yet today will be different. Still a living hell, but June has arrived. Finals are over for the girls, as are the latest round of lessons and extracurricular activities that consumed the weekends. The school year that began in the immediate aftermath of Garvey's downfall has come to an end at last. This morning, instead of heading over to their private high school off York Avenue, Caroline and Annie will be here at home with Marin, along with strangers from the cleaning service who may not turn a blind eye.

Which means you'll have to hold yourself together.

No crying. No ranting. No hyperventilating. No swallowing a couple of the prescription pills her friend Heather gave her to make it all go away—some pills for stress, others for her relentless headaches, still others that let her crawl into bed in the middle of the day to capture the sleep that evades her in the night.

Maybe it's better that way.

When she sleeps, she dreams.

Dreams of a little boy with big black eyes, and he's calling for her.

"Mommy . . . Mommy, please help me . . ."

Not dreams—nightmares. Because she can never help him. Nobody can.

It's too late to save Jeremy.

And maybe, Marin thinks, staring at her haggard reflection in the bathroom mirror, too late to save herself as well.

Brett yawns audibly, evoking a dark glance from his wife. He belatedly covers his mouth and resumes a riveted expression. Too late.

"You're not even listening to me." Elsa sounds more weary than irritated. She reaches for her mug of coffee.

She insisted on brewing it, insisted on sitting here in the kitchen to rehash what happened. In her lace-edged pale pink cotton robe, the front strands of her shoulder-length dark hair caught up in a barrette on top of her head, her lovely face scrubbed free of makeup, she looks more like a young girl than the worried mother of one.

"I'm listening," Brett tells her. "I'm just tired. It's five in the morning, and we don't even have to be up for another—"

"I know, but there's no way I can sleep now."

Maybe not, but *he* certainly can. In fact, after he'd dutifully gone through the entire house clutching a baseball bat, checking inside closets and under beds for prowlers, he'd had every intention of climbing right back under the covers. He saw no reason to lose any more sleep. Even Renny had gone from frantic to drowsy, allowing Brett to tuck her back in with reassurances that there were no monsters.

Not in this house, anyway.

And the man—the monster—responsible for Jeremy's death is behind bars, so . . .

"It was just a nightmare," Brett had told Renny— and he tells Elsa the same thing now.

"But the window was open."

"Maybe you just thought you'd closed it."

"What about the screen? I never open that. Ever."

"Maybe you did, and forgot."

She gives him a *look*. One that says, *I'm not crazy.*

He knows she isn't. Really, he does.

Though there was a time when he'd thought . . .

No. He'd never believed Elsa was actually crazy, had he?

But back when Jeremy was newly missing, she'd gone through a frightening period when she'd completely lost her grasp on reality. Most of the time, she was completely out of it—dissociative behavior, Brett later learned, was the psychiatric term. He would hear her talking to Jeremy as if he were still here, or find her frantically looking for him as if he'd just disappeared, so distraught that he feared she might harm herself. She even talked about wanting to die, but he convinced himself that she was just grief-stricken, that she'd never really try to take her own life.

When she did—when she overdosed and nearly died—he'd blamed himself.

From that moment on, he'd vowed to save his wife. From therapy to medication for what was diagnosed as acute stress disorder, from rehashing the tragedy to sidestepping the topic, from avoiding children to considering parenthood again—he swore he'd do whatever was necessary to help Elsa recover.

And she had. The sorrow never left her, but she was stable. For years.

When they learned last August that Jeremy had been murdered, Brett was poised for a relapse. She'd been grief-stricken, as had he—but there was no frightening dissociative behavior.

None that he's seen, anyway.

What about now? he wonders uneasily, but promptly pushes the thought away. No. No way. After a decade and a half of torture, having found the answers she sought so desperately, Elsa is finally healing—or perhaps, healed.

Renny's arrival in their lives has given her a sense of purpose again.

And yet, watching his wife with their soon-to-be-adopted daughter, Brett has worried all along.

She's trying so hard to be the perfect mother—from preparing organic food and limiting treats and screen time, to what would probably be considered hypervigilance by any standard. Constantly fearing the worst has made her overprotective of Renny; maybe even paranoid.

Who can blame her? Their first child was kidnapped and murdered.

But that doesn't mean it's going to happen again.

It doesn't mean there really was someone in Renny's room in the dead of night.

So you do think she imagined it, is that it?

"I think we should call the police," Elsa announces.

"You can't be serious."

"I am."

"The press is finally off our backs. Do you really want to stir it all up again?"

"The press doesn't have to be involved. I'm just talking about calling the police and—"

"You don't think it's going to get out somehow that the mother of Jeremy Cavalon thinks someone is prowling around her new kid's bedroom?"

Now she's irritated, setting down her coffee cup. "New kid?"

"Sorry, I didn't mean it that way."

New kid. As in replacement for old kid.

God. Brett rakes a hand through his hair. That's not what he meant at all. What's wrong with him? He knows how fragile she is when it comes to this—when it comes to everything. For years now.

"If you honestly think there's a reason to call the police," he tells his wife, "go ahead. You know I would never take a chance with Renny."

"I know that." She toys with a dry pink petal that dropped from the vase of rhododendron blooms in the center of the table.

"Don't make yourself nuts with this." Brett reaches out and pats her thin shoulder. "Everything is fine. Renny is fine. There's nothing to worry about."

"There's always something to worry about when you have a child."

"Yes, but not . . . not like that. Not what you're thinking."

Elsa just looks at him. She can be so damned stubborn . . .

So can I.

"Look, there's no reason to call the police just because a window was open."

"How did it get open?"

"Maybe Renny sleepwalked and did it herself."

Elsa tilts her head. Clearly, she hadn't thought of that.

Brett hadn't, either, until it popped out, but who knows? Maybe it's true. And if it's not, there are countless other explanations for the open window. Explanations that don't involve a monster creeping around their little girl's bedroom—or his wife going crazy. The simplest answer is usually the right one.

Brett presses on. "Think about it. The adoption isn't even finalized. You don't want to risk it, do you? How do you think Roxanne is going to react?"

Something else she hadn't thought of, obviously. Sharp-eyed Roxanne Shields, Renny's latest social worker, makes Elsa nervous.

"She's just not what I expected," Elsa said the first time they met the young woman, with her multiple piercings—including her nose and tongue—and black-everything, from her clothes and dyed hair to her eyeliner and the ankh tattoo on her forearm.

Brett was also taken aback by her appearance, though he didn't admit it to his wife.

As always, Elsa has enough to worry about.

For that matter, so does he. They've been laying off employees at work again, and rumor has it another round is coming. If he loses his job, his family loses their sole source of income, aside from the fostering stipend—which would certainly make the agency think twice about allowing the adoption to go through.

Yeah. So would a police report.

"Look, if we bring the cops in, it's going to go on the records," he reminds Elsa. "Roxanne will have to become involved."

"I know."

Brett glimpses a spark of uncertainty in Elsa's beautiful dark eyes. They've both heard the horror stories about would-be adoptees being removed from their prospective parents over the slightest incident.

Just last month, Todd and Zoe Walden, a couple who had gone through the training program with the Cavalons, lost their foster daughter after their biological son was suspended from school for fighting. Never mind that he was defending himself from a bully. Apparently it doesn't take much to trigger the beleaguered foster agency staff to decide that it's not in the child's best interest to remain in the home.

"I'm scared, Brett. I just don't know whether I'm more scared of the agency taking Renny away, or of something happening to her like it did to Jeremy."

"Lightning doesn't strike the same spot twice."

"Is that a scientific fact, or just a meaningless old saying?"

He shrugs. "Elsa, we can't take a chance and call the police about this. Absolutely not. That would pretty much guarantee that we'd lose her."

"But if we explain—"

"They're still going to err on the side of caution, and you know it."

"You're right. We can't call."

He nods, relieved.

And yet, what if . . . ?

No, he tells himself firmly. *Just like you told Elsa—and Renny, too—there's nothing to worry about. Nothing at all.*

* * *

Ah, there's the rental car: conveniently parked on a quiet waterside street several blocks from the Cavalon home—a perfect spot, near the marina. Fishermen, rising in the early hours to pursue the day's catch, often leave their vehicles here.

It would probably have been a good idea to have some poles and a tackle box in the backseat. Just in case someone came along.

Oh well. Next time.

The engine turns over with a quiet rumble.

Mission accomplished.

For tonight, anyway.

With a crunching sound, the tires begin to roll along the gravel lane that leads back to the main road.

There's no other traffic at this hour, not out here. It might pick up in a few miles, closer to the southbound interstate, but it's still pretty early for that. Without rush hour congestion, it's only about two hours' drive from Groton to New York. With traffic, it can be considerably longer. That's okay. There's no hurry.

Plenty of time for a detour along Thames Street. Not a soul to witness the car pulling up in front of the tiny post office, or its driver hurrying over to drop a stamped manila envelope into the curbside mailbox. Local delivery; the package should arrive the day after tomorrow. No—it's well past midnight. Make that *tomorrow.*

Not a creature was stirring, not even a mouse . . .

What the heck was the rest of it?

Not even a mouse . . .

Not even a mouse . . .

Oh, the next line is: *The children are nestled all snug in their beds . . .*

Ha. Isn't that fitting. Renny Cavalon certainly was nestled all snug in her bed just a short time ago.

Then she opened her eyes and screamed.

No wonder.

That hideous rubber mask—now tucked safely into the glove compartment—would scare anyone to death, looming in the dead of night.

Night . . .

Night . . .

'Twas the Night Before Christmas . . .

That's it!

It wasn't a nursery rhyme after all; it was a storybook, one Mother loved to read aloud, years ago, in the soft glow of Christmas tree lights.

Is Elsa Cavalon planning to read it to Renny when the holidays roll around?

Ha. Come December, Renny will be long gone.

Just like Jeremy.

CHAPTER TWO

Peeking into her daughter's room for what must be the hundredth time this morning, Elsa finds Renny awake at last.

Ordinarily, the little girl bounds noisily out of bed the second she opens her eyes. Today she's just lying there, staring at the faint outline of the plastic stars overhead.

Maternal anxiety, like the phosphorescent Milky Way on the ceiling, had all but faded in the bright morning light. Now, with one look at Renny, Elsa feels it flare again.

"Good *mor*-ning." She forces her usual cheerful singsong as she walks over to the nearest window, lifting the shade with a snap.

Sunshine spills into the room. There—that's better.

She turns to the other window—the one that was open in the night.

"Wait—don't!"

She turns to see Renny sitting up behind her, watching warily. "What's wrong, honey?"

Her daughter starts to say something, then seems to think better of it.

"Renny? What is it?"

"Nothing. It's okay."

Elsa hesitates, then raises the shade. Blinking into the glare, she surveys the heavily landscaped backyard.

Lush shrubs and blooming perennial beds surround the ranch home's foundation, courtesy of a vegetation-loving previous owner. The property's perimeter is a dense natural border of hedges, vines, and trees. Last year, Elsa took it upon herself to keep everything pruned. This spring, with Renny here, she hasn't had time.

Now everything is overgrown. There are plenty of places where someone could hide.

Fifteen years ago, in a backyard a hundred miles away from this one, a stranger was watching her son as he played in the sun with his new superhero action figures. Watching, waiting to pounce—

Oh, Jeremy.

If only I had suspected . . .

And now . . . she does suspect. There's no evidence of an intruder, yet Elsa can almost sense a lingering presence in the dappled shadows.

Her instinct is to grab Renny and flee. But that's crazy, isn't it?

Even for a woman whose child was kidnapped and murdered?

Who could blame her for reacting—or overreacting—to an open window in her daughter's room in the dead of night?

But it's not nighttime anymore; the window itself is closed and locked.

"Lightning doesn't strike the same spot twice," Brett told her earlier, and in that particular moment, she'd found it as comforting as his sleepwalking theory.

Yet it's not impossible, is it? Lightning striking twice in the same place?

Maybe she should look it up.

Maybe that's a bad idea.

She crosses to Renny's bed and gives her a hug.

"I've been waiting for you to wake up." Enveloped in the comforting scents of strawberry shampoo and fabric softener, she smooths her daughter's tousled hair and adjusts the sleeve of her pink nightgown. "I've got a fun day planned for us. I thought we'd go to the aquarium and walk around the seaport."

Mystic, just a few miles away, is one of Renny's favorite places in the world. Ordinarily, she'd jump at the chance to visit, but not today.

"No thanks."

"No? Um, how about if we go to Teppanyaki for lunch, then?"

Once again Renny, who loves to sit at the Japanese restaurant's grill-side table and watch the hibachi chef's flaming antics, shakes her head.

"Okay, well . . . We can go to the mall to get you some new summer clothes, and have our nails done . . ."

Did you really just say that? Shopping and manicures?

Never in a million years would Elsa have thought she'd hear herself suggest such a thing. As the only child of Sylvie Durand, one of the world's first supermodels—who became famous for creating an aura of mystery with the vintage blusher-veiled hats she always wore in public—Elsa had been force-fed girly pursuits. Groomed to follow in Maman's glamorous footsteps, she'd done just that—sans chapeau, of course—until she was twenty-one. Then she met her unlikely soul mate: a preppy nautical engineering student from New Rochelle, who'd never heard of her mother and didn't know haute couture from prêt-à-porter.

Head over heels for Brett, Elsa gladly traded her promising modeling career for family life.

That was the plan, anyway. Through years of heart-breaking infertility, Elsa could do little more than fantasize about what kind of mother she'd be. Unlike Sylvie, she'd *never* impose upon an impressionable daughter the rigid standards of fashion and beauty . . .

Yet here you are, grasping at straws, trying to lure Renny to the mall and salon. Nice going. While you're at it, why don't you just invite Maman over to pluck Renny's eye-brows and parade her around with a book on her head?

The very idea makes her shudder.

It isn't that Maman is a horrible grandparent. Quite the contrary. When Jeremy went missing, Maman was bereft and supportive—in her own self-centered way, of course.

The alluringly tragic Sylvie Durand was all over the airwaves, tearful behind her black veil, pleading for the return of her missing grandson. Elsa and Brett figured it could only help bring attention to the case. It did—and also revitalized Sylvie's career, landing her a multimillion-dollar cosmetics contract. In Paris for a shoot, she reconnected with a childhood sweetheart, fell passionately in love—a frequent habit of hers—and decided to stay.

Elsa fully expected her to return to New York when the affair fizzled, but so far, it hasn't. Maman keeps her Manhattan apartment just in case. She has a lav-ish wardrobe there and another in Elsa's guestroom closet, as she refuses to travel with luggage. But she remains happily settled into Jean Paul's countryside chateau.

Once in a while, Elsa misses her. But Maman flies home every couple of months—for holidays, and Fash-ion Week. And for the most part, Elsa's glad to keep her at a healthy distance—particularly from impres-sionable Renny, who's fascinated by her charming and glamorous "Mémé," as Sylvie prefers her granddaughter to call her.

"Can we just stay home today, Mommy?"

Pushing aside the bitter memory of her own past, Elsa looks at her daughter. "Sure, we can stay home. Are you feeling all right?"

"No. The monster . . ." The child casts a fearful look at the window, and a chill slithers down Elsa's spine. "He's out there."

"No, Renny, he's not. He's in *here*." She gently presses her index fingertip against her daughter's temple. "You dreamed him. He isn't real."

Renny says nothing.

"Look around." Elsa sweeps a hand around the sun-splashed room, with its lavender ruffles and Disney princess theme. "There's nothing to be afraid of here."

"Are you sure?"

"Positive."

"Promise?"

Elsa hesitates.

Before he left for the office earlier, Brett kissed her on the cheek and said, "I promise you everything is fine."

She wanted desperately to believe him. And when she realized that he'd never made any such promise before, about Jeremy, she did believe him—until now.

Now, when she knows just how easy it is to let the right words roll off your tongue to reassure someone you love.

She turns away, not looking Renny in the eye. "I promise."

Things are different here.

In Manhattan, unlike the Connecticut shore towns,

people live in towering, guarded fortresses. You have to be creative here; you can't just climb in a window.

Well, maybe if you're Spider-Man.

Spider-Man . . .

Now *there's* an ironic thought.

Park Avenue is bustling on this cool June morning. People scurry or sometimes even push past, late for work, talking on their cell phones, trying to beat the light. No one casts a second glance in this direction, and even if someone did . . .

I'd never be recognized. Not here. Not in Groton, either— not even by the Cavalons.

One last look at the tall apartment building with its rows of windows high above the street . . .

Somewhere up there, does Marin Quinn really believe her children are safe in a concrete fortress, protected by locks and alarms and uniformed doormen?

She'll learn.

She'll find out what it's like to feel your skin ooze with cold sweat as your heart seems to splinter your fragile ribs with every violent beat. She'll know what it's like to cower, helpless, aware that your darkest fears are going to come to fruition. Most importantly, she'll know that it isn't Jeremy's fault that he did what he did.

No, it's her own fault, and Elsa Cavalon's, for failing the child they were both, in turn, supposed to protect.

"Mom! She took my—"

"Don't listen to her, Mom, I did not!"

Standing at the kitchen counter listing to the commotion from down the hall, Marin closes her eyes for a long moment. Then she wearily resumes what she was doing: pouring the last dredges from the coffeepot into her cup.

The girls have been up for less than an hour, and at each other's throats the entire time. At first, Marin attempted to referee. Now, she's doing her best to ignore.

Is this what it's going to be like every day, all summer long?

"Give it back! Mom!"

"Mom!"

Marin sips the coffee.

Bitter.

Just like me.

She sips again, makes a face, and dumps the cup into the sink.

Maybe she should brew a fresh pot. But so much caffeine isn't good for her. Maybe that's why her nerves have been acting up so much lately.

"Mom!"

"Mom!"

Her shoulders are tense. Stress. Not good.

I need something stronger than coffee.

But not now, in the middle of the day, with the kids home.

God help me.

God? Yeah, right.

She never believed in God before the ultra-conservative, religious Garvey came into her life, nor during most of the forced churchgoing years they were together. She *certainly* doesn't believe now. Not after the merciless ordeal she and her family—and the Walshes, and the Cavalons—have endured.

On the first Sunday morning after Garvey's arrest, the girls dressed in their church clothes, as always. Marin told them to go change.

Caroline was thrilled; Annie dismayed. "Why aren't we going to church?"

Marin blamed the media. "The press knows our

routine. They'll be there waiting for us. I can't subject
you girls to that circus."

She got a lot of mileage out of that reasoning for—
quite literally—a month of Sundays. After all, it was
true: the stretch of Fifth Avenue in front of the Church
of Heavenly Rest swarmed with reporters intent on
snapping photos of Garvey Quinn's family and slap-
ping them all over the tabloids with captions that ridi-
culed their phony piety.

In the months since, Annie has occasionally asked
when they're going back to church, and Marin is running out of excuses—conflicting plans, headaches, the
weather. She hates herself for not having the strength
to admit her own hypocrisy to her daughters; hates
herself more for having gone along with something in
which she had absolutely no sense of conviction.

But as she told her dubious, agnostic parents back
when she was first falling in love with Garvey, she
believed in her future husband more than she *didn't*
believe in God.

And then, for a while there, she even found fleeting
comfort in both. Maybe there really *was* something to
this God stuff. Maybe that was why Marin Hartwell
had been handed a chance at happily-ever-after with
a hero who could have had anyone, but miraculously
wanted *her*.

Concealing her first pregnancy and giving up her
newborn son for adoption soon shattered her fledgling
religious faith—yet, curiously, not her faith in Garvey,
who coerced her into making those decisions. She convinced herself, somehow, that if there was a God, he
had betrayed her; even that she had betrayed herself.
But not Garvey. No, never Garvey. She never realized
the truth about him until last August, when it was too
late.

Down the hall, Caroline and Annie continue to

squabble. As usual, Caroline is accusing her sister of snooping through something—her room, or her laptop, or her phone . . .

Marin closes her eyes and presses her thumb and fingertips into her throbbing temples, wondering when the ibuprofen she'd taken earlier is going to kick in.

"I told you not to . . ."

"Why do you always have to . . ."

"I'm telling Mom!"

When the ringing telephone chimes into the melee, the girls don't miss a beat. They never bother to answer anything but their own cell phones.

Normally Marin doesn't, either, because you never know whether it's going to be a reporter or Garvey calling from jail. Both tend to register—as this call does—as "private number" on the caller ID.

But anything is better than listening to World War III.

She picks up the receiver.

"Marin! There you are!"

Heather Cottington—the one old friend who's stuck by her in the wake of Garvey's scandal. Countless rounds of "I told you so" have been a relatively small price to pay for an adult confidante who, despite a high-profile allegiance with the opposing political party, wouldn't dream of capitalizing on her proximity to the notorious Quinns.

Plus Heather—who is married to a doctor and whose home medicine cabinet is a veritable pharmacy—is always happy to share her Ambien and Xanax with Marin, who, as Heather often says, needs it more than she does.

"I've tried your cell twice this morning. I was getting worried."

"Sorry. I didn't hear the phone."

"Really?"

"*Really.* Maybe I accidentally silenced the ringer. Or maybe the battery's dead."

Maybe she even lost the phone somewhere. Who knows? Who cares?

Heather, who wears her Bluetooth headset like a diamond tiara, pauses dubiously before continuing, "So anyway, I thought I'd better check in and see how it's going so far."

"You mean the cleaning service?" Marin knows very well that's not what this is about, but she isn't in the mood for another head-spinning ride on the I-told-you-so carousel.

"Not the cleaning service—but how *are* they doing?"

"So far, so good."

Actually, beyond the cursory apartment tour and going over the daily chore list, Marin has had very little interaction with the two women, which is fine with her, and also seemed fine with them. They rolled up their sleeves and got right to work. At the moment, they're behind the closed French doors of the living room, vacuuming and moving furniture around.

"What about your summer plan?" Heather asks, and adds, "Or should I say, nonplan?"

"Actually, that's going pretty well, too."

"*Mom!*" Annie shrieks from down the hall. "She—"

"Oh my God, you are such a nosy little brat!" Caroline bellows.

"*Stop it!* Who do you think you—"

"*Owwwww!* Get off me! Mom!"

"Yeah," Heather says dryly on the other end of the phone, "sounds great. There's still time to reconsider, you know."

Slipping into the half bath off the kitchen and closing the door, Marin sighs. "No, there isn't. Registration was months ago for all the decent sleepaway camps."

"Which is why I was trying to get you to do it back then. Do you want me to see if I can pull some strings with Chelsea's camp, or Jack's?"

Heather's youngest child, as horse-crazy as Marin's daughters once were, is attending camp in Wyoming; her big brother will be a CIT in Maine. Their middle sibling, Spencer, is bound for a summer-long academic program in South America.

Naturally, the uber-efficient Heather made all the arrangements before Christmas. In the past, Marin would have been just as proactive; this time, she was just trying to survive the season at hand. Forget summer; she could barely think ahead to New Year's Eve—which she wasn't sure whether to dread spending alone, or look forward to because the horrific year would finally be over.

As it turned out, holiday salvation came unexpectedly, from the last person Marin would ever have expected. Now, six months later, a bond that began with a stranger's New Year's resolution has become Marin's sole source of support—from someone other than Heather, anyway. Someone who understands what it's like to be betrayed by a husband, shunned by a community, left alone with devastated children . . .

Lauren Walsh—the suburban widow whose three children had been kidnapped and whose husband had been murdered, if not by Garvey's own hand, then on his command—had shockingly reached out to Marin as a step along her own healing path. But Marin had needed the contact—and the forgiveness—just as much as, if not more than, Lauren herself.

"You know I wouldn't mind making a couple of calls to see if your girls could—"

"No, it's okay," she assures Heather. "They can't do camp this year, not with the move and everything."

Perched uncomfortably on the closed toilet seat,

Marin pictures Heather lounging on her silk sofa, lazily twisting a strand of long blond hair around a jeweled finger.

"Why don't you at least get out of the city for a while?" Heather suggests. "Spend some time on the beach, clear your head . . ."

"You know there's no way I'm going to Nantucket."

"Of course I know that."

It's no secret that Marin has never liked to spend much time with her blue-blooded Massachusetts in-laws; this year, especially, visiting their rambling island summer home is out of the question. The place has been in the family for generations, shared by the clannish Quinn siblings and their families. Their few obligatory efforts to connect with Garvey since his ordeal seem to have been carefully orchestrated by lawyers and, Marin suspects, by publicists hired to refurbish the tarnished family name.

Having distanced themselves from their disgraced brother, the Quinns wouldn't exactly welcome Marin and the kids to the rambling seaside home—*if* she were willing to visit.

Garvey's defense is working on the theory that he has a sociopathic disorder—which is, in all likelihood, genetically inherited. No one would dispute, in retrospect, that his grandmother Eleanor fit the bill. Who knows what other branches of the family tree are affected? Marin intends to keep her distance from the Quinns, at least for the time being.

As for her own side of the family—she's an only child, and her mother passed away years ago, when the kids were little. Her father, diagnosed with dementia, is in a Brighton nursing home.

And now you're feeling even sorrier for yourself. With good reason, but still . . .

"I didn't mean you should go to Nantucket,"

Heather is saying. "Ron and I are headed to St. Tropez on Saturday, so our cottage will be empty for another couple of weeks."

Cottage—Marin's lips twitch at that description. The Cottingtons' summer house in the Hamptons is an imposing three-story architectural masterpiece perched in the dunes. Last summer, Marin and the girls spent quite a bit of time out there.

Her smile fades as she remembers that Garvey even paid an unexpected visit once, just before all hell broke loose. She was so shocked and happy to see him, so touched that he'd driven all that way in the midst of his hectic campaign. Little did she know . . .

"You and the girls are welcome to stay out there if you want."

"Thanks, Heather, that's sweet of you, but . . ."

But I just can't go back there yet. Or maybe ever again.

Only last fall, after her life had been destroyed, had she found out that Garvey hadn't come to the Hamptons that weekend because he missed her and the girls; he was there to establish an alibi for one of the murders he'd engineered.

How could she not have known? All those years, he had her fooled.

Not just me. The whole world. What if he'd won the election, become governor of New York?

Not that he'd have been the first duplicitous politician in that role, but . . .

"How about coming with us to France, Marin?"

"Heather, you know I would never horn in on—"

"Believe me, you wouldn't be horning in. Ron golfs all day, every day there—same as here. You could keep me company. We'll shop, and drink good wine, and sun ourselves on the boat . . ."

Ah, the "boat": a hundred-foot luxury yacht kept moored on the French Riviera.

"It sounds great, but what about the girls?"

Heather hesitates just long enough for Marin to realize they weren't included in the invite.

"Maybe you could leave them here with someone."

Someone. Like whom? Henry the doorman? The cleaning service ladies?

Anyway, she can barely leave the apartment these days. How is she supposed to get on a plane and fly to Europe?

"Thanks, Heather, I really appreciate the invite, but I have a lot to do around here, and I can't be away from the kids right now."

They're all I have left.

"Then bring them along. I'm sure there'd be things for them to do."

"You're sweet, but we'll be fine here. Really."

"Are you sure?"

"Yes," Marin lies, trying to remember the last time she felt sure of anything at all.

Chinese checkers, potholder weaving, a book of brain teasers, TV . . .

Trying to keep Renny occupied, Elsa has pretty much exhausted the contents of the special rainy day toy bin she keeps filled with games, puzzles, craft kits, and art supplies. And it isn't even raining. Far from it: Beyond the living room picture window, a glorious day beckons.

Renny, sitting on the couch in the next room watching *The Little Mermaid*, wants no part of it.

"What do you want me to do? Drag her out the door?" Elsa whispers to Brett, on the phone from work. He's called several times to check on her.

She wanted to ask why he even bothered to go in if

he's so worried about them—but she knows he had little choice. He's worried about losing his job, with good reason. His boss, Lew—a three-times divorced, childless workaholic—hasn't exactly been thrilled with the many personal days Brett's had to take since he got involved with foster parenting and brought Renny home.

"Maybe you can get her to go out if you promise her something fun."

"Like what? Disney World?" Elsa sorts a handful of Crayolas back into their cardboard slots. "Because we already promised her that, remember?"

"I remember. Why don't you take her to the seaport? She loves that."

"I already tried. She's not interested. And I don't think it's a good idea to force her to go out, do you?"

"If she doesn't confront her fear, it might snowball, and she'll end up . . . I don't know, agoraphobic or something."

"Brett . . . come on." Elsa dumps the crayon box back into the rainy day bin. "Think about that. *Renny*?"

Renny, who has the opposite problem?

According to her psychiatric evaluation, the little girl's claustrophobia is a result of being locked away for hours at a time by her birth mother. Paulette Almeida suffered from schizophrenia and was ridden with delusions—including one that her small daughter was a ferocious jungle animal who had escaped its cage and was trying to kill her. She would corral a desperate Renny into a closet and keep her there until someone—usually Renny's father, Paulette's deadbeat boyfriend, Leon—came along.

Presumably it went on for years before a suspicious new neighbor reported the situation to the authorities.

"I never laid a hand on her," Paulette Almeida

reportedly told Michelle, the social worker who handled the case before it was turned over to a woman named Peggy, who came before Roxanne.

No, Renny's birth mother didn't inflict the brand of torture that leaves telltale marks that can be seen by would-be rescuers. The child's wounds are hidden on the inside.

Once in a while, Elsa glimpses evidence of those emotional scars, but for the most part, Renny's been doing so well. She's no happy-go-lucky first grader, but she does laugh more than she used to, and Elsa actually saw her skipping down the hall to her room the other day. She even overcame her shyness enough to make a friend at her new school.

Please don't let there be setbacks now.

"I just don't like this, Elsa," Brett tells her.

"I don't, either, but we both know she's been through a lot worse than spending a summer day indoors."

"But she shouldn't be afraid to go outside. Why don't you just take her outside and show her that there's nothing to be afraid of?"

"Because she won't—" Suddenly aware that the living room has fallen quiet, Elsa peeks through the doorway and sees that Renny has turned off the TV. Either the movie is over or she's getting restless.

"Brett, I've got to go." She hangs up the phone quickly and goes in to find Renny sitting with her chin in her hands.

"Movie's over?"

"No, but I already saw it."

Elsa smiles. Understatement of the year. Renny knows *The Little Mermaid* by heart, usually mouthing the dialogue along with the characters.

"Was that Daddy again, on the phone?"

"Yup."

"Is he coming home?"

"Not yet. He's at work."

"I wish he could come home."

"He will, tonight. What do you want to do now?"

The little girl sneaks a wistful peek at the window before turning her back and surveying the room. "I don't know. I guess maybe we can play Don't Break the Ice again."

"We can. Or there are some other fun things in the rainy day bin. An Etch A Sketch, or this paint-with-water book—"

"I don't really feel like playing with anything else."

"Well, we can go outside and have a picnic like we did yesterday. Wouldn't that be fun?"

Renny is shaking her head even before Elsa's done speaking. "I don't want to."

But she *does* want to. Elsa can tell.

"Well, you know what? I think I'm going to go out and take a walk around the yard."

Renny's dark eyebrows shoot up toward her bangs. "To check for monsters?"

"I already did, honey. There aren't any. I just want to get some fresh air. Want to come?"

"Maybe."

Carefully nonchalant, Elsa holds out her hand. "Come on."

Renny hesitates. Then, silently, she comes over to take Elsa's hand. Her fingers are so small, and cold.

They walk to the door. As Elsa opens it, Renny holds back, clenching her hand.

"It's okay, honey. Come on."

She doesn't exactly drag Renny outside, but she does have to give her a little tug over the threshold.

The sun is warm, and a slight breeze stirs the forsythia, whose April yellow blooms have long since given way to a dense, summery green. Elsa does her best not to peer at the boughs as she leads a reluctant

Renny around the corner of the house toward the backyard.

She can feel her daughter's grasp relax a bit.

"See?" she tells Renny. "Everything is fine."

"Are you sure?"

"Sure I'm sure. Look around."

As they stroll across the yard, taking in the ordinariness of the June afternoon, Elsa feels Renny's grip relax a bit. Fat bumblebees buzz over a clump of pink peony blossoms, birds call from the trees, and higher overhead, a humming jet trails a white path across the blue sky.

Suddenly, a voice calls out from somewhere close by.

Elsa clutches Renny and spins around.

Oh. Meg Warren. Thank God.

Ordinarily she wouldn't be thrilled to see her next-door neighbor, but today, Elsa practically throws her arms around the woman in sheer relief.

"Well, aren't you two a couple of nervous Nellies!"

"Hi, Meg." To her own ears, Elsa's voice sounds an octave higher than usual. Renny cowers against her, saying nothing.

"Beautiful day, isn't it? What are you up to?"

"Not much. How about you? No work today?"

"I don't go in until five," Meg tells her. "All nights this week. Half shifts."

"Well that's nice. At least you get to enjoy the weather."

"I can't enjoy it when I'm worrying about paying my bills and they're cutting my hours. Anyhoo"—she gestures with the shears in her hand—"I just stepped outside to snip some fresh basil for my salad. Would you two like to join me for lunch?"

"No, thanks, we—"

"Wouldn't you know something got into my herb

patch and trampled the bed? I'd blame my kids, but they're off spending a week with their father. You wouldn't happen to have any basil over there, would you?"

"I have dried basil in the kitchen, if you want to—"

"Lord, no!" Meg throws up her hands in horror. "Fresh basil or nothing—that's what I always say."

It's not the only thing she always says. As she launches into one of her monologues, Elsa reminds herself that the woman means well.

But Meg Warren—a lonely, chatty divorcee—is one of those people who sorely lacks audience awareness. She tends to park herself in the yard or driveway and prattle on, with no regard to whether Elsa might have someplace to go, or has any interest whatsoever in Meg's bunions—one of her all-time favorite conversational topics. She blames the bunions—like everything else—on her deadbeat ex-husband, because she's on her feet all day as a Macy's cashier, her only means of support other than his frequently late alimony payments.

For a while there last August and September, Meg spent far less time talking about her feet and her ex, instead wanting to know all about the Cavalons—specifically, their experience with Jeremy.

"I just can't believe you never told me you had a child who was kidnapped and murdered!" she mused, after discovering—via the satellite news trucks parked at the curb—her neighbors' tragic past.

Karyn, who runs Tidewater Animal Rescue, where Elsa sometimes volunteers, said exactly the same thing.

They're not the only ones. In all the places they lived after Jeremy's disappearance, Elsa never told anyone about Jeremy—other than her therapists, of course. Not that she made new friends, ever—or even kept in touch with the old ones. Isolation was easier.

But now that she has closure, and Renny's here, maybe it's time to branch out, let people in.

She lets Meg talk for a few minutes more about the benefits of fresh herbs, until she inevitably segues down a familiar path.

" . . . and do you know I read that there are herbal remedies for bunions? Turmeric, for example, is—"

"Mommy?" Renny, mercifully, cuts in. "Can we go do something now?"

Ordinarily, Elsa would reprimand her for interrupting. Now she apologetically tells Meg they have some mother-daughter time planned, and they'll have to excuse themselves. After an extended good-bye, Meg leaves at last.

"Okay, so . . . want to swing?" Elsa asks Renny, gesturing at the cedar play set she and Brett bought last fall, right after they received their foster parenting approval. They were supposed to be shopping for a new washer and dryer, and they couldn't afford both, but somehow this seemed more important.

At the time, Elsa couldn't help but think how much Jeremy would have loved the towering playhouse topped by a lookout tower with a plastic telescope and striped awning. It was impossible—and felt so wrong—to imagine another child romping on the slide, swings, and climbing wall . . .

Then Renny came along.

"I want to build a sandcastle." She tugs Elsa toward the sandbox. Molded of pink plastic, it arrived not long after she did—and already Elsa had gotten over the feeling that this backyard, like so many others over the years, should have belonged to Jeremy.

"A sandcastle. Great idea. I'll help you."

Together, they remove the plastic cover and assemble the necessary tools: buckets, molds, shovels.

"We need water, Mommy."

Elsa glances down at the pale yellow sleeveless shift she put on this morning, when she assumed they were going to the seaport. She should probably change into something more sandbox-friendly.

Then again, now that Renny's had a breakthrough, she doesn't dare risk losing momentum. Who cares if her outfit gets wet and dirty?

Maman would care.

As she picks her way through overgrown pachysandra to reach the coiled garden hose against the wall of the house, Elsa can almost hear Sylvie Durand chiding her about mixing sand, water, and French silk. She'd undoubtedly have plenty to say about the pink striped top and orange plaid shorts Renny chose to wear this morning, too.

When she visited over Christmas, she voiced her disapproval over Elsa's habit of allowing her daughter to pick out her own clothes. When Elsa explained that it's important for children to express creativity, her mother's legendary blue eyes rolled back to her fake lashes.

"And it isn't important to learn to look halfway decent in public?" asked Maman, who favors fully accessorized designer outfits, complete with one of her trademark veiled chapeaux, often riding atop one of her elaborately coiffed auburn wigs.

Elsa long ago learned to accept her mother's limits. She is who she is. But sometimes, she simply has to be put in her place.

"Believe me, Maman, wearing plaid with stripes isn't the worst thing that can happen to a child."

Yes, *that* shut her up—for the time being, anyway.

As she unspools a length of green garden hose, Elsa glances over the foundation shrubs. The rhododendron was in full bloom just a day or two ago, when she cut some fat pink blossoms to bring into the house.

Those that remain are droopy and faded. She read somewhere that you're supposed to deadhead them so that they don't go to seed. Maybe she should—

Elsa's random thoughts skid to a screeching halt.

A large, freshly snapped bough dangles from the shrub that sits directly below Renny's bedroom window . . . and a footprint is plainly visible in the dirt beside it.

CHAPTER THREE

All morning and well into the afternoon, people have been coming and going at the luxury apartment tower across the street. Deliverymen, maintenance workers, and the well-heeled residents themselves.

Sooner or later, Marin Quinn or her daughters are bound to appear at the building's front doors, and when they do, they'll be easy to spot from here.

Sooner would be much appreciated; the odor is becoming stronger as midday heat permeates the narrow alleyway between a pub and a sushi restaurant: stale beer and rancid fish. A few feet away, something scurries between the foundation and the row of metal garbage cans.

Not a creature is stirring . . .

Except for a rat.

Make that plural. How fitting that there are dozens, maybe hundreds of the filthy rodents here, just a stone's throw from the Quinns' fancy doorstep.

Fitting—and convenient.

Undaunted by human companionship, another rat brushes past, just as the doorman across the street tips his hat to a familiar-looking female exiting the building.

Ah, it's *her*. Perfect timing.

* * *

"But I didn't even hear the phone ringing," Renny protests as Elsa swoops her out of the backyard and into the house.

"I did. You were too far away." Elsa sets her on her sandy feet just inside the door and locks it behind them.

"What are you doing?"

"Answering the phone."

"But it's not ringing!" Renny looks as though she isn't sure whether to giggle or worry.

"I know, I guess I missed it."

"But—"

"I bet it was Daddy. I'll call him back." She's already dialing Brett's number, keeping a wary eye on the yard.

As it rings, she sees Renny watching her. She reaches for the rainy day bin and hurriedly sets it in front of her. "Here, pick out something that you haven't played with yet."

"But . . . I'm making a sandcastle."

"I know, but—"

"Brett Cavalon's office."

"Cindy, it's Elsa."

"Elsa! How are you?"

"I need to talk to Brett right away. Is he there?"

"He left a little while ago for a meeting. He'll be back soon. Do you want me to have him call you?"

"Please. Tell him it's important."

"Is everything okay?"

Pretending she didn't hear the question, she hangs up and turns back to Renny. "Come on, honey, we have to run a few errands."

"But what about the sandcastle?"

"We'll get back to that later."

"What? When?" Poor thing, she looks alarmed, and no wonder. Her mother is acting crazy.

Elsa grabs her keys from the hook by the door, along with a canvas tote bag hanging beside it. Embroidered in pink thread with Renny's name, it's filled with Barbie dolls and an elaborate collection of clothes, courtesy of her grandmother.

Maman would have preferred to start a collection of antique French porcelain dolls for Renny, as she had for Elsa, but Elsa put her foot down.

She offers the Barbie bag to Renny. "Here, take this to play with in the car."

"I don't want that."

"But you always take it with you when we go someplace."

"Well, I don't want to go anywhere today."

"I know, but we have to. Come on." Juggling the bag with her keys and cell phone as she dials it, Elsa hustles her out the door.

Please pick up, Brett.

The phone rings on the other end.

Pick up!

It rings again as she opens the back door for Renny, who reluctantly climbs in.

"You've reached the voice mail of Brett Cavalon . . ."

Elsa's heart sinks. "Brett, Renny and I are going . . ."

Where are they supposed to go? What are they supposed to do?

" . . . someplace," she tells his voice mail. "I'm not sure where. Please call as soon as you get this."

She hangs up. Seeing Renny obediently strapped into her booster seat, Elsa tosses the tote bag onto the backseat, climbs behind the wheel, and starts the car. They have to go. They can't stay here alone, knowing someone really was prowling around in the night.

Are you sure of that?

A broken branch, a footprint.

Yes. She's positive, sick-to-her-stomach positive that someone was in the bushes beneath the window—the one Renny had said the monster climbed through.

Someone really was in her room last night.

Every time Elsa allows that thought to fully form, a wave of disbelief sweeps it away.

Maybe you're wrong. Maybe . . .

But . . .

A broken branch. A footprint.

Please don't let it be happening again. Please, God . . .

Caroline Quinn glumly sips a gigantic frozen Starbucks coffee drink that tastes like a milk shake and probably has a gazillion calories. She really didn't want it, but she had to order something. And she really doesn't want to be here, but she has to be somewhere, right?

Somewhere other than home, where Annie's being a nosy little pain in the butt as usual, Mom has a depressing plan to clean out the basement storage unit in preparation for the move, and the cleaning ladies are making such a ruckus that you'd think they were expecting the president for dinner.

There was a time when such a concept wouldn't be all that far-fetched. But now that Congressman Quinn has become Inmate Quinn, the era of high-profile dinner guests is over—at least for now. Someday, she's certain, Dad will straighten out this whole mess and come home. Until then, it's going to be a long, lonely summer, and she'd better figure out where she's going to spend it, because anything is better than being at home. Even sitting in the crowded neighborhood coffeehouse with nothing to do but eavesdrop on the world's most boring conversations.

"So then I told him . . ."

"Oh no, you dih-unt!"

"Oh yeah, girl, you *know* I did!"

The two women seated at the table to Caroline's right, close enough to touch, erupt into ear-splitting laughter once again.

"Mo' whip cweam, Mommy!" demands the bratty little kid at the table to Caroline's left, also mere inches away.

"Is that how we ask for something, Dakota?"

"Mo'!"

"You need to say please."

And you need to say "cream," not "cweam," Caroline wants to put in, fed up with the doting mother and bratty kid with the cowgirl name that seems downright stupid here in Manhattan.

Wincing as Dakota lets out a shrill "*Noooooo,*" Caroline fumbles to unzip her shoulder bag on the back of her chair. She already checked inside for her iPod, and it wasn't there. Normally, she doesn't leave home without it, but she was pretty desperate to escape earlier. She feels around inside the bag, thinking maybe the iPod will magically appear now that she's desperate for headphones to block out the kid.

"*Whip cweam, whip cweam, whip cweam . . .*" Dakota rhythmically bangs the table with her fists.

"You're my little drummer girl, aren't you?" her lame mother croons, and one of the women to Caroline's right, in the midst of an exuberant fist bump, elbows her in the arm.

"Oops, sorry about that, hon."

"It's okay," Caroline mumbles, and glances around for an empty spot far, far away from these annoying people. Not only are there no vacant tables, but the line at the register snakes almost back to the door.

She supposes she could always get up and go . . . but where?

Not home. Not yet.

Shopping?

If Dad were still around, she'd have a pile of cash and probably at least one of his credit cards in her wallet. He always told Caroline to get whatever she needed—or wanted, for that matter. But those days are over for the time being, and she's never felt so alone in her life.

To the rest of the world, her father was a public figure, revered or abhorred, depending on the timing, the press, or the party affiliation. But to Caroline, he was just Daddy—the center of her world, the person who made her feel so important, so loved, so special, that her friends had called her Daddy's Girl for as long as she could remember. She took it as a compliment—whether or not it was intended that way.

Oh, Dad.

As always, Caroline feels her eyes begin to sting as she pictures him, sitting in a jail cell somewhere . . .

And all because of me.

Why is she the only person in the whole wide world who understands that Garvey Quinn did what he did out of love? Even Mom doesn't seem to get it. Obviously she, unlike Dad, wasn't willing to do whatever was necessary to save her daughter's life.

Last year, while snooping through her parents' files, Caroline discovered that she'd been born with a rare genetic illness. Only a transplant could save her—and Dad made it his mission to find a donor, at any cost.

He loved me so much.

Taking a hard gulp of her frozen drink, Caroline

winces. Head freeze. She puts down the cup and presses her cold fingertips against her temples, closing her eyes.

The thing is, it wasn't like that boy, Jeremy, meant something to Dad. And it wasn't like Dad actually *killed* him.

No, it wasn't like that at all.

Caroline isn't sure, exactly, what it *was* like, because no one will tell her. Mom did her best to shelter her and Annie when the news first broke, and Caroline was so shell-shocked, she didn't even care about the details. By the time she did care, she found out that the press still didn't have the whole story. She tried snooping through her parents' files for information—which was how she'd learned last year about her own rare illness, and a lot of other stuff her parents apparently didn't want her to know—but found nothing. And Mom still wasn't talking.

"You're better off not knowing," she told Caroline.

What kind of bullshit is that? She's better off not knowing why the one person in the world who loves her enough to die for her is—

"Excuse me, is anyone sitting here?"

Caroline looks up to see a guy standing beside her table with a steaming cup of coffee.

"Um, yeah. I am."

The guy doesn't look the least bit fazed by her sarcasm. "I meant is anyone sitting in the empty seat?"

"You mean you don't see him?"

"See who?" He follows her pointed gaze across the table.

"My friend George."

Now he looks fazed, raising an eyebrow at the empty chair, then at Caroline. "Uh, no. I don't see him."

She sighs, shaking her head. "No one ever does."

"Okay, well, uh . . . thanks anyway." The cute guy starts to back away, obviously convinced she's some kind of nut.

Caroline bursts out laughing. "Relax, dude. I was kidding."

"You were?"

She nods, reaches out her sandal-clad foot, and pushes the empty chair in his direction. "You can take it."

"Thanks." He looks around, obviously trying to figure out where to drag it. In the meager surrounding floor space, there are half a dozen tables, at least twice as many people, plus a couple of baby carriages.

"You can just sit here, if you want," Caroline offers. "I'm getting ready to leave anyway."

"Yeah?"

No, but . . . "Yeah."

"Thanks." The guy sits down, smiling at her. He's got great teeth. So white. Caroline wonders if they're bleached.

She really should get going.

She sneaks another peek at him.

He's totally laid back, with a surfer kind of appeal: casually shaggy, sun-streaked hair, a natural-looking tan you don't typically see in Manhattan, even in the summer, and a Rip Curl T-shirt. He's the antithesis of Caroline, with her creamy complexion and dark hair salon-styled in a long, chic fringe that cost even more than her two-hundred-dollar jeans.

But then again, she *did* learn to surf last summer, out east in the Hamptons. And anyway, opposites attract . . . isn't that what they say?

Surfer Boy smiles at her.

Yeah. She'll get going in a minute.

Maybe two.

* * *

"I want to go home, Mommy," Renny says yet again from the backseat. "I want to make my sandcastle."

"I know, we will—but not just yet."

Jaw set, Elsa drives on, wishing Brett would hurry and call her back on her cell phone.

Driving around and around the most well-populated local areas, it's all she can do to maintain her composure for Renny's sake. Hands clammy on the steering wheel, she keeps an eye on the rearview mirror. She's pretty sure the coast is clear so far, yet her heart is pounding as if someone is following—no, chasing them.

When at last her phone rings, she's stopped at a light on U.S. 1. Startled by the sound, she jerks her foot off the brake for a split second. The car moves—less than an inch toward the bumper of the car ahead of her, but still . . .

You shouldn't be behind the wheel in this state.

She looks around for a place to pull over, reaching for the phone with a trembling hand. "Hello?"

"Elsa! Are you all right?"

Brett. Thank God.

"We are, but . . ." She darts a glance over her shoulder. Renny meets it with a head-on, inquisitive stare.

"What's going on?" Brett asks worriedly. "Where are you?"

"We're on U.S. 1."

"On U.S. 1? Why? *Where* on U.S. 1?"

"Long Hill Road"—she looks around—"by the Sunoco."

Darting a glance at the dashboard gauge, she sees that the needle is almost on E. She hadn't even thought to check it until this moment.

Stupid, stupid, stupid!

What if they had run out of gas? She and Renny would have been sitting in the car like bait in a trap . . .

No. You're getting carried away. It's broad daylight; there are people and cars all around. Calm down.

She quickly turns into the gas station and pulls up to a pump. "Brett, listen, just hang on for a second, I need to talk to you."

Reaching for the door handle, the phone clutched in her other hand, she tells Renny, "Stay buckled in, okay?"

"Where are you going?"

"To get some gas," Elsa murmurs, and climbs out of the car with the phone.

Stopped cold by a fleeting imaginary image— a stranger pushing her aside and driving off with Renny—she reaches back to grab the keys, and locks the door before closing it.

"Mommy! Noooooooo!"

Elsa spins around to see her daughter's frantic expression, her palms splayed helplessly against the window.

"Oh, Renny!" She swiftly unlocks the car and the child hurtles herself out in a sobbing panic. Elsa grabs on to her, wraps her arms around her violently shaking little body. "Oh my God, I'm so sorry."

"You shut me in!"

"I didn't mean it, baby, I was just trying to keep you safe . . ."

"Elsa, please, what is going *on*?" Brett is asking in her ear. "Elsa!"

She wants to scream at him to shut up, to just let her deal with Renny right now. But of course he's alarmed, clueless, thinking God only knows what.

"Wait, please, Brett, just give me a second! Renny, it's okay. You're okay. I'm sorry, I'm so sorry."

Her worst fear. How could I do that to her?

Elsa is zapped by a white-hot bolt of fury—at herself, at whoever was prowling around their home in the middle of the night, violating her little girl's safe haven.

Was it a random incident? A would-be burglar? Or . . . someone else? Someone who knows them, knows about Jeremy . . .

Fear mingles with fury as Elsa guides her daughter gently back down into the car seat. "Just sit right here, you don't even have to strap in yet, and we'll leave the door open . . ."

Conscious of Brett impatiently waiting on the other end of the phone, she settles Renny in as quickly as possible and turns toward the gas pump, furtively checking out the other customers, the cars, the vegetation alongside the parking lot . . .

If anything happens—if anyone makes a move toward Renny—she'll use the nozzle like a gun and—

Something catches Elsa's eye, on the ground beside the open back door of the car. In disbelief, she bends over to take a closer look, because it can't be . . . it just can't be.

But it *is*.

Dear God. Dread slices through her.

Taking out a laptop, Surfer Boy looks across the small table at Caroline, "Do you mind if I . . . ?"

"Oh. No." She moves her own drink cup to make room. She really was just leaving, but for some reason, she can't seem to make herself get up and go.

Some reason?

He's cute. That's the reason. Not your type, but cute.

Her type—the wealthy, well-bred boys who travel in her family's social circle—have given her a wide berth since the scandal broke. So have most of the girls at school, aside from Desdemona and Emily, her two closest friends. Too bad they're both out of town until September.

Across the table, Surfer Boy sips his coffee, presses a button on the keyboard, and sips again, obviously waiting for the laptop to boot up. "This thing is so slow," he comments—to himself, or to Caroline?

She decides to answer, just so he doesn't think she's ignoring him if he was talking to her. And if he wasn't . . .

Well, whatever. "Yeah . . . they all are."

She really should go.

She will . . . right after she finds out how old he is. "So do you go to school?"

He nods, pressing buttons on the keyboard.

"Where?"

"Right now, I'm taking a summer course at Columbia."

Yeah. She had him pegged for older.

"What about you?" he asks, still focused on the screen.

"Done for the summer."

"Yeah?" He looks up. "Where do you go?"

She hesitates. "Billington."

Maybe he'll think that's a private college some-where, and not a high school. If he knows it's a high school, she'll mention that she'll be a senior this year.

And he'll care because . . . ?

This is so stupid, trying to impress some random guy she'll never see again.

But he does seem interested, resting his chin on his hand and looking at her across the table. "Billington? Where is that?"

Maybe she should make up some New England town that sounds like it would be home to a charming college campus.

Yeah, or maybe you should just tell the truth.

"It's over on York. It's a high school," she adds, almost apologetically. "But I'm a senior. I mean, I will be. In September."

"Cool. So you live around here?"

"A few blocks away. How about you?"

He tells her he's from the West Coast, where he goes to college. He's got a summer internship here in the city at some corporation she's never heard of. She finds herself telling him about her friends, and music she likes, and cool places to hang out. He's easy to talk to—until he says, "Hey, I don't even know your name."

She hesitates. What are the odds that he's heard of Garvey Quinn, even if he wasn't in New York when her father was front-page tabloid news?

The odds are definitely good. Daddy was a congressman; she's pretty sure the scandal made national headlines.

Now it's time to go. Saying simply, "I'm Caroline," she pushes back her chair.

"Jake."

"Nice meeting you." Caroline stands, putting her bag over her shoulder and finding herself boxed in by tables, chairs, and the lolling, jean-clad limbs belonging to a trio of teenage boys and a lovey-dovey couple behind her. The cackling friends have been replaced by a young, bespectacled woman engrossed in a book and someone—a man, judging by the hairy knuckles—whose face is hidden behind today's *New York Times*.

The most direct escape route is partially blocked by Dakota's mother, now talking on her cell phone. She's oblivious to her daughter pouring out sugar packets all over the table, and to Caroline's polite "Excuse me."

She says it again, is ignored again. Feeling helpless, she looks back at Jake, and finds him grinning.

"Trapped?" he asks.

"Sort of."

"Is this place always this jammed?"

"I don't know . . . I hardly ever come here."

"Really?"

Realizing he looks kind of bummed, Caroline wonders if he might actually be interested in her. "But sometimes I do," she adds. "Come here, I mean."

Brilliant. You hardly ever come here, but sometimes you come here.

"Yeah? Maybe I'll run into you again sometime, then."

She grins. "Maybe you will."

"Or I can just call you and meet you here tomorrow afternoon. Or somewhere else."

"That, uh . . . that would be cool."

"Let me get your info. Just call me on my cell and then I'll have your number. Where's your phone?"

Trying not to act thrilled, she unzips her bag and shoves her hand inside, feeling around for it.

Something moves inside—something warm, and furry, and—

Caroline screeches and throws the bag, then watches in horror as a fat brown rat emerges and scuttles away.

"Brett! Oh my God . . . oh my God . . ."

"What? What is it?"

"It's . . ." She bends over and retrieves the object from the ground beside her car. "Spider-Man."

"What are you talking about?"

"A Spider-Man action figure."

Brett is silent for a moment.

But he knows what it means. Of course he does.

On the day Jeremy disappeared, they'd gone shopping at Wal-Mart and Elsa had bought him a pair of

Spider-Man action figures. He'd been playing with them in the yard when he vanished. One of the toys was left behind in the grass. The other, presumably, had been clutched in Jeremy's hand when he was taken away.

"Where?" Brett is asking. "Where is it?"

"I think it just fell out of the car." She looks in at Renny. Beside her booster seat, the tote bag is open. Several Barbies and outfits are strewn across the backseat.

Could Spider-Man have been in the bag, too?

"Hang on, Brett." She leans into the car, showing Renny the toy in her hand. "Honey, was this in with the Barbies?"

Renny glances up and frowns. "That's for boys."

"No, I know, but . . . I'm just wondering if it was in your tote bag."

"Why?"

"I think it was. Was it?"

"I don't know."

"Did you see it when you took out your dolls?"

"I didn't take them out. The bag tipped over. They fell out. I told you I don't want to play with them."

"No, I know, I just—"

"Elsa," Brett says on the phone, "you need to talk to me. I still don't know what's going on. You found Spider-Man, and what?"

She turns back to the gas pump, cradling the phone between her ear and shoulder. In a whisper, she tells Brett what she found beneath Renny's bedroom window.

The broken branch . . . the footprint . . . and now Spider-Man?

She half expects him to say she must have been imagining things, but he doesn't.

"Stay where you are. Just pull over and don't move. Lock the doors, stay in the car. I'm on my way."

"What are we going to do?"

There's a pause.

Then Brett, who hours earlier promised Elsa that everything was fine, says in a tone laced with uncertainty, "I have no idea."

Stepping into the storage unit in the basement of her building, Marin flips on the overhead light and sucks in a lungful of musty air.

This is not going to be fun.

But then, what *is* anymore?

Maybe she should save the task for another day, when she's feeling more . . .

What, more ready to deal with the past?

And that will be when?

The truth is, she's never going to feel ready, but it makes sense to tackle this today. There's certainly nowhere to hide upstairs in the apartment. One cleaning lady is in Marin's bedroom, the other in the den, and Annie is in the kitchen engaging in her new favorite hobby: baking.

Marin doesn't have the heart to point out that her younger daughter really should lay off the sweets, having transformed from lithe to chubby amid the upheaval of the past year. It seems cruel to take away something she enjoys so much, especially when she's been deprived of so many other things.

Then again, it's probably even crueler to subject her to the teasing and scrutiny that accompanies being an overweight adolescent—particularly from her older sister.

At least Caroline went out somewhere for the time being. She's probably off brooding in the park, or window-shopping on Madison.

Marin had considered forcing herself to do the

same, figuring she can't stay in seclusion forever, especially now that summer is here and the kids are home.

But if she went out, she'd have to make herself pre-
sentable, because you don't walk around the Upper East
Side in this state: worn jeans and sneakers, makeup-
free, hair pulled back in a coated rubber band. Unless,
of course, you're a preschooler. Or a supermodel.

She doesn't have the energy to get all fixed up, and
she's certainly not in the mood for prying gazes from
those who might recognize her.

Might as well stay here and get this over with.
Clutching a box of garbage bags, she surveys the room.
Closest to the door are the boxes she hauled down here
yesterday, filled with framed photos and the contents
of Garvey's office.

Beyond are stacks and stacks of plastic tubs, accu-
mulated over the lifetime of the Quinn marriage. The
contents of each are neatly identified with a strip of
masking tape and a Sharpie-scrawled label: "Letters
and Cards," "Photos," "Press Clippings". . .

Tangible mementos of a bygone era. These days,
so many of those relics are stored only in cyberspace.
All it would take is the click of a delete button, and
whoosh! It would be as if they never existed at all.

Too bad you can't do that with this stuff.

Or with Garvey.

She can't help but smirk at the thought of deleting
Garvey from her life with the press of a button. There's
something to be said for black humor.

Okay, so, where to begin?

Opening the lid of the nearest container, Marin
finds it filled with DVDs. Ah, store-bought and impersonal: a good place to start. This should be painless.

She glances over the titles: *The Sixth Sense, Saving
Private Ryan, The Big Lebowski* . . .

When the girls were little, she and Garvey would

put them to bed early on Saturday nights and curl up on the couch to watch movies together.

So much for impersonal.

She has to wipe her eyes on her sleeve a few times as she starts sorting through the DVDs. The goal is to create a pile of keepers and throw away the rest. But after a few minutes, the garbage bag remains empty; she can't find anything she's willing to part with. Maybe the memories here are just too fresh. She dumps the entire tear-splotched pile back into the tub and replaces the lid.

For a moment, she just stands there with her eyes closed, longing to go back upstairs and crawl into her bed—*and* the orange prescription bottle in her nightstand.

No. She can't let herself do that.

She pushes her way to a stack of tubs against the wall. Ancient history back here—maybe this will be easier to deal with.

The topmost one is full of clothing.

Marin lifts out the first item, a plain old blue T-shirt. *Why would I have saved this?*

Then she spots the flaps in the bodice and realizes it's a nursing top. There are a dozen more; nursing bras, too, and nightgowns, even maternity dresses. She saved them all.

Didn't she realize, after the disastrous circumstances of Annie's birth, that there would be no more babies? Was she really holding out hope for another child?

She remembers being terrified that Caroline wasn't going to survive her illness; terrified that after bearing three children, she would be left with only one.

Tears fall freely as she sorts through the remnants of early motherhood, remembering the days of morning sickness and labor pains and endless wee-hour feedings . . .

With Annie, anyway. She's such an easygoing kid now that Marin rarely remembers what a demanding, fussy, colicky baby she'd been.

After a few exhausting months, the pediatrician said she didn't need to nurse in the middle of the night. "She's not hungry, she just wants attention. She'll learn to comfort herself if you let her cry it out."

Cry it out? Marin was aghast.

Not Garvey, though. He'd wanted to let her cry it out beginning when she came home from the hospital.

Garvey had his reasons, Marin knows, for resenting Annie from the moment she was born. No . . . even *before* she was born. When prenatal testing confirmed his worst fears, he was faced, for the second time in his life, with an unwanted child. And for the second time, he told Marin they weren't going to keep it. *It*, like some castoff object and not a person.

Bastard.

Marin had learned the hard way not to let anyone rip her own flesh and blood from her arms. All that talk about what a great gift she'd bestow upon a perfect stranger . . .

This time, she ignored it, determined to keep her baby, to raise Annie with enough love to make up for everything.

And I have. I've done all that . . .

For Annie.

I've done for her what I didn't have the strength to do for Jeremy.

If I'd found the strength to do the same for Jeremy, would he be alive right now?

Marin wipes away her tears, dumps the heap of nursing clothes into a black garbage bag, and ties it shut.

There.

One bittersweet chapter of her past, closed forever.

Driving over to the Long Hill Road Sunoco in midday traffic, Brett found his imagination carrying him to some dark places.

Now, spotting Elsa's dark blue Volvo sitting at the edge of the gas station parking lot, he exhales for what feels like the first time since he spoke to her back at the office.

He pulls up alongside Elsa's car. Sitting behind the wheel, she raises a fingertip to her lips and gestures at the backseat.

Seeing Renny curled up back there, small and defenseless, sound asleep, Brett feels sick inside. If Elsa is right—and *she's* not the one who's imagining things—then someone, some monster, in the truest sense of the word, was in Renny's room last night as she slept.

God only knows what might have happened if she hadn't woken up and called for help.

It was Elsa who went in there, not you. You rolled over and went back to sleep. How could you?

If anything had happened to his little girl . . .

But nothing did.

And nothing will.

Because Brett knows, deep down inside, that his wife is sometimes frighteningly fragile; that her imagination can be vivid and powerful; that her mental health history includes episodes of delusion . . .

But he'd thought—hoped, prayed—all that was behind her now.

Brett turns off the car and climbs out. Elsa does the same, leaving the door open. Wordlessly, she shows him the Spider-Man action figure.

He stares down at it.

"Is that . . . ?"

"Jeremy's?" Elsa swallows hard. "Maybe. I don't remember exactly what it looked like—the one that went missing with him—but—"

Her voice breaks, and Brett pulls her close, his thoughts whirling through the possibilities:

It might be a colossal coincidence. Maybe it didn't even fall out of the car. This is a public place. Maybe some little boy lost it . . .

Or maybe it was tucked somewhere among the Cavalons' possessions for all these years and Renny came across it and carried it with her . . .

Or maybe Elsa herself found it somewhere, or bought it somewhere, and—and she forgot about it, or she's delusional, or . . .

"Brett, say something."

"Don't worry," he says automatically. "It's going to be okay."

"You don't know that."

He opens his mouth to contradict her, but thinks better of it. She's right. He *doesn't* know that. Christ, right now he doesn't know anything.

"Did you discuss this with anyone?" he asks, releasing her.

"Not yet. I didn't want to make any calls until I'd talked to you."

"We have to report the break-in now . . . don't you think?"

"Yes." She pauses. "I mean, I think so."

They stare at each other, and Brett is glad Elsa can't read his mind.

Just because she had some problems before, years ago—that doesn't mean she's unbalanced now. It doesn't mean she herself is responsible for the Spider-Man doll being here. It doesn't mean that, fueled by

Renny's nightmare, Elsa imagined the intruder, and there's a logical explanation for footprint and the broken branch—if they do exist.

He wants desperately to believe that they don't, even if it means accepting that his wife is still suffering the psychological fallout of Jeremy's kidnapping— or that learning of his death triggered a relapse into dissociative behavior.

Anything is better than believing that Renny is in danger.

"What's Roxanne going to say, Brett? If we call the police and she finds out?"

"She will find out, and what do *you* think she'll say? It's her job to make sure that Renny's in a safe environment."

"That's *our* job, too."

"And we're doing it."

"Roxanne might not agree." She shrugs, hugging herself, her thin arms bared by a simple, butter-colored dress.

Even now, Brett finds himself marveling at his wife's striking beauty: black hair and eyes offset her flawless complexion and delicate French features.

Before Jeremy came, and after he was gone, Brett had convinced himself that he could be happy if it were just the two of them for the rest of their lives. Yes, they longed for parenthood, but they had each other. Maybe that was enough.

Now he knows that it can't be; that their lives wouldn't be complete without Renny. Now that he's had a true taste of what it's like to love a child so completely . . .

He would never admit to Elsa that it was different with Jeremy. Maybe she knew, deep down, that try as he might, Brett couldn't quite connect with him, couldn't quite . . .

Love him?

Even now, acknowledging it only to himself, shame sweeps through him.

He'd cared for his son, had tried to protect him, had thought he was doing everything in his power to help Jeremy overcome all his problems. Even after what happened that day at Harbor Hills Country Club . . .

Brett rarely allows himself to think about that particular incident. But whenever the memory rears its ugly head anyway, he's swept by the same sense of helpless foreboding he experienced when he saw what his son had done to the sweet, innocent little girl with the big blue eyes and blond braids.

"I didn't mean it," Jeremy had said, standing there with a red-streaked seven-iron in his hand. "She laughed at me, and I got mad."

Mad.

Violently so. All that blood . . .

He'll never forget those terrified blue eyes, dilated with shock, staring up at him as he stood over her holding his son's shoulders—holding him back.

The child survived, thank God. Miraculously, her wealthy parents didn't press charges, reportedly wanting to avoid a messy lawsuit.

Even after what Jeremy had done that day, Brett would have given anything to find him after he vanished.

But maybe you didn't really love him. Not enough. Not like you love Renny.

"Sometimes I think it's a miracle that we were even approved as foster parents after what happened."

Brett looks up, startled, wondering if Elsa really has read his mind, or if she's known all along about Brett's secret failure as a father.

"That wasn't our fault," he tells her. "Jeremy."

Elsa says nothing to that; of course she disagrees.

She was the one who was home the day he was abducted, not Brett. She was in the kitchen making dinner as Jeremy played in the fenced backyard, same as every sunny afternoon. She kept an eye on him, same as always—but not every second.

And in a split second, a child can disappear forever.

Brett always wondered if Jeremy had run away. He was a troubled child. It wouldn't be all that far-fetched.

Intuitive Elsa never bought into the runaway theory. She was certain he'd been kidnapped, and she blamed herself. But when she finally found out why Jeremy had been taken, and by whom . . .

It wasn't her fault, can't she see that? No parent spends every moment of every day standing guard over a seven-year-old. Every mother has to turn her back at some point. And someone was there, watching, waiting for Elsa to do just that.

Jeremy never had a chance.

"This is unbelievable, Brett. Spider-Man . . ." Elsa clutches his arm, and he can feel her body quaking. "Spider-Man just appearing out of the blue on the day after someone broke into our house, and was in Renny's room—"

"That was probably—"

Your imagination.

"—just a burglar," he says instead. "I'm sure it has nothing to do with what happened to Jeremy."

"*Just* a burglar? You're *sure*? Come on, Brett, you're not sure of anything." She keeps her voice low, but he has a feeling that if Renny weren't sleeping a few feet away, she'd be shouting at him.

"So you think that it *does* have something to do with Jeremy?"

"Or with Renny. Who knows? Her birth mother is a lunatic, and her birth father might be out of jail again. What if—"

"Elsa, come on. They signed away their rights without batting an eye. Do you really think they're going to track us down and—and do you really think they know about *Spider-Man*?"

"I don't know. I'm not saying it's them. It could be anyone. It's no secret around here who we are. Maybe someone saw the coverage on TV or in the paper about Garvey Quinn and Jeremy, and decided to look us up."

She might have a point. Sensational stories like theirs must bring all kinds of kooks out of the woodwork.

Still, he shakes his head, unable to grasp—or maybe, accept—that one tragedy could possibly beget another.

"So what do we do?" he asks her. "Call the police? Even though Roxanne will have to know, and something like this . . ."

He doesn't have to finish the sentence. She knows.

Something like this could destroy their fragile new family. If the agency decides it's in Renny's best interest to remove her from their custody, they'll lose her forever.

It happened to Todd and Zoe Walden, for a far less compelling perception of threat. The agency zoomed in and snatched away their daughter without warning, almost as if . . .

She'd been kidnapped. Or had died. One moment she was there, a part of Todd and Zoe's lives; the next, she was gone.

Brett can't let that happen to his own family. It's absolutely in Renny's best interest to stay with him and Elsa; her parents. They would never let anyone harm her. *Ever.*

But if Elsa is right, then what is he supposed to do to keep Renny safe? Hire a private, armed bodyguard until they figure out what the hell is going on?

Yeah, right. Like that would escape Roxanne's attention the next time she pays one of her unscheduled visits—which, come to think of it, is long overdue. She's going to pop up any second now.

So, no bodyguard, no police. No proof, even, that this is real. But Brett will be damned if he's going to take a chance with his kid's life.

"I know what we can do," Elsa tells him. "We can go see Mike, and tell him about what's going on."

"Elsa, that's—"

"If you don't come with me, then I'm going myself. With Renny."

"You're going to just show up there? Why can't you call?"

"I'll call and tell him we're coming, but we need to go in person." She holds out the Spider-Man figure. "We have to show him this. Maybe there are finger-prints or something."

"I don't know . . ."

"Brett, if we don't do anything, and something ter-rible happens, I couldn't live with myself."

Looking at her, he realizes she means it. He man-aged to keep her from taking her own life once before. Next time, he might be too late—for her, and for Renny.

"Okay," he tells her. "Let's go."

Caroline Quinn's bloodcurdling scream seems to reverberate even after she's been hustled off to a back room by the mortified Starbucks manager.

Amid the chaotic mass exodus of rodent-fearing cus-tomers, a skittish employee quickly gathers Caroline's scattered belongings and expensive leather shoulder bag and disappears into the back room as well.

God only knows what's going on back there. Is she crying hysterically? Threatening a lawsuit?

How I'd love to slip back there to see what's going on. Do I dare?

A quick glance around reveals that the hipster baristas behind the counter are probably too caught up in rehashing the rat event to notice the lingering customer who's reluctant to trail out the door after the others.

Still . . . no matter how tempting it is to get another glimpse of the stricken Caroline, it would be foolish to risk arousing anyone's suspicion.

Then again, who would ever imagine that the rat didn't find its way into her bag on its own, but was planted there by a human hand?

Why would anyone want to scare the living daylights out of a beautiful young girl?

Why, indeed.

It was supposed to be enough just to shake them up, to see them suffer, the way Jeremy had.

Somehow, though, it isn't nearly enough.

Now that the line has been crossed . . .

Now that I've felt human blood on my hands . . .

Now that I know what I can do . . .

This is only the beginning.

Back out on the street, a quandary: where to go next?

Find a concealed spot nearby and watch for Caroline to emerge? Head back to the alley across from the Quinns' building?

Now that there's been contact, though, why bother? It's only a matter of time before the apartment itself will be accessible, and then—

A sudden pocket vibration suitably curtails the thought.

That can mean only one thing . . .

Frustratingly, the glare of the midday sun obliterates the small screen. But a few steps away, beneath the shade of a bodega awning, the alert is instantly visible.

One of the Cavalons' vehicles has just traveled beyond the designated area.

No question, now, where to go next.

They're heading north.

And so will I.

CHAPTER
FOUR

The drive up I–95 through Rhode Island and Massachusetts is long and silent, other than the necessary calls Brett has made to—and received from—the office. There's much to be said, but Elsa and Brett don't dare say it in front of Renny.

Maybe it's better that they can't talk right now. Elsa didn't miss the dubious expression on Brett's face back there in the gas station parking lot; she knows he isn't entirely taking her seriously. She doesn't have the energy to argue with him now. All that matters is that they tell Mike what's going on.

"Is this Boston?" Renny asks from the backseat.

"Almost." Elsa turns to see her gazing out the window at the billboards and strip malls, redbrick schools and chain hotels, clusters of Capes and saltbox Colonials.

The landscape is foreign territory for Renny, but achingly familiar to Elsa and Brett. They lived in Nottingshire in the south suburbs of Boston fifteen years ago, with Jeremy.

"Boston drivers are the worst," Brett mutters, and Elsa has to agree. At high speed on the highway, or flying through the city streets, drivers in this part of the country tend to careen unpredictably, or tailgate.

Glancing into the rearview mirror, Brett shakes his head. "Look behind you."

Elsa glances back to see an SUV hugging their bumper. "Just pull over and get out of his way."

"There's no place for him to go."

"No place but into our backseat with Renny," Elsa tells him pointedly, and he flips on the turn signal and moves into the other lane without a word.

Predictably, traffic slows to a rush hour crawl. Anxious as she is to get to Mike's, Elsa decides there's something to be said for sitting in a traffic jam—a momentary reprieve from harrowing drivers and concern about shadowy intruders.

But the longer they sit, the more restless Renny becomes. "Did we forget my Barbies at the gas station?"

"No, they're in the trunk," Elsa tells her reluctantly.

"Can we get them out?"

"Not now."

"Why not?"

"Because . . ."

Because that bag and everything in it might be evidence.

"Just because."

For the moment, Renny seems satisfied. Then she asks, "How long until we get there?"

"About another half hour." Brett jerks the wheel, moving from the slow lane to the less slow lane—which promptly grinds to a halt in front of them. He slaps the wheel in frustration and leans his head back against the headrest.

He's more anxiety-ridden than Elsa, if that's even possible. She knows the reaction from Lew when Brett tried to explain why he'd left the office so abruptly—blaming it on Renny being sick—was definitely not sympathetic. Elsa, who's never held a corporate job in her life, had to bite her tongue to keep from telling Brett to tell Lew to shove it. If he gets fired, they're screwed.

"How long are we going to *be* there when we get there?" Renny asks.

"We don't know," Elsa replies, looking over her shoulder at the traffic as Brett tries to merge back into his original lane, which naturally is now full speed ahead.

"Why do we have to visit this man now?"

"Because he's our friend."

"Do I know him?"

"Go ahead, Brett, he's going to let you in," Elsa tells her husband, as a driver in the next lane waves them to get in front of him.

Or maybe he doesn't. A horn blasts angrily as Brett begins to merge. With a curse, he swerves, narrowly avoiding an accident.

In the backseat, Renny asks again, as though nothing has happened, "Do I know him?"

Brett swears again and shakes his head at Elsa. "I thought you said he was waving me in!"

"I thought he was!"

"Mommy?"

"We could have been killed," Brett tells her. "All it takes is a split second, and—"

"Do you think I don't know that?" She presses her palm against her pounding heart.

"Mommy!"

"What?" she snaps. "What do you want?"

"Never mind."

Elsa turns to meet her daughter's reproachful gaze. "I'm sorry."

Renny shrugs, wounded, and Elsa finds herself thinking of Jeremy.

What? What do you want?

How often did those words spill from her mouth in the past? Jeremy was such a demanding child, so needy, so impetuous. He constantly tried her patience.

Renny isn't anything like him, and yet, just now . . .

But you didn't mean to be short with her. You're only human, Elsa reminds herself. *You can't be the perfect mother, and . . .*

And history doesn't have to repeat itself.

That's what's really bothering her, isn't it? That's why she's on the verge of falling apart here.

She reaches over the seat and touches Renny's arm. "Remember, I told you before—Mr. Fantoni came to see us in the winter, so he could meet you. He brought you something."

"What?"

"I'm not sure . . . it was a toy." Something age-inappropriate, Elsa vaguely recalls, and remembers noting at the time that Mike seemed to know very little about kids. He doesn't seem to have any, though she's pretty sure he's married—at least, he had been at one point during the long search for Jeremy.

In all those years, she never felt comfortable asking the details of his personal life. Or maybe it was more that she was so absorbed by her own trauma, she didn't care enough to ask.

Funny how you can know so little about someone who played such a pivotal role in your life. If it hadn't been for Mike, she'd never know what happened to Jeremy.

Brett has always preferred to keep Mike at arm's length. He tends to do that with anyone he hasn't known all his life—a Yankee tradition, he claims.

While it's certainly true that many New Englanders tend to keep a polite distance, Elsa always wondered whether it was more than that, with Brett. She wasn't convinced Brett really believed in Mike.

And right now, she's not convinced he believes in her, either.

"I really think she's overreacting, Mom. I mean, listen to that."

Marin looks up from the congealed vegetable chow fun on her plate to see Annie across the table, shaking her head. "What?"

"That." Annie points over her shoulder in the general direction of the hallway.

Oh. *That.*

In her room, Caroline is loudly sobbing on the phone long-distance with one of her friends, once again rehashing this afternoon's dramatic rodent encounter.

"I don't know . . ." Marin picks up her chopsticks again. "If I reached into my purse and found a rat, I think I'd be pretty upset, too."

"Upset. But hysterical?"

Marin shrugs. "I don't know what to tell you, Annie."

She didn't know what to tell an inconsolable Caroline, either, when she burst through the door sobbing frantically a few hours ago.

It took Marin several minutes to even comprehend what was wrong.

Not sure what to do, and worried about rabies though Caroline hadn't been bitten, Marin called the doctor. To her relief, he assured her that rats don't carry rabies—not in this country, anyway.

"Just make sure she cleans her hands really well," he advised. "And of course, call me right away if she develops any strange symptoms."

"What kind of symptoms?"

"Symptoms? Symptoms of what? What is he talking about?" Caroline was hovering at her side, listening.

"The usual . . . headache, fever, chills . . ." He went on to explain that there's a rare disease called rat bite fever, transmitted through rodent saliva and mucus. "Chances are that Caroline is fine, but you should keep an eye on her."

Unfortunately, Caroline overheard that and was beside herself. Ever since she found out about her childhood illness, she's been something of a hypochondriac. And really, who can blame her? She's been through hell.

We all have. Including Annie.

Annie, the one bright spot in Marin's life these days.

Maybe not just these days.

Caroline has always accused her of playing favorites, but of course Marin loves both her children equally. It's just that Annie has such an easygoing temperament, and Caroline—like her father—can be . . . intense.

Please, God, let that be all it is. An intense personality and not another inherited genetic flaw, courtesy of the Quinn family tree.

"She's such a drama queen." Annie rolls her eyes.

"Eat your egg roll, Annie." Marin pushes the waxed-paper pouch across the table to her.

"I did. That's Caroline's. Can I have it?"

"No."

"She said she isn't hungry."

But one egg roll is enough—they're fattening, and unhealthy.

"She might be hungry later. Here, have some broccoli."

Annie wrinkles her freckled nose. "Can't. I'm allergic."

"You aren't allergic to broccoli."

"I think there's something in the sauce. Last time I ate it, I got hives, remember?"

Maybe. Poor Annie has so many allergies that hives are a frequent occurrence.

Before Marin can reply, her cell phone, in the back pocket of her jeans, buzzes with an incoming text message. Probably Heather, wanting to see if she's changed her mind about the beach, or France.

But when Marin pulls the phone out and checks it, she doesn't recognize the incoming number.

She clicks on the message. "What in the world . . . ?"

Jeremy first returned to the Northeast last autumn, after Dr. Jacobson had conducted a surgical follow-up and given him the green light to leave Texas.

There was still a little tenderness and swelling around his nose and eyes, reminding him of all the injuries that had shattered and bruised his features over the years. But the doctor assured him that it would eventually subside, and that he'd be left looking like . . .

Well, not like himself, that was for damned sure.

As long as he was going to have his long-broken bones repaired, he'd figured he might as well go all out. Having found his way to Texas after seeing Dr. Jacobson featured on a television documentary about facial reconstruction, he knew the plastic surgeon was capable of creating a whole new look. That was what he wanted: to look like a different person.

Maybe, he reasoned, he would actually *feel* like a different person, too.

He had no way of knowing, at the time, that he really *was* a different person: Jeremy Cavalon, and not Jeremy Smith, as he'd been called all these years.

Smith.

Maybe Papa just couldn't be bothered with coming up with a better pseudonym for himself and thus, for Jeremy.

Or maybe it was his real name.

Jeremy might never know for sure, and he no longer cares.

By the time he had the surgery, Papa had been dead and buried for a year.

As he drove north from Texas, Jeremy occasionally caught a glimpse of his own reflection in the rearview mirror, and marveled at the change in his appearance. It was well worth the pain and the expense—though he'd be hard-pressed to think of a more fitting use for his inheritance.

Papa had smashed up his face. Papa should pay to fix it. Papa should pay for a lot of things.

There was plenty left over after the hospital bills. Enough to keep Jeremy from having to work for a couple of years, at least—though he figured when he got to where he was going, he'd find some sort of job to keep himself busy.

That was what normal people did, wasn't it? And now, at last, he was going to be a normal person, living a normal life.

Jeremy took his time along the way. He spent an entire day winding along Virginia's picturesque Skyline Drive, stopping at overlooks to take in the fall foliage. It was nice, but nothing compared with the scenery when at last he reached New England.

The leaves were at their peak in Groton on that dazzling Indian summer afternoon: a brilliant canopy against a royal blue backdrop that reminded him of a western sky.

But his home wasn't out in California anymore, and it wasn't in Texas. His home was with the Cavalons.

He'd known that ever since he'd first spotted Elsa

on the news that day in the hospital. A dam had burst
in his brain and his past gushed forth, flooding him
with memories.

Suddenly, he knew he'd had another life, before
Papa. He remembered Elsa; remembered Brett as
well—but not as vividly. He wasn't around as much.

No, it was Elsa who'd taken care of Jeremy; Elsa who
always made him feel safe and loved.

The warm, cozy memories weren't the only ones
that came rushing back. There were others as well—
gradually, a torrent of troubling memories he'd just as
soon forget. He tried—but once they'd been unleashed,
they floated around his brain like flotsam from a dev-
astating wreck.

*And I'm the survivor doomed to relive it, over and over
again . . .*

"Is this it? Are we there?" Renny asks Elsa from the
backseat as Brett wedges the car into a tiny parallel
space along the narrow brick sidewalk.

"Almost. We just have to go find the restaurant
where we're meeting Mr. Fantoni."

"And then I can have ice cream."

Elsa smiles faintly, remembering her earlier promise. "Yes, and then you can have ice cream."

"Pink ice cream."

"If they have it."

"And can I watch a movie on Daddy's iPad while
you talk to your friend?"

"Daddy?" Elsa looks at Brett.

"Definitely."

They don't even discuss the decision to violate
their own policy against using sweets and screens as
bribes or rewards. In the grand scheme of things, anything they can do to keep Renny happily distracted—

even if it means plugging her into headphones and plying her with sugar—is necessary in light of the situation.

The North End bustles with locals on their way to or from work, college students, school groups and tourists following the red-painted Freedom Trail through this ancient, historic part of town. Brett and Elsa navigate the narrow, winding sidewalks as swiftly as they can with Renny between them, holding both their hands and playing her favorite game.

"One, two, three, *swing!*" she shouts over and over, erupting with glee every time they simultaneously swing her into the air.

Elsa notices affectionate glances from passersby in a tour group led by a Paul Revere clone in period clothing. To them, she knows, she and Brett and Renny must appear to be just an ordinary family. No one would ever imagine that the parents are hanging on to the child for dear life.

They're meeting Mike at the usual spot: an Italian café off Hanover Street. Elsa suspects he lives somewhere in the vintage neighborhood, but again, she never asked.

The café is quiet in the pre-dinner hour, occupied only by a couple of college students, a pair of elderly women in double-knit pantsuits, and Mike. He's waiting in one of the red vinyl booths, sipping a cup of black coffee.

It's been less than six months since she's seen him, but Elsa is taken aback by the salt and pepper in the dark, wavy hair that brushes the collar of his Nike T-shirt.

Is Mike getting old? He was in his early thirties when she met him; a brash and hungry private eye who promised he'd do what the police wouldn't—or couldn't—to find Jeremy.

Closing in on fifty now, he's still handsome, still has the muscular build of a much younger man, still exudes a roguish charm . . .

But those dark eyes of his have seen a lot, and it shows.

"Elsa . . ." He stands to hug her. He smells familiar, of cologne and coffee, and she's swept by an unexpected wave of emotion. All those years, sitting here across from Mike, begging him to find her son . . .

And that's what he did.

Elsa swallows hard.

"Good to see you again, Brett."

"You too." Clean-cut Brett shakes Mike's hand, looking vaguely out of place here in his crisp white shirt, Brooks Brothers suit, and silk tie. "Renny, say hello to Mr. Fantoni."

"Hello."

"Don't you look pretty today."

"Yes," Renny agrees demurely, hands buried in the pockets of her orange plaid shorts. "Do you know if they have pink ice cream here?"

Mike looks amused. "What flavor would that be? Bubble gum? Strawberry?"

"Um, it doesn't really matter," Renny tells him. "Just so long as it's pink."

"I'll see what I can do."

"Thank you," she remembers to say, and glances to Elsa for a nod of approval.

They've been working on basic manners from the day Renny came to live with them. She's come such a long way since then.

As soon as they settle into the booth, the waitress meanders over to take their order—espressos for Elsa and Brett, raspberry gelato for Renny.

When it arrives, she spoons it rhythmically into her mouth, her eyes riveted to the small screen of Brett's iPad. Elsa explains the situation to Mike, well aware that Brett is leaving the talking to her.

"Spider-Man." Mike slowly rubs his five o'clock shadow. "This isn't something that was ever released to the public . . . unless either of you brought it up to the press during all the commotion last fall?"

"That Jeremy was playing with Spider-Man when he disappeared? Never."

"And there was no mention in any of the missing person's reports . . ." That isn't a question. Mike is more familiar with those reports, perhaps, than they are.

"No."

"Where's the other one? The one you found on the grass when he disappeared? Do you still have it?"

"It's in the cedar chest in our bedroom," Brett speaks up at last. "Elsa keeps it there with some of Jeremy's other things . . . his blanket, and a couple of his shirts . . ."

Elsa keeps it there. Not *we* keep it there.

Elsa feels a familiar flicker of resentment. Brett, the father who rolls over and goes right back to sleep.

"Are you sure it's still there?" Mike is asking—her, not Brett, she notices. He gets it. Of course he does. He's been around them for years. He knows that they both might have lost a child, but that she's the one who clings to the memories.

"Because I'm thinking maybe it's the same one you found in the parking lot," Mike goes on, despite her nod. "Maybe Renny came across it and put it into the bag with her toys."

"No way. I keep that chest locked. She couldn't have gotten into it. And anyway, this Spider-Man is different."

"Are you sure?" Brett asks her. "Spider-Man is Spider-Man."

Elsa doesn't bother to answer. Of course she's sure.

She spent years clinging to the last thing her son ever touched, even slept with it under her pillow. She knows exactly what it looks like: similar enough to the toy she found on the ground today, but certainly not the same.

"A lot of little boys are into superheroes," Mike points out.

Elsa bristles. "So you think—"

Mike cuts in, "I don't know *what* to think. I'm just trying to gather information. To the best of your knowledge, are there any pictures of Jeremy holding a Spider-Man toy, or wearing a Spider-Man costume . . . ?"

Brett looks at Elsa, who again shakes her head. "He was never interested until that day at Wal-Mart. And anyway, I've spent fifteen years going through every photo album we have. There are no pictures anywhere of Jeremy in a Spider-Man costume."

"What about before he came to you?"

"Before he came to us, there were no toys, and no pictures—other than the ones the foster agency took." Maybe Elsa is exaggerating, but not all that much.

Jeremy bounced from one foster home to another before he landed in theirs, having been deprived of just about everything—toys, fun, love . . . particularly love.

"As far as I'm concerned, there's only one way anyone would link Spider-Man to Jeremy . . ." She pauses meaningfully before delivering the bombshell: "And that's by having been there when he disappeared fifteen years ago."

"What is it, Mom?"

Marin frowns at the text message on her phone. "I don't know . . . I just got this text. I guess it was meant for someone else."

"What does it say?"

"It doesn't *say* anything."

"Is it porn?" Annie asks with interest.

"No, it's not *porn*!" Wait—it's not, *is* it?

"Can I see?"

Marin shrugs and hands over the phone.

Annie takes a quick glance and announces, "That's an emoticon, Mom."

"A what?"

"You know how people type a row of symbols—like, to show that you're making a joke, you do a sideways smiley face made out of a colon for the eyes and a close parenthesis for the mouth?"

"Yes . . . so you think this is something like that?"

"Probably. See?"

Marin looks over Annie's shoulder, trying to see the cryptic text message as an image.

~~(=:>

"What's it supposed to mean?" she asks her daughter, still stumped.

"I have no idea." Together, they silently study the symbols.

Annie gasps. "Whoa! I think I know what it is."

"What?"

"Okay, don't freak out, Mom . . . but that totally looks like a rat."

"A rat?" She squints at the image. "I don't see—"

The phone cuts her off, buzzing with another message. It's from the same sender. Marin opens it, and her blood runs cold.

That was nothing, Mrs. Quinn. Stay tuned.

That first day in Groton last fall, Jeremy had found the Cavalons' home with no problem. Incredible, what you can find on the Internet with a little bit of searching.

Yet somehow, no one ever managed to find me *in fourteen years.*

Once he got to the house, he wasn't sure what to do. He sure as hell wasn't going to march right up, ring the doorbell, and say, "I'm your long-lost son."

Anyway, the place looked deserted; there were no cars parked in the driveway. So he sat in his rented pickup truck down the street and studied the house.

The long, low ranch was different from the home he remembered, back when they were living in Nottingshire. But this one was just as inviting. The yard was carpeted with leaves from the huge old trees surrounding the house, and potted mums and a couple of pumpkins sat on the front step. It looked like a wonderful, cozy place to live, and Jeremy was dizzy with homesickness by the time a car pulled into the Cavalons' driveway.

Seconds later, *she* stepped out of the driver's seat.

He braced himself for his first glimpse of Elsa in over fourteen years. His recent obsession with news footage of her must have lessened the impact, though. Seeing her in person brought a fleeting wave of nostalgia and comfort, and none of the anguish he'd anticipated.

Swept by the urge to run down the street and hurtle himself into her arms, he was about to do just that . . .

Then she opened the back door of the car and leaned inside as if to remove a bag of groceries or something.

Something? No. It was *someone.*

Jeremy froze.

A child.

Elsa—*Jeremy's mother*—was holding the little girl's

hand, just the way she used to hold his. She bent over and planted a kiss on the little girl's hair, just the way she used to kiss Jeremy.

He knew, then, that it could never be the same; knew that he could never, ever go home again.

Someone had taken his place.

CHAPTER
FIVE

Caroline can't sleep.

That's not unusual—not since her father left, anyway.

Left?

Oh please, Daddy was ripped from their lives without warning. He might as well have been gunned down in the street that day—in fact, maybe that would have been better. An assassination, or an innocent victim of a drive-by shooting . . .

An image of her father lying on the sidewalk, bleeding all over his Italian wool suit, flutters through Caroline's head. She won't let it roost there; she doesn't wish Daddy were dead. Of course not. She loves him more than anything, and she knows he'll be back one day.

It's just . . .

Right now, it's hard. On her. If he were dead, he'd be a hero. People would have pity for her, instead of contempt. Neighbors in the elevator, kids at school, strangers on the street—even now that the press coverage has died down and the photographers no longer stake out their building, Caroline can sense people watching her, recognizing her, whispering about her.

That's why she's starting to think that what happened today—with the rat—was no accident. That it didn't just crawl into her bag. Maybe someone put it there, a cruel prank, because she's Garvey Quinn's daughter.

The coffeehouse was crowded, so many people jostling past her table, walking—or sitting—within arm's reach of her purse. Anyone could have unzipped the bag as it hung on the back of the chair, dropped the disgusting creature inside, and zipped it up again.

Anyone?

Well, anyone with a seriously warped mind.

Not that cute guy, though—Jake. Caroline is pretty sure it wasn't him.

For one thing, he's not from here; he doesn't even know who she is . . .

Or so he said. How do you know it's true?

She tries to ignore the nagging little voice in her head. Why would he lie?

She remembers reaching into her bag a few times before he got there, to check for her iPod. There was no rat . . . not until after he arrived.

But that doesn't mean it was him. And it doesn't mean the whole place isn't infested with rodents, and one didn't happen to crawl into her purse.

Yeah . . . one that managed to work the zipper with its paw?

She has other things to worry about right now, though. Like dying from rat bite fever.

No wonder she can't sleep.

Someone knocks on Caroline's bedroom door.

Daddy! she thinks for an exhilarating moment. Then she remembers, and the fragile shimmer of hope shatters like crystal on granite.

In the old days, he'd come home late and check to see if she was still awake. He'd come into the room and tickle her toes, always hanging out at the bottom of the mattress. They both sleep that way—not wanting to be confined like mummies by tightly tucked sheets.

Sometimes, she'd get up and sit in the kitchen with Daddy while he ate a sandwich or sipped a cup of tea. Mom never joined them, and Annie was always asleep—or perhaps just uninvited.

It was no secret to anyone that Dad loved Caroline best.

She cherished those late night encounters.

Another knock, louder this time. She checks the digital clock, irritated at the interruption to her thoughts, if not her sleep.

Then again . . . only nine-thirty? Why does it feel like the middle of the night?

"Caroline?" Mom calls through her door. "Are you awake?"

"No."

The door opens. "Very funny."

The light from the hallway spills into the room. It's not that bright, but Caroline throws her arm up to shield her eyes, pointedly letting her mother know she doesn't welcome the visit.

Mom used to be such a classy lady, always dressed to the nines, meticulously styled with scarves and jewelry. These days, she spends a lot of time in old jeans that are much too big for her, her blond hair in a bedraggled ponytail, like right now.

Way to let yourself go, Mom.

Between Mom wasting away and Annie blowing up a couple of sizes, Caroline wonders if Daddy will even recognize them when he comes home.

I'm the only one who's holding it together, she often tells herself. *Daddy will be so proud of me.*

"I wanted to make sure you were okay, Car."

"Sure. I'm great. No big deal at all that I found a live rat in my bag."

Mom closes her eyes, like she's counting to ten. When she opens them, she asks, "Do you think we can have one conversation without sarcasm?"

Caroline tilts her head, mulling it over. "Mmm, no," she says, "I don't think we can. We wouldn't want to squelch my creative personality, would we?"

"Oh, is *that* what we're calling it now?" Mom manages to crack a grin.

"Hell, yes."

"Don't swear, Caroline."

"I wouldn't dream of it, Mom. Daddy says 'hell' isn't a swear word."

Her mother's mouth straightens into a firm line. Watching her, Caroline pretty much knows what she's thinking about Daddy and hell.

But Mom quickly shifts gears, as she has a habit of doing. "Annie and I saved you some Chinese. Want me to heat it up?"

"No, thanks. I'm not hungry."

"Are you sure?"

"Even if I was . . . I mean, Chinese? Really? They use rat meat in kung pao chicken."

"Who told you that?"

"Everyone knows that."

Mom crosses the room and bends over to pick up the sandals Caroline had been wearing this afternoon. She opens the closet door, places them neatly on the shoe rack, closes the door.

Then she turns and says, "Listen . . . about the rat . . ."

Caroline tenses, realizing that her mother isn't just here to tidy up or make her eat leftover takeout.

"I thought all along that it must have crawled into your bag. But now I'm wondering . . . maybe I was wrong."

Her heart beats faster. Yes, she'd been thinking the same thing. But hearing Mom say it . . .

Suddenly, she's frightened—*and* irritated with her mother for scaring her.

She isn't Daddy. She doesn't protect Caroline the way he did. So why would she come in here and make things worse?

"Is there anyone you can think of who might want to upset you?"

Other than you? "No," Caroline tells her. Then, to be fair, she adds, "I mean, a lot of people hate me—*us*—because of . . ."

Daddy. She can't say it. It's so unfair, the way they judge.

"That's what I was thinking, but . . ." Mom peers at her in the dark, maybe seeing the look on Caroline's face, because she quickly says, "Who knows? Maybe the rat just crawled in there. This is New York, after all."

"Yeah, and everyone knows that New York rats have outstanding fine motor skills. Zippers? Totally not a problem."

"I'm trying to help you here, Caroline."

"You're making me feel like someone is out to get me."

"I didn't say that. All I said—"

"Was that someone put the rat there on purpose. Why would you even come in here and bring this up now?"

Mom hesitates, looking as though she wants to say something.

Caroline waits.

"Did you give them your name?"

"What?"

"When you reported the incident to the manager . . . did you tell him who you were?"

"Report it? You think I, like, calmly went and 'reported it'?" Caroline can't believe that her mother doesn't get it. "Basically, I screamed and went hysterical, and they hustled me into the back room."

"Did you tell them your *name*?"

Suddenly realizing what her mother's getting at, she shakes her head. "Are you kidding? Do you think I wanted it to get out? The next thing you'd know, they'd be calling me Rat Girl on the front page of the *Post*."

"So no one knew you were—"

"No, Mom. No one knew I'm related to the dreaded Garvey Quinn."

"I was just worried that . . ."

"Someone's out to get me."

Even in this light, she can see her mother's eyebrows shoot up. "You think so?"

"No, but you do."

"Oh, Caroline . . . I didn't mean to . . . Here, just get some sleep." Mom kisses her forehead and bends over to snugly tuck in the sheet and blanket around the foot of the bed.

Caroline waits until her mother has left the room before she angrily kicks them all loose again.

Brushing her teeth over a motel sink clogged with cloudy, saliva-tainted water and God only knows what else, Elsa can just imagine how Maman would feel about this place.

"Zee peets!" she would say, wrinkling her perfect French nose.

Then again, she once said just that about her suite at the Grand Hotel et de Milan, which had previously been occupied by the queens of Belgium and Sweden—sufficient for foreign royalty, but not for the fair Sylvie Durand.

This low-budget chain motel somewhere off I–95 is a far cry from the Grand Hotel et de Milan. And room 103 definitely isn't what Elsa had in mind when she and Mike convinced Brett that it wasn't a good idea to sleep at home tonight, just in case.

As she turns off the tap, the pipes make a horrible groaning sound.

They probably should have stayed right in Boston, where there are plenty of nice hotels, but Brett wanted to get closer to home—and the office. With no reservation, no vacancies at the halfway-decent places they tried, and an overtired little girl, they settled on this.

"It's just for one night," Brett reassured Elsa, as she checked beneath the fitted sheet for evidence of bedbugs in the mattress seams.

"Mike said we should find someplace to stay for a while."

"I know he did, but either way, it's not going to be here."

"Either way? We can't just go home, Brett, like nothing ever happened."

Brett looked like he was about to say something, but then he shrugged. "Never mind. We'll figure out something in the morning."

Or maybe, Elsa couldn't help but think, *we'll wake up and find out this is all just a bad dream.*

Now, gazing at herself in the mirror, cast in a greenish tint from the overhead light, she knows it's all too real. Yet she can't help but wonder whether Brett's thinking that she's overreacting—and whether he might be right about that.

No. No way. I know what I saw.

Anyway, Mike took her seriously. He took the bag of dolls and the Spider-Man figure, promising to get right on it. He seems to think there's a possibility that someone might want to hurt them.

Someone who knows about Spider-Man's significance.

Garvey Quinn keeps popping into her head. Unless he's broken out of jail—which would surely be front-page news—he wasn't the one prowling through their house last night. Yet he's proven that he's not beyond getting others to do his dirty work.

To what end, though? He has nothing to gain by hurting the Cavalons.

Someone must.

What happened makes no sense, but she keeps telling herself that it might, if she thinks it through logically; that she might be missing something.

She's too exhausted for logic at this point, though.

A toilet flushes in the adjacent bathroom, on the other side of the paper-thin wall.

Exhausted *and* disgusted, Elsa takes one last look in the mirror, wishing she'd thought to pick up some eye makeup remover when they'd stopped at Walgreens to buy the toothbrushes.

The sliver of cheap motel soap succeeded only in smudging this morning's mascara around her lash line. In her modeling days, makeup artists used that trick to make her eyes look bigger. Now it only accentuates the haunted expression in them.

She flicks off the bathroom light and hurries into the next room, not wanting to imagine what might crawl up through the drains in the dark.

God, this is depressing. What are we doing here?

The moment of self-pity immediately gives way to self-contempt.

We're protecting our daughter, that's what we're doing. And I'd live in this dump for the rest of my life if that were what it took to keep Renny out of harm's way.

Feeling her way across the unfamiliar room, Elsa can hear traffic from the nearby highway, and distant voices, and what sounds like a bottle being thrown across pavement into a chain-link fence. Through it all, of course: Brett's peaceful snoring.

Claustrophobic Renny wanted the room door left ajar, which of course was out of the question. They agreed to leave the curtains open instead.

Uneasy, Elsa goes over to the window and looks out into the night. When they checked in, there were only two other cars. Now there are three.

Not a soul in the parking lot, and yet she has the sudden sensation that someone is lurking . . .

She darts a quick look over her shoulder. Her heart stops; a figure is standing in the shadows across the room.

Her mouth opens.

A scream lodges in her throat.

Then she sees that it's just Brett's clothing on a hanger dangling from the outer hinge of the closet door—the closet itself too musty-smelling for clothes.

Her heart beats again, fast and hard, her senses on full alert. She checks the window latch, the chain and lock on the door. It's a dead bolt, but the kind that opens with a key, rather than an electronic key card. Any previous guest could have made a copy . . .

But it's not the previous guests I'm worried about.

She quietly lugs the lone chair over from the desk and puts it in front of the door, where a would-be intruder will trip over it. A feeble trap, perhaps, but it makes her feel a little better.

She returns to the window and takes one last look at the parking lot before tugging on the vinyl-lined curtains. They don't quite meet in the middle; red neon from the "Vacancy" sign falls through the crack. Anyone could see in . . .

But no one even knows we're here.

Swiftly, she strips off the yellow dress she's been

wearing all day and gingerly drapes it over the lone chair in the room. Then she pulls on the polyester blend T-shirt she picked up at Walgreens.

About to climb into the double bed with Brett, she thinks better of it.

Instead, she slips beneath the flimsy, satiny quilted bedspread of the other bed. Careful not to wake Renny, she wraps a firm arm around her, not entirely convinced she's safe anywhere—not even here.

That was nothing, Mrs. Quinn. Stay tuned.

Lying awake in the California king she once shared with Garvey, Marin can almost hear the words in her head, spoken in a menacing, disembodied voice.

Spooked, she saved the text message on her phone, along with the other one—the emoticon that really does, as Annie pointed out, look like a rat.

Marin made her promise not to say anything to Caroline about it, though. "It'll only make her more upset if she thinks someone did it on purpose."

"Is that even possible, Mom?"

"That someone put a rat into her bag?"

"No—that she can get more upset," Annie said dryly, and they both listened for a moment to Caroline still carrying on loudly in her room, on the phone with her friend.

"Just don't talk to her about it, okay, Annie? She's having a hard time."

"I know. Don't worry. I get it, Mom."

God, I love Annie, she thinks now, staring at the shadowy ceiling.

She loves Caroline, too, of course.

Equally.

If that's the case, why do you always seem to be reminding yourself of that lately? Is it because Caroline reminds you so much of Garvey? Is it because she has that cold, sar-castic side to her that makes you wonder about things that run in the family, and what she might be capable of?

No! Of course not.

Marin will not allow herself to go there. Not tonight. Not when she's worried that someone out there wanted—or *wants*—to hurt Caroline.

She could have very easily chalked up the first message to a stray text sent to the wrong address—a text containing a bunch of symbols that just happened to look like a rat . . .

Although not to me.

Not at first, anyway, and certainly not at a glance.

It took Annie to point that out because Marin, apparently, is too old and out of touch to have even realized the message was a—what was it called? An emoticon.

Does that mean it was sent by a kid, then?

That concept is much more comforting than her initial reaction to the second message.

That was nothing, Mrs. Quinn. Stay tuned.

It seemed sinister.

And the use of her name—clearly, the text messages didn't go astray; they were meant for her. She just isn't sure if they were sent after the fact—by a witness who had recognized Caroline and thought it would be fun to further torment the Quinns—or if they were sent by someone who had planned and executed the whole ordeal, targeting Caroline in the first place.

That's why she had gone into Caroline's room earlier. To see if her daughter had noticed anything strange lately, maybe even to give her a heads-up to be extra careful.

Instead, she succeeded only in scaring a kid whose steely veneer, until now, has been largely impenetrable.

Nice going there, Mom. While you're at it, you might as well put Annie on a starvation diet.

She rolls over, restless, wondering if she should take a sleeping pill now, or wait another hour or two. They only knock her out for a short window of time. It would be nice to sleep past dawn for a change.

Again, she finds herself thinking of Elsa Cavalon.

It would be healthy to have one less piece of unfinished business hanging over her head. After all, this summer is supposed to be all about healing and moving on.

She knows how to contact Elsa. Presumably, Elsa could figure out how to get in touch with her, too.

But she hasn't.

I wouldn't blame her if she doesn't want to have anything to do with me.

Still . . . despite Marin's connection to Garvey, despite what he did . . .

Maybe Elsa is waiting for Marin to make the first move.

Tomorrow, she tells herself, as she sits up in bed and reaches for the orange prescription bottle on the nightstand. *Tomorrow, I'll call her.*

Three floors above the Italian butcher shop on Hanover Street, Mike Fantoni paces across the ancient hardwoods, Elsa Cavalon's words ringing in his head.

There's only one way anyone would link Spider-Man to Jeremy . . . and that's by having been there when he disappeared fifteen years ago.

The only witness to Jeremy's kidnapping—the person who snatched him from his own backyard—has been dead for almost a year. Jeremy himself has been dead for fifteen.

Who, then?

Mike stops at the refrigerator and yanks open the door.

Empty.

And you were expecting . . . what? A nice tray of leftover homemade lasagna? Tiramisu?

It's been years since he's tasted homemade anything.

It's been years since he lost Tanya, who loved to cook, and loved to eat, and loved him . . . or so she claimed when she married him.

Mike closes the fridge. It's even more disconcerting to open the one at home and find it empty—his *real* home, the one he shared with her. He doesn't spend much time there anymore. Instead he stays here, in the city, in a dumpy apartment that was meant to be simply a place where he could run his business.

There are no memories of his ex-wife here. Tanya never set foot in this apartment; never wanted to. Irony of ironies: She didn't approve of his being a private detective—not at first, anyway—because it took him away from her at all hours, sometimes for days at a time. Nights at a time.

Caught up in whatever case he was working on, Mike didn't always think to call to check in. Then one night, he did—and sensed that she wasn't alone. That was the beginning of the end.

How many philandering spouses had he nailed through his work? Too many. But somehow, he seemed to have compartmentalized his life, convincing himself that his own marriage was different, overlooking classic signs that would have been red flags if he were investigating a case.

What Tanya had done just didn't happen in his own little world. Not to him.

And yet, in this business, he'd trained himself to consider every possibility . . . and sometimes, the impossibilities, as well. Because you just never know.

Hell, no. You *never* know.

Determined to ignore the bitter memory of Tanya *and* the rumbling in his stomach, Mike closes the fridge, thinking about the Cavalons.

He'd chalk up their situation to mere mischief, break-in and all, if it weren't for Spider-Man.

That's not a coincidence. No way. If his years in this business have taught him anything—other than that *anything* is possible—it's that there are no coincidences.

Yeah. Coincidences. *They're* impossible.

Mike's head is spinning. Too much to think about.

He resumes pacing.

So far, he knows only that someone out there is up to something.

Someone who knew about Jeremy and Spider-Man.

Who knew?

Elsa and Brett.

A handful of cops on the case.

Garvey Quinn and his pawns.

Jeremy himself.

Not a whole lot of suspects to choose from, particularly since a couple of them happen to be dead.

Okay, so go to the motive. What motive would anyone have for hurting the Cavalons? Revenge?

Among that handful of people who knew about Spider-Man, who would possibly have a reason to bear a grudge after all these years? Certainly not the parents, and not the cops. Garvey Quinn—but he's in jail, his mistress is dead, the hit men won't care, and—

Mike stops in his tracks.

But that's impossible . . . isn't it?

The nightmare is familiar. Jeremy's been having it for years.

Now, though, he knows it's not a nightmare at all.

It's a memory, yet another one that's been let loose to drift through his brain and torment him.

"All you have to do is triple up on his pain meds tonight . . ." the man is saying, and the woman's strange, gold-colored eyes are filled with misgiving.

They don't know Jeremy is watching them, listening to every word, as he plays with his Spider-Man superhero on the floor of the hotel room. They don't know that he understands exactly what they're talking about: that he's going to die tonight. They don't see that his hands are shaking in terror, or that tears are streaming down his cheeks. They don't even look at him.

"You're stronger than you think. I believe in you . . . You do what has to be done, and then you wash your hands and you move on. Right?"

The woman nods in agreement. The man kisses her, then swings his pretty little dark-haired daughter onto his hip and leaves without a backward glance.

Jeremy looks up, and the woman is staring at the closed door after them, shaking her head.

Somehow, in that moment, he grasps that there might be hope, and he swiftly wipes his tears on his sleeve.

She turns, sees him watching her. "Come on," she says abruptly. "Let's go for a walk."

The foreign city is unbearably crowded. He still doesn't know where they are; only that they flew for a long time to get here, and no one speaks English.

Few people on the street make eye contact with him, but whenever anyone does, he begs for help. "Please, can you help me get home to my mother? I want my mother!"

Sometimes, he even cries. But it's useless. Even when he sees a flash of sympathy in a stranger's glance, he can't communicate that he's been kidnapped, that he's in danger.

There are so many other troubled children on the teeming streets: orphans sleeping in filthy gutters, starving beggars dressed in rags. Children who look just like him, with glossy black hair and enormous, frightened black eyes.

With one hand, he clutches his Spider-Man action figure; with the other, he tries to hold on to the woman, but she keeps slipping out of her grasp. Always, he finds her again, clings to her . . . until an elephant plods slowly past, and a memory stirs within. A memory of home, and being with his mother at the zoo . . .

"Oh look, Jeremy . . ." Mommy is laughing, pointing, "look at the elephant!"

Mommy! Why did you let them take me away? Why aren't you coming to find me?

His eyes blur with tears, and when he brushes them away and reaches for the hand of the woman with the yellow eyes, it's gone. She's gone, and he's alone now, and he knows that he's never going home again . . .

No, it's not a nightmare. It's a memory.

A grown man, alone in the dark in a strange bed once again, Jeremy cries for his mother.

CHAPTER
SIX

Watching his wife cringe as she steps out of the grungy shower onto the Kleenex-thin bathmat, Brett shakes his head. Room 103 is even more depressing in the first morning light—especially on a rainy summer day.

As Elsa attempts to wrap herself in a flimsy bath towel that's more the size of a hand towel, he sighs. "I can't believe it's come to this. Hiding out in a cheap motel—"

"Shh . . ." She reaches past him and pulls the bathroom door shut. Renny is still sound asleep in the next room, and they're not planning to wake her until they're ready to get out of here.

"She's still out cold, Elsa. She'll never hear us."

"I know, but still . . ." Elsa watches him pick up the travel-sized tube of Crest. "Do you think we jumped to conclusions yesterday?"

Holding it poised over his new toothbrush, he looks at her in surprise, wondering if she's suddenly come to her senses. "Do *you*?"

"I don't know. Maybe it was kind of alarmist, going to see Mike. Maybe the whole thing was a huge coincidence . . ."

"Spider-Man?"

"And the branch, and the footprint . . ." She frowns. "Wait—what am I talking about? Why am I trying to convince myself it was nothing?"

Because somewhere in the back of your mind, you're aware that you imagined it in the first place.

No. He can't say that. He can never let her know he doubts her stability.

"You're trying," he says instead, "because you don't *want* to believe it. I don't, either."

"But you do, don't you?"

Brett hesitates, then admits, "I don't know."

He waits for her to lash out and accuse him of not taking her seriously, but she doesn't. Wearing a contemplative expression, she says only, "Mike seemed to believe it."

"I know."

"He said we shouldn't go home."

"I've been thinking about that." Brett squeezes the toothpaste, and turns on the water to dampen his toothbrush. He raises his voice above the groan of old pipes. "Your mother's apartment is sitting empty in New York."

"I thought of that, too."

"Maybe you and Renny should go stay there for a few days. Through the weekend, at least."

"That's what I was thinking. What about you?"

"I've got a job to go to, Elsa."

"It's Friday. You can just—"

"Lew needs me on the project. You know that."

"I can't understand how at a time like this you can be thinking about—"

"If I don't go to work, I lose my job, and we lose Renny. What don't you understand about that?"

For a moment, she just looks at him with those big

eyes of hers; eyes that now seem enormous, thanks to her smudged makeup.

Paulette Almeida—Renny's mentally ill birth mother—always had smudged eye makeup, Brett remembers—and hates himself for it.

Elsa says—as if it's just that simple—"Take some personal days."

"I've used them all up."

"You have some vacation days coming."

"I'm taking a week off for Disney. I can't just decide to use those days now, at the last minute."

"Not even in an emergency?"

"You want me to tell Lew that I can't be there because I'm running scared?"

"Why do you have to tell him anything?"

Exasperated, Brett doesn't bother to respond. She just doesn't get that he's accountable to someone other than his family.

He brushes his teeth vigorously and rinses using his hand as a cup, rather than even touch the smudged motel drinking glass beside the sink.

"The drain is clogged," he observes, turning off the water.

"This place is disgusting."

"Let's get out of here. We'll go home first to pack up some things for you and Renny, and then I'll drive you to the city."

"I'll drive us. You should go to work if you have to," she adds pointedly. "But . . ."

"What?"

"We're not supposed to cross state lines with Renny without getting permission."

She's right. Brett forgot all about that rule. "We already have," he points out. "We're in Massachusetts, remember?"

"I know. I didn't even think of it yesterday. But—"

"Look, no one from the agency is ever going to find out she's here or in New York without permission. It's not like she's got on some kind of homing device that goes off if she crosses a border."

"I know."

"Anyway, they're so short staffed over there, they do things in a half-assed way themselves half the time."

"But that wouldn't stop them from taking her away from us, and you know it."

"I do—but out of all the risks involved in this situation, not getting permission to take Renny to New York is the least threatening, don't you think?"

She nods. "What about you, though?"

"I'll be fine. Don't worry about me."

"But you can't stay in the house alone. What if whoever it is comes back?"

"Then I'll be there. And this will be over."

"What if something happens to you?"

"It won't. I promise."

Oh, but it might. Something terrible might happen to you, Brett Cavalon. Or to your precious family. You shouldn't make promises you can't keep.

Silence seems to have fallen on the other side of the bathroom wall, but it's probably a good idea to wait a few minutes, just to be sure the Cavalons don't inadvertently share any other interesting tidbits.

One would think the two of them would be more careful about what they say, and where they say it.

Although to be fair, they have no way of knowing they've been tracked to this dumpy motel. Gotta love modern technology. Homing device, indeed.

Then again, there's nothing like a good old-fashioned surveillance tool, either.

The water glass, so filmy that no one in his right mind would dare drink from it, has done its job well. Back onto the grubby sink shelf it goes, its fluted sanitary— ha!—paper cap once more in place.

Twenty minutes later, the Cavalons exit their room, blissfully unaware that they're being watched through a crack in the cheap curtains of the room next door to theirs, which was conveniently vacant last night at check-in time.

Conveniently vacant?

The place is just about empty.

Lucky for me. And so, so unlucky for the Cavalons.

The night manager didn't bat an eye last night at the walk-in request for a specific room number. If he had, the explanation was ready: "I was born at 1:04 on October 4, so 104 is my lucky number."

Almost a shame not to get to use the clever cover story. But it's probably best to have as little contact as possible with people who might—should anything go wrong—be questioned later.

Incredible. Even against this dingy backdrop, with yesterday's smudged makeup around her eyes and her hair pulled back from her face, Elsa Cavalon looks beautiful. She and Renny head toward their car in the parking lot as Brett goes into the office to check out. She keeps a protective hand on her daughter's shoulder as they walk, and she does seem to glance from side to side, as if making sure the coast is clear.

But she never looks behind her, back at the motel.

She and Renny get into the car. Before long, Brett joins them, and they drive away. A moment later, the GPS tracker vibrates, indicating that they've left the vicinity.

As if I didn't know.

But it was a good idea to set the device last night, just in case they left unexpectedly in the wee hours.

Now, the onscreen locator indicates that they're heading toward the southbound entrance to I–95.

Too bad I have to go in the opposite direction.

But we'll meet again before you know it . . . and next time, believe me, you will know it.

This time, the sleeping pill only worked until about three A.M. Marin has been up for hours, listening to the rain, worrying about the rat in Caroline's purse and the anonymous texts to her phone, waiting for a decent hour to call the one person who can possibly understand what it's like to fear for your kids' safety in the wake of a public ordeal.

That last text was so ominous. And how did someone get her private number?

Come on—these days, you can get hold of anyone's personal information, if you really want to.

After all, she herself managed to track down both a home and a cell phone number for Elsa Cavalon a while back, when she was thinking she might want to contact her.

Ever since, she's been toying with the idea of reaching out to Jeremy's adoptive mother, though she isn't sure why.

Does she want to grieve with her?

To express gratitude?

To satisfy her own curiosity?

Thinking of the woman to whom she'd given that precious gift—her firstborn—Marin swallows the bitter irony that they'd both lost him, in the end.

She rubs her burning eyes and looks at the bedside clock.

It's past six. Too late to take another sleeping pill, and too early to call anyone.

Nothing to do but brood.
Story of my life.

After surveying the pile of folded T-shirts on the bed, Mike removes two. Then he adds three pairs of boxer shorts, removes one, puts it back, and adds another.

Four pairs of underwear? Is that enough? Is it over-kill?

He sucks at packing.

At a lot of things, really.

At times like this, he desperately misses Byron Gregson.

Not just because Byron was full of great tips—like "always keep a packed suitcase handy by the door"—but because, as an investigative journalist, his old friend had contacts all over the world. With just a few well-placed overseas calls, he probably would have been able to tell Mike that he's way off base with his suspicion—or that he might be on to something huge.

But Byron did one too many favors for Mike when he agreed to look into Jeremy Cavalon's birth parent-age. He stumbled upon the link to Garvey Quinn, then made the mistake of trying to blackmail him—and now he's gone forever.

And that's something I have to live with for the rest of my life.

Without Byron here to guide him toward the right track, he has nothing to go on with this Cavalon case but a hunch. Yeah, terrific. A hunch—coming from a guy who's so intuitive it only took him a year to figure out that his wife was sleeping around with—no, not *his* best friend. *Hers.*

Married to a closeted lesbian, and he never had a clue. Intuitive? Mike Fantoni? What a joke.

But this hunch . . . it actually makes sense. He's not going to discuss it with the Cavalons, though—not yet, anyway. If he's wrong, they'd be devastated all over again. And if he's right . . .

They'll be devastated anyway.

He was up all night going back over the situation, just to make sure he had the details straight.

He did.

Garvey Quinn said his girlfriend had killed the kid—probably on his say-so, but of course he'd never admit it. He said he'd already left the country, with his daughter, when the kid was killed. Claimed he didn't know what had happened until weeks later, when she told him.

What if she hadn't obeyed his orders?

No reason to think that she wouldn't, but . . .

What if . . . ?

Putting himself into her shoes, Mike could imagine what she'd been thinking.

What if she'd simply abandoned Jeremy there, in Mumbai—or Bombay, as it was called back then? Who would ever know the difference? He'd never find his way back. In fact, he'd probably wind up dead anyway, sooner or later—but at least she wouldn't have a kid's blood on her hands.

Somehow, the theory he'd initially considered impossible no longer seems so.

Anything is possible. Anything at all.

Even Jeremy Cavalon being alive.

Yeah. It makes sense.

So what next?

There he is—a seven-year-old kid, abandoned in a foreign country swarming with abandoned kids. Eleven million in Bombay alone that year, according to a conservative UNICEF estimate.

What, most likely, would have become of him?

There's only one way to find out.

As luck would have it, a direct flight to Mumbai leaves from Logan in just a few hours—and there's an available coach seat.

Mike dumps the folded clothes into an open duffel bag, adds another pair of boxers for good measure, and heads for the door.

When the phone rings at precisely nine o'clock, Lauren Walsh is standing on a ladder, paintbrush in hand, about to apply the first coat of semigloss onto the primed molding above the kitchen window.

She hesitates, wondering if she should bother to answer. She just hung up with Sam a few minutes ago, and doubts it's him again. Her two oldest kids, Ryan and Lucy, are both at school this morning in the midst of finals, so it won't be them, either. And her youngest, Sadie, is in the next room, playing with the dog.

Other than Sam and her children, there really isn't anyone else whose call Lauren would jump to answer these days. Her parents, her sister Alyssa, her friend Trilby . . . they all mean well, but every time they call, Lauren feels as though they're checking up on her, convinced she's going to snap any second now.

There had been a time, before she met Nick, when she was strong and independent, a career woman in the city. Marriage changed that—but her marriage didn't last forever. She was already in the process of relearning, last summer after Nick left, how to survive on her own. So she more or less had a head start on widowhood before her soon-to-be-ex-husband entangled himself in Garvey Quinn's web and paid the ultimate price.

But the fact that she and Nick were on the verge of divorce didn't change the fact that she'd loved him once, that he'd been brutally murdered, that her children had lost their father, leaving her to raise them single-handedly, without a break from the overwhelming emotional, physical, and financial responsibility.

Thanks to time, therapy, and a healthy new relationship, she's managed to pick up the pieces, building a new life for herself and her kids.

These days, they're doing as well as can be expected—perhaps better.

Even little Sadie has gone back to sleeping in her own bed, after months of night terrors. She's made her first friend: a girl named Lily, whose mother invited Sadie to visit a water park with them today. And after a rough start to the school year, Ryan and Lucy are now fully back into the swing of academics and athletics.

For their sake, Lauren has no choice but to be strong. After all they've been through—all they've lost—she can only give them strength by example, and love them. She's not going to let them down.

Yes, Lauren believes in herself—even if her family and Trilby do not.

The phone rings again.

Lauren glances down at the paint-coated bristles, not entirely sure about this russet color for the trim. Why was Autumn Mist so much more appealing on a small strip of paper in the store?

Maybe she should hold off on painting for a few minutes. In fact, maybe she shouldn't have let Trilby talk her out of plain old white.

But Trilby is convinced Lauren's fresh start in life calls for a fresh palette—not just in the house, but in her wardrobe, even cosmetics.

It didn't take long for Lauren to realize she's just not a red lipstick or slinky gold dress kind of girl. Maybe, she decides, climbing down the ladder to answer the phone, not an Autumn Mist kind of girl, either.

"Hello, Lauren?"

"Marin! How are you?"

"Oh . . . you know . . ."

Yeah. Unfortunately, she *does* know. She isn't quite in Marin Quinn's shoes, but close enough.

It was Sam's idea to usher in the new year—their first as a couple—with resolutions designed to put the tumultuous past behind them. For Lauren, the first logical step was to get in touch with Marin Quinn. It proved to be a wise decision. Unlike just about everyone else in her life these days, Marin *gets* it. Gets *her*.

"What's going on?" Lauren carefully props the paintbrush on the tray and settles herself on the bottom rung of the stepladder.

There's a long pause on the other end of the line.

Not good.

"Marin?"

"I'm just . . . for one thing, I'm getting ready to put the house on the market, so I've been sorting through piles of old things. It's brutal."

"I can imagine." Lauren's done everything she can to avoid selling this rambling Victorian, the only home her own kids have ever known. Moving might mean leaving town altogether, considering that real estate in suburban Westchester County has skyrocketed over the past two decades, despite the recession.

Regardless of all that's happened under this roof, Lauren simply can't afford to leave.

Unlike Marin, who can't afford to stay.

"I remember how hard it was when I had to go through all of our stuff last summer," Lauren tells her, but doesn't mention that she gave almost everything to a tag sale.

Yes, and look where that led.

"Try to just think of it as a miserable stomach flu,"

she advises Marin. "You feel awful now, and the actual purge will probably be even worse, but trust me . . . you'll feel a lot better once you've done it."

"Thanks. I knew you'd have some helpful advice."

"Yeah, well . . . been there, done that."

Though a drastically different set of circumstances led Marin to become a fellow single mom—circumstances that make them improbable friends—Lauren can relate to her more than just about anyone else in the world.

She wasn't looking for a confidante, though, when she first got in touch with Marin. Dogged by the press herself after the kidnapping nightmare and Garvey Quinn's arrest, Lauren felt a strange sense of kinship whenever she opened a newspaper or turned on a television and spotted Garvey Quinn's wife looking like a deer in headlights.

Poor Marin.

Poor both of us.

"Do you want me to come down there and help you go through everything?" Lauren offers, and holds her breath, waiting—hoping, really—for Marin to turn her down.

She doesn't necessarily think she's overstepping the bound of new friendship—though she might be. But in the six months since she and Marin met, they've seen each other only on neutral turf, meeting for lunch and dinner at various restaurants. She's never been to the Upper East Side apartment where Garvey Quinn presumably plotted the atrocious crimes that destroyed life as Lauren and her kids once knew it. She has no desire to set foot in there.

"Thanks, but I think this is something I have to do myself." Marin sounds resigned. "I just wish I could run away from home for a little while, you know? I'm so sick of dealing with all of this."

"Why don't you come up here today and visit?"

Lauren offers spontaneously—then wonders what the heck she's doing. Why would Marin want to do that?

Then again, why not? They're friends. Plus, Lauren's bloodstained kitchen walls and floor have been gutted to the studs and completely refurbished.

Great. No blood. How positively inviting.

To Lauren's surprise, Marin says, "You know, maybe I will . . . if you don't mind."

Pedestrians scurry past Jeremy at a rate that makes his head spin. They all seem to be lost in thought, headphone music, conversation with each other or on their cell phones. They don't wait for lights to change at crosswalks, weaving skillfully amid gridlocked cars and cabs and buses filled with more distracted, impatient people.

Where are they all going in such a hurry?

What would it be like to be one of them?

Torture, that's what it would be. Pure torture.

Homesick, he wonders what he's doing here. Big cities have always made him nervous.

No surprise there.

Every time he finds himself on an urban street, surrounded by strangers and traffic, he flashes back . . .

What happened right after the woman with the yellow eyes abandoned him is clouded—mercifully so. But there are bits and pieces. People everywhere. Honking horns and sitar music, thousands of voices speaking, shouting, arguing, all in a strange tongue. Steamy air pungent with curry and elephant dung and unwashed bodies.

He was alone for days, perhaps weeks or even months—and it was worse, far worse, than what had happened to him in the foreign hospital. Without his pain medication, he was in agony, crawling and crying, eating scraps of garbage, begging—but not, like the millions of other slum children, begging for food or money. No, he desperately needed someone to *listen* to him, to help him find his way home, and for a long time, no one—*no one*—understood what he was trying to say.

Then, at last, someone did.

In the fading light of another agonizing day, as Jeremy was dreading another terrifying night, someone listened, held out a hand, and said in English—in *English*, thank God!—"Come with me, little boy. I'll take you home."

Tears of joy rolled down Jeremy's filthy cheeks as his prayers were answered.

Then the sun went down, and the nightmare began in earnest.

"Caroline?"

She groans and opens her eyes to see her mother standing over her bed. Closing them again, she murmurs, "I'm sleeping."

"I know. I just wanted to tell you I have some things to do today. I'll be gone for a few hours. I need you to keep an eye on Annie, and try to get along with her, please. And if Realtors call about the apartment, take down a number and tell them I'll call them back. Okay?"

"Mmm hmm."

"Caroline, are you hearing me?"

She forces her eyes open again and yawns. "Yes. I'm hearing you." Then, taking a closer look at her mother, she asks, "Where are you going?"

For the first time in ages, Mom's blond hair is long and loose, tucked behind her ears—and she's actually wearing earrings. And a sleeveless black top and white slacks. And, Caroline notes with surprise, eye makeup. It doesn't cover the dark circles or worry lines, but it helps.

She'd forgotten that Mom really can look pretty when she wants to.

So . . . why does she suddenly *want* to?

"I'm going to take a drive up to Westchester to see a friend."

"Who? Kathy?" Her mother's former college room-mate lives in Rye, and if that's where Mom's headed, Caroline is definitely going, too. There are some great places to shop around there.

"No, not Kathy."

"Well, if you're going to Rye—"

"Not Rye." Mom leans over and kisses her on the forehead. "I'll be back by three or four. And I'll call to check in. Be good."

"You too." Caroline watches her go out the door, pulling it closed behind her.

She rolls over to go back to sleep, but suddenly, she's wide awake.

Where the heck is Mom going? She hardly ever leaves the building lately. Now, all of a sudden, she's rocking the wardrobe and the makeup . . . and driving, besides? She never takes the car out. She never did, even when Dad was around. He didn't drive much, either, relying on cabs, Town Cars, and limos to get around.

"A friend," Mom said.

Clearly, it's someone she doesn't want Caroline to know about, otherwise, she would have told her who it was . . .

Caroline sits up abruptly.

Can it be a man?

Did Mom forget that she happens to be married? It's not like Dad is dead, or they're divorced. Does she think she can go around *dating* while Dad is rotting away in jail?

I have to stop her.

Caroline jumps out of bed and hurries out into the hall. "Mom? Mom!"

Annie appears in the kitchen doorway, holding a rubber spatula. "She's gone."

"Where did she go?"

"To see her friend in Westchester. I thought she told you."

"Which friend?"

"She didn't say. What's wrong? Are you okay?"

"Are *you*?"

"You don't have to be nasty."

Yeah, Caroline thinks, *I do.*

"For your information," Annie goes on, "Mom said we have to get along today."

"Guess that means one of us has to leave, then. I hope you have plans."

"I do. Making brownies."

Annie used to be such a cute kid, blond and super-skinny. Now her face is getting rounder by the second, and so is the rest of her.

Caroline asks pointedly, "Do you really think that's a good idea? Brownies?"

"Why wouldn't it be a good idea?"

Because you're turning into a real tub o'lard.

Maybe it's mean, but someone really needs to tell Annie these things for her own good, and God knows Mom hasn't stepped up.

"Maybe you should, like, go for a run instead."

"I don't run."

"Why not?"

"I have asthma."

"So? Plenty of people who have asthma are runners," Caroline tells her, not certain that's really the case.

"Well, *I'm* not."

"Maybe you should be."

"Why?"

Caroline opens her mouth, but Annie cuts her off. "Know what? Forget it. I don't want to hear it."

That's because she knows what I was going to say.

Annie returns to the kitchen. A moment later, the electric mixer whirs to life.

Caroline shakes her head. It was so much easier to deal with her sister when Daddy was around. She always had the feeling that Annie got on his nerves, too—especially when her asthma would kick in and she'd get that constant, annoying, wheezy cough.

Then Mom would hover with the nebulizer, and Daddy would take Caroline out someplace, just the two of them. They'd go for frozen hot chocolate at Serendipity, or to a movie, or take a walk through the Central Park Zoo.

Yes, Daddy and Caroline were like a team, and Mom and Annie were a team. Now Caroline's stuck alone here with her mother and sister—and today, she's just stuck with Annie, which is even worse.

She heads back toward her room, hating the new emptiness along the hallway walls, formerly a gallery of family photos. On the last day of school, she came home to find that they were gone. Her dismayed cry woke her mother, who shouldn't have been sleeping in the middle of the day anyway.

"What did you do?" Caroline screamed at her as she stood there looking groggy and bewildered. "Did you throw them away? Did you burn them or something?"

"Burn what? What are you talking about?"

"Our family pictures!"

"Of course not! I just packed them away until—"

"Put them back!"

"Not until after the move."

The move. When Mom so brilliantly decided to uproot them, Caroline was appalled. Somehow, she managed to convince herself that it would never happen. Now it looks like it might. Poor Daddy isn't going to like it one bit when he's released from jail and has to come home to a brand-new apartment.

If, she thinks now, *Mom lets him come home at all.*

Caroline pauses at the master bedroom once shared by her parents.

Where, she wonders again, is Mom going today? Does she have a boyfriend in Westchester?

Maybe there's some indication, somewhere behind the closed bedroom door, of a secret romance.

Shuddering to imagine what that might be, she slips into the room. Everything is picture-perfect, ready for potential buyers to traipse through the apartment. Not a personal item in sight, other than a cluster of perfume bottles on Mom's bureau and a couple of generic-looking paintings on the walls.

Now that all the personal stuff is gone, no one crossing the threshold would ever guess that the notorious Quinns live here.

For that matter, no one looking around Mom's bedroom would ever find evidence that she's involved with some guy.

Caroline figures the only place she might be able to find incriminating information is on Mom's phone, and of course she's taken that with her.

She slouches back down the hall to her own room—also devoid of her favorite photos and mementos and reminders of Daddy that were on prominent display, until Mom made her remove them. The room looks so generic now, like it could belong to anyone. The less time she spends hanging out here, the better.

Now what? The whole day stretches emptily ahead. Too bad none of her friends is around, and there's absolutely nothing to do.

You could always go back to Starbucks.

Ha. As *if.*

Then again . . . what about Jake?

She never had a chance to say good-bye to him, never gave him her number. The rat incident happened right after he asked her about meeting her at Starbucks this afternoon.

He doesn't even know her last name, so he'd have no way of finding her if he wanted to. And she doesn't know his last name, either. There are dozens of Jakes and Jacobs at Billington alone; there are probably hundreds of them at Columbia.

Looks like she's never going to see him again, unless . . .

What if he shows up at Starbucks today, hoping she'll be there?

He never mentioned a time, but he did say afternoon. That's a five-hour window . . . but what else has she got to do?

Sitting around a rat-infested—or not—coffeehouse hoping to run into some guy is pretty pathetic . . . but then what about Caroline's life these days isn't?

The rainy drive back from Massachusetts has left Elsa with a queasy stomach, courtesy of too much gas station coffee, or sheer exhaustion, or nerves—probably all three. All morning, she's been dreading the quick stop at home to pack up some things for herself and Renny, certain that once she crosses the threshold, she

won't want to leave again—and knowing that it's necessary.

But now that she's here . . .

I can't wait to get out.

The house just doesn't *feel* right.

It's nothing she can put her finger on, really. She
walks quickly from room to room. Everything appears
just as she left it yesterday: rainy day bin in the kitchen,
a couple of finished jigsaw puzzles on the coffee table,
The Little Mermaid DVD case beside them.

Still, she feels violated. Someone could have been
here in their absence, snooping around.

From Renny's room, she can see Brett beneath the
rain-spattered window, looking for the footprints and
the broken branch.

In the master bedroom, she goes straight to the
nightstand, where she keeps the tiny key, dangling
from a strip of blue satin ribbon. If anyone was rum-
maging through the drawer and found it, he wouldn't
have to look far to figure out what it's for.

She kneels in front of the cedar chest at the foot of
the bed, fits the key into the lock, turns it, lifts the lid.

The contents, at a glance, are undisturbed. The linens are neatly folded.

Beneath her own things lie the items she rarely
looks at: her wedding veil in its protective wrap, lace
doilies handmade by Brett's grandmother, a preserved
baby dress that had been presented to Maman by the
great Coco Chanel herself when Elsa was born . . .

And then there are the little-boy clothes, the ones
she can barely see because her eyes are flooded: Jeremy's worn dungarees, his T-shirts, the red sweater he'd
worn that last Christmas . . .

Elsa braces herself as she digs her way to the bottom
of the chest. If it isn't there . . .

But it is.

Choking back a sob, she picks up the Spider-Man figurine she'd found lying in the grass the day Jeremy disappeared.

"Mommy?"

Renny is in the doorway.

Keeping her back to her, Elsa drops the toy back into the bottom of the chest and hurriedly wipes her eyes.

"I'm going to go pick out the clothes I want to bring to Mémé's house," Renny tells her. "How many dresses do you think I need?"

"Wait, first you need to put away the puzzles and other toys you played with yesterday," Elsa tells her, conscious that Brett is right under her bedroom window. "Oh, and you can choose some things to bring with us while we're away. Come on, let's go see what we can find."

"Okay." Renny skips down the hall. Elsa hurriedly puts the chest back together and locks it. As she returns the key to the bedside drawer, she reminds herself that she needs to pack the keys to Maman's apartment, before she forgets.

In the kitchen, Renny is putting her toys back into the rainy day bin. She's excited about the impromptu weekend in New York—even though Elsa and Brett explained to her that her grandmother won't be at home.

Renny is full of sightseeing ideas—and some of them, to Elsa's dismay, sound like New York, Sylvie Durand style. Pretty impressive, considering they haven't seen Maman since her Mother's Day visit last month—when, fresh from a few days in Manhattan, she regaled them with tales from the city.

Now Renny wants to see Saks Fifth Avenue, Bloomingdale's, Tiffany's . . .

"Tiffany's?" Elsa asked incredulously.

"For breakfast. Mémé told me about it."

Breakfast at Tiffany's. Of course. It was Sylvie Durand's favorite movie, and back then, she traveled in the same circles as its leading lady. When Elsa was growing up, Maman's highest—and most frequently paid—compliment was that Elsa looked just like Audrey Hepburn. Later, when she was modeling, the resemblance wasn't lost on her booking agents, who cultivated her chic, sleek, gamine style.

She might as well wait until they get to New York before she straightens out Renny's misguided impressions. She has a lot to do before they leave, and she definitely needs to grab a quick shower—a *real* shower, as opposed to the earlier one that left her eyes still rimmed with old makeup and her hair limp from cheap shampoo.

In the grand scheme of things, it's such a minor detail, but maybe it'll help her to feel more *normal*.

As if anything could possibly feel normal right now.

Her eyes go to the hook beside the door, where she always keeps Renny's tote bag to grab when they're on their way out.

The thought of someone touching it, desecrating it . . .

Spider-Man. Who would have known? Who would want to remind them of something so painful?

Turning away, Elsa opens the top drawer of the kitchen desk. As she pulls out the set of keys to her mother's apartment, she remembers how she'd laughed when Brett, Mr. Organization, had fastened an identifying tag to the ring.

"It's a Louis Vuitton keychain, Brett. Do you actually think we're going to forget whose keys they are?"

"You never know," he told her, but even he had to grin.

Elsa tucks the keys into her purse. Then, remembering that she left wet laundry yesterday, she heads toward the utility room off the kitchen. The washing machine is on its last legs, but at least this time it completed the spin cycle.

As she opens the dryer to transfer the load of clothes, she hears the door open and Brett calling her name.

"I'll be right there! I just have to—"

"Elsa—right now. C'mere."

Uh-oh. That doesn't sound good. Abandoning the laundry, she returns to the kitchen. Seeing the look on her husband's face, she turns immediately to her daughter.

"Renny, why don't you go into your room and pack your clothes?"

"You said put the puzzles away first."

"That can wait. Go ahead."

As Renny disappears down the hall, Elsa whispers, "Did you see the footprint?"

"No, it must have washed away."

She was afraid of that. "What about the—"

"The branch. I saw it. But Elsa . . ."

She realizes, then, that he's holding something: a manila envelope. "What is that?"

"It just came in the mail. You need to see this."

Marin could tell Lauren was surprised when she took her up on the invitation to visit her in Glenhaven Park today. She herself was perhaps even more surprised.

But after spending yesterday mired in emotion, between packing away—and throwing away—all those mementos, and dealing with the girls' endless arguing, topped off by the rat experience . . . it was as if Lauren had thrown her a rescue ring, and she'd instinctively grabbed it.

Once she'd said yes, she felt as though she were standing at the base of an enormous mountain with no idea how she was going to climb it.

The only thing to do, she realized, was stop thinking about it and start moving. As quickly as possible, for that matter, hoping she'd gain enough momentum to keep on going.

She's made it out onto the rainy street and is all but running toward the parking garage a block away when it happens.

"Hey, look, it's that lady!" she hears someone say. "The one whose husband—"

Suddenly, a camera flashes in front of her.

Blinking, she hesitates for a split second, wondering whether to keep going, or turn around and head back home.

Home sounds better—but she's closer to the parking garage.

And anyway, is she really going to let a couple of shameless, camera-wielding strangers ruin her plans? That would be pathetic.

No. No way.

Holding her head high, Marin picks up her pace once again, heading for the parking garage.

Stepping out onto the sidewalk, Mike hears a cheerful, familiar "Hey, Mike-*ey!*"

"How's it going, Joe?"

The Sicilian butcher, in his usual smoking spot— leaning against a globed lamppost in front of the shop—shrugs. "Aches and pains. I'm getting old."

"Yeah, who isn't?" Mike figures Joe is about a decade older than he is, probably in his mid-fifties. He likes to complain good-naturedly about his mother, his wife, his kids, his grandkids, all of them sending him to an early grave, he claims. But Mike doesn't buy a word of it. What he wouldn't give to have a family. His own parents are both gone, and so is his brother.

None of them lived to see Mike get married—or divorced.

"You going somewhere, Mikey?" Joe asks, waving his cigarette like a pointer to indicate the duffel bag over Mike's shoulder.

"Yeah. The airport."

"Where you headed? Long weekend? Or a vacation?"

Mumbai. Some vacation.

"Yeah," he tells Joe again. "Just for a coupla days."

Joe pushes himself off the lamppost, grinds out the cigarette with his heel. "You take care of yourself."

"I always do, Joe." Mike gives him a wave and steps off the curb.

Suddenly, the sound of a revving engine explodes in his ears. Startled, he looks up, and is stunned to see a car roaring toward him. For a split second, the driver is visible through the windshield—looking right at him, Mike realizes in horror. *Aiming* right at him.

The last thing he hears before it hits is Joe's horrified *"Miiikkee-eeeyyy!"*

Elsa stares in horror at the contents of the envelope, spread before her and Brett on the kitchen counter.

Photographs.

Of Renny.

They appear to have been taken with a long-angle lens, and recently.

Renny in the supermarket. Renny at the beach. Renny licking an ice cream cone in their own backyard, the photo snapped through the trees with their house in the background.

Her embroidered tote bag is over her shoulder in most of the shots.

"Whoever took these pictures," Brett tells Elsa in a

low voice, "knew that Renny hardly ever leaves home without that bag. He knew it wouldn't be long before we stumbled across Spider-Man."

Elsa nods, unable to speak. She'd been wondering why the toy would have been hidden away in the tote rather than left right out in the open for them to discover more readily.

Now she knows.

Placing the toy in Renny's bag sends a far more ominous message.

And those pictures . . .

Someone is watching . . . again.

She finds her voice at last. "Brett . . . we have to go to the police."

"We'll lose her if we do."

"I'm afraid that if we don't . . ." She swallows hard, forces herself to say it, "We'll lose her anyway."

Hurting Mike Fantoni was never part of the plan—not even after it became clear that people would have to die. But it was absolutely necessary. There's no telling what he knows—and what he might do with the information.

It's pretty obvious the Cavalons met with the detective last night. Why else would they have driven to Boston and left their car parked for several hours in the North End, just a few blocks from Fantoni's address?

The moment the GPS registered that the car had stopped in that particular location, it made perfect sense.

Of course, in their time of need, they'd turn to the private detective who'd devoted all those years to their case, and ultimately led them to Jeremy.

Well . . . not really. Mike Fantoni had led the Cavalons to Jeremy's *trail*—a dead end, in the most literal sense.

Or so they believe.

But if anyone could have dug up the truth, it was Mike.

Such a shame to think of him lying in the middle of Hanover Street in a pool of his own blood.

Really, of everyone who's ever been involved—he's one of the good guys. And if anyone could have saved Jeremy . . .

But then he didn't, did he?

No one saved Jeremy. Not even Mike.

That's all right. He doesn't need any of them. Now he knows that there's only one person in the world he can count on, someone who will never let him down like the others have, one by one, over the years.

Now it's their turn. One by one, they're going to pay. All of them.

CHAPTER SEVEN

In good weather, the view from the Gold Star Memorial Bridge high above the Thames River is striking: a picturesque Connecticut shoreline dotted with red brick, gray shingle, or white clapboard buildings; water bobbing with fishing boats, sailboat masts, and the occasional ferry or ship.

Today, however, as Brett drives across the bridge toward the New London train station, the world beyond the windshield is blanketed in dull gray to match his mood. He keeps a close eye on the rear-view mirror. There are so few other cars on the rain-splashed road that he's almost sure no one is trailing them.

Almost.

After seeing those pictures in the mail, Elsa was much too shaken to get behind the wheel herself. Brett wouldn't have agreed to let her do it anyway. Not now.

As they huddled in the kitchen with the horrifying surveillance photos, they weighed every possible scenario . . .

But one.

Brett hates that he's even capable of thinking it; hates the truth even more, but he has to face it.

Elsa herself might have sent the photos.

She wasn't in any of them, and they were taken at times when she would have been alone with Renny.

Just as she was alone with Renny when that window was open after the nightmare, and when she found the footprint in the mud, and Spider-Man . . .

It doesn't make sense, but . . .

What if some paranoid, delusional fragment of her brain just splintered off, and . . .

But why? Why would she—why would her brain— want to create the illusion that Renny is in danger?

He doesn't understand, but then it wouldn't be the first time. He didn't understand how she was seeing and talking to Jeremy after he disappeared, but she was convinced he was really there. And he didn't believe that she would actually try to kill herself even though she talked for months about wanting to die, and . . .

And this time, I know that anything is possible.

No, he's not going to call the police. Not yet, anyway. That would just guarantee that they'd lose Renny, and for what?

If there is an outside threat, then the first thing to do is get Elsa and Renny to a safe place and assess the situation with Mike.

If there's no outside threat, then he has to get Elsa the help she needs.

One thing is certain: No matter how fragile she is, she'd never, ever, ever hurt Renny or let anything happen to her.

They arrive at the station to find the red brick building nearly deserted. Brett hurriedly buys two tickets on the next southbound train, which happens to be running fifteen minutes late.

"Otherwise, you would have missed it," the attendant informs him. "Guess this is your lucky day!"

"Guess so." Brett's smile is strained as he takes the tickets from her.

When he first suggested this morning that Elsa take Renny to New York, he'd been trying to humor her. A change of scenery would be good for her, he figured, and by the time she was ready to come home, her paranoia would have blown over. He never imagined that the situation would escalate the way it has.

Elsa rests her head on his shoulder as they wait beneath an overhang, watching the rain drip miserably onto the tracks. The platform, too, is sparsely populated: just a young businessman in a suit and an elderly woman dressed in so many layers you'd think it was February instead of June. Neither seems to pay any attention to the Cavalons. Brett notices that Elsa is keeping a wary eye on them anyway.

"You don't have to worry," he reminds her in a whisper. "Even you didn't know you were going to be here until an hour ago, so the chances that someone could be lying in wait for you here are—"

"What if the house is bugged, though?" Seeing his expression, she adds quickly, "I know it sounds crazy, but we did talk about the train at home . . ."

Crazy.

Oh, Elsa . . .

"But really," she goes on, "is it any more crazy than anything that's already happened?"

He shakes his head.

Mike. He needs to talk to Mike about this.

As soon as he gets Elsa and Renny on the train, he'll call Mike.

Maybe it was wrong not to go ahead and call the police, he thinks again.

But then he looks down at Renny—at her sweet, hopeful face, waiting for the train to pull in and carry her and Mommy away on an adventure—and he knows he can't risk it. Not yet. There's no way the agency is going to allow her to stay on with them under the circumstances. Not if someone is stalking them, and not if Elsa is losing touch with reality again.

Is it selfish of Brett not to want to give her up—even for her own good?

But who's to say she'd be any safer anywhere else? If she is in danger, Brett refuses to believe that anyone in the world would fight for Renny the way he and Elsa will. They know how dangerous the world can be, and they would die for her, both of them.

I don't care what the paperwork says or doesn't say. We're her parents, and we're not going to let anything happen to her. And if Elsa needs help, I'll get her help. But losing Renny—she couldn't bear that.

He keeps his arm around Elsa and a protective hand on Renny's shoulder as she excitedly watches the track for the train. She's never ridden the rails and was thrilled, back at the house, when they told her of the change in plans.

Now, when a whistle sounds in the distance, Brett can't decide if it's too soon or not soon enough.

Renny bounces excitedly. "It's coming! It's coming!"

Elsa looks up at him and he kisses her forehead. "I hate that we have to leave you here."

"Someone has to stay and figure out what the hell is going on."

"Call me as soon as you get there."

"I will."

"You'll be safe in your mother's building."

"I know. I'm not worried about us."

"I'll be safe, too."

"You've got to talk to Mike."

"I will."

Brett releases her and swings Renny up into his arms as the train clangs into the station. "Have fun on the train and in New York, sweetheart."

"I will, Daddy. I wish you could come with us."

"So do I, but I have to go to work. When it's time for Disney World, though—" He breaks off, his throat thick. He buries his face in her soft, dark hair for a moment, then smooths it as he sets her back on her feet.

Elsa is watching, tears in her eyes further smudging the makeup she never had a chance to remove. Once they'd decided they were going, she threw some things into a couple of bags, hurriedly changed into jeans, and they were on their way.

It's unnerving, seeing her looking so haggard. He can't help but flash back to the old days, after Jeremy, before Renny, when it was all Elsa could do to wake up in the morning . . .

"All a-*bo-ard*!" the conductor calls from his perch in the open door as the train rolls to a stop.

Elsa grips Renny's hand and walks her toward the door. Brett picks up their luggage and follows, looking around to make sure no last-minute passengers have shown up. Coast is clear: The businessman and the older woman are boarding a few cars down.

The conductor takes the bags from Brett, greeting Renny with a jovial "Hello, there, young lady! Ready to go for a ride?"

Suddenly, Renny looks uncertain.

Brett's heart sinks. She's so small standing there, dwarfed by the conductor, the train, even the luggage.

"I don't want to go!" She shakes her head, holding back.

Elsa tries to coax her, which only makes her dig in her heels, starting to cry. "I want Daddy to come, too!"

Brett pastes a reassuring smile on his face, tells her they'll see each other again before they know it.

"Come on, Renny." Elsa reaches for their daughter, her eyes meeting Brett's. Seeing tears in them, he opens his mouth to tell her not to go. But then Renny is in Elsa's arms, squirming and crying, and it's too late: the two of them disappear onto the train, the doors close, and the train chugs away, leaving him alone on the platform.

He wipes his own eyes on the sleeve of the dress shirt he's been wearing since yesterday morning. This is unbelievable. Did he really just ship his family out of town?

Pulling his cell phone from his pocket as he walks toward the steps, he pulls up his address book and presses the entry that bears Mike's phone number.

Papa was an American businessman in Mumbai—then known as Bombay—or so he told everyone who asked. Maybe it was true. Maybe it wasn't.

Jeremy probably didn't ask. Mercifully, he doesn't remember much about that time.

He does recall how relieved he was initially, after living on the streets, to wear clean clothes, and eat hot food, and sleep in a hotel bed—with Papa, who promised to get Jeremy home to his parents as soon as he could. And so Jeremy endured the nights in his bed, and the beatings that came whenever Papa didn't like something Jeremy did or said.

After a while, there was a long, long airplane ride. He remembers that part clearly: it was terribly bumpy. Things were falling from the overhead bins and people were praying and the woman across the aisle threw up. Jeremy was afraid, clutching his Spider-Man with

one hand and the seat arm with the other, until Papa
pried his fingers loose and held his hand tightly.

"It's okay," he said. "Nothing bad is going to happen. We're going home."

It was a lie, of course—though not, perhaps, in
Papa's twisted mind.

Jeremy was still angry with Papa for all the things
he'd done to him. Yet he found himself clasping Papa's
hand anyway, glad he wasn't alone on that scary plane
ride.

"I'll take care of you," Papa promised. "No matter
what."

And he did. When they landed, Papa bought Jeremy
some food at the airport: a cheeseburger in a paper
wrapper, French fries in a cardboard carton, a milk
shake in a paper cup with a plastic lid and a straw.

Even then, even after all he'd been through, Jeremy
recognized that the food was American. He knew he
was home, and he was grateful to Papa for getting him
there at last.

Papa put Jeremy into a car and drove out onto a
highway. After a while, he glimpsed the ocean from
the car window. The smell of salt air and the screech
of gulls were familiar, and he knew for sure that his
house was nearby.

Now, of course, he understands that it wasn't the
Atlantic Ocean, but the Pacific—three thousand miles
away from the seaside town where he'd been raised
before the kidnapping.

When Papa pulled into a driveway and said, "Here
we are, home sweet home," Jeremy was taken aback.
He didn't recognize the house at all, and he started to
cry.

Papa beat him for that.

Later, Papa showed Jeremy around and told him he
would have his own bedroom. He even let Jeremy pick

out the comforter from a catalog, and some toys and books for the shelves—but he never, ever let him sleep in his room.

No, Jeremy was forced to sleep with Papa every night, in a room where the shades were always down, even during the day; a room where terrible things happened to Jeremy. Things he didn't understand, back then.

Now, years later, he grasps what happened to him. Now he knows all about abuse, and pedophilia, and the Stockholm syndrome: the psychological phenomenon in which kidnap victims develop benevolent feelings for their captors. He knows that he did what he had to, and he shouldn't blame himself, and he doesn't.

Papa was a sick and dangerous man. And Jeremy's path never would have crossed his if not for *them*.

Elsa . . .

Marin . . .

Face it, Jeremy. They let you down.

The more he hears those words—spoken aloud, or echoing in his own head—the easier it is to believe them . . . whether he wants to, or not.

Marin was tempted to turn back when she hit bottleneck traffic on the northbound FDR, but that would be the easy way out. She forced herself to keep going, reminding herself—once again—to stay strong.

Now she's moving along pretty well, finally heading north on the Triborough Bridge.

Wait—not the Triborough anymore, she reminds herself. *Now it's the Robert F. Kennedy.*

She remembers Garvey's reaction when the span was renamed a while back. Publicly, he called it a shameless Democratic photo op at the taxpayers' expense, and was roundly applauded by his constituents.

Privately, he promised Marin that one day, a bridge or tunnel here in New York, or perhaps in Boston, would bear his own name.

Typical hypocritical, egotistical Garvey. To think there was a time when she'd been invigorated by what she convinced herself was admirable confidence and ambition.

Just remember—you weren't the only one who was fooled by him.

Cold comfort now, though, to think of the thousands of people who believed in Congressman Quinn.

Ordinarily, Marin enjoys the skyline views as the highway curves away from the city. Today, however— the first time she's been here in months—she can see nothing at all. The landscape is shrouded in mist. It feels like a bad omen.

She's traveled this route out of the city hundreds of times over the years, heading to and from her hometown, Boston, or the nursing home in Brighton. But it's been a while since she's visited any of those places, and she feels a twinge of guilt thinking of her father.

John Hartwell's condition has steadily deteriorated over the past year or so. Dementia, the doctors are saying, though he's only in his late sixties. He's been talking to invisible people, hearing things, seeing things.

Some days are worse than others.

Once in a while, when Marin calls to check in, the nurse will say, "Mrs. Quinn, your father is having a good day," and she knows that's a hint for her to come visit.

Bur her own good days are fewer and farther between than Dad's; she's never quite up to a spur-of-the-moment drive or the curious stares from the eavesdropping staff, let along having her father ask about her husband.

Dad has always adored Garvey, and until recently, frequently exercised bragging rights that his only daughter married into the illustrious Boston Quinn family. He liked to wait until someone—preferably, as many people as possible—happened to be in earshot before he'd ask, "How's my son-in-law, the congress-man?"

Marin felt obligated to explain to him, last September, what was going on with Garvey. But she waited until no one was around to overhear, and she left out as many of the details as possible. She knew her father didn't really comprehend. Sure enough, he'd forgotten all about it by the next visit, and she didn't bother to reiterate.

Today, as she bypasses the exit leading to Interstate 95 and New England, she promises herself that she'll get back up to Brighton soon. Or someday maybe even to Groton, to meet Elsa Cavalon.

She wonders whether Lauren would think that's a good idea. Then she wonders whether it's even a good idea for her to visit Lauren in Glenhaven Park.

Maybe exposing herself to the scene of one of Garvey's many crimes will be another healthy step in the healing process.

Or maybe, Marin thinks grimly, *it'll convince me to leave well enough alone.*

"Please, Mommy . . . I want to get off!"

"I know, I know . . . shh, it's okay." As she tries to settle Renny into the window seat, Elsa wonders how on earth she could have thought the train was a good idea for a claustrophobic kid.

She *wasn't* thinking when she made the decision—that's the problem. Back at the house, reacting to the frightening series of photos, she was in full flight mode. Driving to New York seemed like a terrible idea. But maybe this is worse.

Still, the alternative would have been . . . what? A commuter flight between Groton–New London airport and New York is half an hour at most—Maman always flies in when she visits, sans luggage, of course—but Renny trapped in the cabin of a tiny plane several miles above the ground? Forget it.

Staying at home, waiting for someone to snatch Renny away? Not an option.

Brett wanted to drive them to Manhattan himself, but Elsa talked him out of it.

"I'd feel safer going to New York on public transportation," she told him. "Someone might be lurking around here, waiting to follow our car. But there's no way anyone can follow a train."

He looked at her for a long time before saying, "Someone could follow us from here to the train station, and it wouldn't be very hard to figure out where you're going from there."

"But even if they saw us get on a southbound train, they wouldn't be sure where we were getting off. It could be anywhere from Old Saybrook to Washington, D.C."

Again, he gave her a probing gaze before nodding.

She was right, of course. Unless whoever was following them managed to hop on the train, too . . . and then follow them through the city to Sylvie's doorstep . . . and then—

No. She refuses to let her mind go there. Everything is going to be okay.

But it wasn't okay before, with Jeremy . . .

That's why it *has* to be okay this time.

"Mommy! I don't like this!"

"Here . . . do you want to sit in the aisle?" Elsa had given her the window, thinking she'd feel less trapped if she could look out. But maybe it only makes her feel boxed in.

She stands to let Renny slide over into the aisle seat . . . but Renny keeps right on sliding.

"Renny!"

Elsa chases after her, catching up at the end of the car.

"There's no doorknob!" Panicking, Renny claws at the closed door that leads to the next compartment. By chance, her hand hits the flat panel that unlatches the door. It slides open and she lurches forward into the vestibule between the cars, nearly crashing into an older woman carrying a cardboard tray from the snack bar.

Elsa grabs onto flailing Renny and apologizes to the woman, who stands back against the bathroom door, raised on her tiptoes like there's a rodent on the loose.

"Mommy, open the door and let me off," Renny begs, pointing to the exit where they boarded less than five minutes ago.

"I can't do that, the conductor has to open it when the train stops."

"I want it to stop now!"

Elsa pulls her back, worried this door, too, might open somehow and Renny would be thrown from the speeding train.

Beside them, the older woman purses her dry, pink-lipsticked lips, probably thinking that Renny is an out-of-control brat who needs a good spanking.

Oh, lady, Elsa thinks, helplessly holding her frightened daughter fast against her. *If you only knew.*

The moment she walks into Starbucks, Caroline wishes she hadn't come.

She'd been thinking she could just get lost in the

crowd, but there *is* no crowd today. As she steps up to the counter, she realizes she's already been recognized by the baristas. Not as Garvey Quinn's daughter, but as the girl who had the rat in her purse.

After a brief, whispered consultation with her coworkers, a pale, fashionably ugly goth girl approaches the register. "Do you want to talk to the manager?"

"What?" Caroline frowns. "No, I wanted to order something."

The girl's pierced eyebrows shoot toward her squared-off, too-short black bangs. "Really?"

"Umm . . . yee-aahh," she says in an isn't-it-obvious? tone, and asks for a tall coffee.

"Just coffee?"

"Right. Make it black." She's never had black coffee—or any coffee—in her life, but when Jake shows up, she doesn't want to be drinking one of those milk shake drinks again. She may not be in college yet, but she's not a little kid.

There are plenty of empty tables to choose from today. Caroline sits at one closest to the door, facing it, then decides that makes her look too expectant. She moves to a more distant table, sits with her back to the door, and realizes that Jake could very easily come and go without either of them seeing each other. She switches to the opposite chair, facing the door, so that she'll spot him when he walks in.

If he walks in.

Something tells her that he will.

For a long time after he landed in California, Jeremy saw no one but Papa. It wasn't so bad, other than at night, or when Papa had to punish him for something. When things were going well, he got to eat candy all the time, and watch as many movies and cartoons as he wanted—only on video, though, and later, on DVD.

It took him years to even comprehend that there was such a thing as live television—let alone to speculate why Papa might refuse to let him watch it.

Maybe it was, like everything else the man did, about control.

Or maybe Papa was afraid he'd catch a glimpse of himself on the news.

Or maybe he worried that Jeremy would stumble across some crime drama—an episode about pedophiles or missing kids—and it might trigger something in him.

Who knows?

All Jeremy cared about back in the early days was that he could watch movies and cartoons to his heart's content. Immersing himself in familiar fictional characters was an escape from his frightening new reality.

After a few weeks—months?—Papa started to take him out shopping, or to get something to eat. The first time, he told Jeremy that if he said a word—one single word—while they were out in public, he would be sorry.

A nice man at the Chinese restaurant at the food court in the mall was handing out chunks of chicken on toothpicks. He put one into Jeremy's hand as he and Papa walked by, and Jeremy thanked him.

Not *one* word, two words: "Thank you." Jeremy spoke them automatically—and paid dearly for them later.

It was the last time he ever spoke to anyone in public when Papa was around.

Papa always introduced Jeremy as his son, said he was painfully shy. No one ever questioned the relationship.

After a while, Jeremy himself started to believe it. In

an enormous world filled with strangers, Papa was all he had. He stopped asking questions, and his old life faded away at last.

The rain has stopped by the time Brett turns onto his block after dropping Elsa and Renny at the station. He groans as he turns into the driveway and spots his next-door neighbor walking through her side yard with a shovel. Meg Warren isn't the type to simply wave and retreat.

Sure enough, by the time he's parked the car, she's coming across the wet grass, dragging her feet a little, as always. He learned the hard way never, ever, *ever* to ask about her limp.

"What are *you* doing home at this time of day, Mr. Brett?" she asks cheerfully as he steps out. She always calls him Mr. Brett, in a cutesy, singsong voice. Once, she asked if that bothered him. It probably shouldn't, but it does. He told her it didn't, of course. Meg means well, as Elsa likes to say.

"I'm actually on my way to the office, but I had to stop home to shower and change first."

"Really? I saw that you were home a little while ago. But then you went out again, with luggage."

He sighs inwardly.

"And you weren't here overnight."

"No. Not overnight," he tells her, hoping she can't see the tension in his jaw. All he wants to do is go into the house, draw the shades, and wait for something else to happen.

But that's not an option. His secretary called his cell phone a few minutes ago as he was driving back from the station. When it rang, he snatched it up, assuming it was Mike, who hadn't answered when Brett called him.

"Lew's looking for you," Cindy said. "What should I tell him?"

"Remind him that I called in earlier—I said I'll be in at noon." He'd lied about having to accompany Renny to a doctor's appointment this morning.

"He knows . . . he said to tell you it's past noon and they already rescheduled the conference call twice. Now it's at one. You need to get here, Brett."

He bites back the urge to tell Cindy that he's not coming in at all. That might just push Lew over the edge. Anyway, maybe it's better to go into the office, do the conference call, and tie up some loose ends in case he really does have to take some time off.

"Tell Lew I'll be there in fifteen minutes."

"Really?"

"Twenty."

There's no way, he acknowledges now, glancing at his watch. Maybe he can get there within the half hour, though, if he hurries.

"I noticed that the house was dark all night," Meg is saying. "You guys always leave the outside lights on when you're not going to be home. And you know, Elsa didn't even mention that you were all going someplace when I saw her and Renny outside yesterday."

Wow. That Meg really doesn't miss a trick.

"It was a last-minute thing," he tells her, and nods toward her muddy shovel, needing to change the subject. "So what are you up to? Burying dead bodies in the petunia patch?"

She laughs like that's the funniest thing she's ever heard. "No! I just dug a new bed out back. The ground is nice and soft from all the rain. I'm moving my herb garden. Like I was telling your wife, someone trampled it."

"Really? Because—" He thinks better of saying

anything about the footprints in their own yard. Why even drag her into it?

Because she sees everything, he reminds himself, *so maybe she saw . . . something. If there was something to see.*

"Because . . . what?" she prompts Brett.

"Ah, I was wondering whether you've noticed anyone hanging around our yard when we're not home."

"Like who?"

"I don't know . . . anyone who shouldn't be here, I guess."

"Why? Did something happen?"

Brett weighs how much to admit, and decides on as little as possible. "There were some footprints in our yard, and we thought maybe kids were cutting through. If anyone got hurt on our property, we'd be looking at a lawsuit, so . . ."

"You mean *my* kids? Because they're not even around right now. They're with their father this week, and—"

"No, that's not what I—"

"—believe me, if I ever caught them sneaking around in your yard, I'd have their keisters in a sling."

Brett murmurs an appropriate reply, almost relieved he's put her on the defensive regarding her kids, rather than have her start asking questions he'd rather not answer. "Well, I'll let you get back to moving your herb garden," he tells Meg.

"Oh, I'm finished for today. I'll dig up the plants over the weekend. The ones that didn't get crushed, anyway."

"Yeah? Where are they now?" he asks as casually as possible.

"Right over there." She points to a small garden plot along the dividing line between their two yards—almost directly adjacent to Renny's bedroom window.

Brett nods thoughtfully. "Well, if you do see anyone around, let me know."

"And you do the same, there, Mr. Brett."

"Believe me, I will."

Glenhaven Park is one of those picture-perfect, leafy suburban towns that look like the set of a television drama series. Even a lifelong city girl like Marin is wistful, driving past big old houses with front porches and hanging geraniums, set back along brick-paved streets that are shiny from this morning's rain.

What would it be like to live here?

For a brief, deluded moment, she imagines that things would be different now if she and Garvey had chosen a simple, low-key life here, because nothing bad could ever happen in a place like this.

Oh, come on. Who are you kidding?

Look at what happened to Lauren here.

Anyway, Garvey is who he is. He would have been a monster anywhere. Married to him, no matter where she lived, her life would have eventually been disastrous.

She turns onto Elm Street and looks for the painted lady Lauren described over the phone. There it is, about halfway down the block: a tall mustard-colored Queen Anne Victorian with brick red gingerbread trim.

Her heart pounds as she pulls up in front. She can't help but think of Garvey, pitilessly shattering the lives of the children who live here, just as he shattered his own children's lives, and Marin's.

I shouldn't be here. I need to go.

But before she can act, she hears someone calling her name through the open car window. Looking up, she sees Lauren waving from the wraparound porch.

The few times they've come face-to-face, it's been over lunch in the city—private booths in restaurants where no one would recognize either of them. Lauren has worn skirts, jewelry, makeup. Today, she descends the porch steps in sneakers, jeans, and a T-shirt, her long, reddish-brown hair caught back in a casual ponytail.

Marin immediately relaxes a bit, despite feeling overdressed.

"Hey, you made it!"

"Yeah—after a narrow brush with the paparazzi," she tells the one person she knows who's also been there, done that.

"You're kidding, right?"

"Nope. Someone snapped my picture on the street. I don't think it was really the paparazzi, though—just someone who recognized me." Not that that's much better. Plenty of amateur photographers sold candid shots to the press last summer when the news first broke.

"Oh, Marin—I thought that had died down. It has here."

"Well, you don't run into thousands of people when you step out your door." Marin gestures at the quiet street.

"Not usually, no." She smiles.

Marin reaches back for a Saran-wrapped platter on the passenger's seat. "This is for you."

"Cookies? Are these homemade?"

"Yes, but I can't take credit. My daughter Annie loves to bake. Now that school is out, we've got cookies coming out of our ears, so . . ."

"Ryan will devour these in five minutes flat. I think he's about the same age as Annie."

"She's almost fourteen."

"Ryan's thirteen." Lauren leads the way up the

porch steps, adding somewhat stiffly, "Lucy's fifteen. Sadie's only five. She's at Splashdown today; Ryan and Lucy are at school. So you won't get to meet any of them yet."

Marin hopes her relief doesn't show. Not that she has anything against Lauren's kids. But she doubts she's ready to handle meeting them so soon, and she's willing to bet they feel the same about her—if they even know she's here.

The conversational ball is in Marin's corner, and she tries to think of something to say. What happened to the easy conversational flow she and Marin share over the phone, and whenever they meet on neutral ground?

At last, she asks, "School is still in session?"

"Just finals. Public schools go later than private. So your older daughter is . . . ?"

"In private school. So is Annie."

"No, I meant her name—is it Caroline?"

"That's right. Very good!" Marin tries for a light tone, deciding maybe she's just uncomfortable talking about the kids—hers, and Lauren's.

Maybe Lauren is, too, because there's an awkward silence as she opens the screened wooden outer door. Marin can hear rainwater dripping from the gutters above the porch.

Stepping into the high-ceilinged foyer, she's greeted by the smell of vintage wood and fresh paint. She takes in the old-fashioned wallpaper, the floral draperies, and the ornate woodwork on the stairway, crown moldings, and half-closed pocket doors off to one side.

It's magnificent; the kind of house you often see preserved in touristy New England towns, with guided tours and a brass plaque by the door.

This one looks lived-in, though—kids' shoes scattered near the doormat, a baseball cap draped over a newel post, and a pile of books and spiral-bound note-books on the bottom step, obviously waiting to be carried up.

"You'll have to excuse the clutter," Lauren tells her, bending to scoop up a stray tennis ball. "Between the kids emptying out their desks and lockers now that it's the end of the school year, and being under construction, I can't seem to keep it under control."

"You're under construction?"

Lauren doesn't reply immediately, and when she does, Marin realizes that it's going to be impossible, here on the Walsh family's home turf, to avoid awkward moments and the subject of what happened last summer.

She shouldn't have come. Why is she here? Why didn't she at least take something for her nerves before she left home? That's what Heather would have advised, had Marin told her where she was going.

But the pills can make her sleepy, or loopy—in no condition to drive. It's been long enough, as it is, since she was behind the wheel.

"I had the kitchen gutted," Lauren tells her.

The kitchen. Of course. That's where it happened—the final bloody showdown.

"Want to see?"

Marin really doesn't, but she says, "Sure," anyway.

Maybe it'll be cathartic, she tells herself as Lauren leads the way toward the back of the house.

"It's been a long time coming . . . we really needed a renovation. Old houses, you know . . ."

"Right," agrees Marin, who doesn't know at all. She's never lived in an old house, not even growing up in the Back Bay, where her nouveau riche parents were content living in a modern condo—a far cry from the stately Quinn mansion just a few blocks away.

Lauren's kitchen is large—by Manhattan standards,

anyway. She gestures at a stepladder pulled up to a window, drop cloths draped on the floor beneath it. "When you called this morning, I was about to paint the woodwork."

"And I interrupted you. Sorry."

"Oh please, it was a welcome interruption. I think I chose the wrong color. Here . . ." Lauren pries the can open with a screwdriver and holds it out. "Autumn Mist looks more like dog poop, doesn't it?"

"It's not so bad."

"Really?"

"No. I was being polite. Definitely dog poop."

Lauren joins her in a laugh, and Marin feels a little better.

It isn't so bad, being here, in this house, in this kitchen. She'd been expecting a rush of emotion, or at the very least, an aura of bad vibes.

Maybe it would be different if she'd visited before, or if the place hadn't been renovated. As it is, she's merely a bit uncomfortable. But really, she feels that way everywhere she goes these days—which is why she really doesn't go anywhere anymore.

"Guess I need to go back to the paint store." Lauren replaces the lid and pounds it down with the screwdriver handle.

"So you're doing all this yourself? Choosing colors, painting?"

"Pretty much."

"I'm impressed."

"You're kidding, right?" Lauren looks more closely at her. "You're not kidding. Trust me, it's not that big a deal."

"I wouldn't even know where to begin with a project like this." She and Garvey have always used professional decorators, professional painters, professional everything. Now that he's gone . . .

"When you move into your new place, I can help you, if you want." Seeing Marin's expression, Lauren quickly adds, "Not that I'm any good at it. I mean, don't feel obligated. I just thought—"

"No, it's not that. It's just—the move. Every time I think about it, I get a little worried about doing it alone."

A little worried? She's scared to death. But somehow, seeing what Lauren has accomplished, she feels almost ashamed to admit it.

"Hey, if I can do this"—Lauren sweeps a hand around the kitchen—"you can do that. You can do anything. You're stronger than you think."

"I'm not so sure. I mean, I know I'm an adult, but I've never really been on my own. I went from my parents' house to college to Garvey."

"Well, I *was* on my own, for years before I got married, and I was terrified when Nick left. Half the time, I'm still terrified."

"You don't seem like you are."

"Neither do you." Lauren pats her arm. "But you're going to be okay. Just think . . . the worst is over."

"I wish I could believe that. Right now, I wake up every day feeling helpless—and sometimes, I get overwhelmed by this sense that something horrible is going to happen any second, and . . ."

"That's probably a panic attack, Marin—due to post-traumatic stress. Are you seeing anyone?"

"No! I'm still married to Garvey, even if—"

"No." Lauren is smiling faintly. "That's not what I meant. Listen, my kids went through this after—you know."

She knows. After her husband had them kidnapped, and commissioned their father's cold-blooded murder.

"Panic attacks—a constant feeling of impending doom—that's what you're feeling, right?"

Marin's instinct is to deny it, and yet—isn't that what she just said? That she feels as though something horrible is going to happen?

"Seriously—you need a good shrink."

"I can't do *that*."

"Why not?"

"Because . . ."

Because why? Because everyone in Manhattan knows who she is? Because she can't bear the thought of admitting the truth about these frightening episodes to a total stranger? Because Garvey didn't believe in shrinks?

"There's nothing wrong with needing outside help, Marin. My sister lives in Manhattan, and she got me a bunch of names there back when I was looking for a family therapist who could treat all four of us. I wound up sticking with someone here, but if you want, I could—"

"No. No, that's okay. *I'm* okay. Really."

She hates the way Lauren is looking at her, as though she can read Marin's mind. Maybe she can, because she says, "A shrink isn't the only place to find peace after what you've been through, you know."

"What do you mean?"

"You can lean on your friends, or you can go to church . . ."

"Church? You're kidding, right?"

"No. I've been going lately, with Sam. It helps."

"That's great, but . . . I don't think it would help me."

"I wouldn't have thought it would help me, either. But then I realized I never prayed so hard as I did when my kids—when their lives were hanging in the balance. And those prayers were answered."

That might very well be true.

But how many others—including Marin's own— haven't been?

"I'm fine," Marin tells her. "Trust me, I don't need a shrink, or church. All I need is time, and everything will be just fine."

Case closed.

I may not be able to pay my cable bill next month, Meg thinks as she settles on the couch in her basement family room, *but at least I've been home to watch* Oprah *every day this week.*

Not only that, but the kids aren't even around to drive her nuts. Feeling vaguely guilty for not missing them, she reaches toward the decidedly guilt-free array of healthy snacks she prepared for the occasion. Low-fat Pringles, reduced-fat Oreos, mini rice cakes spread with peanut butter and marshmallow fluff, and a bag of Jelly Bellys, which she recently discovered have always been nonfat, same as marshmallow fluff.

"That stuff's not good for you," her teenage know-it-all daughter—who clearly knows very little—would probably say.

Grabbing a stack of Pringles from the can, Meg waits for the endless array of commercials to give way to *Oprah*. Floor wax, support pantyhose, line-reducing face lotion . . .

And I can't buy any of it, even if I wanted to.

Munching moodily, she thinks about the stack of overdue bills sitting on the kitchen counter. She's managed to pay the most important ones this month—the mortgage, the electric bill—but most of the others, like the orthodontist and her life insurance policy, will have to wait. As she told one of the girls at work last night, it's not as if Dr. Lichtman is going to come over here and rip the braces off her youngest son's teeth, and it's not as if Meg's going to drop dead tomorrow.

Sooner or later, she'll get her regular hours back.

That, or she'll win the lottery. She plays Power Ball every chance she gets, fantasizing about all the things she'll do if she wins even a small jackpot.

First and foremost, of course, she'll have the bunion surgery. It'll be covered by insurance, but she can't afford to be laid up for all the time it'll take to heal unless she has some other source of income. Then—

"Today, on *Oprah* . . ."

Meg sits up expectantly. It's about time. As she reaches for a rice cake, a shadow crosses the small window high in the wall behind her. She looks up, startled, just in time to see a pair of denim-clad legs stride past.

One of the kids, she thinks absently—before remembering that the kids are out of town with their father.

Her next thought is of her trampled herb garden, and it's enough to make her put down the rice cake and jump up off the couch. She hurriedly climbs the steps to the kitchen, licking the peanut butter and marshmallow goo off her fingers, and goes straight to the door overlooking the side yard.

Sure enough, someone is there, apparently having cut through the Cavalons' yard and into her own. A kid, obviously, wearing a big black sweatshirt with the hood up.

"Hey!" Meg calls, determined to give him a piece of her mind.

He goes absolutely still, but doesn't turn around.

"What are you doing?" She descends the steps to the yard, careful not to trip on the flats of herbs she bought from the nursery, or the shovel leaning against the rail.

Why is he keeping his back to her?

He must be someone she knows—maybe one of her oldest son's friends. He's fallen in with a couple of troublemakers lately.

"I can call the police on you, you know," she tells

him as she strides across the grass toward him. "You're trespassing on private property!"

At last, the figure turns toward her.

The face isn't familiar after all.

This isn't going to go well, is Meg's first thought when she sees the look in the stranger's eyes, and she braces for a tense verbal confrontation.

Then she spots the cold glint of the blade as it arcs toward her, feels the burning pain as it slices into her neck, chokes on the sudden hot gush of blood in her throat.

Meg Warren's final stunned, helpless thought, as she falls to the wet grass, is of her lapsed life insurance policy.

Lauren might not have known Marin Quinn for years as she has other friends, like Trilby, but she knows enough about human nature to realize something is seriously wrong today. The way Marin keeps chewing on her lip, toying with her hair, checking her cell phone messages . . .

She obviously isn't going to bring up whatever it is that's bothering her. Lauren has given her plenty of conversational openings as they sit in her living room sipping coffee and eating chocolate chip cookies.

Well, Lauren eats them. Marin has been nibbling the same one for the better part of an hour now, picking it up and putting it down, often without even taking a bite.

She's saying all the right things, but her mind isn't entirely focused on the conversation, which has meandered from kitchen renovation to kid-friendly summer movies to Lauren's upcoming meeting with the estranged former mother-in-law she never met.

Nick's mother had left him and his dad when he

was just a kid, and he never heard from her again—nor did he want to. But after he'd gone missing last summer, Lauren was afraid his mother, wherever she was, would hear about it in the press. With her blessing, the detectives on the case managed to track her down in Hawaii, where she's been living for years.

Now Nick's mother wants to meet her grandchildren. She's flying in tomorrow morning on the redeye, before Lucy and Ryan leave for sleepaway camp in the Adirondacks.

"Sounds like it's going to be an intense visit." Marin fiddles with one of her gold earrings.

"I just hope it's a positive experience for my kids. They don't need any more stress in their lives right now."

"Maybe you should keep this woman away, then. She hadn't even seen Nick in years."

"She's still his mother—their grandmother." Lauren changes the subject. "How are *your* girls doing with the move and everything?"

"We haven't talked much about it. I guess it won't seem real until this place is officially on the market."

Remembering the media encampment in front of the Quinns' apartment building last year, Lauren can just imagine the barrage of nosy strangers—and even worse, undercover reporters—likely to descend on the Quinn household, posing as buyers.

"The whole world knows where Garvey lived. How do you know that people won't just show up to snoop around?"

"For one thing, they might know the building, but it's a high-rise with over two hundred and fifty apartments. They can't know which one is ours."

I wouldn't be so sure about that, Lauren wants to tell her . . . but then, if Marin feels secure after all she's been through, why instill paranoia?

"Plus, we bought the place under an LLC years ago, and my lawyer said it would be almost impossible at this point to trace it back to Garvey."

"So even the Realtor doesn't know who you are?"

"Well, *she* knows—but she's a friend of my friend Heather's, and I trust her, and anyway, we have a confidentiality agreement in place for the sale. I'm sure it'll be fine."

Really? Are you trying to convince me, or yourself?

Marin changes the subject, asking again about her kids and camp.

"I'm dreading letting them go," Lauren admits, "but Dr. Rogel—he's the child psychiatrist—thinks it's best for them to get some distance and have a normal summer."

"Yeah, well, I wouldn't blame you if you didn't listen to him and never let them out of your sight again, after what happened."

After what happened . . .

That's how they refer to last summer's events: "what happened."

It's as if neither of them can find the words to accurately depict the horror. Lauren's stomach churns as she remembers what it was like to come face-to-face with every mother's worst fear.

But it's over. Her children survived. *She* survived.

And they can't spend the rest of their lives looking over their shoulders. Nor should Marin Quinn.

Seeing her friend's fraught expression, Lauren feels another stab of concern. Something tells Lauren that Marin is on the brink . . . of something. Some kind of breakthrough, or maybe a breakdown.

I'm afraid for her. But I have no idea how to help her as long as she refuses to let me in.

*   *   *

Gotta love a woman who digs her own grave.

Granted, the freshly turned patch of dirt at the back of the property probably wasn't meant to conceal a corpse . . .

Probably?

Okay, it *definitely* wasn't meant to conceal a corpse. Apparently, she'd dug it in anticipation of planting all those fresh herbs in the nursery flats she'd left on the back steps.

Well, lady, now the seedlings are in the ground—and so are you.

The good man upstairs has even seen fit to water the new garden. A drenching rain is giving the new little garden a good soaking—effectively washing away the fresh blood, with the added bonus of keeping the neighbors safely in their houses.

Not that anyone in a surrounding yard can possibly see into this one—or into the Cavalons' yard next door, for that matter.

But there's always a chance that someone might come along, and then what?

Then things would get even messier. You'd need another grave, and this time, you'd have to do the digging yourself . . .

No, thank you.

Time to get in out of the rain.

"Next stop: Stamford, Connecticut . . . *Staaaaamford,* Connecticut will be your next stop."

Hearing the announcement, Elsa glances at her watch. Less than an hour from now, the train will be pulling into Penn Station. Then she and Renny will really be on their own.

Not that they aren't technically on their own right now. Yet she can't help feeling relatively safe here. Nothing is going to happen to them sitting in a brightly lit, crowded railroad car. Once they arrive in New York, though . . . all bets are off.

Needing distraction, Elsa tries to grab the magazine in the seat pocket. It's out of reach unless she shifts her position, which would disturb Renny, sound asleep with her head in Elsa's lap.

It was all she could do to calm her daughter's frayed nerves after her full-blown panic attack, with plenty of disapproving passengers looking on.

She looks around the car. A few people are sleeping, others tap away on laptops, and an older couple is playing cards on their tray tables. Across the aisle, a young man plugged into an iPod bobs his head slightly to an audible beat.

As if he senses Elsa watching him, he suddenly glances at her, gives a little nod, looks away.

Unnerved by the eye contact, she turns her head, focusing on the drab industrial landscape out the window.

What if . . .

No, that's ridiculous. He's just some college student. Yale, probably. Elsa saw him get on at the New Haven stop, wearing jeans and carrying a backpack.

Just because he glanced at her and Renny . . . that doesn't mean it's *him*—the man who's been watching Renny.

But he's out there somewhere. Who is he? How does she know he's not right here on the train?

Because that makes absolutely no sense, and you've got to stop doing this to yourself.

She's spent almost two hours now—once Renny was asleep, anyway—watching every movement around her, just in case. She can't help but imagine that whoever sent that package—and planted the Spider-Man and crept into Renny's room in the middle of the night—might be on this train.

But of course that's impossible. No one other than Brett—and most likely by now Mike, if Brett told him—knows they're even here. Certainly no one would think to look for them in New York City, and even if they did, it would be your classic needle-in-a-haystack search.

What about Brett, though? He's a sitting duck back at home—unless he finds out who's behind this, and whether it's a sick prank, or a true threat.

Elsa's thoughts drift to the past, and Jeremy. Clearly, there's some connection—or someone just wants her to think there is.

She's been going over all the people in their lives back then—the disgruntled teachers whose class-rooms Jeremy disrupted; the frustrated therapists who couldn't reach him; the horror-struck members who were at Harbor Hills Country Club the day he went berserk.

Gazing at the sleeping child on her lap, Elsa can't imagine how she'd feel if someone attacked Renny the way Jeremy had attacked poor little La La Montgomery. A coddled only child, she'd been about the same age Renny is now. Elsa will never forget the horror of seeing that tiny form lying on the ground with her head bashed in.

They never went back to Harbor Hills after that day. She'll never forget the groundskeeper calling after them as they hustled Jeremy toward the car, "You'd better get that kid some help before he kills someone!"

Elsa scheduled an emergency appointment with Jeremy's psychiatrist, Dr. Chase, in Boston. He spoke with Jeremy at length about the incident, then called the Cavalons in for a consult.

Dr. Chase seemed to weigh his words carefully, yet they were no less chilling than if he had come right out and said, *Child abuse spawns serial killers.*

What he did say was that children who have suffered at the hands of sadistic adults are statistically more likely to grow up to be capable of violent, even deadly, behavior. He cited, as evidence, Albert DeSalvo, the Boston Strangler, whom a colleague of his had once treated.

"There are a number of theories behind the link between child abuse and later violence," he told Elsa and Brett, regarding them with clinical detachment, bearded chin propped on steepled fingertips. "The domination and isolation that go hand in hand with psychological and physical abuse can rob a child of basic human compassion and—"

"But not every abused kid grows up to become a depraved adult," Brett interrupted. He sounded perfectly composed, yet Elsa could see the veins in his neck straining with tension.

"Absolutely not," Dr. Chase agreed. "And any number of factors can come into play with those who do eventually resort to violent acting-out. For example, blunt force trauma to the head can cause significant injury to the pre-frontal lobe, which can make a person much more susceptible to aggression. Do you know if Jeremy ever suffered this type of injury?"

"My son was beaten relentlessly before we adopted him by people who were supposed to take care of him," Elsa informed Dr. Chase, not the least bit composed as tears ran down her cheeks. "None of what happened to Jeremy before he came to us—or what's happening now because of it—is his fault."

"No one is saying that it is, Mrs. Cavalon. I'm only saying that given Jeremy's history, we need to consider that he might be suffering a neuropsychological disorder, and that such deficiencies can lead to criminal behavior."

Criminal behavior.

That was the first time Elsa realized that it might be too late to save Jeremy. The damage had been done long before he came to live with them as a four-year-old. She knew that, and yet she was determined to try to heal him.

She'll never know whether she'd have succeeded.

Maybe it's better this way, though. Not better to have lost him—but better not to have witnessed countless other tragedies inflicted by Jeremy's pent-up rage.

How can you even think that way? How can you presume that what happened on the golf course was some kind of omen? It's horrible.

Horrible. Yes. But it happens sometimes. The tortured child grows up to torture others.

Yet here she is, willing to take a chance again, with Renny.

Her name, not that it matters, is—or rather *was*—Meg Warren.

That's easy enough to discover via the stack of overdue bills on her kitchen counter.

Other details about her life become apparent during a quick tour of the house and her computer's Internet history: she works at Macy's, she has at least three kids living at home, and they're conveniently visiting their dad for a week, according to the wall calendar. She has no apparent social engagements planned for the coming weeks, and just one appointment, at the podiatrist.

After turning off the television, polishing off the remains of a snack Meg so thoughtfully prepared, and tidying up afterward, it's time to browse through the closets. They yield a bonanza of potential disguises, all of which fit into a large backpack hanging on the wall in a room that obviously belongs to a teenage boy.

Chances are it won't be readily missed now that summer vacation is here.

Really, this is all working out so very well.

The final order of business is to call in sick on Meg Warren's behalf. Her illness, naturally, will be something that comes with severe hoarseness, making her voice virtually unrecognizable by whoever picks up on the other end of the line.

And—ha—whatever it is must be going around, because wouldn't you know Roxanne Shields had the exact same thing?

"You sound horrible," her coworker at the agency said when "Roxanne" called in sick the other day. "You need hot tea with honey and lemon."

Yes, and at least a few days off to recover.

The call to Macy's on Meg's behalf goes just as well: "Feel better," is the brief, impersonal response from the person who answers the employee line.

Meg was kind enough to leave her car keys right on the counter, so disposing of her little Toyota will be a breeze. With any luck, it'll take a couple of days, at least, for anyone to realize something's happened to Meg Warren—and chances are, they'll never think to start their search here at home.

By that time, the nightmare next door at the Cavalons' will be in full swing, and a missing middle-aged woman will be the least of the local police department's worries.

CHAPTER
EIGHT

On the west side of Broadway between Seventy-third and Seventy-fourth Streets, the eighteen-story Ansonia is, as Maman has always liked to say, as close as she could get to home without hopping an Air France flight to Charles de Gaulle.

Constructed during the Belle Epoque, the massive historical landmark—with its elaborate balconies, arches, masonry curls, and iron grillwork—evokes a romantic Parisian flair befitting the Champs-Élysées.

To Elsa, as a little girl, it looked more like an over-sized haunted mansion, with its looming turrets and mansard roof. There was a time when she dreaded her after-school journey from the lobby to her door. Leery of the creaky old elevators, she'd race instead up the dizzying stack of marble stairways and through the yawning maze of corridors on their floor, lined with shadowy nooks where sinister bad guys and ghosts might be lurking.

Breathless by the time she reached her own door, she'd unlock it in a hurry and slam it closed behind her—only to be scolded by Maman's longtime maid, Monique, or by Maman herself, who had no patience for what she considered silly, childish paranoia.

Looking back now, from a maternal standpoint, Elsa finds it hard to believe that her mother hadn't simply met her in the lobby—or better yet, at school several blocks away—to escort her safely home in the afternoons.

But, then, it was a different world back then; less threatening. And parenting wasn't as hands-on . . .

And let's face it, Maman wasn't the most nurturing mother.

Then again, maybe she did me a favor.

Forced to deal with her daily childhood anxieties, Elsa eventually got over them. Had she been coddled, she might never have developed the strength that allowed her to survive her worst fears becoming reality in adulthood.

How ironic that Maman largely left Elsa to her own devices in the big, bad city, and nothing terrible ever happened. Yet Elsa herself—the ultra-vigilant parent—couldn't prevent the tragic loss of her child in their own bucolic suburban backyard.

"It's spooky here," Renny whispers as they climb endless flights of wrought-iron-railed stairs. The elevators have been renovated, but they're out of the question for claustrophobic Renny.

"When I was your age, I thought so, too." *Still do—* but it's probably not a good idea to admit it. Her goal is to make Renny feel safe—like they're on a fun adventure.

A far cry from Disney World, that's for sure.

A familiar unease steals over Elsa.

The vast stairwell is deserted, as it often seems to be, and their footsteps echo as they ascend toward the shadowy domed ceiling seventeen stories above. Once, it was probably a dazzling glass skylight, though nobody knows for sure. Presumably, it's a relic of the Second World War, covered in blackout paint for almost seventy years.

At every floor, a wide balcony landing houses the main elevator banks, shut off from the rest of the building by closed doors.

When they reach Maman's floor, Elsa is thoroughly winded—thanks in part to having to carry her bag and Renny's, along with a shopping bag from the Fairway market across the street.

There's no way I could run down these halls the way I used to, even if my life depended on it.

She cringes at the thought, and forces herself to note that the wide corridors are much less foreboding now, thanks to new carpet, wallpaper, and paint.

Still, there are twists and turns, and plenty of niches along the walls that would make perfect hiding places if someone wanted to lurk here. Heart racing—and not just from the strenuous climb—she reminds herself that whoever sent those photographs of Renny can't possibly know they're here.

Not only that, but it would be impossible for a random person off the street to even get up here. If Elsa hadn't been recognized by both Ralph the doorman and Ozzy, the longtime security guard, she and Renny would never have gotten beyond the lobby.

Trying to sound cheerful as they reach Maman's door, she tells Renny, "This is it!"

Yet her voice sounds hollow even to her own ears, echoing through the deserted corridors, and Renny all but cowers at her side.

The sprawling apartment lies in a far-flung corner of a high floor, creating as private a residence as possible in an immense urban apartment building. Like many other residents, Maman bought and combined several apartments as their tenants vacated after the building went condo. The original entrance doors remain intact along the hallway, but only one is in use. The others, their knobs removed, have become nothing more than recessed decorative panels.

It takes Elsa a few tries to get the key into the lock, all the while fighting the urge to grab Renny and flee.

Her malaise doesn't make sense, really. This is supposed to be a safe haven.

But what if . . . ?

There you go again, being ridiculous. There's no way anyone could be lying in wait for you here. Absolutely no way.

Though she's careful not to slam the door, the noise seems to echo loudly through the rooms. She half expects a French-accented voice to reprimand her, but of course, no one does. The place is deserted and has been for months, other than the cleaning service that comes in once a week.

She sets down their luggage and flips a light switch to illuminate the overhead crystal chandelier. "There, that's better, isn't it?"

"I guess." Renny takes in the circular foyer with its seventeenth-century paintings, wall-sized gilt-framed mirror, and French Classical Baroque chairs that always seemed to Elsa as though they might as well have a velvet rope across the seats. "How come this room is round?"

"It's special. A lot of rooms in this building are round," she tells Renny, who seems more suspicious than intrigued as they make their way across the room.

"It was so loud outside, and it's so quiet in here," Renny whispers as their footsteps tap on the herringbone hardwoods. The only other sound is the hum of the refrigerator.

"That's because the walls in this building are three

feet thick," Elsa tells her, repeating a bit of Ansonia lore she frequently heard as a child.

Maybe the measurement was exaggerated a bit, but the apartment is undeniably soundproof.

Evidence: Temperamental Maman's equally temperamental across-the-hall neighbor Lucia—a soprano at the Met ten blocks down Broadway—liked to practice her arias at the same hour Maman needed her afternoon beauty sleep. The dueling divas had their share of confrontations over the years, but never about noise.

"Can I have my snack now?"

"Sure. Come on. And you don't have to whisper."

"Okay," Renny whispers, then, with a faint smile, "I mean, okay. Why can't I see out that window?" She points to a large opaque pane in the wall of the hallway just beyond the foyer.

"Oh, that's actually an airshaft." Remembering how her mother explained it to her when she was little, Elsa tells Renny, "It's like a vertical alley that comes all the way up through the middle of the building from the ground to the sky. On hot days, back before there was air conditioning, people would open these panels and let the fresh air in."

"Can I see?"

"Sure . . . if it still works." It's been years since Elsa opened the airshaft. Maman hasn't used it in decades, squeamishly convinced roaches would crawl in from other apartments.

Surprisingly, it takes little more than a tug to raise the window.

"It's like a tunnel," Renny comments, standing on her tiptoes to peer into the shadowy column.

"Exactly. When I was your age, there weren't many kids in the building. I always wished I had a friend living in one of the other apartments on the airshaft, so we could sneak back and forth along the ledges."

"That would be dangerous! What if you fell all the way down?"

"Ouch!" Elsa says lightly, and closes the airshaft.

As they move on down the hall, Renny asks, "What's behind all those doors?"

"A bathroom and a bunch of closets." This place has more storage than the Cavalons have had in any house they've ever lived in. Maman needs it, too, for storing half a century's couture and modeling portfolios.

Leading Renny to the kitchen, Elsa can't help but note the utter absence of oohs and aahs and ooh-la-las Maman would have expected if she herself were escorting a first-time guest into her home. Lacking any frame of reference, Renny can't possibly grasp the fabulousness of Maman's quarters in comparison to the traditional cookie-cutter Manhattan apartment.

At two thousand square feet, it feels more like a house, really, with its unique oval living room, ornate moldings, antique hardware, and turn-of-the-century cabinetry. Twelve-foot ceilings and tall French windows make it feel extra-spacious—very important for a small, claustrophobic houseguest. Beyond many of the windows are narrow Juliet balconies with lacy ironwork railings.

The kitchen is outfitted with professional-quality appliances, including a custom-designed Gaggenau fridge and a built-to-order La Cornue range. A collection of shiny Mauviel copper cookware hangs from an overhead rack, and the granite countertop holds a block of Michel Bras chef's knives—none of which, Elsa suspects, has ever been used.

What a waste of a great kitchen.

She opens a cabinet and finds a juice glass. Baccarat, of course.

Behind her, Renny announces, "I don't like it here."

"Why not?"

"I like regular square rooms."

Elsa can't help but smile.

"I like home."

Elsa's smile promptly fades. "I know you do. But . . ."

But home is supposed to be a haven, and ours has been violated.

"This place is too fancy, right?" she asks Renny, who shrugs.

Elsa herself isn't particularly fond of the elegant Louis XIV decor: velvet and damask upholstery and draperies, fringe and tassels galore, marble and gilded wood, scrollwork and marquetry . . .

Growing up in a showplace that rivaled the Palace of Versailles, Elsa used to dream of the kind of home that was comfortable and lived-in.

Now she has it, and she'll take it any day over this—aging Sears appliances and all.

I like home, too, Renny. I know you wish we were there right now, and so do I.

" . . . and the girls really want to stay on the Upper West Side"—Marin toys with the braided piping on a throw pillow—"but I'd almost prefer to start over in a new neighborhood."

Lauren frowns. "You mean the Upper *East* Side, don't you?"

"Hmm?"

"You live on the Upper East Side, right?"

"Right." Marin lets go of the pillow and picks up the mug of coffee she's been nursing. It's good coffee—Lauren ground fresh beans to make it—yet she's found herself forcing it down like bitter medicine.

"You said Upper *West*."

She blinks and looks up to see Lauren watching her, looking concerned.

"Did I? I meant to say Upper East. I guess I'm distracted."

She *guesses*? The truth is, all afternoon, she's been spacey, her mind a million miles away.

She shouldn't have come here.

She keeps thinking about what happened yesterday, with the rat, and the text message . . .

Maybe she should just come right out and tell Lauren about it. Maybe Lauren will convince her that it was just a prank, or a fluke, or a mistake.

That was nothing, Mrs. Quinn. Stay tuned.

It doesn't sound like a mistake.

But kids can be cruel, and she knows Caroline's classmates have been giving her a hard time all year. There's no reason to think there's anything more to what happened than some stupid kids with too much time on their hands now that summer vacation is here.

She should go. She needs to get home, make sure the girls are okay.

Earlier, she called to check in on them, and of course, no one answered the home phone. Annie must have been on her cell, because it went straight to voice mail, and Caroline didn't pick up hers. No surprise there.

Groggy as she was when Marin left this morning, Caroline still managed to express resentment at having to spend the day at home with Annie.

They've probably been making each other miserable.

Yes, Marin definitely has to get back there.

Before she can make a move, there's a jangling of dog tags from Chauncey, curled at Lauren's feet. Head cocked, he looks expectantly toward the foyer.

A split second later, the front door opens.

Lauren glances at her watch. "That must be Lucy."

"Oh . . . I should get going. I don't want to get stuck in rush hour traffic."

Marin carefully sets her mug on a coaster and prepares to make a speedy exit, hoping Lauren doesn't point out that the bulk of the traffic will be coming *out* of the city, not headed into it.

"Mom? Whose car is that out front?" a female voice calls from the foyer.

Lauren's daughter arrives in the doorway a moment later, and it's clear from the look on her face that she immediately recognizes Marin.

"Lucy . . ." Lauren seems apprehensive. "This is Mrs. Quinn. She's . . ."

She's the woman whose husband had you kidnapped and nearly killed, and—

And why, oh why, did Marin come here today? This was such a stupid idea. Poor Lucy. Poor Lauren.

Poor me.

"She's a friend of mine," Lauren concludes innocuously.

"Hi, Lucy." Marin does her best to offer a friendly smile and holds her breath, unsure she can hold up if Lucy says something hurtful. Caroline certainly would, under the circumstances.

But Lucy smiles and holds out her hand to Marin. "It's nice to meet you."

"It's nice to meet you, too," Marin manages to say around the sudden lump in her throat, gratefully shaking Lucy's hand.

"How'd your math final go?" Lauren asks.

"Oh, you know . . ."

"Mmm, actually, I *don't* know, or I wouldn't have asked."

"I would say that it went as well as could be expected," Lucy replies, with all the confidence of a surgeon delivering dubious news.

Lauren points to the stairway. "Then get moving. Go on up and study for the physics final."

"It's not until Monday. I have all weekend to study."

"Dad's mother is coming, remember?"

"Oh. Right." Clearly, Lucy isn't thrilled by the prospect of meeting her grandmother for the first time. "Well, can't I have, like, two seconds to decompress, Mom?"

"Sure. One, two . . . go."

Lucy goes, with a groan.

Lauren looks at Marin. "It's never easy."

"No," Marin agrees with a faint smile, "it never is. Listen, I really need to get going, so . . ."

"Wait, Marin, before you do . . . is everything okay?"

Marin shifts her weight on the sofa. "Everything is . . ." Not *okay*. That would be a ridiculous claim, and Lauren knows it.

She settles on, "Everything is as well as can be expected."

"Are you sure?"

Should I tell her about the e-mail, and the rat?

Will she think I'm crazy and paranoid if I do?

Or, even worse, will she think that Caroline is crazy and paranoid?

"I'm positive, Lauren. I'm hanging in there. We all are. But thanks for asking." She stands up, her car keys already in hand.

"Wait, I know you didn't just come here to drink coffee and check out my new kitchen. I know something's bugging you . . . and I think I know what it is."

Marin raises an eyebrow. "I doubt it . . . but try me."

Meg Warren's car is sorely in need of some routine maintenance—not that she'll be needing it anymore, but still . . .

It's a wonder the thing even made it to New York City, what with the horrible creaking beneath the pedals every time the steering wheel makes the slightest turn.

Oh well. This Bronx neighborhood is the end of the road. Other than being a great place to abandon a stolen car, the area has very little going for it. But at least it's right off the highway, and there's a subway station with a southbound express train.

Oh, and one more perk: On this rainy day, the streets are teeming with furtive-looking, backpack-carrying young people wearing baggy jeans and hoodies. It's easy to blend into the crowd here and on the downtown Number Five train.

It won't be the same in Manhattan, though. Rush hour will be under way on this summer Friday; well-dressed office workers will have begun their mad dash toward home. That means it'll be a good idea to slip into the bathroom at Grand Central Terminal and swap out the black hoodie and baggy jeans for something more suitable for midtown.

And after that . . . East Side, to Marin, or West Side, to Elsa?

Guess I'll just have to start walking uptown and see which way the wind blows.

Elsa looks at her watch.

Does she dare call Brett at the office again? She'd spoken to him when they first arrived at Penn Station, just before hailing a cab to take them uptown. The conversation was harried, and she could tell he wasn't alone in the room on his end. Maybe he is now.

She settles Renny at the table with the fresh orange juice and organic granola cookies they picked up at the Fairway.

"Wait, Mommy, where are you going?" Renny protests as Elsa starts for the hallway, fishing her cell phone from her bag.

"Just into the bedroom to . . . to make sure there are clean sheets on the beds. I'll be right back."

"Can I watch TV?" Renny gestures at the flat screen mounted in the custom cabinetry.

There are probably a dozen good reasons not to park her daughter in front of the television again, but Elsa decides they're far outweighed by the need for some semblance of familiarity to put her at ease.

As the silence gives way to the reassuring cartoon commotion, even she finds herself breathing a little easier.

"Okay, holler if you need me."

Fixated on the screen, Renny barely nods.

In her childhood bedroom, Elsa sits on the white Matelasse coverlet—something she'd never been allowed to do as a girl—and takes out her phone.

Uh-oh—she's down to one battery bar. Did she even remember to pack her charger? She thought of it, amid the scramble to get out of the house—but did she actually do it?

She dials Brett's cell phone, promising herself she'll make it a quick call, then check her bag for her charger. If it's not here, she's going to have to go buy one.

He picks up on the first ring. "Are you okay?"

"Yes. No." The sound of his voice makes her homesick. "I mean, nothing happened to us . . . I just want this to be over. It's crazy."

There's a pause before he says, "I know," and she wonders if he's not alone.

"Did you hear from Mike yet?"

"No. I've left him a couple of messages now, but he hasn't called back."

"That isn't like him, Brett."

"I know."

"When you left those messages for him, did you say where Renny and I were going?"

"No!"

"I was just worried you might have left it on his voice mail, or . . ."

"All I told him was to call me, and that it was important." Brett clears his throat. "Listen, I'm in the middle of something, so . . ."

Oh. Okay, she gets it. "Is someone right there?"

"Yes."

"Call me when you get home."

"I will."

As she hangs up, frustrated, her gaze falls on an antique Mardi Gras eye mask sitting on top of a gilded bombé chest across the room. She remembers being severely reprimanded at Renny's age for parading around wearing it. Like so many of Maman's objets d'art, the mask was meant to be admired, not touched.

Back in the kitchen, she finds Renny staring bleakly off into space, cartoon gone to commercials, cookies and juice untouched.

Time for a new distraction. "Hey, Renny, want to see my old bedroom? I had a collection of dolls when I was your age, and they're still here."

"Can I play with them?"

"Definitely," Elsa tells her with a touch of smug satisfaction. When she herself was young, Maman insisted on keeping the antique Jumeau porcelain dolls displayed well out of her reach, behind protective glass.

She leads Renny back down the hall to her room and shows her the dolls. "What do you think? Should we take them out and play with them?"

"I don't know . . . maybe later."

"I guess Barbies would probably be more fun, huh?"

"Pro'ly."

Renny is equally unenthusiastic when Elsa points out the row of first edition leather-bound storybooks in her bookcase, offering to read to her.

"Maybe later." She wanders across the room.

Watching her stop abruptly at the bombé chest, Elsa sees that she's staring at the Mardi Gras mask. She can't recall ever having mentioned that she herself got into trouble once for touching the mask, but she must have, because her daughter takes a wary step back, dark eyes troubled.

"Don't worry, Renny. You can touch it if you want to."

"No, thank you."

"What's wrong?"

"The monster."

"What?" Startled, Elsa looks around. The room is empty, and Renny is fixated on the mask.

"Renny? What monster?"

"The one in my room, back at home." She shudders, and Elsa feels sick inside. "He had on a mask."

"Are you sure? You mean it covered his eyes?"

"No, it covered his whole face. Like a scary monster on Halloween."

"You mean he was wearing a rubber mask?"

Renny nods vehemently.

Dear God. It never occurred to Elsa that the intruder really *was* masquerading as a monster.

"I'm afraid, Mommy."

"Don't be afraid." The words are automatic, but it's such a stupid thing to say. *Don't be afraid?*

"*You* are, and so is Daddy." As if sensing that Elsa is about to deny it, Renny adds, "I heard you talking."

Oh no. How much did she hear? There's no use denying anything now. Renny's a smart kid. Smarter, perhaps, than Elsa even suspected.

"Tell me about the monster, Renny. What was he wearing?"

"A mask."

"What else?"

"A jacket." Renny responds so readily that Elsa realizes the vivid image is fresh in her mind, poor little thing.

She wants more than anything to drop the subject, but now that it's out in the open, she has to get as much information as possible. She has to let Brett know, and Mike, too, as soon as they reach him.

"What kind of jacket was he wearing?"

"The kind with a zipper and a hood. It was black."

"Did you see his hair?"

"No. The hood was up."

"Was he tall or short?"

"Tall."

That doesn't help. Anyone would seem tall, looming over a child in the dead of night.

And anyone who would do such a thing really is a sick, twisted monster.

Last October, around Halloween, Jeremy found his way from Groton back to Nottingshire, in the Boston suburbs.

Thanks to all the news accounts that recapped his kidnapping, he knew where he'd lived—not just the town, but the street as well. He was pretty sure that if he drove along Twin Ponds Lane, he'd recognize the two-story house where he'd lived with the Cavalons.

He didn't know why it seemed so important to return to the scene of the crime, but it was all he could think about.

He drove around and around Nottingshire that day, checking street signs, looking for landmarks. He found a few that seemed familiar: a big blue water tower, a redbrick library, a Shell gas station.

The gas station had—and still has—an attached mini-mart where Elsa once bought Jeremy an ice cream Drumstick on a hot summer day. She told him it wouldn't drip out the bottom of the cone because the point was plugged with a chunk of fudge.

"I always loved to eat my way down to it," she told him. "It was like a bonus treat at the end."

Intrigued, Jeremy couldn't wait; he bit off the bottom of the cone first. Somehow, it didn't taste as good as he'd expected. He spit it out on the ground, dismayed.

When they went to get back into the car, Elsa saw the melted ice cream dripping all over his hands and realized what he'd done.

He'd expected her to get angry. But she didn't. She just seemed disappointed that he hadn't saved the fudge for last the way she used to, and that he hadn't even liked it. Her disappointment made him feel worse, probably, than he would have if she'd yelled at him for making a mess.

It was so long ago, it's pretty amazing that he even remembers the incident—especially since he didn't even remember her until recently.

But ever since the dam burst, he'd been piecing together his childhood, the only childhood he ever had, even though it was another decade—an endless, excruciating decade—before he actually became an adult.

That day, his first back in Nottingshire, Jeremy parked the car and went into the mini-mart. There, he found a freezer full of Good Humor novelties . . . but no Drumsticks.

"Can I help you find something?" asked the middle-aged woman behind the register, who was eyeing him suspiciously, as if he were going to shoplift a Popsicle or something.

"Just this." He grabbed a chocolate chip sandwich and plunked it down on the counter.

"Sure that's all?" she asked, obviously wary of a grown man who'd wander in for ice cream on a blustery autumn day.

"Actually, there is something else you can help me find—but it's not in the store."

"What's that?"

He hesitated. What if something clicked when he mentioned it, and she recognized him?

That's nuts. You don't even recognize yourself these days when you look into the mirror.

"Twin Ponds Lane," he told her, and she looked relieved that he only wanted directions. "I thought it was around here someplace, but . . ."

"Oh, it used to be. But that's been gone for a few years now. They tore down all those houses and built a new development back there. McMansions . . . you know."

Maybe that was just as well, Jeremy decided as he drove away, eating his ice cream sandwich. He'd already figured out that you can't go home again.

Funny, the things you remember—and the things you forget.

On his way out of town that day, he passed a sign that read "Harbor Hills Golf." It jogged something in his brain.

Harbor Hills . . .

Something had happened here.

Something important.

Something *bad*.

* * *

"You're thinking about divorcing Garvey, right?"

Seeing Marin's salon-arched brows disappear beneath her blond bangs, Lauren immediately wishes she hadn't said it.

Judging by Marin's expression, her hunch is way off base—and even if it isn't, she, of all people, has no business doling out advice on the state of Marin's marriage to a cold-blooded murderer. What was she thinking?

She *wasn't* thinking. She was feeling—feeling sorry for Marin, and worried about her.

"At some point, I will—but I can't deal with it just yet."

"I don't blame you. One day at a time—that's all you need to face."

Marin nods, picks up the pillow, begins twisting the fringe again.

"Look, you don't have to tell me what's bothering you, but it might help. Does it have to do with the girls?"

Bingo. Marin looks up at her and nods. "Caroline."

"What's going on?"

"Yesterday, she was out, and she thinks someone put a rat into her handbag."

"*What?*"

"I know it sounds kind of . . . out there. But then I got this text message last night, and it made me think . . ." She pulls her cell phone from her pocket, presses a few buttons, and hands it to Lauren. "What does this look like to you?"

She examines the screen, frowns.

"It's an emoticon. A rat." Marin takes the phone from her, presses a couple more buttons on the keypad, then hands it back. "Read this."

Lauren does. "Who sent it?"

"I have no idea, but . . . it's scaring me."

"I don't know . . . it looks like something my kids do."

"Mine, too. But it's really bothering me."

"Maybe you should go to the police."

"And tell them . . . ?"

"And tell them you're getting menacing text messages, and someone put a rat in your daughter's purse."

"And they'll tell me it goes with the territory. This isn't the first time since last fall that some jerk has tried to get us worked up."

"I know . . . we've had to deal with gossip and the press, too—and we've had some crank calls, that sort of thing."

Marin sighs. "You're right. If I call the police, they'll just chalk it up to one more loser with nothing better to do trying to make our lives miserable."

"I didn't say that. And if you don't call the police, then what other option do you have? Ignoring it?"

"I guess so." Marin tilts her head thoughtfully. "Do you think she's dealing with this kind of thing, too?"

"Who?"

"Elsa Cavalon."

It's Lauren's turn to raise her eyebrows. "I don't know . . . why? Do you?"

"I wonder. I feel like maybe we should ask her."

"Are you serious?"

Marin nods.

"But—look, Marin, it's all I can do to handle my ex-mother-in-law showing up here this weekend. I don't think I could deal with—"

"No, I know. It's just me. It's just—she was raising my son."

But he wasn't your son anymore, Marin. He was hers.

Does Lauren dare say it? Does she really even have to? Surely Marin doesn't think of Jeremy Cavalon as her son.

"It sounds crazy, but sometimes I feel like she's the only one who can relate to my loss."

It *does* sound crazy.

"That was different, though," Lauren tells her gently. "You lost him so long ago, and it was your choice to give him up . . ."

She trails off, seeing the flash of anger in Marin's blue eyes.

"You're wrong about that. It wasn't my choice. It was Garvey's."

"I'm sorry. I didn't mean you *wanted*—"

"No. I didn't. I never wanted to give him up, but I was too weak, and Garvey was too strong."

"I'm sorry," Lauren says again.

"It killed me. Handing over that baby to a stranger . . . I wish I could tell Jeremy that, but now it's too late, and . . ."

"And you need to tell someone."

"Maybe I do. You said it yourself, Lauren. When you were talking about Nick's mother. It doesn't matter that she hasn't seen him in years—she's still his mother."

Lauren swallows hard and leans over to put an arm around Marin, half expecting her friend to crumple at the contact. But Marin stoically keeps her composure: the epitome of grace under pressure, courtesy of all those years in the spotlight.

"So what do you think?" she asks Lauren after a moment.

I think it's a huge mistake. I think you're setting yourself up for more heartache. I think you're on the verge of a nervous breakdown as it is, and . . .

And I don't think it matters what I think.

"Just be careful, Marin. If you decide to reach out to her, it won't be easy—for either of you."

"Yeah, well, you know what they say. Whatever doesn't kill you makes you stronger."

For some reason, those last words linger ominously in Lauren's mind long after Marin has driven off into the pouring rain.

It all came back to Jeremy as he drove out of Nottingshire that day last fall, past the familiar sign: "Harbor Hills Golf."

That was where he'd bashed in a little girl's head with a seven-iron.

He didn't remember her last name, or even her first—not her real one, anyway. He remembered only that she had some silly nickname everyone called her—Cha Cha or Lulu or something—and he remembered her blond braids.

He remembered other things, too: how angry he felt about having to take golf lessons. How impossible it was to get the ball into that tiny, faraway hole—only for him, though, not for the others. How mercilessly the little girl with the blond braids had taunted him about it . . .

He remembered her mean-spirited laughter every time he'd cry out in frustration after his turn; remembered how he'd sort of waved the seven-iron at her as a threat; remembered her scoffing at that, saying his swing was so bad there was no way he could hit her with the golf club.

He remembered proving her wrong. Over and over again.

He remembered her screams, then her moans; remembered the blood in her hair and on the club and spattered all over him, blood everywhere; remembered the voices as people came rushing.

"What happened to her?"

"Is she breathing?"

"Does anyone know CPR?"

He remembered Brett Cavalon grabbing him by the shoulders and shaking him, shouting, "What did you do?"

And he remembered the look on Elsa's face.

The memories were relentless. They haunted him. Finally, he had to do something about them.

It was November when he returned to Nottingshire and snuck onto the grounds of Harbor Hills. Dressed in a golf shirt and khakis, Jeremy meandered his way to the clubhouse, where he hit pay dirt: a series of framed photographs of junior golfers over the years. He didn't recognize any of the faces, but one name jumped out at him from a photo caption: La La. That was it. Not Cha Cha or Lulu. It was La La. La La Montgomery.

The picture must have been taken maybe a year or two after he'd known her. He never would have recognized her, and not just because her blond braids had been exchanged for a pixie cut. Her whole face looked different—and he wondered if that was because of what he'd done to her.

Probably.

Well, she wasn't the only one who'd been beaten beyond recognition. She wasn't the only one who'd had plastic surgery.

Suddenly, Jeremy wanted to see her . . . even if she didn't want to see him. No, he didn't just want to see her . . . he *had* to see her.

Luckily for him, she wasn't hard to find.

CHAPTER
NINE

The sky opens up in earnest as Elsa and Renny stand waiting for the light to change on Broadway. Carrying take-out Chinese food in a soggy plastic bag, Elsa wishes she'd thought to ask the restaurant for a few extra bags, since she has no umbrella and no raincoat.

Oh well. At least you're finally getting that shower you missed earlier.

When she'd suggested to Renny that they go browse around some stores and have dinner at a neighborhood restaurant, she was hoping to kill a solid hour or two. She figured she might even have a glass of wine—take the edge off and relax a little, since her stress isn't doing Renny any favors.

But Renny wasn't interested in browsing or dining out—particularly once they had ventured out into the downpour.

"When can we go back?" she kept asking, and Elsa didn't have the heart to keep dragging her around in the deluge.

She's hardly thrilled about returning to her mother's apartment, though. Intellectually, she knows there's no real reason to feel threatened there, yet she can't seem to help it.

The light changes at last, and they join the mass of pedestrians swarming the wide thoroughfare as lightning flashes overhead. Honking yellow cabs clog the street on either side of the landscaped median, headlights glaring in the gloom. A lucky few commuters huddle beneath the shelter at the bus stop; the rest crowd along the curb between the rushing gutter and the parade of black pedestrian umbrellas heading toward the express subway station two blocks down.

High above the chaos, the Ansonia's mansard roofline is shrouded in a misty curtain of rain, towering like a haunted mansion in some vintage, monochromatic film.

The light changes again before Renny's short legs can make it all the way across, and they're forced to wait it out on the median with a few other stragglers.

"You okay?" Elsa looks down at Renny, who nods unconvincingly.

"Can we go to Tiffany's for breakfast tomorrow?"

Oh, right. Breakfast at Tiffany's. "We'll see."

Elsa figures the necessary disillusionment can at least wait until they're inside, out of the miserable weather.

Anyway, tomorrow morning the nightmare will be over and they'll be on their way home to Connecticut.

Please, please, please let it be over.

Before they left the apartment, she'd called Brett again to tell him about the rubber monster mask. She could tell that Lew was still hovering, because while Brett listened to what she had to say, he didn't comment, other than telling her he'll call her as soon as he gets home.

"Still no Mike?" she asked hopefully before hanging up.

Still no Mike.

Something is wrong. She knows it, and so does Brett. Either something terrible happened to him, or . . .

Something terrible must have happened to him.

Why else would he not have checked his messages? If he had, and if he'd heard theirs, he'd have been in touch by now.

You're jumping to conclusions. Stop being such a pessimist. There must be other logical reasons why he hasn't called back.

Right. She just can't think of a single one.

Unless he has called back, and Brett doesn't want to tell her what Mike has to say, because he's trying to shield her . . .

I need to call Brett and tell him that if he's hiding something from me, he'd better stop right now, because I can handle it.

Finally the light changes again. Reaching the other side of the street, they skirt around a large puddle and step onto the sidewalk. The building's main entrance is around the corner on Seventy-third Street, beneath a stone portico framed by globed sconces and the tall, gargoyle-embellished façade.

A uniformed doorman standing outside holds open the door as they approach—not the same one from this afternoon. This guard, who told them his name is Tom, was just starting his shift when they were on their way out. Elsa reluctantly introduced herself and Renny as Sylvie Durand's daughter and granddaughter.

"But don't hold it against us," she wanted to add, well aware that Maman always sweeps grandly from her cab or Town Car to the elevator without giving "the help" a second glance. The building staff has never been very fond of her—or of Elsa, purely by association.

Maybe Tom doesn't know her snobbish mother very

well, though, because he just held the door, tipped his hat, and wished her and Renny a pleasant evening.

"Back so soon?" he asks now. "Guess I don't blame you. It's a real gullywasher out here, isn't it?"

"Definitely," Elsa agrees, thinking that it's an odd comment. Gullywasher—it sounds like something you'd hear out in the Southwest, not in the heart of Manhattan.

"That smells great." Tom gestures at the bag of take-out. "Moo shoo pork, right?"

"Wow, you're good."

"Oh, I don't fool around when it comes to Chinese. Hope you got extra."

She grins. "Do you want some?"

"No, but your mother might."

"Chinese food? My mother?" She laughs, shaking her head. "Anyway . . . I don't think Rainbow Panda delivers to Paris, so . . ."

"Paris?"

So he *is* pretty new here. "That's where she lives now," Elsa explains.

"I know that—but I thought you were here to see her."

"Oh—no. We're just spending a night or two at her place. She's in Paris."

Tom shakes his head. "She's here. She showed up a little while ago, while you were out."

"What?"

"Mémé's here?" Renny lights up immediately. "Why didn't she tell us she was coming?"

"I'm not sure, little lady. See, your grandma's not the type to stop and chat on her way in. Or out, come to think of it."

Elsa is incredulous. "Are you sure it was her?"

"You know anyone else who goes around in a fancy hat and veil like an old-fashioned movie star?"

"Did you mention that we were here?"

"I figured she knew, but if it's a surprise, don't worry because—"

"Did she say anything at all?"

"To me? Nah. She was all wrapped up in a shawl and under a big black umbrella when she came in. I don't even think she needed the umbrella, with that gigantic hat she had on, but to each his own. I did mention to her that it's bad luck to keep an umbrella open inside, but she just kept on walking. I guess she's not the superstitious type."

No, she isn't.

Nor is she the type to show up in New York without warning.

What in the world is going on?

Staring at the pouring rain beyond the plate-glass window, Caroline wonders if she should have given up hours ago. Technically, it's no longer even afternoon. Yet here she is, parked at the same table in Starbucks, waiting for some guy to show up. And why *would* he? It's not like people can read minds. It's not like she's sent him some telepathic message to meet her and, voilà—here he'll be.

That is *so* not going to happen.

So what are you doing here, then? How did you, of all people, turn into this pathetic loser?

Dejectedly, she sips her third—or is it fourth?—cup of tea. Herbal this time. She'd discovered earlier that coffee made her sick to her stomach, and regular tea made her antsy. But she couldn't just sit here for hours without buying something every once in a while—even if all this hot liquid makes her have to pee constantly.

Maybe she missed Surfer Boy during one of her countless visits to the bathroom.

Yeah, or maybe you're never going to see him again.

This is crazy. A year ago, she was on top of the world. Now she's, like, some peerless—

"Hi, Caroline! What are you doing here?"

She looks up, startled . . . then breaks into a slow smile.

It's him.

Rounding the corner into the hallway that bisects Maman's wing of the building, Elsa can see that the main apartment door is ajar.

That's strange.

Unless Maman arrived, saw their luggage by the door, realized that they're in town, and didn't want to lock them out . . .

But she knows I have the keys. How else would I have gotten into the apartment in the first place? And why wouldn't she just call me on my cell phone to see where I was?

She sticks her head in and calls, "Maman?"

No reply.

"Is she here?" Renny asks.

"She must be. Come on." Opening the door wider, she sees that the lights are off, just as she left them. No bags have joined their own in the foyer—because, of course, Maman doesn't travel with luggage—but no dripping black umbrella, either.

Elsa sniffs the air for a waft of Parisian perfume, but smells only the Chinese food in the bag she's carrying.

"Maman!"

Silence.

She closes the door, again wondering uneasily why her mother left it open. After a moment's hesitation, she slides the dead bolt.

Immediately, she wonders if that was a mistake.

What if her mother isn't the only one who's waiting for them here? What if Renny's stalker somehow found his way to the apartment, and broke in, and . . . Oh God, what if Maman showed up and surprised him?

"Where is she, Mommy?"

"I'm not sure. Come on, let's go see." She gingerly moves toward the hall, her hand firm on Renny's shoulder. Again, she calls to her mother, wondering if the doorman might have been mistaken.

Renny chimes in with a singsong "Mémé! Mémé!"

In the kitchen, Elsa flips on a light. Again, everything is just as she left it: the untouched cookies on a plate, the juice in a glass.

Remembering every horror movie she's ever seen, she glances at the knife block. All the handles are accounted for. Good. That's good.

See? Everything is fine.

She sets the bag of Chinese food on the counter beside the knives. "Maman! Are you here?"

"That man said she is, Mommy. I bet the walls are so thick she can't hear us."

"I guess so," Elsa agrees, not bothering to point out that it's the walls between the apartments that are soundproof. Most of the interior ones are just regular drywall partitions installed over the years as the rooms were reconfigured.

They resume the search in the dining room, the living room, the library. Back in the entry hall, she looks again at the locked door. If Maman isn't here, who left it open while they were out? Elsa distinctly remembers closing it earlier, before they left.

"Do you think she's sleeping, Mommy?"

At this hour? Even with jet lag, Maman stays up late.

Then again, she's getting older, and anyway, where the hell else could she be?

"Probably. Let's go look."

But when they reach the master bedroom, it's not only dark; it's deserted.

"Maybe she's in the shower," Renny suggests.

"I don't hear the water running." Elsa can't hear anything at all, in fact, but the distant hum of the refrigerator. "Anyway, Maman takes baths."

Chanel-scented bubble baths—but never in the middle of the day.

"Come out, come out, wherever you are!" For Renny's sake, Elsa tries to sound playful as they cross the master suite toward the adjoining bath.

"Do you think she's playing hide-and-seek?"

Maman is hardly the playful type, but . . . "You never know," Elsa tells Renny as she knocks on the door. No reply.

"Ready or not, here we come!" She opens the door.

The bathroom, too, is empty. Renny jerks back the shower curtain to make sure.

Visibly disappointed, she says, "I thought she was going to jump out and yell surprise."

"I know, sweetie, but I just don't—"

Suddenly, Renny clutches her arm. "What was that?"

"What was what?"

"Shh, I just heard something in the other room."

They stand absolutely still.

After a moment, Elsa whispers, "I don't hear any—"

And then she does. She hears . . . something. A faint thumping sound.

"See? She's here!" Renny takes off running through the bedroom to the hallway, calling, "Mémé!"

Elsa follows, relieved.

But not for long.

There's no sign of her mother. Elsa trails Renny from room to room until they end up in the empty foyer again.

"I really thought I heard something."

"I heard it too," Elsa assures Renny, "but this is an old building. It makes noises. Or maybe it was someone walking around in the apartment upstairs."

"I thought it was soundproof."

Yeah. So did I.

Elsa glances again at the door. If no one was here, then why was it ajar when they got back?

And why, she wonders in alarm as she takes a closer look, is it no longer dead-bolted from the inside now?

Jake is just as good-looking as Caroline remembered. Maybe better-looking, with his hair all damp and kind of spiky from the rain, as if he ran his fingers through it. Caroline wouldn't mind doing just that, she decides, watching him walk toward her again, this time carrying the cup of coffee he just bought.

His rain jacket is already draped over the chair opposite her, and his backpack is resting on the floor at her feet where he left it, after saying, "Be right back."

Now he sits down, shaking his head. "I still can't believe you're here."

"Why can't you believe it? I told you I come here sometimes," she reminds him, hoping she doesn't look as stale and wilted as she feels. Too bad she didn't think to put on some lip gloss when she last visited the ladies' room, about twenty minutes ago. By then, she'd all but given up hope that he'd show up.

But he's here! He's here!

He shrugs. "After what happened to you yesterday, I can't believe you'd ever come back."

"*You* did."

"I'm not the one it happened to."

"Whatever. It was random. I'm fine."

Yeah, sure. Fine. Totally laid back about a rat crawling out of her purse.

But his being here really does make it seem all better.

"You know"—Jake sips the coffee, and makes a face like it's too hot—"I tried to wait around for you for a little bit after they took you into the back room, but then I thought that might seem weird, so I left."

"Why would it seem weird?"

"You don't think it would have?"

"No." She smiles at him. "I think it would have been sweet."

"Oh . . . too bad I didn't do it, then. Because I really am a sweet guy."

"Yeah?" She gives him a flirty little smile.

He smiles back, and for the first time, Caroline notices his eyes.

With his blond hair, you'd expect them to be blue, or maybe brown.

But they're dark—as dark, perhaps, as her own.

The door *was* dead-bolted. Elsa is sure of it.

Now it isn't. She's sure of that, too.

Numb with fear, she calls out to her mother, hearing the doubt in her own voice. There will be no reply, because Maman isn't here.

But maybe she *was* here, and she unlocked the door on her way out just now . . .

No. If Maman had been here, she'd have heard them calling her. She'd have answered.

But if she wasn't here . . . then who came into the apartment while they were gone, left the door ajar, and now unlocked it?

"Mommy, what are you doing?"

Opening her mouth to answer Renny's question, she can't seem to find her voice.

Okay, don't panic. Just stay calm and think this through. There must be an explanation.

Elsa rests a hand on Renny's shoulder, as much to steady herself as to reassure her daughter.

Think. Think.

Tom said he saw Maman. Was he imagining things? Or lying? But why would he lie?

Who is Tom, anyway? A doorman. A stranger. He wasn't even in the lobby, she realizes, when they came and went. He was standing outside. He could have been anyone.

Oh God. I can't trust him. I can't trust anyone.

Someone knows she and Renny are in Maman's apartment. Someone was waiting for them just now.

Yet she's positive they weren't followed here from Connecticut, or even from Penn Station.

And she didn't even decide they were coming to New York until this afternoon. She hasn't discussed it with anyone but Brett. They didn't even buy tickets until right before they boarded the train.

Yet someone found them.

That means they weren't just being watched and photographed. Someone must have been listening to their private conversations. Someone heard them talking about the trip in their kitchen, or over the phone. Either the line is tapped, or the house is bugged. Maybe both.

She has to call Brett and tell him—

No! You can't call Brett. You can't call Maman, either.

You can't call anyone. You can't talk about it to anyone, not even Renny.

Someone might be listening right now. Someone might hear her shallow breathing, her heart pounding like crazy, blood roaring through her veins . . .

"Mommy?"

"Shh!"

Whoever was here might have wanted her to think he was leaving. But he might still be here, hiding, watching, listening.

Clutching Renny's shoulder, she glances warily around the foyer.

Dear God, someone is there—standing right behind her.

Elsa cries out—then realizes it's her own reflection in an enormous gilded mirror. She looks like hell: hair straggly from the rain, pupils dilated in sheer terror, yesterday's mascara rendering her gaunt, almost otherworldly.

"Mommy!"

"It's okay, Renny." She hugs her shaken daughter. "I didn't mean to scare you."

But someone is sure as hell trying to scare *her*—and doing a damned good job of it.

Arriving home after an agonizing day of going through the motions at the office, still with no word from Mike, Brett is relieved to see that Meg's car is no longer parked in the driveway next door. He's definitely not up for another round of Q&A.

Reminded that Elsa's car is still sitting at the Sunoco station—or, by now, in a tow yard somewhere—he wonders again about that Spider-Man toy she'd found lying in the parking lot. Even if it had fallen out of the car . . .

What if Elsa herself had been the one who was carrying it around? Caught in the throes of acute stress disorder, she'd done that back in the beginning, for months after their son disappeared. She'd clung fiercely to that toy, even talked to it, as if it were Jeremy himself. The day she'd tried to kill herself, when he'd found her unconscious, she'd been clutching the toy in her hands.

So, what? You think she lied to you about how it might have gotten into the car and onto the ground next to it?

No. Her terror was too real. She didn't lie.

But maybe her subconscious mind is up to something again. Losing touch with reality. Dissociative behavior. Maybe learning of Jeremy's death really did push her over the edge, and Brett was just too distracted or busy to notice the signs.

But it isn't just that she thought someone was in Renny's room, or that she thought she saw a footprint, and found that Spider-Man by the car.

What about the envelope of pictures?

Wait a minute.

She wasn't in any of them.

Could she have taken them, and mailed them, herself?

It would mean his wife is seriously mentally ill.

No. I can't accept that. I won't.

He strides toward the house, casting a wary eye across the surrounding landscape, relieved to see nothing unusual. It isn't until he's reached the front door that he spots the small rectangle of paper stuck to the frame.

Heart racing, he grabs it.

Mr. and Mrs. Cavalon: I'll be Renata's new caseworker, and I came by this afternoon to introduce myself. Please give me a call to schedule a meeting at your earliest convenience.

The ink is wet and smeared in spots, particularly at the bottom, making the scrawled signature difficult to read. It looks like Melissa—or perhaps Melvin?—Jackson, or Johnson. The phone number is legible, though.

Brett hurriedly unlocks the door and shoves the keys into his suit coat pocket along with the note, wondering why the new social worker didn't just call in advance to introduce herself.

Then again—why *would* she call? Pop-in visits are a necessary evil when it comes to foster care, and a heads-up would obviously ruin the spontaneity.

After stepping over the threshold, Brett locks the dead bolt behind him and leans against the door, head tilted back, eyes closed.

The threat of an unexpected visit from Roxanne was bad enough. Now another new caseworker breathing down their necks? That's the last thing he and Elsa need right now.

What they do need right now is help. But Mike seems to have fallen off the face of the earth, and the only other person to whom he can consider reaching out is Elsa's therapist, Joan.

There must be some kind of patient privacy protocol, but he can only hope that Elsa signed a release in the beginning that would allow him access to her mental health records.

He has to call Joan. He knows he does. He dreads the thought of it, but it's time.

He pulls his cell phone from his pocket and checks to make sure he didn't somehow miss a call. Nope.

He finds Mike's number and hits redial, wanting to give it one more try before he gets in touch with Joan.

This time, someone answers the phone with a gruff-sounding hello.

"Mike?"

"No," the unfamiliar voice says.

"Sorry, I must have the wrong—"

"Are you looking for Mike Fantoni?"

"Yes . . ."

"This is the right phone. Who is this?"

"I'm . . . a friend of his."

"Yeah. So am I."

Wondering what's going on, Brett asks, "Can I please speak to him?"

There's a long pause. "I'm sorry. They just gave me his phone, and I heard it ring, so . . ."

"They?"

"The nurses. I'm at the hospital. Mike is . . . he's been in an accident."

Elsa desperately wants to believe she and Renny are alone in the apartment.

If they are, then the safest thing to do would be to barricade the door and stay right here until this is over . . .

Whatever "this" is.

But if that isn't the case—if whoever unlocked the dead bolt is still here—then they have to escape, before—

No. Don't even think about that. It's going to be fine. You can get through this. Just stay calm.

Okay. An escape. The door is just a few yards away. It would be so easy to grab Renny and run for it . . .

Her eyes go to the coat closet beside the door. What if someone is hiding in there, watching them through the crack? Or that tall armoire positioned against the curved wall between the door and where they're standing now: Someone could be lurking in the shadows on the far side of it. If she makes a move to leave with Renny, he'll pounce, and then what?

Elsa could scream for help at the top of her lungs . . .

And no one would hear.

Soundproof. Oh God.

Her eyes are starting to sting.

How could she have thought it was a good idea to leave Brett, to travel so far from home alone with Renny, to a city filled with strangers who—

"Can we eat now?" Renny's voice startles Elsa.

She blinks, takes a deep breath, tries to focus. Her throat dry with fear, she repeats Renny's question slowly, as if it had been spoken in a foreign language. "Can we eat now?"

Can . . . we . . . eat . . . now . . . ?

Can . . . we . . . ?

The words aren't registering. All she can think of is fleeing this gilded cage, getting her daughter to safety . . .

"Mommy?"

Food. She's talking about the Chinese food in the kitchen.

"No, we . . ."

Wait a minute. The kitchen . . .

The knives are there, right on the counter. If she were armed, she'd at least be able to fight back if someone attacked.

Yes. That's what she'll do. She'll grab a knife and then make a break for the door with her daughter.

"Come on," she tells Renny, trying to keep panic from edging into her voice. "Let's go eat."

Peering into every shadowy nook along the way as they move toward the kitchen, Elsa keeps one firm hand on Renny's shoulder and the other in her pocket, clamped around her cell phone. If she had to, she could probably dial 911 blindly, with her thumb.

But how long would it take for help to arrive?

Too long.

And no one will hear their screams.

Oh God . . . Oh God . . .

In the kitchen, the Chinese food waits on the counter.

Keeping Renny close beside her, Elsa walks over. Her hand is shaking like crazy, her thumb poised on the 9 button, as she starts to reach past the bag . . .

Calm down. You have to calm down. If he's watching, he'll think you're going for the takeout, and—

Stunned by what she sees, she involuntarily loosens her grip on her phone. It clatters onto the granite counter as she stares in disbelief at the knife block.

Minutes ago, the handles were all accounted for.

Now one of the slots is empty.

Stunned, Brett listens as Joe, the man who answered Mike's phone—his neighbor, and a witness to the accident—explains the situation.

Mike Fantoni is in a coma.

"It was a hit-and-run in front of his building. This car came barreling out of nowhere. Hit him, and kept on going."

"Did you get a look at it?"

"Not a good look, no. I was in a state of shock, trying to help Mikey . . ." He pauses, clears the emotion from his throat. "A couple of other people saw it, though. The cops found the car abandoned a coupla blocks away. Stolen."

"Do they have any idea who was driving it?"

"Probably some crazy-ass kid out joyriding." Joe sighs heavily. "You know, another few seconds, and he woulda been outa there, on his way to the airport."

"What? The kid? How do you know—"

"Not the *kid*. Mike!"

"*Mike* was going to the *airport*?"

"Had his bags all packed and everything."

"Do you know where he was going?"

"On vacation."

"Do you know *where*?" Brett repeats, his heart pounding.

"Nah. Why?"

"Just . . . he was working on something for me. Is there any way you can find out where—"

"I told you, he's in a coma, on a respirator. I can't—"

"No, I know," Brett says quickly, guiltily. "Forget it. It's not important."

But it *is* important.

Just last night, Mike promised to figure out where that Spider-Man figurine came from. Why hadn't he mentioned he was going away this morning?

Was it a sudden decision?

Or . . .

Could the trip have had something to do with the case?

With a burst of adrenaline, Elsa grabs her daughter by the arm and drags her out of the kitchen.

Renny starts to cry out in protest.

"Shh, no! No!" Elsa grabs her by the shoulders. "I know this doesn't make sense, Renny, but just do what I say right now, please. Okay?"

At her frightened nod, Elsa releases her and turns to see if there's any sign of an intruder.

The menacing presence seems as blatant as the gaping hole in the knife block, yet the long hallway is deserted.

Could she have imagined that a handle was missing? Fear does strange things to a person . . .

Or maybe it was missing all along, and she just thought she saw all the knives accounted for when she checked earlier . . .

Am I losing my mind?

Maybe it's crazy to acknowledge—even to herself— that she might be seeing things. But is that any crazier than assuming someone is creeping around the apartment, armed with a kitchen knife, like a murderous maniac from a horror movie?

Renny tugs her arm, and Elsa glances down to see that her face is etched in worry.

I can't take any chances. I've got to get her out of here.

Motioning with her forefinger against her lips, Elsa pulls Renny into the dining room, past the Baroque dining set and antique sideboard. She keeps an eye on the drawn gold brocade draperies at the windows for any sign of movement.

All is still. But that doesn't mean they aren't being watched from a gap in the curtains, or . . . or a crevice in the wall, or around a doorway . . .

Why, oh why, didn't Elsa think to grab one of the knives before she left the kitchen? Now she's utterly defenseless; the door might as well be on the far side of a crocodile moat.

Incredibly, Renny is cooperating. Does she realize their lives are hanging in the balance?

Or is she merely humoring Elsa, thinking she's gone off the deep end like her schizophrenic birth mother?

I'll explain everything to her later—as soon as I get her out of here.

Moving in absolute silence, they make it to the large, circular living room. The elaborate decor creates plenty of potential hiding places. Still, no hint of anyone lurking as they tiptoe across the carpet. Elsa keeps an eye on the French doors, where the wrought-iron Juliet balcony extends off to either side, beyond her view. What if someone is lurking there?

Then he can't see me, either.

Step by stealthy step, they cover the home stretch.

In the foyer, acutely aware of the closed closet door and the shadowy recess beside the armoire, Elsa reminds herself again that slow and steady is the only way to escape with Renny. Her instinct is to get the hell out of here; if she were alone, she'd make a run for it. But she can't do that with Renny. She has no choice.

Inch by inch, they make their way across the herringbone hardwoods. The apartment is silent but for the sound of the ticking clock and the humming refrigerator.

Holding her breath, Elsa reaches for the doorknob. Painstakingly, she turns it, pulls it open, bracing herself for the attack from behind.

When it doesn't come—when she finds herself crossing the threshold into the hall with Renny—it's all she can do not to collapse in relief. She leaves the door ajar, just as she found it, afraid the sound of it closing might alert the person who's lurking in the apartment—if, indeed, anyone is really there.

"Mommy," Renny whispers, "what—"

"Shh, sweetie, we just have to get out of here, and then I'll explain."

Oh, you will? What are you going to tell her? That you're afraid someone wants to kill you, or her? That this was meant to be a refuge, but we aren't safe here? That we aren't safe anywhere?

If they manage to get out of here in one piece, what next? Should she call the police?

She reaches into her pocket for her phone, just in case . . .

But it's not there.

What the . . . ? She knows she had it earlier. She was going to call 911, right before—

Oh. She must have dropped it in the kitchen when she saw that the knife was missing.

The knife . . .

She can't go back for the phone. It doesn't matter. All that matters now is getting Renny out of here.

Please, God, let us get out of here . . .

The wide, deserted hallway stretches ahead of them. Short corridors branch off in several spots. There's an ancient stairwell no one ever uses—for all she knows, it might be locked or blocked off once they get inside.

No. Not worth the risk. They pass the stairwell, the garbage chute, the door to a utility room.

Just ahead looms a shallow recess that holds a fire extinguisher and enough room for someone to hide, flat against the wall.

But the danger lies behind them, Elsa reminds herself—not ahead.

Still, her chest aches with tension as they pass it and round the corner. No one follows; no one jumps out at them, yet she won't breathe easily until they're outside.

Not even then. Not until you know what you're dealing with, and why, and who . . .

Stop. Just focus. One thing at a time.

Ahead, the door to the main elevator bank and stairs beckons like the proverbial light at the end of the tunnel. She hustles Renny toward it, her brain ping-ponging between escape route options.

Stairs or elevator?

Stairs or elevator?

Stairs . . .

No. They'd be out in the open, easily spotted descending the stairwell from anyone on a landing above.

Once they got into an elevator, though, they'd be safe—as long as it showed up in a hurry. There are six of them; the odds are good. They'll take the elevator.

She pushes through the door and heaves a sigh of relief that they've made it this far.

She's about to press the down button when her daughter speaks for the first time.

"No!"

"What? What's wrong?"

Oh—oh no. Renny shrinks back, staring fearfully at the elevator doors.

"I can't."

"You can. Please, Renny . . ." Elsa jams her palm

down hard on the button, repeatedly, and hears an elevator lurching up from below.

"No!"

"Shh! You have to." It's all Elsa can do to speak over the awful lump in her own throat. "We need to get out of here, and I promise it's going to be okay."

The doors glide open; the elevator is empty. She reaches for Renny, pulls her inside, and hesitates, thoughts careening again.

Lobby or ground floor?
Lobby or ground floor?

The security desk is right in the lobby—along with creepy Tom.

There's a service entrance in the basement, along with the door to the adjacent parking garage. They'll sneak out one way or another, and once they're on the street, she can figure out where to go next.

Elsa presses the ground floor button. The doors start to close.

Relieved, Elsa leans back her head, closes her eyes, and at last breathes a sigh of relief.

With an anguished cry and a fierce lurch of her little body, Renny wrenches herself free of Elsa's grasp. She throws herself back out through the elevator doors at the last second before they slide closed.

In a panic, Elsa presses the door open button, but it's too late. The descent is under way, and she's helplessly trapped inside without her daughter.

"Is there anything I can do from here?" Brett asks Mike's friend Joe.

"Do you pray?"

Brett hesitates, remembering all the years he'd gone faithfully to church—and all the years he hadn't.

He and Elsa were married at St. Mary's, the parish where he'd been christened, confirmed, served as an altar boy, and eventually cried at his parents' funerals.

"Will you accept children lovingly from God?" Father Nolan asked solemnly during the wedding ceremony. Brett and Elsa vowed that they would.

And they did. They accepted Jeremy lovingly from God—by way of the foster care agency back in Boston—and they did their best to make him their own. Brett even took him to church a couple of times, thinking it might be good for both of them.

Looking back, he remembers the disapproving glances from other parishioners and his own discomfort over Jeremy's behavior more than he remembers anything spiritually positive.

He thinks about what Jeremy did to the Montgomery girl, and of Jeremy's disappearance, and how he finally stopped going to church for good when his prayers weren't answered.

Then he thinks about Elsa, who tried to kill herself, and Renny, so close to becoming their daughter . . .

"Yeah," he tells Joe. "I pray."

"Then pray for Mikey. That's all anyone can do."

Elsa keeps pressing buttons, but the elevator descends to the ground floor without stopping.

Trapped inside, on the verge of panic, she flashes back to the first moments after she realized Jeremy was missing from the backyard.

She remembers running back into the house, thinking he might have gotten past her and was safely inside; screaming his name; racing back outside, combing the yard, the block, a nearby field . . .

Later, years later, she wondered if her own terror

had precluded her from getting to Jeremy while there was still time. If she'd only stayed calm; if she'd called the police right away; if she hadn't been hysterical . . .

Yes. She blamed herself. All these years, she's blamed herself.

And the same familiar firestorm of panic is sweeping toward her now.

Yet she's helpless, trapped; there's nothing to do but wait for the elevator to hit bottom.

The second it does, she jabs the button for her mother's floor.

The elevator begins the excruciating ascent and Elsa prays it won't stop along the way, prays Renny will be right where she left her.

Of course she will. Where else would she go? She'd know I'm coming back for her.

Wouldn't she?

Yes. She'd know I wouldn't just abandon her, ever.

But what if he gets to her first?

What if . . . ?

At last, at last, the elevator bumps to a stop. The doors begin to open. Elsa springs through the opening the moment it's wide enough.

Renny is gone.

It's all she can do not to collapse in despair, or shout her daughter's name.

No. Don't. Stay focused.

Think. Think . . .

Would Renny have left of her own accord? Or did someone grab her?

Dizzy with fear, Elsa rushes over to the wrought-iron railing and leans over, scanning the vast stairwell for Renny.

No sign of her daughter below, or above, either.

Again reliving the nightmare of Jeremy's disappearance, Elsa runs blindly back along the corridor.

She tries to reassure herself exactly as she did on that awful day fifteen years ago—that her child is simply hiding, or lost; that nothing bad can happen to someone who's already endured so much pain in a short lifetime.

But it did, and Jeremy is dead, and now Renny . . .

"Renny!" she calls recklessly, no longer in control of her instincts.

She races around the corner, retracing the path to her mother's apartment. The door is still ajar.

Did Renny go back inside?

Was someone waiting for her there?

Would she have left the door standing open exactly as Elsa had?

Without a thought to her own safety, Elsa dashes inside, dizzy with fear, calling her daughter's name.

It takes her a minute of frantic searching, maybe less, to determine that the apartment is empty—just as the house and the yard were fifteen years ago.

Back in the round entryway, she grasps the edge of an antique table as the world seems to spin around her like a carnival ride.

"Renny! Oh God, Renny, where are you?"

She's gone.

Gone.

At last, the bottom drops out and Elsa falls to her knees.

CHAPTER
TEN

Driving down the Saw Mill River Parkway, Marin can't stop thinking about Lauren's daughter, Lucy. A pretty, wholesome-looking brunette, she's really got her act together.

Not that Caroline doesn't, in her own way . . .

Yet Marin can't help comparing the two—especially when she remembers Lucy's polite response when Lauren introduced her; the way she managed to put Marin herself at ease. Whether or not her warmth was genuine—though Marin sensed that it was—Lucy sure sailed through the potentially awkward moment with grace.

No way would Caroline display that level of maturity under those particular circumstances. No, she's always put her own needs first, just as Garvey did.

It's easy to blame him for Caroline's character flaws—after all, he spoiled her rotten.

But I'm her mother. Aren't I partly responsible, too?

Marin's always told herself that she could love Annie enough to make up for the way Garvey treated her—but what about Caroline? Did she love Caroline enough?

Or did she resent her for being the center of Garvey's world—or for being so sick that—

No. Absolutely not. I'm her mother. Of course I love her enough.

Yes, Caroline possesses some of her father's more disagreeable personality traits: she's self-centered, sarcastic, and can be mean-spirited. But, like him, she's also charming, and quick-witted, and brilliant.

She'll probably turn out to be just fine, Marin assures herself.

So what? Everyone has faults. Why, all of a sudden, are you dwelling on Caroline's?

She knows exactly why. That thing yesterday, with the rat—it's been in the back of Marin's mind all day. What if . . . ?

No. She would never, ever do that.

And yet . . . Caroline thrives on attention. She always got plenty of it from Garvey. With him gone, she's taken the histrionics to a whole new level. The way she pitched a tantrum the other day over family photos, accusing Marin of burning them . . .

I couldn't even listen to her. I turned around and walked away from her in mid-tirade.

And yesterday, when the girls were fighting—Marin chose to ignore that, as well. Numb. That's it—she's been numb for so long, ignoring, denying, overlooking, overmedicating . . .

How far would Caroline go for her attention?

Did she make up the bizarre story about the rat?

Did she send the text message herself, so that Marin wouldn't doubt her?

She sighs, staring bleakly through the windshield as the wipers sweep the rain from side to side.

Maybe I should have called her on it last night.

But I will. I'll talk to her as soon as I get home.

* * *

Crumpled on the herringbone floor in her mother's foyer, head buried in her arms, Elsa tells herself that as bad as it seems, she can't give in to tears now. That won't do Renny any good.

"Mommy?"

Hearing her daughter's voice, Elsa lurches upright, praying it wasn't her mind playing tricks on her.

No—it's Renny!

She's standing in the doorway of the apartment.

About to cry out in relief, Elsa realizes that someone is standing behind the little girl.

It's Tom the doorman, his hand firmly planted on her shoulder.

Lauren's knock on Lucy's bedroom door is greeted by a gruff "Ryan, I told you, I don't know where it is, so stop bugging me!"

"It's not Ryan." Lauren pushes the door open a crack. "What did he lose this time? His phone? His wallet? His iPod—again?"

Lucy, sitting at her desk in front of an open notebook, shakes her head. "I told him I wouldn't tell you."

"Either your sibling loyalty has done a major about-face, or you're blackmailing him to keep quiet."

Seeing the look on Lucy's face, she wonders why—then realizes the blunder. *Blackmail? You idiot.*

Blackmail was what triggered Garvey Quinn's heinous plot last summer.

"Stupid thing to say. I'm sorry, Lucy. You know I didn't mean—"

"It's okay."

Someday, Lauren hopes as she crosses her daughter's bedroom, this whole thing might really be behind them once and for all, and they'll never have to worry about stirring up painful memories.

But somehow, she doubts it.

One man's evil has scarred so many innocent people for life: Lauren and her children, Marin and hers, the Cavalon family, even Sam . . .

All of them are forced to live with the fallout.

Live . . . that's the key word, Lauren reminds herself. *It could have been so much worse.*

She looks down at her daughter. "I just wanted to tell you how proud I am of the way you handled yourself when you met Marin Quinn."

"Oh . . . yeah. Well, what did you expect me to do? And, I mean . . . it wasn't her fault, right? What her bastard husband did?"

Ordinarily, Lauren would reprimand her for using bad language. In this case, it's well deserved. In fact, nothing she can think of is strong enough for Garvey Quinn.

"No," she tells Lucy, "it wasn't Marin's fault."

"She seemed nice. But nervous."

"Yes." Nervous, and frightened, and dangerously fragile . . .

"Is she okay, Mom?"

"I hope so, Lucy. I really do."

Garvey Quinn has claimed enough victims.

Please, God, don't let there be any more.

As Elsa stares at the uniformed stranger behind Renny, her thoughts race from one wild scenario to another.

Is he armed?

Has he taken Renny hostage?

Does he want something in return for her release?

"I couldn't find you, Mommy!" Renny's expression is accusatory—but not frightened.

"She got off an elevator in the basement. Ozzy spotted her on one of the surveillance screens, wandering around down there."

Tom's words fail to register, but his avuncular tone certainly does.

"I . . ."

Dazed, Elsa looks from him to Renny and back again, trying to assess the situation. Are his words meant to be informative, or menacing? She wants desperately to snatch her daughter from his clutches, but does she dare?

Before she can make a move, Tom releases Renny.

"I've got to get back downstairs to work." He ruffles her dark hair playfully. "No more running away from your mother, you hear me?"

"She ran away from me."

He laughs and shakes his head, then heads down the hall.

Elsa slams the door shut behind him and grabs on to her daughter, burying her face in Renny's shoulder with a sob.

"Why are you crying?"

"I'm so relieved. How did you . . . did you actually take an *elevator*?"

Renny nods. "I was scared when you left. I kept calling you but you didn't come back, so I pressed the button."

"But . . . you don't like elevators."

"I was brave," Renny tells her matter-of-factly. "I had to find you."

"Thank God you did."

"Tom helped me."

"I know."

At least, for now, they're safe. And it's time to go . . . somewhere.

As if she's reading Elsa's mind, Renny asks, "Can we go home now?"

"Oh, sweetie . . ." *You have no idea how badly I want to say yes.* "Not just yet. You don't really want to get back on the train tonight, do you?"

"We can call Daddy to come get us."

Call Daddy—another fierce stab of longing. Elsa desperately wants to connect with Brett.

Forget the possibility that her phone is bugged. Right now, all that matters is hearing her husband's voice.

I've got to find my phone and get us out of here.

She hurries Renny to the kitchen, plotting their exit from the building.

They'll avoid the lobby, she decides, still not sure whether to trust Tom. He did say he saw her mother, and her mother isn't here. Why would he lie? If he wasn't lying, then is it possible . . .

The idea is so far-fetched that Elsa refuses to allow herself to consider it.

In the kitchen, she sees the bag of Chinese food on the counter, the ominously empty slot in the knife holder.

But no cell phone.

A quick search, then a more thorough one, and there's still no sign of it.

Maybe she was mistaken about dropping it here in the apartment.

Maybe she lost it while she was chasing through the building, or—

Or maybe whoever was here and took the knife came back and stole my phone as well.

Brett rummages through the drawer, looking for the little address book where Elsa keeps all the household phone numbers: the take-out pizza place, the plumber, the pediatrician . . . and presumably, Joan.

Brett has to call the therapist, and the sooner the better.

If Elsa is losing touch with reality, finding out about Mike's accident might push her over the edge.

A hit-and-run.

Unbelievable.

The way Mike's friend Joe described it, Mike had just stepped out of his building on Hanover Street, and the car came barreling at him.

Almost like someone was lying in wait.

Joe didn't say that. But Brett sure as hell thinks it.

Mike is a private eye. He's made his share of enemies. It's not that far-fetched to imagine that someone might have sought vengeance for an extramarital affair Mike had uncovered, or a jail sentence resulting from one of Mike's investigations . . .

Brett finds the phone book and flips the alphabetical pages, looking first under J for Joan—no luck—and then under T for therapist—again, no luck.

He has no idea what her last name is, but he thumbs through every page in the book, looking for any entry that bears the first name Joan.

There is none.

"Now what?" he mutters aloud.

He certainly can't call Elsa and ask her for her therapist's contact information.

No, but he can at least call her to check in and see how she sounds.

After that, I'll figure out how to reach her therapist.

Grimly shaking his head, he dials Elsa's cell phone.

It was all so perfect, right from the moment Elsa Cavalon and her kid showed up at the Ansonia with their take-out dinner, looking like drowned rats.

They could have stayed out for hours, which would have been okay, too—eventually they'd have returned to discover that their would-be safe house wasn't safe at all.

But at least the way it happened—their arrival within a half hour of "Sylvie Durand's" supposed grand entrance—prevented this thing from dragging on all night.

The veiled hat—purchased a mere two hours ago from a Scarlett O'Hara display at a costume shop in the Theater District—certainly served its purpose, as did the black pashmina and umbrella: twenty bucks from a street vendor near Columbus Circle. Now the hat, pashmina, and umbrella are carefully positioned on the edge of an alley Dumpster off West Seventy-third Street, where some poor homeless person can probably put them to good use.

See? Who says you don't have a heart?

The duplicate keys to Sylvie Durand's apartment almost landed in the Dumpster, too—after all, it's a safe bet Elsa Cavalon won't be coming back to the Ansonia anytime soon. But it seems like a shame to throw them away after going to all the trouble of stealing them, along with a spare set of keys to the Cavalons' house, having them copied, and returning them before anyone noticed they were missing.

All the trouble?

Okay, it was a piece of cake to walk in through the unlocked door while Elsa and her kid were out in the backyard the other day, having a cozy little picnic under a tree. So easy to keep an eye on them while snooping around the house, finding not just the keys, but planting the listening devices that had proven just as handy.

The best part was unlocking the door in the dead

of night to replace the keys, and taking a little detour, wearing the rubber mask, to scare the shit out of the kid.

Yeah. Good times.

Staying one step ahead—or rather, behind—the two of them in the apartment just now was even more fun. What a great setup for hide-and-seek—plenty of places to hide, though a few times, when Elsa looked over her shoulder, it seemed certain that the jig was up. Grabbing the knife from the kitchen was meant to be a scare tactic, but for a minute there, it almost seemed like it would have to be put to use.

That would have been a real shame, to end it all just as the real fun is about to get under way.

How fitting that it was Scarlett O'Hara herself who said it: *Tomorrow is another day.*

Marin can't recall the last time she filled the car—*any* car—with gas. No wonder the fuel level is on E by the time she reaches the southbound Hutchinson Parkway. Figuring it's better to fill up now than within city limits, she pulls into a roadside service area.

Once she remembers how to work the pump, it takes only a few minutes to fill the tank.

There's something to be said for having your own means of transportation, she decides as she replaces the nozzle and removes her receipt from the machine. Throughout Garvey's gubernatorial campaign, and even before that, the Quinns traveled mostly by car service and limo.

It's kind of nice to be fully in charge, once again, of where she goes, and when she gets there.

Slipping back behind the wheel, she's planning to merge right back out onto the highway.

Instead, she finds herself pulling into a parking space near the on-ramp.

You sure you're in charge, there?

Yes. But once she gets home, she'll have to deal with Caroline, plus she and Annie will be in earshot.

If you're going to make that call, she tells herself as she pulls out her cell phone, *you'd better make it now.*

After the first killing, it got easier.

That's how it is.

The first time, even while it's happening, you don't know quite what to expect when it's over. You don't know how you'll feel, or what you'll do, or where you'll hide the corpse, or even if you should bother. You don't know whether you're actually capable of taking a human life, though it feels good—*so damned good*—to try.

To succeed is just . . . well, it's a gust of pure, exhilarating supremacy, and you know, in that moment, that you can accomplish anything. Anything at all.

Eventually, though, the feeling subsides.

And you feel a pang when you realize it'll never return, unless . . .

You have to kill again.

The more often you experience the addictive rush of power, the harder it is to hold off until you get to feel it again.

You don't want to get sloppy, though. You don't want to start doing it just for the hell of it. You have to have a plan; it has to be a means to an end. Otherwise, it's wrong: killing for the sake of killing.

This isn't like that. This is about vengeance, and about love.

Like the lyrics of that old song . . .

It was by The Who. What was it?

"Behind Blue Eyes." Right.

And the lyrics, all of them, are true. So true. No one knows what it's like.

No one but Jeremy . . .

The sudden ringing of a telephone curtails that line of thinking. The ringtone is unfamiliar. It can only be Elsa Cavalon's phone—the one she so carelessly left on the countertop in her mother's apartment.

Too bad. It's mine now.

Is she calling it herself, aware she lost it?

Or is someone else trying to reach her: her husband, perhaps, or her mother in France? It sure as hell isn't Mike Fantoni—or, for that matter, Roxanne the social worker. Ha.

One look at the caller ID window provides the shock of a lifetime.

Of all the names that might have come up, this is by far the least expected—and the most intriguing.

"Hi, you've reached Elsa. I can't take your call right now, but if you leave a message I'll get right back to you."

Marin takes a deep breath. "Elsa, this is Marin Quinn. I'm . . ."

Oh please. She knows who you are.

"I need to talk to you. Over the phone or in person, whatever . . ."

She can hear the quaking in her voice, and knows she'd better hang up before she bursts into tears—which would pretty much ensure that Elsa Cavalon won't be calling her back.

Do you really think she's going to do that anyway?

"I, um, understand if you'd rather not talk to me after . . . after all this. But I hope you will."

Marin pauses.

Is there anything more to say? This might be her only chance.

"I'm sorry," she blurts, and hangs up.

Out on Broadway, it's still raining. The mass weekend exodus is well under way; the streets are jammed with traffic, the sidewalks crowded with people and umbrellas.

Spotting a cop issuing a traffic ticket over on the corner, Elsa considers—for a fleeting moment—pouring out the whole story and asking him for help.

But what proof do you even have that anyone was even after you?

What if he thinks you're crazy?

There will be an official report. That much is certain.

And having taken Renny across state lines without permission will be the least of her worries when the agency gets hold of it.

Right now, her priority is to find a safe haven for herself and Renny—then figure out what the hell is going on.

"Where are we going?" Renny asks.

"Home," Elsa tells her resolutely. "We're going home."

" *. . . can't locate next of kin . . . touch and go . . . maybe we should . . .*"

Snatches of far-off voices reach Mike's ears, bewildering him.

Where is he?

Not at home. If he were at home, he'd be alone. There are people here; he can feel movement all around him;

can hear, in addition to the murmuring voices, some kind of steady electronic beep.

With tremendous effort, he opens his eyes.

At least, that's what he thought he just did.

But still he can see nothing at all. He's surrounded not by the darkness of a night room, but a solid pitch black that scares the shit out of him. What the hell is going on? Has he gone blind?

He opens his mouth to ask someone, but he can't seem to move his jaw. He can't move anything, he realizes, not even his fingers.

As terror cloaks Mike like a straitjacket, he struggles to stay conscious, desperate to piece together what might have happened to him.

The last thing he remembers is standing on the street . . .

He was talking to Joe . . .

"You going somewhere, Mikey?"

Yeah. That's right . . . he *was* going somewhere. He had luggage. But where . . . ?

Oh no. Oh Christ.

In a flash, it comes back to him: the Cavalons' visit, his suspicion that Jeremy might be alive, deciding to go to Mumbai . . . and the speeding car that gunned right toward him.

That was no accident—the car hitting him.

Again, he struggles to speak; again, he can't move a muscle.

He can hear two women talking nearby, and a rattling sound, as though someone is pushing a cart around.

"I don't know . . . I probably shouldn't . . ."

"Come on, they have two-for-one happy hour margaritas."

"Yeah, but I'm on the early shift tomorrow."

Listening to their mundane chatter, Mike is helpless. Don't they realize he's trapped in here? Don't they care that someone tried to kill him?

Someone tried to kill him. Someone almost succeeded. Or maybe they did. Maybe he's dying.

He's always wondered what it would be like. Is this it? Is he living his last moments?

Or has it already happened? Is he dead?

Something comes back to him then—a thought so disturbing that Mike is certain he's still alive, because everyone knows that when you're dead, there's no pain. And this is painful.

Not physically. There is no physical pain, only immobility.

But remembering how he glimpsed, for a split second through the windshield, the person who was behind the wheel of that car—the person who was gunning right for him—he realizes he'd been wrong about something crucial to the Cavalon case.

Mike Fantoni doesn't like to be wrong. He prides himself on the fact that he rarely ever is. He's built a reputation on it. His clients count on it.

His clients . . .

Mike Fantoni's last thought before he drifts back to the peaceful silence is that someone needs to warn Brett and Elsa.

CHAPTER
ELEVEN

Located almost midway between New York and Boston on the busy I–95 corridor, New Haven, Connecticut, is a prime location for drug dealers and the addicts and prostitutes who go with the territory. As a longtime vice detective with the NHPD, Bill Ellsworth has seen it all—and then some—particularly here in the neighborhood of Fair Haven on the banks of the Quinnipiac River.

A light rain is falling as he strides toward the overgrown vacant lot in a seedy stretch just off Chapel Street. It isn't the first time he's been summoned to this area, a favorite haunt of hookers and their johns, many of whom are from the surrounding shore towns. It isn't even the first time he's seen a woman lying facedown here amid the broken glass and syringes.

But it's the first time this particular area is cordoned off with yellow crime scene tape, and the woman on the ground isn't passed out cold from last night's crack binge.

She's dead.

Not an OD, though. She got her throat slit. And she's been here at least a day or two, judging by the insects nesting in her flesh.

Jim Novak, the first officer on the scene, had been summoned by a couple of twelve-year-olds who found her while cutting through the lot. Spotting Bill, Novak turns away from his animated conversation with a uniformed rookie.

"Look who's here. When'd you get back?"

"Late last night," Bill tells him, fighting a yawn. More like early this morning, by the time he and his wife had gotten their luggage and driven home from the airport.

"Where'd you go this time?"

"The Caribbean."

"Nice."

Bill nods. *Nice* doesn't begin to cover it.

If there's anything he's learned on this job, it's that life is short and unpredictable. You'd better do everything you want to do and see everything you want to see while you have the chance, because you never know whether you're going to be around tomorrow.

He and Tina won't retire young or rich; they've spent every vacation day and every dime they have on travel, mostly by ship. At ports of call all over the world, they've seen ancient ruins and exotic wildlife, cathedrals and pyramids, volcanoes and caverns, and, on this last trip, the most breathtaking beaches on the planet.

And now, back to reality.

Bill surveys the corpse. "Any ID on her?"

"What, are you kidding me?"

"You never know."

"That'd make life too simple, Ellsworth." Novak goes back to the rookie, shooting the shit about the Red Sox.

Pulling on a pair of plastic gloves, Bill steps past Dave Rivera, the police photographer, who's snapping his bubble gum as he shoots the scene from every angle.

"How's it going, Bill?"

"TGIF," Bill mutters dryly, studying the victim.

He can't see her face, but she's skinny and pale with jet black hair, wearing a black skirt, black top, and—oddly—black platform-soled boots with studded buckles. Not exactly typical footwear for a working girl around here.

There's dried blood matted in her hair and on her shoulders beneath the wounds on either side of her neck. Her right arm is bent up near her head, as if she'd tried to shield herself from the attack.

"Such a shame to see a nice religious kid like her killed right down the street from St. Rose's, huh?" Rivera comments, leaning in to get a close-up of what Bill had assumed, at a glance, was a bruise on her arm above a leather-studded bracelet.

"What do you mean?"

"Her ink. She's got a nice fancy cross there, see it?"

Bill waves off a fly and bends over to take a closer look at the corpse.

"First of all, she wasn't killed in this spot. There's not enough blood. Someone dumped her here. The other thing is . . . that's no cross," he informs Rivera, pointing at the tattoo. "It's a hieroglyphic symbol."

"What makes you think that?"

Bill levels a look at him. "I don't think it—I know it. I've been to Egypt. And by the way—it's called an ankh."

This was the longest stretch Marin's been away from home in months. Maybe that's why the apartment feels oddly empty as she crosses the threshold.

"Hello . . . girls, I'm back!"

She can't help but compare the sterile entry hall to the Walshes', with its pleasant clutter of personal belongings. Here, everything is perfectly staged for the real estate sale; a reminder that soon the place will belong to somebody else.

Why does it already seem as though it does?

But it's not just the absence of stray shoes and books and framed photos on the walls and knickknacks on the shelves.

The apartment is still. *Too* still.

And dark. This might be one of the longest days of the year, but the dreary weather calls for lamplight. She tosses her keys on the bare surface of the hall table and flips a wall switch. There—that's a little better.

"Anybody home?"

No reply. She kicks off her shoes as she walks, wincing.

It's hard to believe her feet were once accustomed to wearing heels morning, noon, and night. Today, they merely carried her a block and a half from the parking garage back to the building, and they're killing her.

Since she usually doesn't bother to wear shoes around the house—and around the house is pretty much the only place she's been lately—she's out of practice.

With shoes, and driving.

But you did it, she reminds herself. *You made it up to Westchester and back all by yourself—no pills, no tears, no . . . panic attacks.*

Remembering what Lauren said about her episodes, and about finding a shrink, she wishes she'd never mentioned anything about it. True, she went up there to find some moral support, thinking Lauren might be the one person who might understand what she's going through . . .

But even *she* can't quite relate. Lauren's never lost a child. Not like Marin. Not like . . .

Elsa.

Will Jeremy's adoptive mother call back when she gets Marin's message?

Why wouldn't she?

Why *would* she?

Marin's head is throbbing again.

"Girls!" she calls, walking down the hallway toward their rooms. They're probably both plugged into headphones, as usual.

Annie's door is ajar. Marin sticks her head in. No Annie.

Caroline's door is closed. Are they in there?

Together?

An image flashes through her head: two little girls sitting side by side, heads close together—one blond, one brunette—over an open storybook across their laps, the older sister reading to the younger.

Oh please. That would never happen.

It never did, even when they were younger. Her girls were never close.

There's no way they're both cozily occupied in Caroline's room, yet she knocks anyway. "Caroline? Annie?"

No answer.

"Caroline!" Uneasy, she tries the knob. Sometimes, her daughter locks it when she's inside.

Not today.

The door isn't locked, but Caroline's not inside.

Marin surveys the empty room, wondering where she is.

And where, she wonders, her pulse beginning to race, is Annie?

Brett is sitting at the kitchen table in front of an open laptop, scrolling through the online listing for local therapists when the phone rings. He jumps on it, certain it's going to be Elsa. He's been nervous ever since he tried her earlier and she didn't pick up.

He keeps reminding himself that her battery might be dead, and she might not have thought to pack her charger.

But when he tried calling the regular line to her mother's apartment, no one answered there, either.

Maybe, not thinking it would be for her, Elsa didn't bother.

Or maybe she took Renny out to eat and couldn't hear the phone in a crowded restaurant . . .

Or maybe they went to a movie, and she had to turn it off . . .

Come on—would she really do that under these circumstances?

She might. She might have been trying hard to distract Renny.

Really, there are any number of scenarios that might explain why Elsa's cell went straight into voice mail—and has continued to, several times—but Brett can't quite accept any of them.

Now, he eagerly checks the incoming call. His heart sinks.

It isn't Elsa.

He doesn't recognize the number on the caller ID screen, nor, for a moment, the voice that greets him when he picks up.

"Hi, sorry to bother you again . . ."

Who . . . ?

Oh. Joe. Mike's friend.

"Is Mike . . . ?"

"No change."

"Thank God." Brett closes his eyes briefly.

"Listen, you asked me if I knew where he was going. You know, on vacation?"

His eyes snap open. "Yes."

"When the nurses gave me his phone, they gave me his other stuff, too. You know—to hang on to. After I talked to you I got to thinking . . . I know it probably wasn't right, but I looked through Mikey's stuff. He had the printout of the e-mail with the confirmation number for his flight. It was in his pocket."

Brett holds his breath, waiting.

"Funny thing is, the confirmation e-mail had a time on it—and it was from early this morning, so I guess it was some kind of last-minute trip."

"Where was he going?"

"That's the funny thing. It's a hell of a place for a vacation—even at the last minute."

"Where?"

At the reply, Brett lowers himself into the nearest chair, stunned.

Mumbai: the city where Jeremy was killed.

Creeping up the rain-slicked West Side Highway in Friday night congestion, Elsa keeps a close eye on the headlights and changing traffic patterns in the rear-view mirror.

Breathing easily—or perhaps, just *breathing*—for the first time since they left the Ansonia, she's fairly certain they've managed to shake whoever was dogging them there.

They definitely weren't trailed as they walked over to the car rental place on West End Avenue. They made several turns—more than were necessary—and she made sure they eventually lost all the pedestrians who'd been behind them from the start.

It was surprisingly simple to rent a car—complete with a booster seat—on short notice. Or maybe not so surprising. Maybe people do it all the time in Manhattan, where so few residents own cars. Maybe that's why the man behind the counter didn't give her a second glance as he ran her credit card and handed her the keys.

Renny pretty much dropped off to sleep within minutes after they pulled out of the rental agency garage. Poor kid has been dragged from Boston to Groton to New York and now back again; from car to train to cab to car; up and down steps, into a dreaded elevator, along the streets in the rain . . .

For a fleeing moment, Elsa wonders what kind of a mother would put a child through all that.

Maybe she isn't fit to—

Wait a minute. What are you thinking? Stop that right now!

She's the best mother Renny could ever have because she loves her with all her heart. She's gone to such extremes today for one reason alone: to keep Renny safe. No one in this world is going to do a better job at that.

Less than two hours to go, and they'll be home. Then at last she'll be able to tell Brett what's been going on—but not while they're inside the house. It must be bugged, like their phones. She'll have to take him outside to talk—or write it down on paper. She'll figure it out when she gets there.

All she wants is to get there.

Home . . . home . . . home . . . home . . .

The windshield wipers beat in time to the refrain in her head.

Taillights blur into red splotches in front of her, and she wipes her eyes with the back of her hand. She can't cry now. She can't cry at all. There's no reason to. Renny is fine, and she's going to stay that way.

Please . . . please . . . please . . . please . . .

* * *

Caroline's cell phone rings just as she's telling Jake one of her best stories: the one about her top falling off while she was surfing on Long Island last summer. It's a particularly good story because it makes her seem adventurous and sexy and funny all at the same time. Plus he must surf, too, so he'll realize how much they really do have in common.

"Aren't you going to get that?" he cuts into the story when she ignores the phone.

"Nah."

It rings three more times, then bounces into voice mail.

"You know," Jake says thoughtfully, "I've been kicking myself since yesterday that I didn't stick around to get your phone number—but maybe that's not the best way to get in touch with you?"

"Oh, I'd answer it if it was *you*. But obviously, it's not, because you're right here, so . . ."

"So why don't you give me your number now?" Grinning, he reaches for his backpack.

"Right this second? You mean, before a disgusting rodent comes crawling out of *your* bag?"

"No rodents." He pulls out a pen and pats the bag. "Not yet, anyway." He writes her number on a napkin, and she does the same with his.

As she tucks it into her pocket, her phone rings again.

Again, she ignores it.

Again, it goes into voice mail.

Less than a minute later, it starts ringing again.

"You should probably get it," Jake advises. "Maybe it's me."

She laughs, then reluctantly pulls out her phone and glances at the caller ID. "It's my mother."

"Go ahead. Pick it up."

She rolls her eyes. "Hello?"

"Caroline!"

Her mother practically screams her name. Caroline winces and holds the phone away from her ear.

"Where are you girls?"

"*I'm* at Starbucks. Annie's home."

"No, she isn't!"

"What?"

"*I'm* at home. I just got back. Where is she, Caroline?"

"I have no idea. She was there when I left."

"When did you leave?"

"Umm . . . I guess around eleven-thirty."

Her mother starts going on and on, freaking out about Annie. Shaking her head, Caroline holds the phone out away from her ear again.

"Don't mind her," she whispers to Jake. "She's kind of nuts. But then, I guess, aren't they all?"

"What?"

"Mothers. You know—they're all crazy."

Jake doesn't reply.

"Well, mine is, anyway," she mutters, wondering if he gets along great with his own mother or something. Whatever. His mother probably isn't dealing with half of the crap that's going on with Mom. No wonder she's ranting and raving on the phone . . . not that Caroline can make out a word of it with the phone held at arm's length from her ear.

"She sounds really upset," Jake tells her. "Maybe you should go home and make sure everything's all right."

Go *home*? Is he trying to get rid of her?

Or is he just trying to be helpful?

Or maybe he just thinks she's a terrible person, not talking to her own mother.

Quickly, she puts the receiver back up to her ear. "Hey, Mom, listen, you need to chill. I'm sure she's okay."

"I can't believe you left her!" Mom's voice is shrill. "I asked you to keep an eye on her!"

"It's not like she needs a babysitter. She's thirteen."

"She's gone, Caroline. Oh my God. She's *gone*."

There's only one therapist named Joan in the area—and her phone goes into voice mail.

"Hi—this is Brett Cavalon. My wife, Elsa, is a patient of yours and . . . I'd like to talk to you, as soon as possible."

He left his cell phone number, and ended the call asking Joan to please not mention to Elsa that he'd gotten in touch.

He has no idea whether she'll be willing—or even able—to heed that request, or to call him back. He can only hope.

After changing into jeans and a polo shirt, he tries again to reach Elsa.

Her phone bounces straight into voice mail again.

"Elsa, it's me. I'm getting worried. Why aren't you picking up? Is your battery dead? That's probably it. Call me on my cell when you get this message. I'm . . ."

Wait a minute. He'd better not say he's going to Boston, because she'll wonder why, and he can't tell her about Mike. Certainly not in a voice mail.

Nor does he want to mention he'll be back tonight, because he might not be. He should probably stick around Mike's bedside, in case he regains consciousness.

After all, the guy was working Brett's case. He wasn't going off to Mumbai on the spur of the moment without a good reason. Brett needs to find out what it is—and what it has to do with his family.

If it gets late, he can grab a room someplace—not last night's fleabag motel, though. Just someplace where he can get some rest without having to keep one eye open in case someone comes prowling around.

Not that he's *afraid* to sleep here at home.

No, of course not.

"Just get a good night's sleep, you and Renny," he finishes the message to Elsa. "I love you both. Hug her for me."

After hanging up the phone, he opens the desk drawer where his wife keeps her phone charger. Sure enough, there it is.

Okay, at least he knows why she's not picking up. Hopefully she'll figure out that the battery has died and that she's forgotten her charger, and she'll get herself to a store to buy a new one. But that might not happen until tomorrow morning.

In the meantime, she'll probably try to reach him from her mother's phone. When she doesn't get him at home, she'll call his cell.

Okay. So he's good to go . . .

As soon as I figure out what the heck I did with my keys.

They aren't in any of the usual spots: on the kitchen counters or dangling from the hooks beside the door.

But there's the suit coat he wore today, draped over the back of a chair. The keys are in his pocket—and so is the note from Renny's new social worker. He rereads it.

He can't call. Not just yet. Elsa doesn't even know that the case has been handed off yet again, and Renny's not even in town.

No, she's across state lines without permission. That'll go over well with the agency.

It's not a good idea to ignore caseworker requests, but . . . no one even knows he got it for sure. The Post-it could have fallen off the door and blown away, right? Or the ink could have smeared in the rain so that the whole thing was illegible, and not just the signature.

Frustrated, Brett tosses the note onto the kitchen counter. He'll deal with it later. Right now, he's got to get to Boston.

"So as you probably figured out, my idiot sister is missing," Caroline informs Jake as she hangs up the phone—with a slight twinge of guilt over her choice of words.

Okay, so maybe Annie's not a *total* idiot. Not *all* the time.

What if something terrible actually happened to her?

"She's *missing*?"

"Yeah, and my mom is a basket case. I guess she thinks she's going to have to, like, put up missing kid posters all over town or something."

She means it as a joke, of course—but seeing the look in Jake's dark eyes, she realizes he doesn't find it the least bit funny. Maybe he just doesn't get black humor.

"I wouldn't say that if I didn't think Annie was okay," she tells him hastily, but the damage seems to be done.

He pushes back his chair. "You should go help find your sister."

"I'm sure she just—"

"It sounds like your mother needs you. Anyway, I have to go to—uh, class."

No, he doesn't. She can tell he's lying. It's just an excuse to get away from her.

"Okay . . . I guess I'll see you around?"

"Sure."

But he doesn't say he'll call her.

Too bad, because there was something about him—a

real connection, the kind you usually don't feel with a stranger. And she'd been pretty sure he was into her, as well.

Now she'll probably never see him again.

Oh well. His loss.

Mine, too, she thinks wistfully, watching Jake sling his backpack over his shoulder and walk away.

Sick with fear, Marin paces the apartment clutching both the cordless and her cell phone.

How can this be happening?

Her younger daughter is missing, her older daughter doesn't give a damn, and . . .

My son is dead.

And Lauren was wrong. I'm not strong enough to deal with all this.

Her hands are trembling so violently that it takes her a couple of tries to dial Annie's cell phone number again. As before, it goes straight into voice mail.

"Annie, it's Mom again. Where are you? I'm home, and you're not, and I'm worried, and . . ."

She trails off and hangs up, swallowing over the painful lump in her throat.

Should she call the police again?

When she called the first time, the desk sergeant transferred her to a female officer who asked a few questions—including Marin's full name, which didn't seem to strike a chord—and wanted to know whether she had reason to believe her daughter might be in danger.

"Of course she might be in danger! She's out there somewhere alone! And—oh God—yesterday, someone put a live rat into her sister's purse."

There's a pause. "Excuse me? What was that?"

Even as Marin hurriedly explained about the rat and the text message, she could tell it wasn't making much sense to the officer.

"And this happened to your daughter just yesterday?"

"To my other daughter. Her sister. We thought it was a prank."

"It sounds like one. Getting back to today—are you sure your daughter didn't just go for a walk, or to a friend's house, or maybe out with a boyfriend . . . ?"

"She doesn't even have a boyfriend!" Marin shrieked into the phone.

"Ma'am, please, I'm trying to assess the situation."

She managed to control herself long enough to answer several other frustrating questions, all of which allowed the officer to conclude that this isn't an emergency.

"You don't think a missing child is an emergency?" Marin asked incredulously, certain she was being regarded as an incoherent, overreaching maternal lunatic.

"At this juncture, we—"

"You have to do something!"

"Ma'am, please," the officer said again, all but sighing. "You're welcome to come down to the precinct with a recent photograph of your daughter and a description of what she was wearing—"

"I have to come down *there*? How can I leave here when she might show up any second? You can't send someone here?"

"At this stage, no. As you said, she'll probably turn up safe and sound any second, but—"

"That isn't what I said!"

"Ma'am, please—"

That was when Marin banged the phone down in frustration.

The woman has no idea. No idea who Annie is, or what their family has been through, or why they don't take missing children lightly.

Marin should have told her.

Why didn't she tell her?

What the hell is wrong with me?

God, I wish Garvey were here.

It isn't the first time she's missed him, but it's the first time she's *needed* him. For all his faults, at least he'd know what to do. He always did. He was the one in control, the one who took care of things—of *her*; the one who—

Her phone rings in her hand, startling her. She answers with a breathless "Hello?"

"Is this Marin Quinn?" an unfamiliar voice asks.

"Yes . . ."

"I'm calling from Lenox Hill Hospital. It's about your daughter Anne."

According to the GPS planted in Brett Cavalon's car, he's on the move again.

Surely he's not on his way to rescue his wife and daughter—unless he thinks they're somewhere up north, toward Boston.

Are they?

That's highly unlikely. They're probably holed up in a hotel somewhere here in New York. Who knows? Maybe even this one.

It doesn't really matter where they are, though.

I'm finished with them for tonight. They've had enough, and so have I.

It's been such a long day—so tempting just to stay in Manhattan for tonight, as planned, and let Brett go wherever he's going.

But then, Elsa's husband might be dangerous, left to

his own devices. More dangerous than Elsa herself, for the time being.

So much for a reprieve.

Might as well hop a shuttle to Logan and see what he's up to.

One quick phone call, a cursory check of the room, and it's time to go.

Downstairs, the Times Square hotel is teeming with weekend tourists checking in, bellhops pushing luggage carts, and locals grabbing pre-theater cocktails at the posh lobby bar.

A doorman opens the door with a friendly tip of his hat. "Do you need a cab?"

Yes. But I'm not going to let you get one for me.

"No, thank you." It wouldn't be a good idea to draw any extra attention. That would only increase the risk of being remembered later, should anything go wrong and investigators find their way to the hotel.

"All right, then. Have a good night."

"Same to you."

Down the block, across Seventh, down another block, around the corner onto Sixth. It's much quieter over here; flagging a taxi is surprisingly easy on this rainy evening.

"La Guardia airport, please."

The cabbie nods and hits the meter. "You want me to take the bridge, or the tunnel?"

"The bridge, please. I'm claustrophobic."

The cabbie mutters disinterestedly, "Oh yeah?"

No.

But I know someone who is. And she's got a big, big day ahead of her tomorrow.

Marin doesn't give a damn who recognizes her as she races to the nursing station; doesn't care who overhears her frantic "My daughter is here. Her name is Annie—Anne. Quinn. It's Anne Quinn, and I don't know what happened, but I got a call—"

"All right, let me see here . . ." With maddening precision, one of the women behind the desk types something on a computer keyboard.

At least she didn't say, *Ma'am, please,* like the female cop had, over and over. At least she's not looking at Marin like she's some kind of nutcase. She's not looking at Marin at all.

"And you spell that—"

"With an E."

"Q-U-I-N-N-E . . ."

"No! We spell Anne with an E! There's no E on the end of Quinn!"

She goes back to typing as Marin grips the edge of the counter, fearful that her legs are going to give out. The lights seem garish and she closes her eyes, praying that she won't faint right here.

"All right, come with me," someone is saying, and Marin's eyes snap open to see a scrubs-clad nurse with a clipboard.

Somehow, Marin's feet carry her down the hall to a curtained-off area, and then . . .

There she is.

"Annie!" She rushes to the bed, swept by a massive wave of relief at finding her daughter lying there, physically intact, with her eyes open.

"Hi, Mom." Annie smiles wanly behind the oxygen tubing that snakes up her nostrils.

"Oh, Annie—" Her voice breaks. She clears her throat, turns to the nurse. "What happened?"

"She was running in the park and she had a severe asthma attack. She collapsed, and luckily, someone called 911."

Marin looks at Annie, trying to wrap her head

around it. "You were running in the park? Was someone chasing you?"

"No! I was running. You know—jogging."

"Jogging? But . . . you don't jog."

"Caroline said I should."

Caroline.

Marin opens her mouth to ask why she'd tell Annie
to run, then closes it again. She knows why, and she
shakes her head, her bewilderment rapidly giving way
to rage.

The nurse is talking again, saying something about
paperwork, and that she'll send a doctor in to speak
with Marin.

Annie's going to be all right. That's all that matters, she
tells herself, sinking into a chair beside the bed.

But in her heart, she knows that isn't true.

Caroline, who looks so much like Garvey, acts so
much like Garvey, treats Annie with as much resentment as Garvey did . . .

Caroline.

Caroline did this.

CHAPTER TWELVE

Despite the crummy weather, it seems that a good portion of the metropolitan New York population is headed to the New England coast for the weekend. Thanks to relentless traffic, Elsa's two-hour trip has taken nearly five.

By the time she reaches Groton, the last two frantic days and virtually sleepless nights have taken their toll. Her shoulder blades are ablaze, her head is pounding, and her eyes desperately want to close. All she can think of is falling into her own bed—with Renny safely tucked between her and Brett—and going to sleep.

She doesn't give a damn about anything else. As long as the doors are locked and Brett is there—

But as soon as she turns onto their block, she can see that the house is dark, the driveway empty. At this hour?

She pulls over to the curb, thoughts racing.

Maybe he's taking advantage of their absence and working late.

Maybe he's on his way to New York after all. Maybe he's been trying to call her and got worried when she didn't answer.

That must be it.

Why didn't she try to reach him? Even if the phones are tapped and the house is bugged, she could have let him know that she and Renny are okay. How could she have been so stupid?

Stupid, scared, deliriously tired . . .

And now, alone once again.

Even Meg's house next door appears unusually deserted. Oh, that's right—she mentioned that her kids are out of town, and she's working nights.

Ordinarily, Elsa would be glad for the opportunity to have her nosy neighbor MIA. But right now, it might be nice to have someone within earshot, just in case . . .

In case she needs to scream for help.

Yet no one can be in two places at the same time. Whoever was back in New York prowling around Maman's apartment isn't here waiting for them now, inside the house—not unless he read Elsa's mind and somehow managed to beat her back to Groton.

For now, they're safe here.

All we have to do is get inside.

Then I can call Brett and tell him where we are.

No—she'd better not do that. Not from the home phone. If it really is tapped, or the house is bugged, Brett wouldn't be the only one who knows where she and Renny are.

Oh, come on. Do you really believe this guy wouldn't think to check here sooner or later?

But this isn't her car. Hers is still in the parking lot of the Sunoco—or, for all she knows—or cares—it's been towed away by now.

If she parks this rental car, with its Florida plates, around the corner, and doesn't turn on any lights when they get inside the house, it'll look like no one is home.

And Meg Warren should be home from work any

second now. Elsa can run over and call Brett from her phone. Of course, Meg will want to know why she's doing that . . .

I'll just tell her we're having trouble with our lines.

Then Meg will want to know why she doesn't just use her cell phone.

I'll tell her the battery is dead.

She'll ask why I don't just plug it into the charger.

I'll tell her I lost it, or that the power lines aren't working either, or . . .

Something. Anything. Right now, it's the best she can do. This is the end of the road—not just literally. She's depleted; far too weary to figure out where else she can possibly go, much less get herself and Renny there. It would be dangerous to keep driving in her condition.

Mind made up, she shifts into drive and passes the house, turns the corner. A little ways down the next block, she parks the car, turns off the engine, and pulls the keys from the ignition.

Renny barely stirs as Elsa picks her up, whispering, "It's okay, Mommy's got you."

The child's arms wrap around her and her legs straddle Elsa's hip. Her sleepy head rests on Elsa's shoulder and she yawns softly, exhaling a whisper of warmth against her bare neck.

She's too heavy for Elsa to carry her very far . . . but Meg Warren's yard is right beyond that stand of trees in a nearby lot. They can cut through and go in the back door at home. If anyone is watching the house from the street . . .

No. You know they're not.

But just in case . . .

The rain has stopped at last, having left the ground spongy beneath Elsa's feet as she walks through the moonless night, picking her way around tree trunks and shrubs. Around and above her, branches drip steadily and the crickets have taken up their nightly chorus. Her ears strain to pick up other sounds—snapping twigs, footfalls other than her own . . .

But they're alone out here tonight. Elsa feels it with just as much conviction as she felt the earlier presence in Maman's apartment.

As she crosses into the Warrens' yard, her feet suddenly start to slide out from under her. Managing to keep her hold on Renny and regain her balance, she looks down. Even in the darkness, she can see that she's mired in a large rectangular patch of mud dotted with seedlings.

Meg must have planted a new garden . . .

And I've gone and trampled right through it. There will be hell to pay when she finds out.

For a moment, the thought strikes her as so ludicrous that Elsa is on the verge of hysterical laughter. Just as quickly, the humor disappears, though the burgeoning hysteria threatens to burst forth as a violent sob instead.

Good Lord, she's an emotional wreck—and now is not the time to fall apart.

Gingerly, her arms beginning to sag under Renny's weight, she picks her way across the muddy plot to the grass. Seconds later, she's unlocking her own back door.

The last thing she wants to do is walk across the threshold without Brett waiting on the other side. But she has no choice.

Opening the door, she whispers to her sleeping daughter, "Everything's going to be okay now, Renny—we're home."

* * *

Caroline is lying on her bed, staring at the ceiling, when she hears footsteps in the hall and an abrupt knock on her bedroom door.

Startled, she sits up. "Who is it?"

The door jerks open. "Who do you *think* it is?" Her mother is standing there, still wearing the clothes she had on this morning. But her makeup is smeared around her eyes, and her hair is a mess—like it got wet, and she let it dry without bothering to comb it.

"You were out when I got home." Looking like that, besides. Sheesh. "Did you find Annie?"

"Yes, I found her."

"Where is she?"

"Right now, she's in bed. I just tucked her in."

Tucked her in? Caroline opens her mouth to point out that her sister isn't five years old, but sees her mother's expression and thinks better of it. Clearly, Mom is in a bad mood.

Instead, she asks, "So where was she?"

"In the hospital."

"What? Is she okay?"

"She will be."

"What happened to her?"

"You sent her out to run in the park. That's what happened. In the rain, all alone, with her asthma . . ."

Uh-oh. Remembering her earlier conversation with Annie, Caroline feels a twinge of guilt—not that she'll admit it.

"I didn't send her anywhere!" she tells her mother. "I wasn't even here."

"Exactly."

Caroline frowns. "What does that mean?"

"I asked you to take care of things around here."

"That's *your* job. Not mine. Anyway, where were you? What were you doing in Westchester?"

Her mother's blue eyes flash. "We're not talking about me. We're talking about you, and Annie, and how you could have been so irresponsible to—"

"Stop it!" Caroline bolts from her bed. "Stop blaming me! Not *everything* is my fault!"

As they stand there glaring at each other, Caroline waits for her mother to soften and offer an apology.

It never comes.

Renny barely stirs when Elsa tucks her into bed in the master bedroom, still wearing her clothes. She had considered trying to get her into pajamas, but that would be sure to wake her, and she'd start talking, and that might be dangerous.

She leaves the bedroom door open and tiptoes out.

Well aware that the house might be bugged, Elsa is careful not to make a sound as she walks through the rooms with a small flashlight. Every door and window is securely locked, the shades are down, the lights are off. She casts light into the far corners, making sure no one is lurking, doubting she could even defend herself and Renny if someone were.

Right now, she barely has the energy to stay on her feet, much less fight off an assailant, or flee into the night with her daughter.

In the kitchen, she checks her own wooden knife block. The handles are all there. She stands with her hand poised over it for a moment. Then she pulls out a utility knife and examines the honed blade glinting in the flashlight's beam.

Are you really capable of using this to harm a human being?

Remembering what happened to Jeremy fifteen years ago when someone violated their own backyard, she knows the answer.

If she had been armed then, and standing guard over her child, she would have killed to protect him. No question about it.

I'd do the same thing now, with Renny.

About to turn away from the counter, she sees a slip of paper with some writing on it. A note from Brett?

She snatches it up.

Mr. and Mrs. Cavalon: I'll be Renata's new caseworker . . .

Elsa's heart sinks as she reads on. The last thing they need right now is this—this *person*—snooping around.

The signature is illegible, but there's a phone number.

She paces, holding the note and the knife, wondering whether Brett called the number on the note, wondering whether she should call him after all.

But if she uses the phone and the line is tapped, all bets are off. She'd have to get Renny out right away.

I just need some time to rest and regroup, figure out what to do.

Brett won't call here—that much is certain. Why would he? He thinks she's in New York; he might be headed there himself.

He doesn't have the keys to Maman's apartment. What happens when he arrives and no one is there to buzz him up?

Is Tom the doorman still on duty?

Is he even a doorman?

He's the one who helped Renny, remember? He could have hurt her, and he didn't. He wasn't the one stalking us in the apartment.

But why did he think he'd seen Maman in the lobby? Was she really there?

I can't even call her to see what the hell is going on. Not from here, anyway.

Peering through a crack in the shade, Elsa sees that Meg Warren's driveway is still empty; the house still dark.

She should be home from work by now. She must have gone out afterward. Of all the nights for someone who frequently complains of having no social life to depart from her regular routine . . .

Oh well. She can't stay out all night—can she?

Her kids are away. Maybe she has a secret lover, and she's spending the night.

No. Meg has made the Cavalons privy to every detail about her life. If she had a lover, Elsa would know about it.

She'll be home soon. When she gets here, Elsa will go over—with Renny, of course—and use her phone.

For now, there's nothing to do but sit on the couch, clutching the knife, and wait.

Still shaking from the confrontation with Caroline, Marin jerks open the drawer on her bedside table and grabs an orange prescription bottle. It takes her a few tries to open the childproof cap. She dumps a couple of pills into her hand and steps into the bathroom to wash them down with a palmful of tap water.

She turns off the faucet and catches her reflection in the mirror above the sink.

"What's happened to you?" she asks the haggard woman in the mirror, who stares back at her with haunted eyes.

She's a mess; utterly depleted. When was the last time she ate anything, or actually even sat down, other than in the cab home from Lenox Hill?

Marin turns away from the mirror and goes back to the bedroom. For a moment, she stands looking at the door she slammed closed a few minutes earlier—after storming out of Caroline's room and slamming her door closed as well.

Should she go apologize?

Maybe.

You shouldn't have lashed out at her like that. She's your daughter.

But so is Annie. When Marin thinks of what might have happened to her, lying on the ground in Central Park, all alone, struggling to breathe . . .

Awash in fresh fury, she turns away from the door and climbs into her big, empty bed to wait for sleep to overtake her.

Brett pauses to read the sign posted just off the elevator outside the ICU.

ABSOLUTELY NO CELL PHONE USE

"They mean it," advises a grumpy-looking woman who just stepped off the elevator with him. "Electromagnetic interference messes with the equipment."

Brett frowns, wondering if that's even true.

"You need to turn off your phone," the woman orders him. "My husband is in there on a ventilator, and the last thing I need is for some jackass to kill him by not following the rules."

Jackass?

Jesus.

But Brett can't really blame her. Like everyone else in this unit, the poor woman is under terrible pressure.

Reluctantly, he removes his phone from his pocket. He really doesn't want to turn it off now, in case Elsa tries to reach him, or Joan does.

But what if it's true about the electromagnetic interference?

"Off," the woman repeats, all but folding her arms and tapping her foot.

Brett presses the button and holds it up to show her that it's powering down. She gives a satisfied nod and walks briskly into the unit.

He stays close on her heels. He's gotten this far without incident, but security has to be much tighter up here on the ICU floor.

Luck is with him: the staff is just changing shifts. He sticks close to the woman from the elevator, acts as though he belongs here just as much as she does, and miraculously, no one stops either of them.

Mike's name is scrawled beside a half-open door at the end of the hall.

Brett stops and stares at the unrecognizably battered and bandaged comatose man in the bed.

"You here for Mike?"

He turns to see that the room has one other occupant: a gruff-sounding, burly guy who seems ill at ease in a small bedside chair.

"Yes. I'm Brett Cavalon. You must be Joe."

The man nods, getting to his feet, and they shake hands. Brett can smell cigarette smoke on his clothes.

"How the hell did you get here?" he asks.

"I walked."

"All the way from Connecticut?" Joe returns his faint grin.

"No, all the way from the parking lot. I tried to call and tell you I was going to drive up, but your phone went into voice mail."

"Yeah, they make you turn it off in here."

"So I hear."

"Have a seat." Joe gestures at the chair.

"That's okay. It's yours."

"Nah, I've been sitting for hours. I don't want to leave the poor guy lying here alone."

"What about his family?"

"Mikey don't have family as far as I know. He's divorced, no kids."

"Parents?"

"Dead."

"That's sad."

"Yeah."

The two of them stand somberly watching Mike breathe, assisted by the machines.

"Has he said anything at all?"

"No." After a moment, Joe adds, "But the nurse said he might be able to hear."

Brett tries to imagine what it would be like for Mike to be helplessly trapped somewhere inside that broken body. It's probably better for him if he's completely unconscious.

But it's better for me if he can hear.

He can't help wishing—somewhat guiltily—that Joe would leave so that he might try to ask Mike about Mumbai.

I hate her.

She ruins everything. Daddy's life, her own life . . .

But she's not going to ruin mine.

Pacing her room like a caged animal, Caroline knows she can't stay here. Not for long, anyway—maybe not even for the rest of the night.

But she can't leave until she has someplace to go—and she won't until she works up her nerve to make the phone call.

She keeps finding reasons not to—the most convincing one being that it's too late—yet it probably isn't, and the more she stalls, the later it gets. Pretty soon, it really will be too late—even for a college guy.

Frustrated, Caroline pulls his phone number

from her pocket as she has countless times since her mother slammed her bedroom door and stormed away.

This time, though, she actually dials.

After a few rings, she hears, "Hello?"

"Jake? It's Caroline. What are you doing?"

"Now?" There's a pause. "Why?"

"I was just wondering if you wanted to get together."

"Now?" he says again.

"If you're not busy."

"I'm . . . ah, I was just about to go to bed."

She thinks about making some kind of suggestive comment, but decides against it. That's his department— if he's interested in her.

But all he says is "Yeah. It's been a long day."

Tell me about it.

The thing is, he doesn't sound all that tired. He sounds wide awake.

"Okay. I just thought . . . you know . . ." Trailing off awkwardly, knowing she must seem desperate, she wishes she'd never called.

Then Jake surprises her.

"How about tomorrow?" he asks.

"You mean . . . getting together?"

"Sure."

"Really?"

"Why not? I'll call you, okay?"

"Okay. When?"

"As soon as possible."

"Great. So, uh, have a good sleep."

"Yeah." He yawns loudly. Maybe he really is tired. "You too."

"I definitely will," Caroline assures him, and hangs up the phone.

Tomorrow isn't ideal, but it's better than nothing.

* * *

With a silent curse, Jeremy hangs up the phone.

Caroline's call caught him off guard. He didn't know what to do, what to say.

So you told her you'll get together with her tomorrow?

He was nervous. It just popped out somehow.

Maybe he should call her back now and tell her the truth.

Not the *whole* truth, of course. Just that he's been called out of town, to Boston, and won't be around tomorrow.

Then again, maybe he should see her. Maybe it's time to come clean. Tell Caroline that his name isn't really Jake.

He plucked that from thin air that day in Starbucks. Jake . . . as in Jacobson . . . as in the surgeon who'd given him a fresh start. It seemed fitting.

Still does.

No. Jeremy puts his phone back into his pocket. He won't call Caroline back tonight. Better to wait and see what tomorrow brings.

Sleep tight, sis.

The night drags on past midnight, into morning, and still, there's been no change in Mike Fantoni's condition.

Doctors and nurses check the patient, requiring the visitors to leave the room for a bit. So far, no one has asked Brett who he is or how he got in here. The staff seems too sympathetic, or maybe just too busy, to worry about rules.

"This is torture," Joe comments, rolling a pen back and forth between his right thumb and forefinger and looking at the clock. It's almost two in the morning now.

"I'll stay here with him if you want to go get something to eat, or grab a few hours' sleep," Brett offers, realizing Joe is probably desperate for a cigarette.

"You don't mind?"

"Not at all."

Brett doesn't have to volunteer twice.

Left alone in the room, he sits for a long time in the uncomfortable chair, watching Mike.

Finally, he goes over to the bed. "I don't know if you can hear me. It's Brett Cavalon. I'm so sorry this happened to you." He pauses to clear his throat. "I know you were looking into what happened down in Groton yesterday, and I know you were heading to Mumbai. If you—"

"Excuse me!"

He looks up and is startled to see a scrubs-clad stranger in the doorway.

"Who are you?" So much for the kindly nurses who looked the other way. This one clearly isn't thrilled to find him here.

Brett takes a step back from the bed. "I'm a friend of Mike's."

"You'll have to leave. No one is supposed to be in here right now."

Judging by the no-nonsense expression, Brett figures it's no use arguing—and, considering the patient's condition, no use staying.

He leans over Mike one last time, again whispering, "I'm so sorry. Hang in there. I'll be back when I can."

"Mommy!"

Renny!

Elsa's eyes snap open.

She sits up in bed.

No—she's not in bed. It's dark, but she's . . .

Where am I? What's going on?

Disoriented, she knows only that Renny is calling her. She gets her feet onto the floor, takes a step, and bumps into something.

"Ouch!"

The coffee table? What is she doing in the living room? Why—?

Then the memories hit like a barrage of bullets and she rushes toward her daughter's bedroom, her heart pounding.

"I'm coming, Renny!" she calls out, remembering but not caring that the house might be bugged.

The door is closed. No, no, no . . . they never close Renny's door. Something is wrong.

She jerks the knob, bursts through the door, and flips on the light.

The bed is empty.

She's too late.

Reeling, Elsa flattens a palm against the wall to stay on her feet.

How could she have let this happen? How could she have fallen asleep knowing that someone out there wants to hurt her daughter?

Oh God. Please, God, no.

He can't have taken Renny very far. But if he's armed—

"Mommy!"

She lets out a whimper of relief as Renny's voice hits her, along with the recollection that she's not sleeping in her own bed tonight.

Elsa races back to the master bedroom, terrified of what she might find there.

Renny looks small and defenseless in the king-sized bed—and as disoriented as Elsa herself was just moments ago. A quick glance reveals that the room is empty—apparently so, anyway.

"What's the matter?" She gathers Renny into her arms.

"The monster."

Elsa's heart stops. "He's *here*?"

Renny nods and buries her head against Elsa's breast.

"Where? Where is he, Renny?"

"I don't know. I saw him . . ." A tremendous yawn overtakes her.

Elsa casts another wary look around. "Are you sure you saw him?"

"Mmm hmm," Renny says sleepily.

But there's no evidence of him, and nothing seems to have been disturbed. Was it another of Renny's usual nightmares? Or was the monster sighting as real as everything else that's been going on?

Awash in uncertainty, Elsa strokes her daughter's hair.

Is *any* of it real?

Or was it her own imagination—that someone was stalking her around her mother's apartment, that the doorman had taken Renny hostage, that someone had planted a Spider-Man toy that had once belonged to her dead son.

But what about those pictures that came in the mail? Brett saw them, too.

Unless her mind—fed by her own worst nightmares, and Renny's wee-hour monster ones—conjured that, like everything else?

It happens. It happened to Renny's birth mother.

But she was mentally ill.

Yet Elsa herself was unbalanced enough, at one point, to have completely lost touch with reality. She'd even tried to take her own life, convinced it was the only way to end the pain.

But that means nothing. Sane people commit suicide.

So do insane people.

Dear God.

Who's to say Elsa isn't suffering from acute stress disorder all over again? She wouldn't know it if she were. She certainly didn't realize it when it was happening to her last time around.

Is she suffering the final vestiges of a breakdown that began fifteen years ago, with Jeremy's disappearance?

Is it any wonder?

She lost a child. She's terrified of losing another. The human mind, under duress, is capable of playing all kinds of terrible tricks.

Somehow, right here, right now, in her own familiar house in the middle of the night, it's easier to believe that she's delusional than it is that the whole nightmare—her own, and Renny's—ever happened at all.

Wait! Brett! Don't leave!

The silent scream that seizes Mike's body obliterates everything else—the pain, the fear, the sounds and sensation of movement around him.

It's no use.

Brett is gone.

And even if the staff hadn't come along to kick him out, Mike couldn't have warned him anyway. He can't communicate, dammit; can't even bat an eyelash to let anyone know that he's alive in here, like an undetected disaster survivor entombed in wreckage.

He can only pray that Brett and Elsa will figure it out somehow, before it's too late. Or that he'll have a miraculous recovery and be able to tell them himself. It doesn't seem likely, but . . .

Anything is possible. Anything at all.

Isn't that what he'd told himself when he suspected that Jeremy Cavalon might actually be alive?

Yes—and that was his fatal mistake.

Almost fatal, anyway.

After all, he's not dead. He—

A sudden sound reaches his ears. The slightest sound, barely there—a whisper of movement somewhere nearby.

Startled, Mike realizes he's not alone after all.

Someone is in the room.

It must be a doctor, or a nurse.

He waits.

All is still. Wouldn't the medical staff be bustling about their business?

Whoever it is seems to be just . . . here.

Maybe it's clergy, come to pray over him, or maybe Brett snuck back in, or—

"You should have minded your own business," a voice hisses, its proximity as startling as the ominous words.

Caught up in thoughts of Mike, Brett doesn't remember to turn on his phone until he's in the car, heading back toward the highway.

He must have countless voice mails from Elsa. She's probably worried sick. And with any luck, there will be one from Joan, as well.

Working his phone with one hand while he steers over the unfamiliar road with the other, he sees that his voice mail box is empty.

That can't be. He must have hit the wrong button. They're so small, and his fingers are clumsy.

He fumbles with the phone, trying to find the right one as he merges onto the highway.

Nope . . . that *was* the right button. There are no messages.

It's understandable that Joan wouldn't check her voice mail after hours, or that she wouldn't call him back even if she'd gotten the message, but . . .

Surely, Elsa would have found a way to charge the battery before now. Or she would have realized hers was dead and called him from her mother's house.

He gropes the buttons and blindly dials her cell.

Unlike earlier, it doesn't bounce right into voice mail. This time, it rings a few times, getting Brett's hopes up. Then Elsa's voice comes on the line.

"You've reached the Cavalons. We can't come to the phone right now . . ."

Brett lets out a frustrated curse and tosses the phone aside.

"Where are you, Elsa?" he mutters.

Clenching the wheel hard, he runs through one terrifying scenario after another until a blaring horn jerks his attention back to the road. He swerves just in time to avoid hitting the concrete median and pulls off at the next exit, shaken.

He needs to call someone.

But without Mike, he's at a loss.

It's time to involve the police. There's nothing else he can do. He'll just have to pray that when the time comes, the agency will understand and let the adoption go through.

When the time comes . . .

Please, please, please let the time come.

Let my girls be all right.

It must be a good sign, though, that the phone rang a few times before going into voice mail. It means the battery is no longer dead, right? So she must have charged it. Maybe—

Wait a minute.

You've reached the Cavalons . . .

That wasn't her cell phone's outgoing message.

He really must have hit the wrong button that time, pressing the speed dial number for their home phone, not Elsa's cell.

No sooner does he realize that than his own phone, which landed on the floor in front of the passenger's seat, begins to ring.

"If you could talk, you'd probably beg me to put you out of your misery, wouldn't you?" asks the person looming over Mike, terrifyingly close. "Guess what? It's your lucky day."

Helpless, gripped by fear, Mike senses a swift, furtive movement beside him.

"There. All set. This should be quick."

Quick . . . ?

What should be quick?

Oh . . .

Oh God.

Oh no.

He's suffocating.

Horror seeps in, saturating his body as if to replace the precious oxygen that's been deliberately cut off.

"It's okay . . . Just let it happen."

Just . . . let . . . it . . . happen . . .

The voice seems far away now, fading.

Mike has always wondered what it would be like to die—whether it would hurt, whether the end would come quickly . . .

Now you know.

Funny, he thinks as he plummets into the darkness, that death is an even greater paradox than life.

Death—*his* death—is excruciating yet painless, ago-
nizingly drawn out even as it happens in a flash . . .

It's over.

Another one bites the dust.

Ah . . . that was the title of an oldie but goodie, and
the perfect addition to life's little soundtrack.

Mike Fantoni looks so peaceful, lying there with his
eyes closed. No different, really, than he did a minute
ago, when he was alive.

*I really did do him a favor. Euthanasia. No need to feel
bad about this one.*

It's what lies ahead that remains a bit troubling.

Taking the life of a healthy child isn't exactly doing
anyone any favors.

But it's no less necessary, and there's some comfort
knowing that it will be done out of love.

In the end, as far as Jeremy is concerned, that's all
that's really going to matter.

Straining to keep one hand on the wheel and an eye
on the road, Brett struggles to reach the ringing phone
on the floor in front of the passenger's seat. At last his
fingers close around it.

"Elsa?"

"Brett!"

"Thank God you're all right!"

"How did you know where we were?"

"I—" He's so relieved to hear her voice that it takes
him a minute to grasp the question. "What do you
mean? Where *are* you?"

"Didn't you just call me?"

"I just called—wait, are you *home*?"

"You didn't know?"

"No, I meant to call your cell, but . . . Is everything okay there?"

She hesitates long enough that he realizes she isn't telling the whole truth when she answers that it is.

"Elsa—are you sure?"

"Yes, I was just asleep when the phone rang and by the time I got to it, it had gone into voice mail."

"But why aren't you at your mother's?"

"It's a long story. Where are *you*, by the way? I thought I'd find you here when we got back."

"Another long story," he tells Elsa. "But I'm on my way home. Are the doors locked?"

"The doors, the windows . . . trust me, we're fine. Just hurry home. We have to figure out what's going on . . . if anything even is."

"What do you mean?"

"I don't know . . . I'm starting to wonder if I might not just be . . . paranoid."

Paranoid?

It's not the right word, he knows. But it's the only one she can bring herself to say.

"I love you," he says simply, relieved that she at least grasps the possibility that she's suffering from a relapse. Now they can work together to get her the help she needs.

Hanging up, Brett makes a U-turn back toward the highway.

Was it really just six hours ago that you were about to climb into bed in a hotel in Times Square, exhausted?

It seems like a month has passed since the GPS alert that Brett Cavalon was on the move. Interesting how the human body responds to stress. Just when you think you're too exhausted to even reach over and turn off the bedside lamp, you somehow find the energy to grab a cab to the airport, hop a flight, rent a car, and carry out yet another unfortunate but necessary death sentence.

Adrenaline is a wonderful thing.

But now . . .

It's time to get some sleep at last.

At least this time, it won't be in a cold, impersonal hotel room. Not when there's a huge, vacant house with beds dressed in the finest European linens Montgomery money could buy.

At this hour, with hardly another soul on the road, the fifteen-mile trip from downtown Boston will be a breeze.

Nottingshire, here I come . . . again.

Did I just make a terrible mistake? Elsa wonders as she hangs up the telephone. Lying to Brett about having been asleep when it rang—that was no mistake. Later, when he gets here, and she can explain the whole story, she'll tell him the truth: that she had been afraid the lines were tapped.

Had been afraid . . .

Or are you still?

Answering the call in the first place—*that* might have been her terrible mistake.

Earlier, after Renny's nightmare, she'd convinced herself that she'd conjured the stalker situation in her paranoid maternal brain.

Paranoid?

Try mentally ill.

But as she lay there in the dark, listening to Renny's even breathing and the silence of the house that no longer felt familiar, she wasn't so sure.

Okay. So either she's crazy, or they're in danger.

Which is it?

Some choice.

No wonder you can't decide.

Anyway, when the phone rang, her first instinct was not to take any chances.

A moment later, after it had gone into voice mail, she decided that was ridiculous—particularly when she saw on the caller ID that it had been Brett.

She didn't even bother to listen to his message, just carried the phone into the next room and called him right back.

It's a relief to know where Brett is and that he's on his way home, but . . .

Did she just broadcast Renny's whereabouts to a stranger listening in?

So now you're back to the theory that (A) you're not crazy and (B) you're in danger. Terrific.

She paces over to the living room window and peeks through a crack in the curtains, half expecting to see the silhouette of a man watching the house.

But the street is empty . . . and so, she notices with a frown, is Meg Warren's driveway.

At this hour?

Maybe Meg really does have a secret love life.

Anything is possible, Elsa tells herself. *Anything at all.*

CHAPTER THIRTEEN

Not even five A.M., yet the sky above Regis Terrace is already streaked with dawn's pink glow.

Strolling past one grand brick Colonial after another, Jeremy thinks back six months to the first time he came to Nottingshire. Back then, he'd marveled at how, this far east in mid-December, dusk fell before four o'clock.

He'd come here that day looking for La La Montgomery.

What happened when he found her wasn't what he'd intended—not at all. He'd only wanted to see her, maybe talk to her for a minute, try to explain . . .

As if there was any satisfying explanation he could offer for having taken a golf club and shattered her skull.

His emotions, when he came face-to-face with her, were raw. After so many years alone, keeping everything pent up inside him, he'd gotten carried away. He'd known it was wrong, but he couldn't help it.

Afterward, he'd promised himself it would never happen again.

And now look. Look where you are. Look what you've been doing.

He picks up his pace a little, almost as if instinctively trying to outrun the demons that brought him back here on that cold December dusk.

Haven't you learned by now that you're never going to escape what happened to you?

Even coming back to his old life, revisiting the scenes of the crimes—his own, and Garvey Quinn's—can't help him reconcile the past.

Maybe he does know it's no use, deep down inside.

It's not as if he's going to reclaim his rightful place in Elsa Cavalon's heart, or in Marin Quinn's.

And yet . . .

He can't walk away, either. Not until it's over.

It will be. Soon. Today.

He just can't take it anymore.

Can't take *her*. He can't take seeing her this way, seeing what she's become, wondering what might have been . . .

He can't take the guilt, the waiting, the wondering if there's a part of her that really does love him . . .

Just as there's a part of him that hates her still, even after all these years.

Hearing a car on the street, Elsa peeks through the curtains.

Brett!

Thank God.

She hurries to the front door, opening it just as he turns off the ignition in the driveway. Hesitating just a moment, she weighs the wisdom of leaving Renny alone and asleep in the house for a minute.

But she has no choice. There's a lot to say to Brett, and she doesn't dare say it inside the house.

Granted, she's spent the last few hours combing every room for bugs and found nothing. But she didn't even know what she was looking for, exactly. What does a listening device look like? Where might it be hidden? The clueless search did little to ease her fear.

Brett is out of the car in a flash, looking worried. "Where's Renny?"

"Inside."

"Alone?"

"She's sleeping."

Brett sweeps Elsa into a fierce, fleeting hug, releases her quickly, and starts toward the house.

"Brett, no, wait. We need to talk."

"We can talk inside. Renny won't hear us if she's asleep, and—"

"Renny isn't the only one who might hear us in there."

He stops walking. Pivots to look at her. "What do you mean? Who's there?"

"No one's *there*, exactly, but . . ."

Elsa takes a deep breath. This is it. If she tells him everything that's happened—everything she's *thought* has happened—there will be no going back.

If it turns out she's delusional, Brett will have to decide whether she's any more fit to parent Renny than Renny's birth mother was.

But I would never hurt her. Never. No matter what.

Still . . . could she ever really trust herself again, knowing her mind is capable of playing such terrible tricks on her? Could Brett ever trust her?

Hopefully, she'll never have to find out. But she has to tell him.

"Brett, someone followed us to New York."

Jeremy had expected to have Regis Terrace all to himself at this hour.

However, just up ahead, right in front of the Montgomery house, as luck would have it, a neighbor is walking her dog.

She's one of those upscale housewife types you see around here—fit and attractive, wearing yoga pants and sneakers, holding a mug that's presumably from her nearby kitchen and filled with hot coffee.

She glances up, making eye contact with Jeremy as her dog pokes along the curb. "Hello."

"Hi." He's careful not to be too friendly, but not unfriendly, either.

"Looks like it's going to be a nice day, doesn't it?"

He nods, slowing his pace a bit, wondering if he should keep right on walking. Sneaking a peek at the house, he notes that the shades are drawn.

"Did you know them?"

The question catches him off guard, and he looks up to see the woman following his gaze.

"The Montgomerys, I mean."

His instinct is to lie, but what if she's seen him around here before?

He settles on a vague "Not very well."

She shrugs. "It's just such a horrible thing. I know it's been six months now, but every time I look at that house, I feel sick just thinking about what happened. Poor La La."

"Yes," Jeremy agrees, his heart pounding, even though she can't possibly *know*. "Poor La La."

"Well? What do you think?" Elsa watches Brett, waiting for him to say something now that she's spilled the whole story.

Uneasy, he looks away, back at the house, where Renny lies sleeping.

His daughter.

But she won't be, if the adoption doesn't go through.

What do I think?

About someone stalking my wife and child with a butcher knife?

He looks again at Elsa. Finding out her son is dead, combined with the renewed strain of foster mother-hood, must have plunged her back into the nightmare of acute stress disorder.

She actually admitted that she might have imagined the part about the knife—or even more.

Still . . . what about those surveillance pictures of Renny? Did she actually go to such great lengths? Taking the pictures, mailing them, claiming not to recognize them—or perhaps really not recognizing them, in her state of mind.

Oh God. If that's the case; if she really is that ill . . .

Yet maybe there's some other explanation. Something not as sinister as it seems. Maybe the photos were taken by the press.

Or maybe they were from someone who wants to blackmail the Cavalons to keep their new child out of the media . . .

And the person forgot to put in the blackmail note? Yeah, right.

Well, maybe that envelope was sent by the foster care agency, as some kind of . . .

What? Official procedure? Why wouldn't there be any paperwork?

Well, maybe the paperwork that was supposed to accompany the photos was accidentally missing, or . . .

All of those scenarios seem pretty far-fetched. But really, are they any more unlikely than the house being bugged, and someone following Elsa and Renny to New York, and—

And what about Mike?

Chances are, the hit-and-run really was a freak accident.

But why would he bother to follow a dead-end trail overseas after all these years? And why—since the trip obviously has some connection to Jeremy's kidnapping—didn't he bother to tell Brett and Elsa he was going?

Unless . . .

"When was the last time you checked your cell phone voice mail, Elsa?"

"I don't know, but I told you, either I lost my phone in New York, or—"

Or it was stolen from her mother's apartment by the knife-wielding intruder.

Yeah. He knows.

"Maybe you should check it. I know your battery was dead—"

"But not until yesterday afternoon. I called you from my phone when I got to New York, remember?"

That's right. She did.

He'd been thinking that Mike might have tried to call Elsa yesterday morning, before the accident. But she'd presumably had her phone with her the whole time. She would have heard it and picked it up.

But we were traveling, and in that motel room . . .

If Mike had tried to call when they were in a no-service area, it would have gone into voice mail.

"You should check your messages," he urges. "You don't even need the phone to access the mailbox, you can dial it from the house."

"What if the line is bugged?"

He pulls his own cell phone from his pocket. "Dial it from here."

"It might be bugged, too."

"If it is, then it's too late to do anything about it anyway. I've been using it nonstop. Here. Hurry up and call."

He glances again at the house as she dials. She

left the front door ajar so they can hear Renny, just in case . . .

"Hurry," he urges Elsa again.

"I *am*!"

It isn't like her to snap at him.

He bites his lip to keep from snapping back, knowing she's under terrible pressure. They both are. He can feel his jaw clenching painfully as he watches her punch in her PIN.

"I have messages," she murmurs after a moment.

"Some are from me. I left you a bunch."

She nods, listening. Her eyes grow wide.

"What? What is it? Is it Mike?"

"No, it's . . ." She presses the replay button and passes the phone to him, her hand trembling. "Listen to this. Oh my God, Brett. Oh my God. She's the one who did this . . ."

She? She who? What on earth is she talking about?

Brett quickly raises the phone to his ear. The message is already under way.

"—need to talk to you," an unfamiliar female voice is saying. "Over the phone or in person, whatever . . . I, um, understand if you'd rather not talk to me after . . . after all this. But I hope you will. I'm sorry."

The caller hangs up.

"Who?" Brett asks Elsa, his pulse racing. "Who *is* this?"

"Marin Quinn. Jeremy's birth mother," she adds, as if he doesn't know.

"What is she talking about? What is she apologizing for?"

"What do you *think*? It must have been her. She's the one who took those pictures of Renny."

"But why? Why would she do this to us?"

"She's a mother who lost a child, Brett. That does terrible things to a person."

Yes. Nobody knows that better than we do.

"She gave him up when he was a newborn, though," Brett points out. "It's not the same thing as raising a child and having him kidnapped and murdered."

Elsa is shaking her head before he even finishes speaking. "She still lost him. You can't assign degrees to the pain. That's like saying that losing Jeremy didn't hurt me as much as it would have if I'd given birth to him. He was my son. He was her son. She's probably torturing herself, thinking that if she hadn't given him up, he'd—"

"Or blaming us," Brett cuts in as it dawns on him.

Elsa presses a hand to her mouth. "You think . . . ?"

"She wants to punish us for not taking care of her son."

"By harming our daughter?"

"Or at least by threatening to."

"But that's . . ."

Crazy. Yes. Better Marin Quinn than his wife.

"You said it yourself, Elsa. Grief does terrible things to a person. Anyway, she reached out to us. That message made it sound like she'd thought better of it."

"You're right. So you think it's over?"

"I didn't say that." Brett shakes his head grimly. "I don't know what to think. But at least we know who we're dealing with now."

Opening her eyes, Marin sees that her bedroom is brighter than usual. Frowning, she turns her head to look at the bedside clock and is startled to find that she slept through the night for a change. She must have been really exhausted. Or—thinking back, she remembers that she'd had an empty stomach last night. The medication must have hit her harder than usual.

Last night . . .

She yawns, stretches—then sits up abruptly.

Annie.

Marin bolts from the bed.

Annie was sick, in the hospital . . . what if something happened to her in the night?

Marin hurries down the hall to her younger daughter's room. The door is closed. She doesn't bother to knock. Annie's probably asleep, and even if she isn't, she's not the privacy fanatic her sister is.

Opening the door, she's relieved to see that her child is resting peacefully: eyes closed and mouth open, snoring as usual.

Reassured, she closes the door quietly and starts back down the hall.

Caroline's door is closed, too.

Should I look in on her?

Remembering the way they'd left things last night—in anger—Marin hesitates.

Caroline's attitude problem was increasingly difficult to handle even before yesterday's near-disaster. Marin probably still has some cooling off to do before she can possibly have a rational conversation with her.

Probably?

Even now, thinking of poor Annie in the hospital, she's furious all over again.

In fact, she can't even picture herself and Caroline forgiving each other and moving past this.

There's nothing wrong with needing outside help . . .

Lauren Walsh's words ring in her ears . . . yet so do her own.

All I need is time, and everything will be just fine.

Yesterday, she honestly believed that.

Today . . .

I don't know what to believe. I don't even know who I am anymore . . .

Or, she thinks as she keeps going, right past Caroline's door without a backward glance, *who my daughter is.*

"I still can't believe it," Brett murmurs, shaking his head.

"I can't, either."

Sitting across from Brett at the kitchen table, coffee mugs in front of them, Elsa notes that this is exactly where they were forty-eight hours ago—after Renny's first nightmare about the monster in her room, and the open window . . .

Despite what she told Brett earlier, trying to rationalize Marin Quinn's actions as a mental imbalance brought on by profound maternal grief, she finds it almost impossible to believe that Jeremy's birth mother would actually sneak into their house in the dead of night, wearing a rubber mask . . .

And that's the least of it.

Incredible. *Beyond* incredible, and infuriating, and bewildering . . .

But there's no denying that bizarre phone call out of the blue.

And here I thought I was the one who'd gone off the deep end.

Brett, too, had thought so, remembering what she'd gone through after Jeremy disappeared. For all he knew, in her dissociative state, Elsa herself could have been capable of crawling in someone's window in the middle of the night.

That's why he hadn't told her about Mike's accident right away, or that he was headed for Mumbai when it happened. He was afraid, he said, that it might push her over the edge.

Elsa watches Brett sip his coffee, wondering if he's

thinking about Marin Quinn. His theory is that Marin convinced herself that Renny is Jeremy, and she wants to rescue—

Brett's cell phone rings, startling them both. He pulls it from his pocket as Elsa glances at the clock.

It's past six—not the middle of the night, but still early enough for a call at this hour to threaten bad news.

Brett glances at the caller ID pane. "Oh no."

"Who is it?"

He holds up a finger, already answering the phone. "Hello?"

She can hear a male voice on the other end of the line, though she can't make out what he's saying. Judging by the look on Brett's face, she can tell that she was right. It's bad news.

"When?" he asks hoarsely. After listening for a moment, he nods. "Was anyone with him?" He listens again, shaking his head, and Elsa sees that there are tears in his eyes.

Comprehending, she whispers, "Mike?"

He nods, and a lump of unexpected sorrow clogs her throat.

She closes her eyes, seeing his familiar handsome face—not as it was this last time, etched by age and stress—but as it was when she first met him, years ago.

Mike Fantoni had promised, that first day, not to give up until he'd found out what happened to her lost son.

He never gave up.

If there is a heaven, she thinks, wiping away a tear that managed to squeeze through her lashes, then one thing is certain: they're both there: Mike Fantoni and the little boy he'd so longed to bring home alive.

* * *

A few hours in the downy cloud of a featherbed that once belonged to La La's parents was hardly enough.

But it will have to do for now. The sun is up out there beyond the drawn shades, and it's time to get moving.

The first floor of the huge house on Regis Terrace is dim and still this morning. Moving through the rooms, it's hard to remember that the place was actually lived in, a comfortable family home like any other in this quintessential small New England town.

Once upon a time, a clock ticked steadily on the marble mantel in the living room. But it was the kind that needed to be wound nightly, and there's no longer anyone here to bother.

The silence is unnerving.

It's going to be another long, exhausting day. Some caffeine would be helpful.

In the kitchen, there's a percolator, a canister filled with dark roast coffee, even milk that isn't yet outdated. But the beans would need to be ground, and the grinder is loud enough to wake the dead, as Candace Montgomery, La La's mother, used to say.

Interesting turn of phrase.

The dead.

No one was ever meant to die.

Certainly not *her*.

But on the stormy December night of Jeremy's first visit to this house, as soon as she realized who he was, she opened her mouth. Opened her big, fat, loud mouth and said all the wrong things.

I couldn't help it. I just snapped.

Maybe if she hadn't been standing at the top of the back stairs when she started blabbing . . .

But she was. Standing with her back to the tall, steep flight, her heels just inches from the edge of the top step. It was so tempting to just reach out and . . .

And I tried to fight it. Really, I did.

But in the end, it was no use. It took precious little effort to shut her up. Just one swift and mighty shove, and over she went, tumbling down the steps with a bone-crunching commotion.

After she hit bottom, all was silent . . . at first.

Then a faint moan floated up the stairs.

It wasn't over. She was still alive.

But not for long.

Her blue eyes were wide open, staring in helpless horror until the last moment, when the pillow—a plush European down pillow from La La's own bed—came down over her face.

Wow—what a way to start the day, with such a grim memory.

Coffee probably would have been better.

But not this morning. Not here, anyway.

The last thing I want to do in this house is wake the dead.

If it wasn't too late to call Jake last night, Caroline reasons, then it probably isn't too early to call him this morning. Right? Right.

She dials his number quickly, before she can question her own logic.

Who knows? Maybe he didn't sleep any better than she did, as anxious to see her today as she is to see him.

She almost expects him to pick up on the first ring, but he doesn't. It takes several before she hears a click and a "Hello?"—a groggy-sounding one, at that.

"Jake?"

"N— I mean, yeah. Yeah, hi."

She forces a laugh. "Did you forget your own name there, for a second?"

"No, I . . . sorry, I'm just . . . sleeping."

"Really? I guess no one told you this is the city that never sleeps," she says lightly, trying to make the best of having woken him up so early.

"Yeah . . . about that . . ."

Uh-oh.

"I'm kind of . . . not exactly in New York."

Her heart sinks. " 'Kind of not exactly'?"

"I'm *not*. I got called away yesterday by . . . a friend."

"Oh." Bummed, but trying not to sound it, she asks, "Where are you?"

"Just outside of Boston. I might need to be here for a couple of days."

"Boston? That's not so bad."

"*Bad?*"

"Far, I mean. I could meet you there," she blurts.

Are you crazy? In Boston?

"In *Boston?*" he echoes her incredulous thought aloud.

"Sure, why not?"

Why not? Really? Why not?

She can think of a thousand reasons why she can't just take off and go to Boston to meet some guy . . . beginning with the fact that he didn't invite her.

But she can think of an even better reason why she should—the only reason she really even needs.

She has to get away from this apartment and her mother for a while.

Maybe even for good.

She hears herself say, "Just tell me where to meet you, and when, and I'll be there."

"Are you serious?"

"I am *dead* serious, Jake."

Renny is still in their bed, but when Brett checked her a few minutes ago, in the room to grab his laptop, she was beginning to stir. They need to make this quick.

Opening the Internet search engine as Elsa hovers behind his kitchen chair, he types "Marin Quinn." He hits enter and almost immediately, a list of hits pops up on the screen.

"What are we even looking for?" Elsa asks as they scan the results.

"Anything. Anything we can find out about her. Anything that might tell us what she's been up to lately, and—whoa. Look at this."

He quickly slides the mouse, moving cursor over the third item down: a *New York Post* entry.

Elsa leans in closer. "That's today's date!"

"Exactly." Brett holds his breath and clicks on it. Waiting for the screen to pop up, he wonders why Marin Quinn is in the news. Did she do something drastic, like . . . kill someone? Kill herself?

But he finds himself looking at a grainy photo of a woman on a city street. She's attractive, but a far cry from the polished political wife in all the file photos shown back when the news first broke about her husband.

"That doesn't even look like her," Elsa tells him.

"I guess it does now."

"When was it taken?"

Brett points to the accompanying caption.

Reclusive Marin Quinn emerges for a rainy day stroll on an Upper East Side street yesterday morning.

"Yesterday morning? Brett—you said that's when Mike was hit by that car in Boston."

"Right." He nods slowly. "So she couldn't have done it."

"You said you didn't think it was deliberate anyway."

"No . . . I know."

He said—*thought*—a lot of things. But he isn't positive about any of it.

Isn't it too coincidental that Mike was mowed down just hours after Elsa and Brett went to him for help—and just as he was leaving for Mumbai? Now he's dead.

"She doesn't strike me as a cold-blooded murderer," Elsa comments, gazing at the woman onscreen.

"Neither would her husband, at a glance. But look what he did."

Eyes hardening, Elsa turns away.

Brett takes another long look and closes out of the screen, wondering where Marin Quinn is right this moment and hoping—*praying*—that she's far, far from here.

Drenched in a cold sweat, her heart racing frantically, Marin huddles on her bed. Her gasping breaths are coming too hard and too fast, terrible pain gripping her chest every time she inhales.

What's going on? Is she having a heart attack? Is she *dying*? Having some kind of reaction to the medication? Did she accidentally take too much of it last night?

She could have sworn she'd had the usual dose, but maybe she was mistaken.

I need to call someone . . .

Ron.

Heather's husband is a doctor; he'll know what to do.

Wait—he's not even here. They're on their way to the Riviera.

Marin clutches her aching ribs, feeling as though she's going to pass out.

Then I have to call 911.

But if she does that, she'll have to tell them that she took medicine that wasn't prescribed for her. The press might get hold of it, blow it up into some nightmare scandal.

Even through the haze of pain and panic, she can see the headlines—*Quinn's Wife Admits Drug Habit,* or even *Quinn's Wife Attempts Suicide.*

No—she'd never kill herself. Never leave her girls alone. But . . .

Does she have a drug habit?

Of course not. She's only taking prescription medications to help her sleep, and to ease the pain of her headaches, and to calm her nerves.

But the pills weren't prescribed to her. It's illegal to take them. And *dangerous.*

This is crazy. You've been acting crazy. Maybe you are crazy.

But she can't let this go on, can't continue to drown herself in grief over her lost husband and son. They aren't coming back.

But she has two daughters who need her.

Two daughters.

Caroline is impossible. But she's my child and I love her.

Lauren was right.

I need help.

We all do.

Marin has to pull herself together.

Yes. She'll talk to Lauren and get the name of a good family therapist.

And after she does that, she'll go straight into Caroline's room, call a truce, and tell her they're going to make a fresh start—beginning today.

* * *

Pouring a bowl of organic cereal for Renny, Elsa asks, as she does every morning, "Do you want milk in it, or just on the side?"

"Just on the side today."

Comforted by the sense of ordinariness that's settled over the house now that Renny is up, Elsa pours milk into a plastic cup, then sets it and the dry cereal on the table. "Here you go."

"Thanks, Mommy."

Elsa leans over to kiss her daughter's head, loving Renny so much her heart actually hurts.

All I want is to be her mother. Why does it have to be so complicated?

Though Elsa and Brett know who's behind the threats now, one thing hasn't changed: they still can't risk losing custody of Renny—particularly with a new social worker on their case, one who doesn't know them at all and might be tempted to go by the book. Undoubtedly, "the book" won't allow any leeway to foster parents being stalked by a lunatic who wants to harm the child.

It isn't fair that their future as a family is hanging in the balance; that the slightest misstep now could destroy any chances of adoption.

Elsa pats Renny on the head and leaves the room, surreptitiously wiping her eyes on her sleeve.

She finds Brett in the master bathroom, lathering shaving cream onto his jaw. She slips in and closes the door behind her.

"What?" Brett turns to look at her. "Is everything okay?"

"She's eating her breakfast. She hasn't even mentioned what happened yesterday or last night. Maybe she thinks it was all just a bad dream."

"I wish it was."

"Too bad we can't get her out of here for a little while, Brett—send her someplace safe while we figure out what to do about this."

"We tried that. You went to New York. Look what happened. *She* was there. Marin Quinn." The name sounds strange on Brett's tongue, and Elsa wonders whether he's ever even said it aloud before.

For that matter, has she? She's thought it countless times, and read it in the news over and over again . . . but has she ever had reason to say it?

I wish I didn't now.

Brett turns on the water and picks up his razor. "How could she have known where you and Renny were, though?"

"I told you—this house is bugged."

"I know you did."

Elsa frowns. The last two words make all the difference.

He's not saying, *I know the house is bugged.*

No, he's saying, *I know what you told me.*

Even now, she realizes, he's thinking she might be off her rocker—like Marin Quinn.

Maybe he's right. Just a little while ago, she was thinking the same thing.

"Or maybe she really did follow you," Brett says, carefully running the razor along his cheek, leaving a trail like a toboggan track on a snowy slope.

"But I kept looking."

"Do you think it's possible that you missed her?"

Considering that, she shrugs. "I mean . . . maybe. I wasn't looking for a woman. I know that's crazy, but I just assumed we were dealing with a man. I guess she could have been right there on the train, or on the street, and I didn't even notice her. But I was so sure . . ." She trails off, shaking her head.

"What?"

"Marin Quinn . . . wouldn't I have recognized her if she were following me?"

"When you saw that picture in the paper you said yourself that she doesn't look the same."

"No . . . but . . . I mean, it's not like she had plastic surgery and has a whole new face. You can tell it's her. She just looks older, and tired. Not like a different person. I think I would have noticed her."

"So maybe she really did bug the phones or the house. May—ouch! Dammit!"

He's cut himself. A scarlet trickle runs down his cheek like a bloody tear.

Seeing it, Elsa shivers, seized by an inexplicable chill of foreboding.

CHAPTER FOURTEEN

Striving for normalcy—for Renny's sake, and their own—Elsa and Brett have spent the last few hours watching television on the couch with their daughter between them. Elsa has almost managed to convince herself that it really is just any other Saturday morning—until the doorbell rings.

She looks at Brett in alarm, even though she knows Marin Quinn is hardly likely to show up boldly on their doorstep.

"It's probably UPS," Brett says unconvincingly.

"Do they even deliver on Saturdays?"

"Sure they do."

"Shh, I love this song." Renny is fixated on the screen, where Ariel the Little Mermaid is singing the "Part of Your World" reprise.

"Stay here with her," Brett tells Elsa in a low voice. "I'll go see who it is."

She instinctively pulls Renny a little closer to her side as he leaves the room.

Even if Marin Quinn really were at the door, Brett would never let her get past him.

But what if she has a gun, and forces her way in?

Elsa's heart pounds wildly as she waits, her whole body tense.

Oblivious, Renny sings along with a plaintive Ariel, longing to stay and live where she is now.

Elsa hears Brett open the door.

For a moment, the swelling music and Renny's voice drown out whatever's happening in the hall.

Then Elsa hears Brett. ". . . nice to meet you. Please come in."

Relief courses through her. He would never say that to Marin Quinn. Never in a million years.

"Elsa?" Brett calls from the hall. "Bring Renny in. Her new caseworker is here."

Caroline's offer to come meet him in Boston had caught Jeremy completely off guard. But he'd quickly realized that while it hadn't been his own idea, it was a good one.

He can't leave New England until he takes care of business once and for all, and he wasn't thrilled about keeping the whole Caroline situation on hold until that's over.

She's already on her way here, having caught an early Acela. "It's a high-speed train," she told him excitedly. "I'll be in Boston in a few hours, tops."

"That's great. I'll meet you by the Dunkin' Donuts in South Station."

"Can't wait."

"Me either."

Lying, Jeremy realizes as he hangs up the phone, is getting to be a regular habit.

Thank God I left the kids at home, Lauren thinks as she hikes toward the terminal at JFK airport. She wound up parking what feels like—and might actually *be*—miles away, after wasting half an hour circling around hoping to find a vacant spot in the jammed short-term lots.

At least her mother-in-law's flight from the West Coast landed late, according to the arrivals board. Hopefully, she's already collected her luggage and hasn't been waiting too long.

If she's anything like her son, patience isn't her strong suit. Nick always hated flying for that reason. He couldn't stand to wait at the gate, or on the runway, or at the baggage claim . . .

Nick. Even now, Lauren feels a little stab of shock. Never in a million years would she have imagined that he'd leave her, or—

Or what about this? Being here, today?

She'd certainly never pictured herself coming face-to-face with the mother-in-law who hadn't even seen her own son in decades.

That's partly why she didn't want to drag the kids down here this morning. Not just because they act more human when they sleep in—they probably won't even wake up for at least another hour—but because she wanted to meet their grandmother before thrusting her upon the kids.

She seemed cordial enough on the phone—even wistful. But what kind of woman turns her back on her own young son?

As Lauren hurries into the crowded baggage claim area, her cell phone rings. It's probably Nick's mother now, wondering where she is.

Taking it out of her pocket, she glances at the caller ID window.

Marin.

Yesterday's worry for her friend comes rushing back at her. About to answer the phone, she hears a voice calling her name.

"Lauren? Lauren Walsh?"

She looks up.

A woman is coming toward her—a woman with silver hair and Nick's eyes and Nick's smile and tears rolling down her weathered cheeks . . .

Marin momentarily forgotten, Lauren shoves her phone back into her pocket and opens her arms to her mother-in-law.

Brett can see that Elsa's hand is shaking a bit as she pours hot water from the whistling tea kettle into a trio of bone china cups on the counter.

She's doing everything she can to convince the new caseworker that this is a carefree household; that they're the perfect parents for Renny.

He notices that she leaves the box of tea—expensive, fair trade organic green tea—prominently placed on the counter. No one wanted it, but she made it anyway.

Maybe she's trying too hard; maybe they both are.

"Would anyone like some fresh fruit?" Elsa asks as she sets the cups into saucers waiting on the table, careful not to spill the scalding water. "I have some berries . . ."

"I love berries!" Renny exclaims over the rim of her milk cup.

"You sure do." Elsa goes promptly to the fridge, takes out a container, and starts to carry it over to the sink. "Oh."

"What's wrong?" Brett asks, seeing her stop in her tracks.

"They're moldy. They're organic," she adds hastily, with a worried glance at the caseworker. "They never last long enough."

"It's okay, Mrs. Cavalon. Actually, I don't have much time today anyway. I was thinking that I could take

Renata out for a bit this morning so that we can get to know each other."

"Oh . . ." Elsa looks at Brett. She can read his mind: he's thinking the same thing she is.

We have to let her go.

This, they both know, is how the system works. Unannounced visits. Private outings and conversations between the social worker and child.

"We're so close to finalization, Mr. and Mrs. Cavalon . . . I'm hoping we can get this paperwork pushed through in the next couple of days."

Elsa's breath catches in her throat.

Finalization.

Adoption.

It's really going to happen.

Not overnight, of course, but once the paperwork is finalized, the agency interaction will all but cease—and so will their power to arbitrarily take Renny away. It'll just be a matter of time until it's made legal with an adoption hearing in court.

Elsa opens her mouth, but can't seem to find her voice.

"That would be . . ." Brett clears his throat, sounding hoarse himself. "Wow. That would be absolutely great."

"I know you're going to be a wonderful family." Melody Johnson, a statuesque, beautiful blonde, smiles at the three of them and stretches out her hand. "Come on, Renata. It's a beautiful day."

When no one picked up Lauren's home phone, Marin tried her cell, but got no answer there, either.

Now what?

"Talk about helpless . . . you need help just *finding* help," she whispers aloud, forcing a grim little smile.

She can't, given her circumstances, just start dialing random psychiatrists' numbers. She knows better than to trust just anyone; she needs someone who comes highly recommended; someone guaranteed not to betray her family's privacy.

Clearly, people are still interested in the Quinns. Look what happened just yesterday, when Marin was ambushed on the street with a camera.

Okay . . . so, no Lauren.

Her next step was going to be confronting Caroline, but maybe she should wait a little while, just so she has a plan in place when she approaches her daughter. Maybe, if she gets a couple of names from Lauren, she can even call and get an appointment right away, and tell Caroline about it.

Yes. A concrete plan. That's the way to go.

For now, she just has to settle back and wait.

Setting the phone on the bedside table, she shoots a longing glance at the orange prescription bottle sitting beside it.

No.

She looks at it.

But why not?

Suddenly, she can't remember.

Here you are thinking you're helpless, and you're not. Not at all. Sleep always helps.

She picks up the bottle.

If she took a couple of pills, she could rest for a while. She's going to need all her energy for what lies ahead.

Yes.

Marin carries the bottle into the bathroom, flips on the light, and turns on the water. Waiting for it to run cold, she catches a glimpse of her face in the mirror.

Once again, she's struck by her reflection—and she remembers all the reasons why not.

She turns off the water abruptly, whispering, "No."

She unscrews the plastic childproof cap, opens the toilet lid, and holds the open bottle over the bowl.

Go ahead. Get rid of them.

It's absolutely what she should do—dump these pills, and the ones still tucked away in her bedside drawer. It's the only way to guarantee that she won't take them—and with Ron and Heather out of the country, she won't have access to more.

Hurry up and do it, before you change your mind.

A moment later, she returns to the bedroom and jerks open the bedside drawer.

She hesitates only a moment before dropping the bottle beside the others and closing the drawer.

Just in case.

Just so you won't be helpless.

Every time Lauren comes back home after leaving her children at home alone, she flashes back to the nightmare last August, when she stepped over the threshold and found that they had disappeared.

Some scars, she knows, might never fully heal, and yet . . .

She looks at Nick's mom, holding the door open for her. "Come on in."

"Thank you. What a beautiful home."

"Anyone home?" she calls.

Three bedroom doors burst open overhead; three sets of footsteps pound down the stairs, and she smiles.

Truer words have never been spoken.

It's a beautiful home.

"You said yourself you wished we could get Renny out of here for a bit," Brett reminds Elsa, watching her pace to the window again to look out into the street.

"I know I did, but I can't help it. I'm just nervous after everything that's happened."

"So am I." Brett fingers the envelope of pictures. He's been going over them with a magnifying glass, looking for . . .

Well, he doesn't know, exactly. Some kind of clue to when they were taken, maybe?

"Maybe we should call the agency and double-check."

He looks up at Elsa to find her holding the phone. "I don't know . . . you don't want to rock the boat over there right now, do you? And she had ID."

Melody offered her credentials the moment he opened the door. Her photo on her agency identification card was unmistakably her, and the card itself was the same as Roxanne and the other employees carried.

Besides, there was something familiar about her. Brett is certain he's seen her before, probably at the agency.

"Look, chances are everything's fine."

"I know, but . . ." Elsa shakes her head. "I just have this feeling . . . I'm worried anyway."

"About the caseworker?"

"About everything."

"Look, we *know* who did this." He waves the envelope of photos. "It wasn't Melody Johnson. It was Marin Quinn."

Yet even as he utters her name, Brett feels a twinge of misgiving.

Again, he thinks of Mike Fantoni. If his death had anything to do with their case—and Marin Quinn couldn't have been in Boston at the time—then there could be someone else out there. Someone who wanted to keep Mike from going to Mumbai. Someone who wants to hurt them.

Hurt Renny.

Why the hell didn't he think things through more carefully before sending his daughter away with a stranger?

Calm down. Be rational here.

Melody Johnson isn't really a stranger. She's familiar, even if they haven't officially met her before. She's a social worker. Renny's social worker.

Anyway, we did the same thing with Roxanne, and with Peggy and Michelle who came before her. We met them, and then we let them meet alone with Renny. It's fine. This is how the system works. This is how it worked when we adopted Jeremy, too.

Jeremy . . .

No, don't think about what happened to Jeremy.

Anyway, he and Elsa really had no choice. A parent who acts rattled by an unannounced home visit or refuses to allow the child out of their earshot is just begging for trouble. At the very least, a closer look at the household—and what would be found, in this case?

Nothing we want anyone there to know about.

Still . . . his little girl is out there with a woman they've never met.

A woman whose first introduction to the case came by way of a Post-it note stuck to the front door. It's not out of the realm of possibility, given the way the agency operates, but . . .

"Go ahead," Brett tells Elsa abruptly. "Call the agency. Just . . . be careful what you say."

Caroline has ridden the train before. When Daddy was campaigning, he insisted that they take public transportation sometimes. He said it looked good to the voters.

But it's different today, sitting here by herself—no

Daddy to make things fun, no Mom to put a damper on it, no Annie to get up Caroline's butt every two seconds, no security guards or campaign aides, no photographers or chatty constituents.

It's just me.

Caroline expected to find the freedom exhilarating, but instead, it's kind of . . . well, lonely, sitting here in a double seat by herself, watching the scenery fly by in a blur. Lonely, and a little scary.

Not because of the high speed, or anything. That doesn't bother her.

No, she's just feeling like something is wrong, and she can't put her finger on it.

For some reason, she keeps thinking about that rat in her bag; remembering how one minute, she was sitting there at the table with Jake and everything was fine; the next, she was screaming bloody murder.

At the table with Jake . . .

Jake.

She knows he didn't do it.

If she thought he had, she wouldn't be going up to Boston to see him, right?

Right. He's a good guy. You like him. And he likes you, too.

If he didn't, he wouldn't have told her to come, right?

Right.

But then again . . .

Did you really give him much choice? You sort of invited yourself, don't you think?

Um, sort of?

Face it. You did *invite yourself.*

But he didn't say no.

He sounded like he wanted to, for a minute. But then he seemed to think it over, and he got into the idea. He's even going to meet her at the station.

Everything's going to be fine. Maybe she'll stay

in Boston with Jake, or they'll go out to California together or something—someplace where they can surf—and they'll live happily ever after, and she'll never have to see her mother or Annie again.

She thinks things like that all the time, yet today, the thought is oddly disquieting.

Okay, so maybe she *will* see them again.

Who knows? Maybe someday, she'll even want to.

She pictures herself introducing her mother to Jake, and smiles. Mom would probably like him.

Waiting for her call to be routed through the agency's automated phone system, Elsa can feel an irrational wave of panic building in the pit of her stomach.

Maybe she wouldn't be so uneasy about Renny's safety if she thought Brett was still assured of it.

But he's looking pale, thrumming his fingertips on the tabletop.

At last, Debra Tupperman, an office administrator, comes on the line.

"Hi, Debra, it's Elsa Cavalon." She does her best to sound breezy.

"Elsa! How funny—you were on my list of people to call this morning."

"Really?" She looks at Brett, who raises a questioning eyebrow. "Why were you going to call me?"

That news—and the resulting expression of concern on Brett's face—do nothing to ease her anxiety.

"I just wanted to talk to you about Roxanne Shields."

"Oh . . . right." Relieved, Elsa gives Brett a thumbs-up. "We were sorry to see her go," she lies.

"Go?"

Elsa frowns. "She left the agency . . . didn't she?"

"No, she's just been sick for a few days. You were on her schedule, so—"

"Wait, she's *sick*? She didn't *leave*?"

"Leave? No."

Shaken, Elsa sinks into a chair, her head spinning. "So you haven't replaced her?"

"*Replaced* her? Not at all."

Vaguely aware of Brett beside her now, clutching her arm, Elsa struggles to form her next question.

"But what . . . who . . . oh my God. Oh my GOD!"

Brett grabs the phone from her. "Debra, has a woman named Melody Johnson been assigned to our case?"

Elsa can't hear the answer above the full-blown panic screeching through her brain, but she knows.

She *knows*.

It's happening again.

Her worst nightmare has come true: Renny has been stolen away, just like Jeremy.

Her given name was Amelia.

When she was little she couldn't pronounce it, and so, her parents told her years later, she called herself La La.

It stuck.

It was the perfect nickname, because she was always singing. She would use anything at hand as a pretend microphone—a Barbie doll, a carrot, a bottle from her parents' liquor cabinet—and she'd perform.

As she grew older, she told anyone who would listen that she was going to be a huge star when she grew up, like the favorites she mimicked in her "act": Mariah Carey, Gloria Estefan, Madonna . . .

Isn't that nice, they would say politely—the substitute teacher, the woman in the supermarket checkout line, the new babysitter . . .

Then she would sing for them, and their eyes would widen, and sometimes, they'd even call other people over to listen. *You gotta hear this kid*, they'd say, and La La would sing for them all.

"That's my girl," her doting father would say. "She's going to be a huge star. You just wait and see."

Everyone believed in her—especially Daddy. He even built a small, soundproof voice studio in the basement of their home in Nottingshire.

Then, one day on the golf course, Jeremy Cavalon came at her with a seven-iron. He beat her head, her face, her neck.

The tracheal intubation saved her life, her parents were told. But it resulted in vocal cord paralysis. The condition was temporary, the doctors promised. One day very soon, she'd be able to talk again.

They were right.

She could talk.

But she couldn't sing. Not the way she used to.

La La's voice was never the same after the attack.

Nothing was ever the same.

Her parents got her into piano lessons. They figured playing an instrument might help make up for her lost voice.

It didn't.

She was talented. Not so talented that people would stop what they were doing when she played, and say, *You gotta hear this kid.*

But it was something. She admitted as much to Jeremy when he found her years later, still living in her childhood home. By then, her father had died of liver failure brought on by alcoholism. La La knew he wouldn't have drunk so much if it hadn't been for her injury. The brutal attack might not have killed her, but in the end, it was what killed him.

For La La, college was a welcome reprieve. She went to Tufts—close to home, but she lived on campus—and she majored in music.

After returning to Nottingshire after graduation last summer, it didn't take her long to conclude that being around her mother was more depressing than being alone.

Never a particularly warm woman, Candace Montgomery had grown increasingly brittle over the years. She didn't live life so much as she endured it, armed with dry martinis that rendered her a dismal drunk, as opposed to the slaphappy one her husband had been.

La La was planning on moving out last fall when Jeremy found her.

At the time, she wasn't sure where she was going, or what she would do when she got there—and she didn't really care. All she wanted was to get away from her mother, far from the pall that had shrouded the brick Colonial mansion on Regis Terrace since her father's death.

If Jeremy hadn't come along, La La might have had a chance to get away, make something of herself.

But, like so many other things in this life, it wasn't meant to be.

W hy aren't you talking?" she asks the child strapped into the passenger seat of the Mercedes.

Yes, *strapped in.* She's in a hurry to get back up to Boston, and the last thing she wants right now is to have an accident in a car that belongs to her, with a kid who doesn't.

No answer.

Renata just sits staring straight ahead like a zombie. She's been this way for miles now—for over an hour.

At first, she asked a few times where they were going.

"For a ride," she was told. "To get . . . berries."

"My mommy said berries never last long enough."

Nothing does, kid.

"How about ice cream?"

"Pink ice cream?"

Oh, for God's sake. "Sure, why not?"

The kid is breathing loudly, and every time she exhales, the breath trembles.

Yeah. Maybe she's figured out by now that this is a hell of a long drive to get pink ice cream.

It's okay. They've reached the Boston suburbs. It won't be much longer.

It's a relief to be back in the Mercedes after driving around in rentals all week—and Meg Warren's piece of shit car.

Suddenly, the kid reaches for the door handle.

"Hey, what are you doing?" She hits the brakes. A car behind her honks loudly and swerves around her. Furious, she gives the driver the finger as he passes.

"I was just putting down my window," the kid says in a small voice.

"It's already down!" Yeah, she allowed that, trying to make her feel at ease from the moment they got into the car in her parents' driveway.

"I need it more open!"

Right. Because she's desperately claustrophobic. Her worst fear is being trapped in close quarters. That information came from the file folder Roxanne Shields so conveniently brought home the night she died— along with other interesting tidbits.

Like her photo ID.

It was so easy to create an identical one, complete with a recent photo and the perfect alias.

Melody.

Such a shame no one can really appreciate her cleverness.

And Johnson—the second most common surname, after Smith.

As in Jeremy Smith.

As in *Jeremy Cavalon.*

As in the child whose life was destroyed—

Before he went and destroyed mine.

And all because of Elsa Cavalon and Marin Quinn.

"I said cut that out!"

Dammit, the kid's hand has strayed back to the controls on the door handle. The doors are locked, and flying up the interstate at sixty-five miles an hour, she's probably not going to try to throw herself out of the car through the window, but you never know.

Up it goes, all the way, courtesy of the driver's side control. Luckily, there's also a lock button.

"No!" Renata Cavalon screams. "Put it down!"

"If I were you, little girl, I'd settle down and shut up right now."

She calmly pulls the gun from her pocket.

Using it right here and now wouldn't be nearly as much fun as what she has in store for Little Miss Claustrophobia . . .

But then, it's been such a long, exhausting day already.

It might be a good idea to get it over with and go home.

Home to Jeremy.

"Mom! Mom!"

Marin opens her eyes to see someone standing there, shaking her awake.

Something's wrong.

Annie . . . something about Annie . . . she's supposed to be worrying about Annie.

But Annie is here . . .

Isn't she?

That *is* Annie standing over her bed, isn't it?

She tries to sit up. Her body is too heavy to move.

The person says something, but it's as if Marin's head is swathed in layers of gauze—she can barely see, can barely hear.

" . . . police!"

The word cuts through the fog, jolting Marin like a knife. "*What?*"

"The police are here."

The police? The police . . . no. Please, no.

"Caroline . . . where's Caroline?"

"I don't know, in her room, I guess, but Mom . . . you have to get up. They want to talk to you, now!"

Elsa refuses to lose herself in the miasma of fear swirling around her. Not like last time, with Jeremy.

If she doesn't stay strong, stay focused, Renny will be gone for good, just like Jeremy.

So she sits stoically with Brett on the couch as police officers move around them, radios squawking, taking photos, dusting the doorknob and the kitchen chair and table for Melody Johnson's fingerprints.

Was it like this last time, when Jeremy went missing? She doesn't even know. She was too far gone, by the time the police arrived, to notice their specific movements.

She does remember that Brett somehow managed to hold himself together back then. He was always the strong one, the one who kept his head amid chaos.

Not this time. He's trembling, crying on and off, his head buried in his hands as Elsa sits here like the eye of a hurricane.

She can't let it sweep her away.

She won't.

I'm Renny's only hope.

"Keep your head *down*, I said!"

Crouched on the floor of the Mercedes, the kid obeys with a whimper.

Turning on to Regis Terrace, she sees that the neighborhood has stirred to life since she drove away earlier. Kids on bikes and skateboards, pedigreed dogs on leashes, gardeners tending to lush landscapes . . .

Good Lord, the whole world is awake to see her come home. She carefully slips the gun back into her pocket and waves from the driver's seat as she passes people she knows. People who saw the hearse come to remove the body after that deadly stairway accident last fall; people who later came to her door with casseroles and sympathetic hugs for the sole survivor of the Montgomery family.

"We're so sorry," they all said. "We're here if you need us."

But La La doesn't need them.

She needs only one person—and he's here right now, waiting for her.

Elsa watches Detective Gibbs, a no-nonsense African-American man with graying temples and kind brown eyes—the one who seems to be in charge here—hang up his phone.

"Mrs. Cavalon, I know I've asked you this already"— he crouches in front of her, resting his hand on the arm of the sofa—"but is there anyone . . . anyone at all . . . who might want to hurt your daughter?"

"Just Marin Quinn, but—" She shakes her head. "She's the one, the one who called us."

But Elsa has played her message over and over since they realized Renny had been abducted.

It was so easy, given their situation, to interpret Marin Quinn's message as an admission of guilt.

Elsa is no longer convinced.

I need to talk to you . . . Over the phone or in person, whatever . . . I, um, understand if you'd rather not talk to me after . . . after all this. But I hope you will. I'm sorry.

After all this.

After her husband was arrested for his role in Jeremy's kidnapping and murder?

Yes. It makes sense now.

But Elsa is even more frightened to think that she isn't the one behind Renny's disappearance.

Temporarily insane or not, Marin Quinn is still a mother. A grieving mother. She could still be harmless.

"We've got someone over at the Quinn place now," Detective Gibbs is saying. "She's there—at her apartment in Manhattan."

Elsa nods, unsurprised "The only other person— people—I can think of are Renny's birth parents."

"They've also checked out. He's in jail again on drug charges. She's in a mental health facility."

Elsa shakes her head, imagining what would have become of Renny had she been left in their custody.

Then it hits her—Renny wouldn't be wherever she is now.

No.

No, I can't blame myself. Not this time.

La La left home this morning not long after Jeremy arrived, having driven up from New York.

She'd wanted him to catch the shuttle with her, but he's afraid to fly.

He's afraid of a lot of things.

Poor Jeremy.

All these years, she's hated him, and yet . . .

The day he showed up on her doorstep, it was love at first sight. She fell for him before she even realized his identity. He had such kind eyes, and a warm smile, and he looked at her as though he really cared . . .

"Don't you know who he is?" her mother had screamed at her when she came home to find him there.

Of course La La knew who he was. He'd told her.

Told her everything. Begged her to forgive him for what he'd done to her.

How could she *not* forgive him? He was a victim, too.

He understood, unlike anyone else. He knew what it was like to feel like a lost soul, to have your life shattered.

"He's the one who did this to you!"

Candace Montgomery was incredulous that she'd even let Jeremy past the door. She had no idea, of course, that he'd gotten much further than that. By the time she got home, they'd already fallen into La La's bed.

"How can you even look at him? He ruined your life!"

"Well, now he's here to save it, okay?" La La shot back. She knew she had to do something. Her mother was going to ruin things with Jeremy.

I tried to fight it. Really, I did.

But in the end, it was no use. It took precious little effort to shut her up. Just one swift and mighty shove, and over she went, tumbling down the steps . . .

That was it.

La La was left alone.

Alone with Jeremy. He was all she had, and she was all he had. That's how she wants it to be. That's how it is.

They take care of each other. Tell each other everything.

That's how she found out about all the horrible things that had happened to him.

The more he poured out his anguished memories, the more furious La La became. Her heart broke for the frightened little boy who still lived inside this beautiful man, the lost child who had been replaced by Renata and Caroline and Annie . . .

Replaced, as if he'd never even mattered.

He confessed that he dreamed of meeting them— the family he'd lost.

"I'll help you," La La promised. She meant it.

Jeremy didn't even realize that there should be retribution for what they'd done to him—and thus, to her.

But La La knew. And she's going to make them all pay. For his sake, and for her own.

She presses the automatic opener, raising the middle door of the three-car attached garage. She pulls the Mercedes in, parks, and closes the door behind them.

"Home sweet home," she informs the kid. "You can get up now."

The little girl raises her head just in time to see the door close, sealing them in.

She screams.

"Oh, shut up. This is nothing compared to what I have waiting for you. Let's go."

"Mom, drink this."

Someone presses a glass into her hand. Marin raises it to her lips, sips. Water. Cold. Wet. Good. So simple.

"Here, I'll take it so you don't spill it."

"Caroline." She smiles as her daughter takes the glass away, leaning back against the chair cushion and closing her eyes, exhausted. "Thank you."

"No, Mom, it's me, Annie. Caroline is gone, remember? We're trying to figure out where she is."

Marin's eyes open again.

"Gone?" she echoes, confused.

There's Annie.

There are several men she doesn't recognize, men in uniform.

Police.

She grabs the arm of the nearest man. "Something happened to Caroline?"

"We don't know where she is, Mrs. Quinn."

"She takes off sometimes," she hears Annie say. "Like, a lot."

"Caroline! You're here because Caroline—"

"No, Mrs. Quinn, we're here because we're looking for Brett and Elsa Cavalon's daughter, remember?"

Daughter?

No.

Son. Her son is missing.

"Jeremy. You're looking for Jeremy."

"No. Not him."

She remembers, and grief wells up inside her.

"Where is Renata Cavalon, Mrs. Quinn?"

"Who . . . ?"

Why won't they leave her alone? Why won't they let her mourn her own child?

"Dead . . . oh God."

"Did you say 'dead'?

"Yes . . . dead . . . all my fault."

"Are you saying you killed Renata Cavalon?"

"No! No! Jeremy. My son. Jeremy is dead."

Caroline spots him right where he said he'd be, next to the Dunkin' Donuts kiosk.

He doesn't see her yet, though. He's on his cell phone.

She walks over to him.

Still, he doesn't notice her. Should she say his name, or touch his shoulder? Or should she just let him finish his conversation?

He looks upset, she realizes.

"I know you are," he's saying into the phone, "but I

had no choice. No . . . no, I didn't invite her, it was her idea . . ."

Clearly, he's talking about Caroline.

Oh my God. Why am I here?

"Yes, because I thought I should tell her . . . No, I couldn't do it that way . . . No, I need to tell her in person . . ."

Tell her what?

That he has a girlfriend? Is that who he's talking to?

Don't worry, you jerk. You don't have to tell me anything, in person or otherwise. I'm out of here.

She turns to walk away.

"Caroline!"

Too late.

Jake is hurrying toward her, shoving his phone back into his pocket. "Hey, you made it."

Tell him. Tell him right now that you know he doesn't want you here. Tell him you're going back home.

Caroline opens her mouth.

He smiles at her. That smile . . .

"Yeah," she hears herself say. "I made it."

"Great. Come on. I'm going to take you over to the place where I'm staying, down in Nottingshire."

Unbelievable.

He's with *her*.

It's not as if La La thinks anything romantic is going to happen between the two of them. She's his *sister*, for God's sake.

She doesn't know that yet, of course. But Jeremy's going to tell her. He promised.

"Bring her back here and we'll tell her together," La La instructed him.

He didn't think that was such a good idea.

"Who helped you find her in the first place?" she

reminded him. "I'm the one who kept an eye out for her the other day, and followed her to Starbucks and told you where she was so you could meet her, remember?"

What Jeremy doesn't know, of course, was that La La had also been the one who planted that rat in Caroline's bag just before he arrived.

As she sat there, drinking coffee and watching the two of them getting to know each other, she found herself feeling more and more jealous.

Just like now.

But she'll do something about it. They should be here soon.

Then Caroline can join Renny, already entombed in the soundproof basement studio Daddy built all those years ago, where no one will ever hear their screams.

So nice that it came in handy for something, La La thinks. She tries the studio door one more time to be sure it's locked, then goes back up to the first floor to wait for Jeremy.

"You're sure you don't know where your sister might be?" one of the cops asks Annie, who's sitting beside Marin, stroking her hand.

"No. Her bedroom door was closed when I got up. I thought she was in there."

Marin raises the water glass to her lips, taking another sip. The medication is still in her system, but she's coming out of it now. At least she can focus on what's going on.

Caroline is out somewhere . . .

But that's not why the police are here.

They're here because Elsa Cavalon's daughter is missing, and for some reason, they thought Marin might have had something to do with it.

They still might think that, judging by the way they're watching her every move.

But they're definitely concerned about Caroline's absence. Maybe because they're wondering if Marin has something to do with that, too.

She told them about the argument they had last night. "Just normal mother-daughter stuff," she'd called it.

They didn't seem convinced.

They've called Caroline's friends. None of them are even in town, and none has heard from Caroline in the last twenty-four hours.

Marin sets down the half-empty water glass, shaking so badly that droplets slosh over the rim. Annie reaches for her hand and squeezes it.

"Annie . . ." Marin leans her head on her daughter's surprisingly sturdy shoulder. "Thank you."

"For what?"

"For being here with me. *For* me. You . . . you're the only one I can count on. Ever."

Annie strokes her mother's hair in silence.

It should be the other way around, Marin thinks. Mother comforting daughter. No matter what happens— *no matter what*—things are going to change around here.

She's going to change.

I know what I have to do to make that happen.

Right now, before I lose my nerve.

She starts to rise, thinking only of the pill bottles in her bedside drawer.

"Mom?"

"Yes?"

"Wait. There is one thing . . ."

Marin sits again. "What is it?"

"I don't want to get into trouble." She glances anxiously at the police officers who are watching and lis-

tening with interest. "You have to swear you won't tell
Caroline."

"Tell her what?"

"I'll be right back." Annie gets up quickly and disappears down the hall.

Marin and the cops wait in strained silence, but not
for long.

Annie returns clutching something in her hand. "I
was kind of . . . looking through Caroline's room . . . I
do that sometimes . . ."

Marin closes her eyes. How many times has her
older daughter accused her kid sister of snooping?

I always stuck up for Annie.

But Caroline was right.

"I found this in her drawer."

"I'll take it." The cop closest to her stretches out his
hand. She looks at Marin, who nods slightly.

Annie hands him what looks like a crumpled napkin.

He inspects it. "Whose phone number is this?"

"I don't know. But maybe it has something to do
with where she went."

Caroline hasn't said much since Jeremy met her at the
train station, and he wonders what's wrong with her.

Is she having second thoughts about being here?

He's having second thoughts about it, that's for sure.
Maybe he isn't ready to tell her the truth yet. Or maybe
it's just that he doesn't want La La here when he tells
her.

Maybe?

Hell, he doesn't want La La around anywhere. She's
smothering him. He can't take it anymore.

Guilt brought him here in the first place; guilt has
kept him coming back.

But he's had enough. He was going to tell La La that this morning—tell her it's over.

She was gone, though, when he woke up, and then Caroline called, and now . . .

Now everything's a mess.

He turns on to Regis Terrace, thinking again of the first time he came here, last fall.

La La had made the first move that night, but he hadn't fought her off very hard.

Oh hell, he hadn't fought her off at all. She was a beautiful woman, and despite all he'd been through with Papa, he was a red-blooded man. Women had been drawn to him ever since he ventured out the front door of Papa's house and made his way to Texas.

He'd known it would be wrong to get too close to any of them, though. As much as he craved love and acceptance, he was nowhere near ready for a real relationship. Not after what he'd been through.

But it was different with La La Montgomery—or so he'd tried to convince himself just before he got carried away and fell into bed with her. Different because she wasn't really a stranger, and because she wasn't like the carefree young girls he'd met in bars. La La had been through her share of pain; she was, in many ways, older than her years, with a nurturing quality that enveloped him, made him feel momentarily safe and warm.

And yet, after he left her that first night, he'd promised himself it would never happen again, just as he had with the others who'd come before her.

La La might understand him better than anyone, but he still wasn't capable of a relationship, and they both had too much baggage, and anyway, there was something about her—about the intensity of her gaze—that made him uneasy.

He would never have gone back if not for the hysterical phone call from La La the next morning, saying she'd just found her mother, tragically killed in a drunken fall down the stairs.

"Please, Jeremy—please come. I need you."

She's always telling him how much she needs him, how much she loves him, how he's all she has . . .

That much is true. La La lives in complete isolation, alone now in the brick mansion she inherited along with her parents' fortune.

He knows she graduated from college, that she had vague plans of moving away and finding a career of some kind.

"But then I found you instead," she likes to tell him.

As he pulls into the driveway, Caroline speaks at last.

"Whose house is this?"

What do I even tell her? Do I explain here, in the car? Or wait until we get inside?

"Jake?"

Maybe La La won't be here after all. Maybe she's . . . out somewhere. Or sleeping—she couldn't have gotten much sleep . . .

Thoughts racing, Jeremy reaches for the garage door opener.

"Jake!"

Oh. Right. He's supposed to be Jake, and Caroline is waiting for him to answer her question.

"It's a friend's house."

The door opens and he pulls into the garage.

No luck. La La's Mercedes is parked there. He'd known it would be, and yet he feels sick at the sight of it.

He turns off the car, closes the garage door behind them, and gets out.

Caroline hasn't moved.

"Coming?" he leans in to ask her, and she turns to him.

"Is this your girlfriend's house, Jake?"

The question catches him off guard. Her dark eyes are narrowed—eyes that are so like his own that sometimes he feels as though he's looking into a mirror.

How can she not know? Doesn't she realize that we have some kind of connection? Doesn't she sense that the same blood runs through our veins?

"Jake . . . I asked you a question."

"Yeah. The thing is . . . she's not going to be my girlfriend for much longer. It's over."

"Mrs. Quinn?"

Caught up in a wistful reverie, she's startled by a male voice beside her. She looks up to see the cop who left the room a short time ago with the telephone number Annie had found in Caroline's room.

"Two things. Your credit card was used this morning at an electronic kiosk in Penn Station to purchase a one-way ticket to Boston on the Acela."

"*What?*"

"Also, we've checked your daughter's phone records, and she called this number last night and again this morning."

"Whose phone is it?"

"We traced it to a twenty-two-year-old named Jeremy Smith from California."

Jeremy.

"La La?"

Standing with her back to the doorway, she hears her name spoken behind her, but it doesn't register.

Nothing has registered, other than the words that floated to her ears from the garage, when she opened the door to greet Jeremy.

She's not going to be my girlfriend for much longer. It's over.

La La chews her lip, tasting blood.

Really?

Really, Jeremy?

You're going to leave me, after what you did to me?

Arms folded, she stares at a photograph on the mantel. In it, she's with her father, sitting on his lap. He's grinning, and her mouth is wide open. She's probably singing. She was always singing.

Then Jeremy came along.

"There you are."

Slowly, she turns.

There he is.

Not Jeremy the way he used to be—a dark-haired imp with troubled eyes. Not the Jeremy who beat her beyond recognition. Not on the outside, anyway.

This Jeremy looks different.

His hair is blond now.

He had plastic surgery to repair the damage to his face, as did she. But his was more recent: surgery to repair the scars and bruises and broken bones inflicted by the man he called Papa.

Her own scars, bruises, broken bones—her broken voice, her broken heart—were inflicted by Jeremy.

This Jeremy. He's still the same person, deep down inside. The person who destroyed her.

"La La! What are you doing?"

She blinks.

He isn't alone.

She recognizes the girl.

"This is Caroline. Caroline, this is La La."

Looking hesitant—so different from the cocky girl

La La followed in New York the other day—Caroline cautiously takes a step toward her. "Hi, Lila."

"It's La La! Not Lila. You stupid bitch."

"Hey!" Jeremy steps in front of Caroline, almost as if he's protecting her. *Her*—not La La. That's rich.

La La strides toward the two of them.

"What are you doing?"

"I'm just telling your little sister that she got my name wrong."

"Jesus, La La, shut *up*!"

"Oh, and I think she has your name wrong, too. She thinks you're Jake. Isn't that funny, Jeremy?"

Beside him, Caroline Quinn has gone pale, her mouth gaping open as she absorbs La La's words.

Jeremy turns toward her, touches her arm. "Caroline . . ."

"*Sister?*"

He shakes his head, and La La grins.

Caroline touches the door frame, as if she's going to faint. "You're—"

"No, Caroline, I—"

"What is she talking about?"

"She's crazy." He glares at La La.

Rage flares inside her. "It's the truth and you know it."

"Who *are* you?" Caroline takes a step back from Jeremy, shaking her head in disbelief.

"I'm—your parents are—"

Obviously, he can't even bring himself to say the words.

La La does it for him. "Your parents are *his* parents, get it? He's your brother. The one everyone thinks is dead. Surprise!"

Caroline looks from Jeremy to La La and back again. "How—how can . . . You're *alive*?"

"Don't worry," La La can't resist saying as she

reaches into her pocket for the gun. "He won't be, for long. And neither will you."

"Mr. and Mrs. Cavalon . . ."

Elsa looks up to see Detective Gibbs in the doorway of the kitchen, where she and Brett are seated at the table with Lisa, the police sketch artist working on a composite drawing of Melody Johnson. Brett keeps saying he's seen the woman somewhere before, but he can't remember where, and it's driving him crazy.

"We've had a development."

Elsa's heart stops.

No. Please, no.

She braces herself for the worst news.

Brett grabs her hand and squeezes it, asking Detective Gibbs, "Is Renny . . . ?"

"No," he says hastily, "it's not about her. No. We're still working on a couple of leads, but . . . Lisa, would you mind giving us a few moments' privacy?"

"No problem." The sketch artist pushes back her chair, flashes them a concerned smile, and slips out of the room.

Detective Gibbs crosses toward them, carrying an open laptop. "I've been on the phone with New York."

New York . . .

Marin Quinn is in New York. So is Garvey Quinn.

"I need you to take a look at something I just received," Detective Gibbs says, almost gently, as he sits across from them, the laptop facing in his direction. "You might want to prepare yourselves. It's going to be a shock."

Prepare ourselves? Elsa thinks incredulously. *How are we supposed to prepare ourselves? For what?*

He turns the laptop so that they're looking at the screen.

There's a picture on the screen. A photograph of a young man.

Peering closer at it, Elsa is struck by an impossible thought.

No. It can't be.

And yet, Brett gasps. "Is that . . . ?"

"No," Elsa says sharply. "It isn't."

Of course not. Brett just wants so badly for it to be him that he's seeing him, just as Elsa did, for all these years.

Always looking at little boys, at teenagers, at young men who were the same age her son would have been. Always searching for that familiar gleam in a pair of big dark eyes, for the quick smile that could light up a room; always searching for Jeremy.

Even after she knew in her heart that he was never coming home again—she never stopped looking for him.

Never.

Not until they told her, last fall, that he was dead.

Detective Gibbs clears his throat and asks, very softly, "Do you recognize him?"

"Yes," Brett whispers.

"No!" Elsa turns to him. "No, Brett, don't. That isn't him."

The features are different.

"Elsa—"

"Don't let yourself get caught up in . . . in hoping, and wishing. It'll only hurt more."

"But—"

"It's *not him*. It can't be. They told us—"

"Elsa, please, just look at him again. Look at his face."

"Why? He's dead, Brett. We both know it. He's *dead*."

"Mrs. Cavalon," Detective Gibbs cuts in gently, "we have reason to believe that this is your son. He's twenty-two years old, and his name is Jeremy."

"He's . . . twenty-two?" Brett's voice is ragged. "He's alive?"

"He's alive. Mrs. Cavalon . . . ?"

Elsa forces herself to look again, to really look this time.

Look at his face.

Look at his eyes.

She does.

And then she knows. She *knows.*

She presses her fists against her mouth, tears streaming down her face.

"That's him. It's Jeremy."

"Look at you . . . you're scared to death, aren't you?"

Yes, Caroline's scared. She's terrified. Terrified of this . . . this person, this La La, who's clearly insane . . .

And terrified of Jake, who brought her here.

No, not Jake.

Jeremy.

Her *brother.*

"You know, everyone's afraid of something—like being closed into small spaces . . . that's called claustrophobia, did you know that?" La La doesn't wait for an answer, rambling on, "Then there's Jeremy—he's afraid of everything. Including me. Aren't you?"

She abruptly whirls to face Jeremy, standing beside Caroline. She sneaks a glance at him and sees that he's fixated on the gun.

He's going to try to grab it, she realizes.

"He's not a man. He's like a little boy. No—like a little *girl.* How about if I lock you away, too?" She pokes the gun at him and he flinches.

She laughs, a sound that sends chills down Caroline's spine.

She's going to kill us.

Oh God. I'm going to die.

She wants her mother so badly that the pain takes her breath away.

Mom.

Not Daddy.

Mom is the one who's there for her, she realizes. The only one.

There was a time when Caroline was convinced she'd be better off without her mother—and vice versa.

It's not true. I need her. And I'm never going to get the chance to tell her.

Staring at the gun, Jeremy knows he's running out of time. He has to do something.

Any second now, La La is going to kill him, and Caroline, too.

"After all I've done for you . . . you were going to leave me?"

"What have you done for me?" He looks past her, scanning the living room for some way out, or for a weapon . . .

"I've done everything you're too weak to do. I've punished them all for what they did to you, and this is the thanks I get?"

"Who?" he asks, his gaze falling on a pair of andirons beside the hearth, just a few feet away. "Who did you punish?"

"Who do you think?" She laughs again. "Look at you—you're pathetic. You're *nothing.*"

In her eyes, he sees the same streak of mocking cruelty that made him lash out at her all those years ago.

Back then, she was just a mean little girl, and he was a confused, angry, abused little boy.

Now she's a cold-blooded killer . . .

And I'm . . .

I'm not pathetic.

I'm not nothing.

I'm a man.

Looking at her, he sees Papa's face, and he sees the faces of all the others, too, the ones who tortured him before he came to Elsa.

He closes his eyes so he won't have to see, and he claps his hands over his ears, trying to drown out the scornful laughter filling his head.

"What's the matter, Jeremy? Are you scared?"

Scared?

No.

He's not scared. He's been to hell and back, and nothing will ever scare him again.

Jeremy's eyes snap open.

He lunges for the gun.

La La presses the trigger.

Jeremy is alive.

Alive.

And Renny is gone.

Cradling his wife in his arms, Brett tries to grasp the situation—tries to figure out what one unbelievable fact might have to do with the other.

Detective Gibbs seems to be waiting for him and Elsa to absorb the miracle.

"Are you saying . . ." Brett shakes his head rapidly, starts again. "Is Jeremy connected to the woman who took our daughter?"

"He may be."

"No," Elsa says sharply, lifting her head at last. "He wouldn't hurt her."

"You don't even know him, Elsa," Brett can't help snapping. Even now, even after all these years, the old pattern has resumed. Elsa's defense of Jeremy, and Brett's wariness.

"He wouldn't hurt her," she repeats stubbornly, wrenching herself from his arms and standing to face him.

"How can you even say that? Look what he did to—"

All at once, it hits him.

Melody Johnson . . .

He knows where he's seen her before. Years ago, and her face is different, but her eyes . . . those blue eyes . . .

Even the name . . .

Melody.

"La La." Brett turns abruptly to Detective Gibbs. "Her name was—*is*—La La Montgomery."

Numb with horror, Caroline watches Jeremy fall to the floor.

Standing over him with the gun in her hand, La La shakes her head. "I told you you're pathetic."

It's as if she's forgotten Caroline is there.

I have to get out of here.

She turns her head slightly, checking the pathway behind her. The house, when Jeremy led her through, was a maze. Can she even find her way back to the door?

"Don't try it."

Startled, she sees that La La is looking at her. *Aiming* at her.

"Come on." La La calmly sidesteps Jeremy's crumpled, bloody form. "Let's go."

"Go . . ." Caroline whispers, paralyzed with fear.

La La jabs the gun into her ribs. "I said, let's go! *Walk!*"

Caroline walks.

* * *

In the master bedroom, Marin once again stands holding a plastic pill bottle in her hand, poised over the toilet.

This time, though, there's no hesitation. This time, her hand is sure and steady as she dumps the contents into the bowl.

Then she empties another bottle, and another, and when they're all gone, every last pill, she flushes them down the toilet.

Turning away, she sees Annie standing in the doorway.

"Mom," she says, "the detectives want to talk to you. They said they think they know why Caroline went to Boston."

Moving through the big house, prodded along by La La's gun in her back, Caroline struggles to keep her wits about her.

Where is she taking me?

What is she going to do?

No, she *knows* what La La is going to do.

This is, unmistakably, a death march.

They've reached the kitchen now, and the back door is just a few yards away. Beyond it, through the glass window, Caroline can see leafy trees, and sunshine, and a wide blue sky.

Freedom.

But she doesn't dare run for it, knowing she'll be shot in the back.

La La yanks open a door—a different door, and Caroline sees a steep flight of stairs before her.

"Go!"

Caroline hesitates, knowing beyond a doubt that if

she descends into the shadows, she'll never again see the light of day.

This is her only chance.

"Move!"

She moves.

But not forward.

No, she flings herself backward, full force, into La La Montgomery.

Sitting beside Brett in the back of Detective Gibbs's car, hurtling north up Interstate 95 toward Boston, Elsa closes her eyes, seeing her lost little boy—the boy she'd always known, deep down inside, would never come home again.

And Renny . . .

"She's going to be okay," she tells Brett, opening her eyes to see him staring grimly out the window.

He turns to look at her. "How do you know?"

"I just know."

All those years, her heart had told her that her little boy was lost to her forever. She was right about that.

Jeremy the child is gone forever.

But Jeremy the man is alive.

And he's still her son, no matter what.

The wind knocked out of her, La La falls to the kitchen floor with Caroline on top of her.

"Get *off* me!" she snarls, her arms pinned beneath their combined weight, her right hand still clenching the gun.

She can feel Caroline clawing for it.

Keeping her finger tight on the trigger, she summons every bit of strength to heave her upper body from the floor. The other girl goes flying and La La scrambles to her feet.

"You shouldn't have done that." She stands over Caroline with the gun in both hands now, straight out in front of her as she takes aim for the girl's chest.

Then she thinks better of it and changes her vantage, aiming instead for Caroline's head. Yes, that's better. This way, her pretty face will be destroyed, just like—

Sensing a whoosh of movement behind her, La La whirls around . . .

Just in time to see Jeremy, enraged, swinging a golf club toward her head.

No, she realizes in the split second before it hits.

It's not a golf club at all.

It's an andiron.

"Oh my God. Jeremy!"

Standing over La La, seeing the blood pooling beneath her head, Jeremy is vaguely aware of Caroline's shocked horror—but well aware of his own, and of the agonizing pain in his arm.

"You . . . you're bleeding." Caroline has turned to him.

He looks down, sees the blood running down his hand, covering the andiron.

"No, that's hers." All at once, his fingers release the weight of it and it thuds to the floor beside her body.

"Yours, too. Let me see." Caroline touches his arm gently, and her hand comes away red. "She shot you, Jeremy."

"She . . . shot me?" He closes his eyes, feeling faint, then forces them open and looks down at his arm.

Caroline is right. He was shot. He was on the floor, in the living room . . .

"Here, sit down."

He lets Caroline guide him into a chair.

"I'll call for help," she's saying.

All he knew, when he was lying on the floor, was that he had to stop La La before she hurt his sister.

And now . . .

"Don't worry," Caroline tells him, already dialing 911. "It's going to be all right. Just hang in there, okay?"

Hang in there.

Jeremy leans his head back and smiles faintly.

Hang in there. That, he can do.

He's done it all his life.

When her cell phone rings in her hand, Marin literally jumps out of her chair.

"Mom?" Annie is up, too, right beside her. "Is it . . . ?"

Yes. Caroline's number is in the caller ID window.

In the moment before she answers the call, blurting her daughter's name, Marin has a flash of doubt.

The police are certain Caroline is in Boston . . . with Jeremy.

What if I've lost her—lost them both—for good?

"Mom?"

"Caroline," she says again, and then her voice breaks.

"Mom . . . I'm so sorry. I'm sorry."

Caroline—her stoic, unemotional daughter, so like Garvey—or so Marin has always believed—is crying. Apologizing.

Tears streaming down her face, Marin asks, "Are you all right?"

"I am. We both are."

"Both?"

"Jeremy—he's been shot, but the paramedics are here, and he's going to be okay."

"Jeremy . . ."

"He saved my life."

"Jeremy . . ."

"My brother. Your son."

Yes. Her son.

"Mom," Caroline sobs, "I want to come home. I just want to come home."

Through her own tears, Marin smiles.

Riding through the streets of Nottingshire, Elsa is lost in memories of Jeremy. Not, this time, of losing him—but of Jeremy alive, clinging to her hand as they walked down Main Street, and teeter-tottering in the park, and running up the hill toward the red brick school.

But the familiar spots fall away as Detective Gibbs takes them into a part of town they rarely visited. Here, the homes are massive, set wide apart and back from the wide, leafy streets.

As they turn on to Regis Terrace, Elsa spots police cars and ambulances. An icy tide of dread sweeps through her.

Detective Gibbs parks quickly at the curb across from the hub of the action: a stately home Elsa knows belongs to the Montgomerys.

"You folks sit tight for a minute." The detective is out of the car in a hurry, striding toward a cluster of uniformed cops out front.

Elsa's pulse races as she and Brett wait in silence, watching the house.

Renny . . .

Jeremy . . .

Her children . . .

Detective Gibbs strides back to the car. Elsa grips her husband's hand.

"Amelia Montgomery is in custody—and injured, in critical condition," he announces without ado. "Jeremy has been shot, but he's safe. So is Caroline Quinn."

"Caroline Quinn?" Looking bewildered, Brett voices the question Elsa can't bring herself to ask. "What about Renny?"

Detective Gibbs clears his throat. "We don't know where she is. I'm sorry, Mr. Cavalon. But we're doing everything we can to find her."

Propped on the couch where they moved him, away from the bloody kitchen, Jeremy winces.

"Sorry . . . does that hurt?" asks the motherly paramedic who's wrapping a bandage around his wounded arm. A uniformed police officer hovers nearby, keeping a wary eye on things.

On *Jeremy*.

"It's okay," he tells the paramedic. "I'm good with pain."

She raises a dubious gray eyebrow. "This is more than just pain, honey. You've been shot."

Yeah, well, he's been through worse.

Much worse.

"All right," the woman says as she finishes up. "They want to talk to you now."

"Who does?"

"The detectives." She gives him a sympathetic pat on the arm and disappears.

The police officer looks at Jeremy as if to say, *Don't try anything.*

It was self-defense! he wants to shout. *I had to do it. She was going to kill—*

Several men stride into the room, the one in the lead saying briskly, "I'm Detective Gibbs. Are you Jeremy Cavalon?"

Jeremy *Cavalon* . . .

It's been years since he heard the name. Tears spring to his eyes.

They know.

They know it's me.

"Yes," he says simply. "I'm Jeremy Cavalon."

Isolated in the den of the Montgomery mansion with a pair of female police officers, Caroline tries hard to focus on their questions.

But they have so many, and some don't even make sense.

They just showed her a photo of a little girl she's never even seen before, and asked what she knew about her.

"Absolutely nothing."

"So you have no idea where she is?" one of the officers—the one who looks like her face would crack if she tried to smile—asks Caroline.

"I don't even know *who* she is."

"She's missing. Amelia Montgomery abducted her from her home in Groton."

"Amel—"

"La La," the other officer says. "That's what she was called."

Caroline nods. "But I don't know anything about this."

"She didn't say anything about a little girl?"

"No. Nothing at—" Caroline stops, remembering. "She did say something."

The officers wait, pens poised over their notes.

"She said . . ." Caroline closes her eyes, trying to

remember. "She told Jeremy he was like a little girl, afraid of everything . . . she kept talking about stuff like that."

"Like *what*?"

"You know . . . fear. Like, she said something about how some people are afraid of being trapped in small spaces . . ."

The two women look at each other, then again at Caroline.

"The child we're trying to find has a severe case of claustrophobia," the humorless officer tells her. "She might have hidden her somewhere to scare her. Do you have any idea where she might have—"

Caroline gasps. "Yes! The basement!"

"Excuse me . . . I'm sorry to interrupt, but this is urgent."

Looking up to see a female police officer poking her head into the living room, Jeremy welcomes the interruption. Sitting here, telling the detectives about Papa—about what he went through, in Mumbai, and here—it's harder than he ever imagined it would be.

The only other person he's ever told was La La—but that was almost as if he were talking to himself, purging his soul of the horror.

Little did he realize she was registering every last detail, planning to use the information to launch her vengeful crusade.

"We think she might have hidden the little girl somewhere in the basement," the female officer announces from the doorway. "There must be a closet down there, or something."

"There are a few," Jeremy speaks up. "And there's a wine cellar too, and a voice studio."

"Voice studio?"

"It's not like . . . I mean, it's really small. Her father built it for her, because she—"

"Small?" The female officer echoes. "Where is it, exactly?"

"I can show you."

The authorities all look at one another.

"Go ahead, let him take you down," Detective Gibbs instructs. "I'll be waiting outside with the Cavalons."

Jeremy's heart stops. "They're here?"

"Yeah, they're here." The detective's tone is all business, but his eyes aren't unkind. "And they want their daughter back alive."

Elsa can't take it.

Something is going on inside that house.

The way Detective Gibbs comes striding out here so purposefully . . .

"Did you find her?" She rushes toward him.

"Not yet." He rests a firm hand on her arm, guiding her back over to the car.

But he *expects* to find her, or he expects . . . something. The air is unmistakably charged.

Brett's arm is tight around Elsa's shoulders; she can feel the expectant tension in his body as well. He's waiting; they're all just sitting here waiting . . . waiting . . .

The door of the house is thrown open; they all look up.

Nothing could have prepared Elsa for the sight that greets her.

A male figure stands in the doorway, holding something in his arms.

Jeremy . . . with Renny.

With a scream, Elsa races toward them, toward her children, Brett right alongside her.

"Mommy!" Renny calls out. "Daddy!"

Jeremy bends over to gently set her on her feet.

Brett gets to her first, scooping her into his arms and holding her close.

Reaching them, Elsa gives her daughter a fierce hug.

"I was so scared, Mommy."

"I know you were, sweetheart, but you're going to be okay."

"That boy found me." She points at Jeremy. "He let me out."

Boy . . . he's not a boy.

He's a *man*.

Elsa swallows hard and turns toward him. He's just standing there, waiting . . . waiting . . .

He looks nothing like the little boy she lost, and yet . . .

Their eyes connect, and she knows.

My son.

Glancing quickly over at Brett, she sees that his eyes, above Renny's dark head, are shiny. "Thank you," he says raggedly. Balancing Renny on his hip, he holds out a hand.

Jeremy looks down at his feet, then shyly up at Brett. "You're welcome." He stretches out a hand to shake Brett's, but is swept into a bear hug instead.

"You're crushing me!" Renny squeals, and they all laugh through their tears.

At last, Brett releases him and he looks at Elsa.

"Jeremy," she whispers, and opens her arms. "Welcome home."

Epilogue

The airport is packed on this Friday morning, with the line for security snaking across the terminal.

"I hope we don't miss the flight," Elsa tells Brett as they wrestle their bags another couple of feet forward.

"The line's moving fast. Here, Renny, let me take your bag."

"No, I've got it." She wheels her small Vuitton suitcase—a gift from Maman, of course, in honor of this long-awaited trip—and anxiously asks, "What if the plane leaves without us?"

"It won't, I promise."

"But you just said it might," she reminds Elsa, who smiles and shakes her head.

"You don't miss a trick, do you?"

"Nope. And I been waiting for this day for so long."

Brett rests a hand on Renny's shoulder. "We all have."

Fifteen minutes later, they reach the head of the line. The security guard is jovial as Brett hands him their three IDs.

"Let's see . . . we have Brett Cavalon, Elsa Cavalon, and . . ." He looks down. "Renata Cavalon. Is that your name?"

"No." She shakes her head fervently, and he raises an eyebrow.

Elsa and Brett look at each other.

"Sweetie," Elsa says, "it is now, remember? The adoption? You're a Cavalon now."

"But I'm not Renata. It's Renny," she informs the security guard, who grins and hands back the documents.

"All right, Renny Cavalon. You have a good trip. Where are you going?"

"To Disney World!"

As they make their way toward the gate, she gallops along pulling her little bag, singing her favorite Ariel song.

The one about becoming part of your world, Elsa thinks.

Renny still isn't sick of the song, or of *The Little Mermaid*.

And I'm not, either, thinks Elsa, who often goes around singing the poignant lyrics herself. So does Brett.

"It's like our family theme song," he comments now, as he and Elsa pull the luggage along toward the gate, just up ahead.

"They're here!" Renny breaks off to announce excitedly. "Can I run ahead?"

Elsa hesitates. This is a public place, and there are so many strangers . . .

"Just be careful," she tells Renny, who breaks into a happy run.

"Good job, Mom." Brett nods his approval.

"What?"

"Letting go."

"I'm learning," she says with a smile. "And anyway, look—they see her coming."

She points toward the gate, where the rest of the family are waiting for Renny to reach them.

Jeremy, Marin, Caroline, Annie.

The Cavalons and the Quinns may not be technically related, but they've come to think of one another
that way these past few months, with Jeremy as the
bridge between them.

Anyway, no one knows better than Elsa that blood
doesn't create a familial bond.

Love does.